# WARRIOR'S SONG

# Books by Judith Pella

*Lone Star Legacy*

> *Frontier Lady*
> *Stoner's Crossing*
> *Warrior's Song*

*The Russians* (with Michael Phillips)

> *The Crown and the Crucible*
> *A House Divided*
> *Travail and Triumph*
> *Heirs of the Motherland* (Judith Pella only)
> *Dawning of Deliverance* (Judith Pella only)

*The Stonewycke Trilogy* (with Michael Phillips)

> *The Heather Hills of Stonewycke*
> *Flight from Stonewycke*
> *Lady of Stonewycke*

*The Stonewycke Legacy* (with Michael Phillips)

> *Stranger at Stonewycke*
> *Shadows over Stonewycke*
> *Treasure of Stonewycke*

*The Highland Collection* (with Michael Phillips)

> *Jamie MacLeod: Highland Lass*
> *Robbie Taggart: Highland Sailor*

*The Journals of Corrie Belle Hollister* (with Michael Phillips)

> *My Father's World*
> *Daughter of Grace*
> *On the Trail of the Truth**
> *A Place in the Sun**
> *Sea to Shining Sea**
> *Into the Long Dark Night**
> *Land of the Brave and the Free**
> *Grayfox**

*Michael Phillips only

# Judith Pella

# WARRIOR'S SONG

**BETHANY HOUSE PUBLISHERS**
MINNEAPOLIS, MINNESOTA 55438

Published by Bethany House Publishers
A Ministry of Bethany Fellowship, Inc.
11300 Hampshire Avenue South
Minneapolis, Minnesota 55438

Printed in the United States of America.

**Library of Congress Cataloging-in-Publication Data**

Pella, Judith.
    Warrior's song / Judith Pella.
    p.   cm. — (Lone star legacy ; 3)

    1. Frontier and pioneer life—West (U.S.)—Fiction.  2. Cheyenne
Indians—Fiction.  I. Title.  II. Series: Pella, Judith.
Lone star legacy ; bk. 3.
PS3566.E415W37      1996
813'.54—dc20                                                    95–45622
ISBN 1–55661–655–4                                                CIP

To the staff of the Eureka, California, P.A.C.E. program who, with true compassion and dedication, serve troubled young people in my community.

*"Let no one look down on your youthfulness, but rather in speech, conduct, love, faith and purity, show yourself an example of those who believe."*

1 Timothy 4:12 (NAS)

JUDITH PELLA is the author of five major fiction series for the Christian market, co-written with Michael Phillips. An avid reader and researcher in historical, adventure, and geographical venues, her skill as a writer is exceptional. She and her family make their home in California.

# Contents

# PART 3
## SPRING 1889

# PART 4
## WINTER 1893

# WHAT HAS GONE BEFORE . . .

Deborah Stoner's first marriage was a blind attempt to escape the ravages of the Civil War. She found out too late that the man she had married was cruel and abusive. When he was found murdered, she was accused of the crime. Her escape from the gallows was nothing short of a miracle, but it did little to change her heart or her bitterness toward God. She wanted only to be free and independent. In her mind submitting to God was just another form of imprisonment.

When in another attempt to escape capture she was left stranded and alone on the prairie, it seemed she would never find relief, either physically or emotionally. And the last place she would have looked for peace was with a band of wild Indians. But Broken Wing, a Cheyenne warrior, rescued Deborah and gave her shelter among his people. Deborah soon found that she experienced less savagery in the Cheyenne village than among her own people, in her own husband's home. Broken Wing, in fact, proved to be one of the most civilized human beings she had ever known. She couldn't have imagined actually falling in love with a wild Indian, but she did just that. She grew to love the man and his people.

Deborah and Broken Wing were married, and they loved each other with all their hearts. But their love was tested in the fires of historical events that cared nothing for simple love. They were torn between two hostile races—caught in the middle of war, misunderstanding, and deception. Broken Wing had been destined for such division. His mother had married a white mountain man, and though they were not related by blood, Broken Wing and his stepfather grew to love each other. Upon the death of his mother and stepfather, Broken Wing returned to the Cheyenne people and learned to be a warrior. But part of his heart always belonged with the people of his white stepfather, and like his chief Black Kettle, he wanted to hold out his hand to the whites.

Yet the government continually broke faith with the Indians. When Broken Wing's family and his way of life were threatened, he was finally forced to take up arms against the whites—his stepfather's people, his wife's people. Deborah, attached to the Cheyenne people, was far more eager than Broken Wing to fight the whites, but she didn't want to sacrifice her husband to that fight. They now had a son, named Blue Sky, and Deborah wanted to live in peace with her family, following the Cheyenne Way.

Through Broken Wing's influence, Deborah's bitterness toward her own people had been tempered. But when Broken Wing was killed in battle and her Cheyenne home destroyed in the Washita massacre, all the old anger resurfaced.

Then God brought into Deborah's shattered life a godly preacher named Sam Killion. Gently and lovingly, Deborah was nudged back to a faith that had long ago grown cold. She discovered true independence and freedom could only be found in God, and that in Christ, her weaknesses could be made strong.

At last Deborah could forgive her people and move on with her life. She bought a ranch in Texas, married Sam, and raised her two children—Carolyn, the daughter of her first husband, and Blue Sky, son of her beloved Cheyenne warrior.

Deborah taught her young son to love the Cheyenne people, and she instilled in him a deep love for his dead father. She constantly regaled him with tales of the fine deeds of dear Broken Wing. Young Blue Sky, called by the white name *Sky*, wanted to be a warrior like his father. But the Cheyenne way of life was dying as the victorious whites began herding the conquered Indian people onto reservations. What Sky longed for was only a dream. And it was a dream that was constantly buffeted by the harsh realities of bigotry. . . .

# WARRIOR'S SONG

Words by Denella Kimura
Music by Phil Bearce

**VERSE 3**

(Chanting to instrumental accompaniment)

I sing of winding haunted trails
Where snow-capped mountains touch the stars
Through days of fasting, nights of prayer
To lift my spirit, fill my heart;
Come, Father, heal my broken song
Wrapped in your arms where I belong;
Dance in my soul to sweet release,
Your arrows point the way, the way to peace.

**VERSE 4**

(fits tune of vv. 1 & 2)

O God, you shared my guilt and pain,
Caught in two worlds that tore my soul;
You taught my heart to love again
And then forgiveness made me whole:
Show me the pathway through the sky
With healing wind beneath my wings,
You heard this wounded eagle's cry
And gave the song my spirit sings.

# PART 1

# SUMMER 1885

# 1
# AT THE RIVER

Thirty folks lined the banks of the muddy stream. The paltry ribbon of water was hardly the River Jordan where Jesus Christ had been baptized, but in its shallow expanse some might have found a spiritual if not physical resemblance. The worshipers were just glad to have found enough water to perform the holy sacrament for their people.

Young Sky watched closely as Sam Killion dunked his last man. Sky marveled at how detached he felt from the ritual taking place in front of him. In fact, for a few moments his attention had been diverted entirely by a vulture that had swooped down from the sky, curious about the human activity. No one else seemed to notice the ebony-winged creature, but it struck Sky as eerie and gave him a shiver.

Sam pulled his convert out of the water, then all six of the newly baptized believers—two men, two women, and two children—linked arms, with him in the middle. Knee deep in the dirty stream, they began to sing.

*"Take my life, and let it be consecrated, Lord, to Thee . . . take my hands and let them move at the impulse of Thy love . . . at the impulse of Thy love."*

Sky's attention refocused, and he was ready when Sam called to him.

"Go ahead, Sky, finish it for us."

Sky adjusted his guitar, then effortlessly picked out the chords and began to sing in a fine tenor.

*"Take my feet, and let them be swift and beautiful for Thee . . . take my voice, and let me sing always, only, for my King . . . always, only, for my king."*

His voice was soft, almost prayerful. The vulture was forgotten,

17

as were all the other distractions around him. He wrapped himself up entirely in the hymn.

*"Take my lips,"* Sky continued, *"and let them be filled with messages from Thee; take my silver and my gold, not a mite would I withhold . . . not a mite would I withhold."*

He had sung this song many times, perhaps too many. He knew the pose to strike, the tone to take. He didn't have to think about it anymore. That was just as well, for all he *could* think about was that the words might be just a little too simple. Even if you wanted to give your life to God, there were so many things around to interfere with such good intentions. Maybe he didn't want it as much as he thought. Maybe he was afraid of giving up some secret part of himself—something even he could not identify.

*"Take my love, my God, I pour at Thy feet its treasure store,"* he went on. *"Take myself, and I will be ever, only, all for Thee . . . ever, only, all for Thee."*

The last words poured smoothly from his lips, and his fingers nimbly chorded a final flourish.

Sam raised his hands high into the air and cried a fervent, "Praise God! And Amen!"

Then the small crowd erupted into mild mayhem as the dripping converts trailed from the water and were greeted with embraces, slaps on the back, handshakes, and all manner of verbal praise and cheers.

Sky pushed his guitar around to his back and joined the group as they moved up the low embankment. Several makeshift board tables had been laid out with a picnic lunch. Emma Hawkins came up to Sky, giving him a warm, motherly pat on the shoulder.

"I declare, Sky! It never fails to take me back, hearing that wonderful voice of yours. I mean, how marvelous to hear praises to Jesus coming from a dark-skinned Indian boy. Your mama did well with you."

A stiff smile bent Sky's lips. "I reckon so."

At that moment Sam walked by and Emma caught his arm. "Reverend Killion, it's just wonderful how you've taken this here boy under your wing and Christianized him."

Sam gave Sky a covert wink before answering the woman. "Well, Mrs. Hawkins, I wish I could do the same for several of the other young men in these parts."

A look of alarm crossed the woman's face. "I didn't think there were any other Indians hereabouts."

"I'm talking about your own neighbors, ma'am. There are some

18

ranchers' sons who sure could use a dose of 'Christianizing'—"

"But, Reverend—"

"Excuse me," Sky interrupted. "I'm gonna get some chow, if you don't mind."

"Okay, son," said Sam. "In fact, I think I'll join you. Nice talking with you, Mrs. Hawkins." He tipped his hat and strode toward the food with Sky.

"Ya know, Sky," Sam said, "when you sing that song, it brings tears to my eyes. You've got a real talent."

"For an Indian boy?"

"Aw, Sky, don't you know me better than that?"

"Sorry, Sam. You didn't deserve that. Anyway, I guess I shouldn't get bothered if folks notice I'm an Indian—shoot, I *am* an Indian!"

"And always remember that's something to be proud of."

"Sure."

Sky took a plate and began piling it high with roasted turkey, ham, grits, beans, succotash, and bread. He thought of how often he'd heard Sam, or his ma, say those very words to him. Although the words were true, they had been a lot easier to accept when he was younger and had stayed close to home. Back then he would listen to the stories of his wonderful father, Broken Wing, and see the proud light in his ma's eyes as she spoke of him. Sky had known without a doubt that the Cheyenne warrior had been a real man, whose noble measure would have been the same regardless of the color of his skin.

But Sky was too old for stories now.

At seventeen he was nearly a man himself, and the shining image of his father was growing dim. The stories seemed just that—*stories*, fairy tales told to an innocent child. Even the memory of that visit many years ago by his uncle Stands-in-the-River was hazy in his memory. A man needed more than stories and dull memories when the realities of life began to press in upon him.

The spiritual things Sam taught were often elusive, too. Sky was beginning to feel as if nothing would fit in that widening hole in his soul.

Sky swung away from the food table and found a place to sit in the grass with a few other young people his age. He didn't know any of them well, for this was one of the furthermost churches on Sam's circuit, and he saw them only occasionally when he accompanied Sam.

"Is it okay if I sit here?" he asked.

"It's a free country," replied a boy of about Sky's age.

The group grew noticeably silent. Ignoring the slight awkwardness, Sky dug into his food. He wasn't much of a talker, anyway, so the quiet suited him fine. Then, one by one, the teens rose and departed, reforming their group elsewhere.

Well, Sky thought to himself, I ought to be thankful that's all they did. Probably if Sam hadn't been around, one of the boys would have picked a fight with me.

It had been ten years since the last of the Indian wars in northern Texas, but resentments—even hatred—still ran high. In a way, Sky couldn't blame them; many of these very folks were still grieving over personal losses from Indian raids and massacres. Sky could not permit himself similar grief, however. Even though his father had been killed by whites, he'd always had to closely guard his own resentments. After all, he was half white, and many people he loved were white—his mother, Sam, Carolyn, Griff, Longjim, and Slim. In fact, he knew and loved no Indians at all, except for some vague images from the past.

Sky deposited his empty plate in a washtub and ambled over to a cottonwood near the stream. Leaning against the tree, he studied the group in the objective way of an outsider. The folks on Sam's circuit weren't always rude to him. They could be friendly and accepting at times. There was no end of the praise for his singing. But in all the years he had traveled with Sam visiting the churches on his circuit, he had never really gotten close to anyone. Sam said he felt that way himself; you just couldn't develop close relationships when you only saw folks ten times a year. Maybe Sam was right. Maybe it had nothing at all to do with Sky's blood.

The blue eyes which had inspired his name suggested that there was probably a bit more white blood in him than Indian. Not that it mattered to most people. Having any Indian blood at all made him inferior. In fact, Sky often got the impression that being a *half-breed* only made it worse. To be pure anything was somehow better than being a . . . mongrel.

But often Sky looked at himself and thought his skin was no darker than many of the cowboys with their sun-blackened, leathery hides. He had taken to wearing his black hair cut short, and he almost always wore a hat. He thought he looked very white. He certainly *felt* white.

# 2

# CONFRONTATION

It was hot. Too hot.

Spring had turned too quickly into summer. It hadn't rained in weeks, and it was only the first of June. Sky was riding the northern sector of the Wind Rider range, and he was glad to be back at work. Going with Sam on his circuit was not as much fun as it used to be. And it never had compared with riding free over the endless prairie where the brilliant blue sky seemed to come right down and touch the yellow grass.

That's what Sky loved most—even in the heat.

Sky nosed his mount a bit to the west. He was riding a piebald mustang stallion which he had jokingly named Two-Tone. He had drawn range riding duty this week—checking out the cattle, treating screwworm, and making sure the cattle had enough water. It would take him about three days to cover this sector, sleeping under the stars, cooking coffee and tinned beans on a campfire. The good life!

He headed toward the big pond that was used by the Wind Rider Ranch and several other outfits in the summer when they drove their cattle north. It was their most reliable source of water, especially this year. It had been a dry spring and looked as if it would only get worse.

Sky wiped a sleeve across his sweaty brow. "Hey, Two-Tone, how'd you like to take a little dip in the pond?" The black and white stallion snorted and shook his head as if in reply.

Horse and rider picked their way up the rocky hill. In a few moments, as they crested the rise, the shimmering expanse of the pond became visible, like a desert mirage Sky had read about in books. He could almost taste the cool water and feel it tingle over his hot skin.

21

He quickly made the descent and dismounted the minute he reached the water's edge. There was nothing to tie his reins to, but Two-Tone wouldn't wander off, especially within sight of water. Sky dropped the reins and immediately stripped off his shirt and boots.

"What'd you think you're doing?"

The voice startled Sky and made him jump like a skittish colt. Sky spun around, then groaned inwardly. Billy Yates.

"I'm gonna take a swim," answered Sky, matching Billy's defiance. "You got a problem with that?"

"You bet I got a problem, 'cause I'm gonna swim and I ain't gonna swim with no dirty Injun."

Billy hadn't changed much from the first time Sky had encountered him at Fort Griffin, when Billy had been eight and Sky five. That meeting had come to blows, as had nearly every encounter since. Billy Yates was still big and thick like his father, appropriately called Big Bill. But the initial height advantage Billy had once had over the younger Sky had diminished over the years. Sky had shot up to and exceeded six feet. Billy still had twenty-five pounds on Sky, with every ounce pure muscle. Still, the last time the two had tangled, a year ago in Danville after Sky's mother had been arrested, Sky had proven himself an even match with the older, heftier Billy.

"Billy, don't start any trouble." It was a new voice, feminine.

Sky hadn't noticed that Yates wasn't alone. The glare of the sun, combined with the bulk of Billy's frame, had obscured the figure standing behind him. Jenny Yates, Billy's younger sister, stepped forward.

"I ain't starting nothing," said Billy. "We was here first, that's all."

"The pond is big enough—" Sky began.

"It won't cover your smell—"

Sky started toward Billy, fists clenched, violence in his blue eyes.

In an instant, Billy had a six-gun in his hand.

"Billy, don't!" Jenny screamed.

Sky stopped. "You're crazy, Yates."

"I'd be a hero to most folks for clearing out one more Injun."

Sky had no intention of letting a simple swim erupt into bloodshed. He quickly pulled his boots back on, then mounted his horse without even taking time to slip into his shirt. He didn't worry about the cowardly appearance of running away. It would have been pure foolishness to argue with a drawn weapon, especially when it was in the hand of a mean-spirited mule like Billy.

But Sky couldn't resist a final word over his shoulder. "Someday, Billy, you're gonna really make me mad. Then you better watch it."

Sky rode away at a deliberate, easy canter. When Billy's gun exploded and a bullet zinged over Sky's head, Sky did not wince or speed up. He would not give Billy the satisfaction. He rode as if he hadn't heard a thing.

When Sky was well out of sight, he yanked on his shirt and allowed himself to fume. He wished now he had pulled his own gun. Billy wouldn't have expected that, and no doubt he would have turned yellow. Another thing that would have surprised Billy was just how good Sky was with a gun.

During those long winter months when there was less work on the ranch, Griff had taught Sky how to handle a Colt 45. And Sky had learned well. He could outdraw and outshoot all the cowhands except Griff and Longjim. Sky didn't like to advertise his skill, though. A lot of folks were apt to get nervous around an Indian with a gun.

"I wish I could show them all!" he declared to the empty prairie.

It was getting harder and harder for Sky to control his temper. The volcano of fury inside him had been simmering for years, and it didn't take much to make it erupt hot and dangerous. But he constantly had to suppress his resentments. It would tear his mother apart if she knew just how much wrath was burning inside her son.

When his sister, Carolyn, had been around, they had talked sometimes. But now she was gone to Stoner's Crossing, running the ranch she had inherited from her grandfather. Sky usually ended up pouring out his feelings to the four-legged creatures that were part of his life. At least the animals didn't care who he was, or what color his skin was, or who his father happened to be.

His ma and Sam tried to be understanding, but not only were they white, they were just too old to fathom his complex emotions. They were always telling him how proud he should be. But he wasn't proud. How could he be, when all he ever received was derision for who he was? It was no longer enough that his family accepted him. There was more to the world than them. But Sky couldn't tell his parents that. They wouldn't be able to hear it, or understand.

He used to be able to talk to God. But God seemed so far away, and Sky needed relief and answers *now*. Besides, wasn't God a white man? More than that, weren't nearly all the whites who belittled Sky supposed to be God-fearing people? They were Christians, churchgoers. Why, Big Bill Yates was a deacon in the Danville church!

Sky came upon a handful of grazing cattle. He stopped and dismounted, moving in among the dozen or so animals.

"So, how're you fellows doing?" He began checking them over one by one.

"Sam's got an answer to that argument, you know," he said, murmuring his thoughts out loud to the cows. "He'd say Christians aren't perfect. They got their faults like everyone else. And maybe some of them that profess Christ ain't truly Christians. Of course, it ain't for us to judge. God will deal with them. That's what Sam says, anyway."

Sky stopped by one cow and shook his head as he spied a nasty invasion of screwworm in its thick hide. He returned to his saddlebag for a can of medicine.

After roping the animal and tying him down, Sky took his wooden paddle and rubbed the gooey, foul-smelling cresylic concoction into the animal's infected hide, digging out as many worms as he could. It was disgusting work, but the worms made the animals miserable. The cattle didn't fight treatment, so in their dumb way, they must have appreciated Sky's efforts.

"Well, I'll tell you what I say," Sky continued his one-sided conversation as he worked. "It don't look to me like God's doing much about it at all. Maybe there's too many phonies out there for Him to get around to, or maybe He don't think it's a big enough deal to bother with." He paused as if expecting the cow to respond.

"Or maybe I'm just looney. I must be, if I'm talking to a cow!"

He finished his job, mounted his horse and rode away. He had been stewing over this too much. That was the one problem with working on the range—so much time alone when all you had for company were your thoughts.

The sun was going down, and Sky set his attention on looking for a campsite. When he found one, he set up camp, built a fire, and cooked dinner.

He smiled as he dug a spoon into the warm can of beans. His sister used to go on and on about how delicious beans over a campfire were. Sky would take Yolanda's cooking over this any day.

By the time he finished eating, the sun was down and the only light came from the half moon and the fading embers of his fire. He took his guitar from his saddle and began chording a song, pausing for a minute to tune the strings. He made it up as he went and hummed a melody to accompany it. But in a few moments he became bored with it and started to pick out a hymn.

*"Amazing grace—how sweet the sound . . ."*

He had always liked that tune, and the melancholy notes suited his mood. He tried not to think of the words.

Unfortunately, most of the songs he knew were hymns, and ignoring the words soon became too much of a strain.

Life seemed so unfair. What right did people like Billy Yates have to ruin his life? It wasn't Sky's fault he was half Indian. All his life he had fought with Billy, defending himself against those slurs. Wouldn't Billy have a good laugh if he knew that down deep Sky despised that Indian half, that he longed, sometimes desperately, to be white. To be like everyone else. Even like Billy. Was that so terrible?

But his parents expected him to be proud, to hold up his head, to ignore the derision he received. What was there to be proud of?

Then Sky thought of his father.

Broken Wing, Cheyenne warrior.

Maybe it would be different if he were still here.

But Broken Wing wasn't here. He had taken the Hanging Road, as the Cheyenne would say. He was happily hunting buffalo beyond the Milky Way. It wasn't his fault that he had left his son behind in such pain. He had not wanted to leave, to die. Sky couldn't blame his father.

"But, Nehuo," Sky murmured into the wind, "do you blame me for feeling as I do?" Without thinking, he spoke in Cheyenne, a tongue he had hardly used for several years.

Odd, how something like that stayed with a person. No matter how hard he tried to suppress his heritage, it didn't go away, just as the color of his skin would never change.

"Oh, Nehuo! I didn't always hate being Indian. When I was young and listened to my mother's stories, I wanted more than anything to be a warrior like you. I saw myself riding your gray Pawnee stallion, victorious over all my enemies. But I'm not a child now, who can face the world armed only with dreams and illusions.

"And that's what they are, Nehuo. Even if you *were* still alive, there are simply no more warriors, no more Indian glory. And

25

those of us who are forced to face the real world have to do it the best way we can. Why shouldn't I try to claim my *white* heritage? That's who I am, too."

Sky desperately wanted to believe he was right, and that his father would understand. He didn't want to think that his desire to be accepted in a white world might displease his father. But after all, Broken Wing had been torn similarly between the two worlds. His father would surely understand.

Sky returned, almost absently, to the little tune he had made up before. He changed it a little here and there until it had more feeling. Instead of boring him, now, it absorbed him. He didn't know how it happened, but somehow the tune reminded him of the lonely plains—lonely but free, harsh but comforting in its mournful way. The very plains his father had once walked.

The wind at his shoulder seemed the perfect accompaniment to Sky's tune. Words formed in Sky's mind, and he began to sing them quietly.

> My warrior's song borne on the wind,
> Blows from the empty pale blue skies;
> Its chanting moan that has no end
> Sweeps teardrops from my heaven turned eyes:
> White eagle soars on broken wing
> For peace and glory long since gone;
> He leaves a lonely shattered dream,
> And hopes to sing his song at dawn.

An hour later, when he laid aside his guitar, Sky was no less confused. But in a way he didn't understand, just expressing his pain in music made him feel a little better. He wrapped himself in his bedroll and, looking up at the countless stars, fell asleep.

# 3

# RESCUE

Two days later Sky was heading back to the ranch, his circuit of the range complete. The day was another scorcher, but the sky was so clear and pretty that he couldn't complain about the heat. He was eager to get home. As much as he liked riding the range, three days of it made even him look forward to some human company. And he missed Yolanda's cooking. She had promised to make him one of her famous pecan pies when he got home.

With his mind on the pie, Sky almost rode right past the riderless horse. A roan mare was dipping her head to nibble at the grass. She was no wild mustang, either. She was saddled and bridled, her reins dragging along the ground.

As Sky turned his mount and drew near, he recognized the animal. Billy Yates's horse.

For all Billy's faults, he was too experienced a cowboy to let his horse graze with her bit still in her mouth. Besides, no good hand would simply lose his horse out on the range. Something must be wrong.

Nothing in the near vicinity indicated anything amiss, so Sky took the mare's reins, hitched them to the back of his saddle, and started moving again.

Only for a brief instant did he entertain the idea of ignoring the mare. What had Billy ever done for him? And if Sky was seen with Billy's mount, he'd probably be accused of horse stealing.

But the code of the range had been too deeply ingrained in Sky. A man without a horse was a dead man, and anyone who left him in that condition was nothing less than a murderer. Sky had to make an attempt to find the roan's rider, no matter who it happened to be.

But the prairie was big, and there was no telling how far the roan had already wandered. Sky spent an hour combing the area in widening concentric rings. All he found was grass, mesquite, and rocks. Nothing living except jack rabbits, lizards, and snakes. Then he saw a hawk circling in the sky about half a mile away.

Sky didn't like Billy Yates, but he sure hoped that hawk wasn't after him.

Sky closed in on the area and finally caught sight of the figure sprawled out in the knee-high grass. He dismounted, grabbed his water canteen, and knelt beside Billy, pouring a few drops of water over Billy's sunburned face. The swollen eyelids flickered and opened to small slits.

"Good, you're still alive," said Sky. He put the canteen to Billy's lips. "Drink some water."

Billy drank, coughing and sputtering a bit before he managed to swallow some.

"Thought I was a goner for sure." Billy's voice was a mere rasp, barely audible.

"What happened?"

"Rattler . . ."

"How long ago?"

Billy turned his head to get a fix on the sun. "Couple of hours." Then he seemed to notice his rescuer for the first time. "Sky Killion?"

"Yeah."

Billy closed his eyes, saying no more.

"I'm gonna try to get some of that venom out before I move you. I just hope it ain't too late. Where was you bit?"

"Back of my lower leg."

Sky set to work. He had never done this before, but treating snakebites was part of a cowboy's training. He ripped Billy's pant leg open. Most of the lower leg was red and puffy, but Sky hoped Billy had had the presence of mind to limit his movement to prevent the venom from spreading. He took off his own neckerchief and tied it into a tourniquet above the knee where the swelling stopped. Then he took out his pocketknife.

"This is gonna hurt."

Billy grunted. "Get it over with."

Sky found the fang marks and made two deep cuts across them. He sucked out a good bit of venom. Maybe it hadn't circulated too much. If only he had some kind of poultice to put on the wound! Then he remembered an Indian remedy his ma had told him about. He searched around for some buckhorn, a simple prairie weed.

After finding a nice clump, he picked a couple handfuls, chewed several leaves until he had a nice mash, then applied them to the wound. Finally, he took Billy's neckerchief and wrapped that around the poultice and wound. It might not cure him, but it certainly wouldn't hurt. He wondered briefly what Billy would think of being the object of Indian medicine. If the situation hadn't been so serious, Sky might have been amused at the thought.

"Okay, Billy, it's time we get you back to town and to a doctor. You up to it?"

"It's just a snakebite," Billy replied defensively. "Why shouldn't I be?"

Sky shrugged silently. It didn't seem a safe question to answer.

It was no easy matter to maneuver Billy's hulk from the ground onto his horse, especially while trying to keep the injured leg immobile. Billy cursed several times, accusing Sky of everything but rescuing him.

They were silent almost the entire way into town, a good three-hour ride. They arrived in Danville in the late afternoon and found the doctor in, just back from several house calls. The physician took Billy into his office, examined the wound, and praised Sky for his nice doctoring. As soon as Sky knew Billy was in good hands, he turned to go.

Billy, lying on the examination table, grabbed Sky's sleeve. "Why'd you do it, Killion?"

"What?"

"You know what."

Sky shrugged as if it had been a trifling matter. " 'Cause I was there."

————————

Billy Yates chewed on Sky's statement for a long time. At first, it made him so mad that for a while he forgot Sky had saved his life. He couldn't quite define what it was, exactly, that angered him. Maybe it was the half-breed's haughty arrogance—as if he had anything to be proud of. He acted as if helping Billy had no more importance than if he had been a sick cow!

Then the doctor said something that sent Billy's mind spinning in another direction.

"Well, Billy, sure looks like you owe that half-breed boy. You'd be pushing up daisies if he hadn't come along when he did."

"I'd have found some other way to get help."

"I'll tell you, if I was Sky Killion right now, I'd be wishing I'd

29

left your ungrateful bones to the vultures."

"Why should I feel grateful? You heard him; he did no more for me than if I was a lame critter."

"But he did do something. He could have just rode by, especially since there's always been bad blood between the two of you. No, Billy, you better face it—you owe that Indian boy big."

Billy fumed silently. His pa had always taught him to be independent. There was hardly anything worse than being beholden to anyone—much less an Indian. It was unthinkable.

Somehow Billy had to find a way to even the score with that half-breed.

# 4

# THE DEBT

A week later, Sky was in Danville with Griff to pick up supplies. Griff was hauling sacks of feed out from the general store and handing them to Sky, who loaded them in the wagon. Sky paused to wipe a sleeve across his sweaty brow.

"Hey, no malingering," Griff called good-humoredly. "There's only a couple more to go. Remember I promised to buy us pie at the cafe when we finished."

"I ain't forgetting that."

Griff tossed another sack, then looked up. "Uh-oh, here comes trouble."

Billy Yates was walking toward them, limping slightly on his snakebit leg. Sky braced himself. He couldn't remember a single encounter with Yates that hadn't erupted into trouble—except the other day, and Billy had been too sick to do much of anything. Maybe now he was going to make up for the lost opportunity. Maybe he had found some reason to hold the incident against Sky. After all, Sky had only saved his life.

When Billy reached them, he spoke in an uncharacteristically soft tone.

"Killion, I want to talk with you."

Griff responded first. "Listen, Billy, we don't want no trouble. Just move along like a smart fellow." Griff rested his hand pointedly on the handle of his holstered six-gun.

"This don't concern you, McCulloch, so butt out."

"What do you want, Yates?" Sky said.

"Just to talk—in private." Billy raised his arms to indicate he wasn't armed. "Just talk, that's all."

"Okay." Sky looked at Griff. "I'll be back in a minute."

Sky jumped from the wagon and followed Billy down the

wooden sidewalk a short distance, then into an alleyway between two buildings. They walked behind a couple of buildings, finally pausing next to Billy's roan mare, which was tied to a back-door latch. Sky glanced around warily. This looked like a good place for an ambush.

"So, what's on your mind, Yates?"

Billy spoke hesitantly. Sky had never seen the town bully act like this. "You know, the other day when you . . . found me out on the range."

Sky nodded.

"I reckon you saved my life."

"I reckon."

"Well . . . I never thanked you."

"I didn't expect no thanks."

"Don't matter. I'm . . . beholden to you. I owe you—"

"Forget it, Billy. You don't owe me nothing. I did what anyone would have done. I don't want your thanks. I don't want nothing from you. You've been giving me grief ever since I can remember. One little thanks ain't gonna erase that."

"That ain't the point. The way I grew up, a man pays his debts. I'm not apologizing for the past."

"Like I said, forget it." Sky started to turn. Billy grabbed his arm to stop him.

"You gotta let me make up for this. You wouldn't want to be beholden to me if the tables were turned, would you? It's just common decency to let a fellow take care of these things."

Sky crossed his arms and eyed Billy smugly. "This is really getting to you. And it's more than owing just anyone. It kills you to be indebted to the town half-breed." An ironic smile slanted Sky's lips. "This is some predicament you're in, ain't it?"

"You're really trying my patience, Killion. You gonna let me thank you or what?"

"That's all your life is worth, a word of thanks?"

"What do you mean by that?"

"You said you was in debt to me. You figure whispering thanks to me back here, all alone, is gonna settle everything?"

"I guess so."

"I figure you owe me more than that. I figure the only way to really settle this is for you to thank me in public—"

"Aw, come on!"

"See you later, Billy." Sky turned again and started walking away.

32

Before Sky went three steps, Billy called, "Okay, I'll do it. Then I'm free and clear."

They walked back around to the front of the buildings.

"There's only one place to do this," Billy said. "Real men settle things between them over a drink. We'll go to the saloon."

Sky hesitated. His ma and Sam had brought him up on the evils of strong drink and saloons. Even at seventeen, he figured his ma would skin him alive if she saw him go near a saloon. Sky was pretty sure Billy knew that. He had probably suggested the saloon for that very reason, thinking that if Sky backed down, Billy would be in the clear. But Sky had been in control of the situation up until now, so why couldn't he just insist that they go to the cafe?

Sky knew the answer to that. Billy was talking about how *men* settle their differences. For the first time in their lives, he and Billy were reacting to each other in an adult way. No scraps in the street or yelling matches. Billy was twenty years old, a grown man, and he was inviting Sky to meet him on that level. Besides, Sky reasoned to himself, Griff frequented saloons and he wasn't a bad person. And it wasn't as if Sky planned to *frequent* the saloon. He'd just go in long enough for Billy to make his announcement. Five minutes.

Besides, Billy's announcement would have the most effect where there were the most cowboys. In the cafe, only women and children and a couple cowboys there for a meal or pie would hear Billy's declaration. But this time of day on a Saturday afternoon, the saloon would have a fair enough representation from the local ranches to make Billy's thanks count for something.

"Let's go," Sky said.

Before they could cross the street to the saloon, Griff called from behind. "Hey, Sky, I finished loading. Let's go get that pie."

"Some other time, Griff, okay?" said Sky. "I got some business to settle with Billy."

"Business?"

"Don't worry, there ain't gonna be trouble."

"Well, if you're sure . . ." Griff didn't sound convinced. "I'll meet you in half an hour in front of the general store."

When Griff was gone, Billy nudged Sky. "You ready?"

"Just a minute." Sky told himself he didn't have anything to hide. Still, he waited until Griff was almost to the cafe, at the other end of the street, before he started moving.

———

About a dozen customers were in the saloon, mostly cowboys, some standing at the bar, some seated at tables. Two saloon girls were circulating around. The piano was quiet and the voices were subdued. It seemed as if everyone was saving up for the wild Saturday night ahead.

No one noticed as the two young men strode in. It didn't matter to any of them that one of the boys was only seventeen and his ma would have a fit if she knew where he was. Young men did a man's work in the West and were entitled to be treated as adults.

Billy strode confidently to the bar. This was obviously not a new experience for him.

"Whiskey," he said.

The bartender set one glass in front of Billy.

"What about me?" Sky asked.

There was no apology in the barkeeper's voice. "It's against the law for me to serve liquor to an Injun."

The words hit Sky like a blow, just like everything else that reminded him of his ancestry. Even in Billy's presence he felt so white. It was easy to forget how he looked.

"He's with me, Jim," said Billy. "This here Indian saved my life. I owe him a drink." Billy turned and said in a louder voice to the room in general. "You fellas hear that? This Indian—Sky Killion— saved my life!" Then, facing Sky, he said in the same strong, clear tone. "Thank you, Sky. I owe you."

Sky suddenly felt very uncomfortable. He wished he had never made Billy do this.

"Now, barkeep," Billy went on, "how 'bout a drink for my . . . uh, for this Indian?"

"They'd close me down if I was caught."

"Well, we gotta settle things with a drink."

The bartender shook his head.

"Okay, then I'll buy a bottle." Billy plunked down some coins on the counter.

The bartender shrugged, scooped up the coins and set a bottle on the counter. Billy took it and motioned for Sky to follow him.

Outside, Sky said, "You did what you said you'd do, Billy. You don't have to do no more."

"This ain't gonna be finished until we settle it with a drink. Unless you're afraid whiskey won't mix with your Injun blood."

Sky rankled and turned on Billy with a menacing glare.

"Okay, that wasn't called for," Billy said with a surprising note of apology in his tone. "But why else wouldn't you drink with me?"

34

"For one thing, Billy, men don't drink with their enemies. So, if we have a drink together . . ."

"It don't mean we gotta be blood brothers or nothing."

"That's for sure."

"Come on."

They went back to where Billy's horse was still tied. Billy immediately opened the bottle and was about to bring it to his lips when he stopped and handed it to Sky.

"You first."

Sky took it and quickly raised it to his mouth. He pointedly kept his mind blank—at least he tried. But uninvited thoughts crept in anyway. It was the first time in his life he'd tasted whiskey, and he remembered something Sam once told him: *"Liquor itself ain't so bad, son. It's what liquor does to some folks that's bad— it's the way liquor takes control of some folks that's bad."*

As the whiskey touched Sky's lips, he told himself that whiskey wasn't going to ever control him. He would prove it. He took a big, almost defiant gulp. The burning liquid nearly gagged him. Coughing, his eyes watering, he spit out half of it.

Billy laughed. "Let me show you how a man does it." He took the bottle but paused before drinking. He started to wipe the rim with his hand, then stopped, shrugged carelessly and lifted the bottle to his lips. He took a long swallow and grinned afterward, wiping a sleeve across his mouth.

"I guess that's it," said Sky, trying not to show that he was impressed.

"You can have another drink if you want. It's a hot, thirsty day and it gets easier with practice."

"Your debt's clear, Billy."

"You saved my life. Least I can do is give you another drink."

They passed the bottle back and forth a couple times. Sky could hardly believe what was happening. Yes, the whiskey did go down easier each time, but more than that he was amazed at what was transpiring between him and Billy. He hated Billy Yates, and Billy had always made it clear the feeling was mutual. They had grown up practically at each other's throats. Now, here they were actually sharing a civil moment. And Sky had never spent time like this with a peer. He'd never had buddies of his own age to pal around with. The closest he ever had to a friend had been Griff and some of the cowhands at the ranch. But Griff was old enough to be his father, and the others were a lot older, too. He'd always been "the kid," never a friend.

35

A couple of friendly drinks didn't exactly make him and Billy friends. Yet Sky had to admit that he was seeing a side to his adversary that had never been revealed before now. There seemed more to Billy Yates than the bigoted bullying.

Or was it just the effects of the whiskey? Sky was starting to feel a bit woozy. He'd probably had enough. Any more and he'd have to answer to his ma.

"I better be on my way," Sky said after a final pull on the bottle.

"I gotta know one thing, Sky. Why'd you do it—save me, that is?"

"I already told you."

"Yeah, ''cause you were there.' But no one would ever have known if you had just gone on by."

"I would have known. And I think you would have done the same thing. You would have stopped, you would have helped me."

"You're wrong there, Sky. A week ago you was just another Indian. I could have rode by real easy. It's different now, though. You're more of a person now. I still don't know what to make of it all."

Sky rolled his eyes with disgust. "I ain't no different. I'm the same 'dirty half-breed' I always was to you. Or else you're gonna have to deal with the fact that I was a *person* before, too."

Billy swore. "I wish you hadn't saved me. All it does is complicate things."

"I'm starting to regret what I did, too," Sky said broadly, the effects of the alcohol emboldening his speech. "It was a lot easier to hate you. Just promise me we don't have to start being friends or anything."

"Don't worry 'bout that! It's the furthest thing from my mind."

"First time we ever agreed on anything!" Sky laughed.

"Yeah, what'd you know!"

# 5

# ULTERIOR MOTIVES

Billy was standing by the corral watching a cowhand break a newly caught mustang. It was a pretty mare, dapple gray and spirited. Billy's sister had been wanting a new horse—her present mount, she complained, was an old nag that could barely walk, much less gallop. Their pa didn't think a gal needed more than that. It was hard to gallop riding sidesaddle anyway, and he'd never permit her to ride astride.

Still, Billy thought Jenny would like the dapple gray mustang, and he had all but promised Jenny he'd ask Pa about getting her a new mount. Billy supposed he was nothing but a softy where Jenny was concerned. But she was such a sweet, pretty little thing, and since she was the only female around the ranch, it wasn't surprising the Yates men tended to spoil her. Even Big Bill melted in his daughter's presence, though he did stay firm where matters of femininity were concerned. Jenny could do nearly anything, as long as it was ladylike. She had wardrobes full of dresses and bonnets—no split skirts, though, like that brazen Deborah Killion and her daughter.

When Billy looked up and saw his pa approach, he decided he'd ask him about the horse. But his pa had something else entirely on his mind.

"There you are, Billy." Big Bill leaned on the rail, propping a foot on the lower rail. "I hear you was in the saloon yesterday drinking with that half-breed kid of the Killion woman."

"We wasn't drinking—they wouldn't give him no liquor."

"It's a good thing! I woulda turned them in if they had. But what was that all about, anyway?"

"Now don't get riled, Pa."

"I ain't riled. Not yet, anyway."

"You know when I got snakebit? It was the half-breed that found me and brought me into town. The doc said I would have died otherwise."

"You don't say?"

"Anyway, I didn't want to be beholden to him. So, he told me I'd be in the clear if I bought him a drink and thanked him publicly."

"He had a nerve!"

Billy shrugged. "Was I wrong to go along?"

"I don't know why you thought you owed him anything. He's just an Injun."

"You always taught me—"

"That's for your equals, Billy."

"But, Pa. He could have just left me out there, especially after all the bad blood between us. I reckon it kinda took me by surprise."

"What's done is done. Now, I figure we can use this whole incident to our advantage."

"What do you mean?"

"At the last Cattlemen's Association meeting there was a fella from up north talking about barbed wire. That Killion woman got all up in arms. She wants no part of wire, and she's got a fair contingent of ranchers behind her."

"Yeah?"

"My Galloway bull is gonna be arriving in a few weeks. I want to improve the quality of my stock, and I don't want no free-range advocates standing in my way. I also just signed a deal with that wire salesman. There's gonna be changes around here."

"So, what's that got to do with me?"

"Well, maybe it wouldn't hurt to get on the good side of the half-breed. Now that the ball's rolling that way, we ought to make the best use of it."

"I can't believe I'm hearing this, Pa. I thought you had no use for Injuns."

"I got several thousand dollars invested in this project, what with the bull and the wire. I'll use anything to keep my investment safe. So keep cozy with the half-breed and win him over to our side."

"What makes you think his ma is gonna put any stock in what he thinks?"

Big Bill shook his head disdainfully. "Boy, don't you pay attention to anything that goes on around here? Why, last year when Deborah Killion was down south in jail, the half-breed ran the ranch. She puts a lot of stock in what that kid thinks. And when she's gone, the Injun is gonna own her big spread. I ain't saying winning him over is a shoo-in for winning her, but did you ever hear the saying, 'Divide and conquer'? That's all we need to do."

"Why don't you just put up your fence and tell 'em all to go to blazes?"

"I'm gonna do that, don't worry. But I'll do what I can to prevent a range war. If it don't work, then I'll fight."

"It ain't an easy thing you're asking me to do. Injun or no, he did save my life."

"So, you're doing him a favor, then, by befriending him. He ain't got no friends around here, especially since his sister left."

"Well, I'll think about it."

"Listen up, boy. You'll *do* it, you hear?"

Billy hated it when his father pushed him around. Maybe he should have been used to it after all these years, but he was too much like his pa to adjust easily to such treatment.

"I'll do it," Billy said sulkily. "But in return, you gotta let Jenny have that there mustang."

"You got cheek, trying to make deals with me." Bill paused, glanced at the horse, then shook his head. "Why not? She'd probably cajole it out of me some other way."

After his pa walked away, Billy cursed under his breath. As if this whole thing with Sky Killion wasn't hard enough, his pa had to make it worse. Billy Yates knew he was sometimes a bully and a blowhard, but one thing he wasn't was a phony. Now his father was making him be that as well. It just didn't set well with Billy, after all his talk to Sky about his debt, to turn around and use that very debt for his father's gain.

But he was stuck. Billy couldn't go against his father, and his pa knew that. Well, there was no reason for Sky to ever know. The minute things quieted down about the fence issue, Billy could just find some reason to drop Sky. And that would be that.

He sighed as he turned away from the corral. At least Jenny would get her horse out of the deal.

# 6

# BARBECUE

Even though the Lowells threw the best barbecues in the county, Sky didn't want to go. Now that his ma's name had been cleared with the law and she didn't have to keep such a low profile, she was wanting to get better acquainted with their neighbors. But Sky didn't see why that should mean he had to do the same.

Still, his ma wanted to do things as a family. Probably she was feeling a touch of loneliness with Carolyn gone. Sky decided to go for her sake. Besides, if he had refused too adamantly, she would have wanted to know why. And Sky didn't want anyone to know just how deeply he was feeling the subtle bigotry of the community.

He would go to the party, eat—the food would be great, that was something!—then leave if things got uncomfortable.

"*If*? More like *when*," he mumbled to himself as he finished dressing.

Nearly a hundred folks turned out for the shindig. A dozen ranches were represented, along with many townsfolk. Sky could have easily faded into the woodwork—and he was wishing he could do just that after Doug Lowell's greeting.

Sky wondered what bothered him more—outright hostility, or the patronizing attitudes of people bending over backward to prove how accepting they were. Lowell had made such a particular point of welcoming Sky that it made him feel more *different* than ever.

The food wouldn't be served for a while, so Sky had to wander about trying to look as if he fit in. Billy Yates was in a tight circle with three or four of his friends. Sky fleetingly thought of joining them, but gave it up because he just couldn't muster the nerve to break into the group. They didn't notice him.

He watched as a newcomer attracted a little group around him—a man dressed in city clothes, with a Yankee accent.

"Now, gentlemen, this is a social gathering. I don't want to mix business with pleasure, you know."

"This may be the only convenient chance some of us will have to talk with you, Mr. Eddings," said Tom Weaver of the Bar W Outfit.

"Well, I don't know. . . ."

"Go on, Eddings," said Doug Lowell, joining the group. "I don't mind a bit of business being discussed. Just keep it friendly."

"Wouldn't think of doing anything else," said Eddings.

"So," said one of the men, "tell us about that wire of yours. You really think it's gonna hold in cattle? I got an ornery bull nothing'll hold."

"Barbed wire has been proven effective, even with the strongest animals," said Eddings. "It's the wave of the future, men! Northern markets are clamoring for a better grade of beef—the Longhorn is no longer going to suffice. There is only one way to insure the quality of your product and protect your investments."

"He's right there," said another. "Those fancy breeds ain't cheap."

"What about us small ranchers? Open range is our lifeblood."

"Of course there is going to be a period of adjustment," hedged Eddings. "But in the long run everyone will benefit from better quality stock."

"There's been problems down south."

"That's right," put in Weaver. "I heard of some shootings and a couple of cowhands getting killed over that barbed wire."

"Most of what you hear is pure exaggeration," said Eddings. "There is nothing that can't be worked out with reason and level-headedness."

"Range wars?"

"But you folks are reasonable people. No need for—"

Big Bill Yates broke in. "Eddings, tell them about the Frying Pan ranch up in the panhandle."

"Ah yes, a glowing tribute to the march of progress."

Having heard enough, Sky turned his head to focus his attention elsewhere—anywhere but on all that gibberish about the merits of barbed wire. A voice spoke his name and he jerked around, startled.

41

It was Jenny Yates. She was so close, he almost bumped into her when he turned.

She smiled apologetically. "I'm sorry, did I startle you?"

"I guess I was too deep in my own thoughts."

"I won't intrude."

"That's okay. I can have my thoughts anytime. You want something?"

"I just saw you here all by yourself—"

"Don't worry about me," he cut in defensively. "I like being by myself."

"Oh. Then I am intruding."

"Naw. I didn't mean that. But you don't have to feel sorry for me or anything."

"I didn't. I just wanted to speak to you alone for a moment, that's all. I wanted to apologize for my brother's behavior the other day at the pond. I don't know what gets into him."

"That's nice of you, Jenny. But do you go around making up for your brother a lot? It must keep you awfully busy."

She smiled, a sweet smile that made her soft brown eyes glow. Jenny Yates was a pretty girl. Funny, he hadn't noticed this before. But it had been a while since he had seen her—not counting the recent encounter at the pond—and she must have blossomed like a prairie flower. Her brown hair was shiny, with a whole bunch of curls that she had pulled back from her face and tied with a red ribbon at the back of her head. It made her round face and rosy cheeks and almond-shaped eyes all the more distinctive. And the red and white checkered dress she wore, all soft and frilly, just made the effect even better.

"I also wanted to thank you for what you did for my brother— you know, saving him after he'd been snakebit. But mostly, I guess I just wanted to talk to you." She blushed, heightening even more the pink in her cheeks. "You don't mind, do you?"

"Not at all. Why should I mind a pretty girl like you wanting to talk to me?"

"You know, you're our closest neighbors and it's too bad we've never been friends. I always thought I would have liked to get to know your sister, even though she's a couple years older than me, but . . . well, it never worked out."

"We were never very sociable."

"My pa doesn't much like me riding all over tarnation, either. I always envied your sister's freedom. I never saw women like her and your ma work a ranch. I'll bet you're proud of them."

42

"I guess they just did what they had to do."

"I'm going to do more riding now, too. I got a new horse. It's back at the ranch, but if you'd like to come by and see her sometime you'd be welcome."

Sky smiled. "Only by you, I think."

"Well, it is my house, too."

Sky changed the subject. "What's your horse like?"

"A dapple gray mare. A pretty mustang. She's small, but she fits me perfectly. She was caught with a wild herd up by Waggoner Hills, you know, about ten miles north of the pond."

"Yeah, we've got some good horses up that way, too. My ma is still trying to get the great white stallion that runs with his herd up there."

"I've heard of the white. Have you ever seen him?"

"I did once. I doubt there is a more magnificent animal alive."

"It would be a shame to capture such a creature."

"I think, down deep, my ma feels the same. She almost had him once, but I think she just didn't have the heart to put a rope on him."

"I'd give anything to see him."

"I'll take you up there sometime."

"The pond is about as far as my pa ever lets me go."

An awkward silence descended. Sky fidgeted, not knowing if they were finished and he should depart, or if she still wanted to talk. Nervously, he glanced around and caught Big Bill Yates's eye. He tried to look quickly away so Yates would think he hadn't noticed. But Sky couldn't feel comfortable talking to Jenny any longer knowing her father was watching them, probably ready to storm in on them.

"I guess I'll be on my way," Sky said as if he had any place to go. "It was nice talking to you."

"There's going to be dancing later. I'll save one for you, Sky."

"That might not be a good idea."

"I don't care what anyone thinks."

"Well, it's a good thing one of us does. But I enjoyed talking to you, Jenny."

"Same here. Let's talk again sometime."

Sky nodded and walked away. Maybe he'd stick around for the party, after all. Maybe he *would* dance with Jenny Yates.

And maybe he'd catch that white stallion, too. Maybe . . . when it snows in July.

# 7

# NEW FRIENDS

Dinner was served outdoors under the three big oaks in the Lowells' front yard. Seated at a long table, surrounded by other guests, Sky felt alone as he ate his barbecue. He had hoped Jenny might eat with him, but she was sitting with some girlfriends. He ate quickly, then went to find his ma to tell her he was leaving.

Billy Yates found him first.

"Hey, Sky, some of us think this party needs livening up."

"Yeah. I was getting ready to leave."

"No need for that."

"What'd you got in mind?"

"Come with me."

Sky followed Billy around back and to the barn. He didn't know what to expect, but it was so rare to be invited to do anything, he was willing to take a risk.

Billy opened the big doors wide enough for them to squeeze through. It was dim inside despite the late afternoon light that slanted in through openings high in the rafters. They climbed up a narrow ladder that led to the loft, and there they were greeted by eighteen-year-old Kyle Evanston and Tommy Ray Lowell, known as T.R., who was Sky's age.

"What you got there, Billy?" asked Kyle, eyeing Sky with open hostility.

"Told you I was gonna get a friend to join us," said Billy.

"Yeah, and look what you came back with."

"You all listen here," Billy replied with conviction. "Sky Killion saved my life—so, if you want me you gotta take him, too."

"I never asked to come here," said Sky, anger welling up in him.

44

"Aw, simmer down," Billy replied. He turned to Kyle and T.R. "So, what's it gonna be?"

"I ain't never drank with no Injun before," said T.R.

Sky spun around and headed for the ladder.

"Now, wait up, Sky," Billy said. "These boys just don't know you for the fine man you are. Let 'em get used to it."

"What for?" snapped Sky. "I don't need any of you."

"Everyone needs friends."

"We agreed—"

"Shut up and give it a chance—all of you," said Billy with authority. He was, after all, the oldest in the group and the natural leader. "T.R.'s got some of his daddy's best whiskey," Billy went on. "If we ain't getting along after a couple of swigs, then we can forget the whole thing."

Sky wondered why Billy was suddenly such a peacemaker. But Yates was right about one thing. Everyone did need friends. There was precious little to choose from in the way of young men his age besides these fellows. There wasn't a rancher's son in the county who wouldn't have been just as bigoted.

What did their motives matter? If it turned out they were just trying to get the "Injun" liquored up for a good laugh, he could pulverize all of them when they started laughing. If not . . . well, it would harm nothing but his pride to take the risk. And he was used to having these boys take potshots at his pride. Maybe, like Billy, they would think differently once they got to know him as a *person*.

Sky turned and faced the group. His shoulders were hitched back, his chin jutted out, his glinting blue eyes challenging any of them to reject him.

T.R. held up his bottle of whiskey. As if meeting a challenge, Sky took it and gulped down a mouthful. He held back the urge to sputter and cough, only biting his lip as the burning liquid seared its way down his throat.

Billy and Kyle seemed to be more accustomed to the strong drink. T.R. had about the same reaction as Sky. It was just his second time, too. Although they were allowed to go into saloons, drink, and pack guns just like their elders, there was another standard by which most of the boys had to adhere. The majority of women, the mothers of these boys, were churchgoing teetotalers and temperance advocates. Many of the women, and a few of the men, would have shut the saloons down in an instant if they could. The ranchers forbid alcohol on their spreads, so the saloons were the only place the cowboys could go to "blow off steam." For that reason saloons were tolerated as a necessary evil—but most definitely an *evil*.

A bartender might welcome them, but young cowboys usually risked the wrath of God if their mothers ever found out. Even at a social function such as the Lowells' barbecue, strong drink was absent in deference to the women. The men might go off alone for a brandy later, but the young men didn't care to be in the company of the stodgy elders.

After two drinks Sky's head was spinning. His limbs felt loose and relaxed, and the sensation must have reached up into his brain, too, because he didn't get mad when Kyle laughed, "We're not only getting an Injun drunk, we're getting the minister's son drunk, too."

"Killing two birds with one stone," T.R. agreed, his tone more friendly than malicious.

"Guess I gotta drink enough for two, then," Sky rejoined with a laugh.

They all laughed and drank some more.

"Hey, you guys notice that dress Becky Sue Weaver was wearing?" Billy asked.

"Didn't leave nothing to the imagination," said Kyle.

"You don't know what I been imagining," Billy leered.

The boys howled in response.

"I'm gonna dance with her tonight, then I'm gonna get her to come up here," Billy bragged.

"That'll be the day!" said T.R. "Everyone knows she's the biggest tease in the county."

"Hey," said Sky, "you planning on going back to the party?"

"Why not? That's what the whiskey's for—to make it more fun."

"But my ma'll skin me alive when she sees I been drinking."

"Don't you know nothing, Sky?" Billy's tone was obviously intended to be superior, but he slurred too much for it to be effective. "We got ways so they'll never know."

"Really?"

"For one thing we ain't gonna overdo it. One more drink and that's it. Then we give things a chance to settle before we go back."

"And finally," said Kyle, "this—" He pulled out some peppermint sticks and tossed one to each of his companions. "The worst we'll get in trouble for is eating too many sweets."

"I dunno," said Sky, "I feel awful woozy."

"Me, too," T.R. said.

"Then maybe we better cork the bottle now," said Billy.

"It's my bottle," said T.R., "and I'll say when to put it away."

They had one more drink, then T.R. corked the bottle and hid it under the hay.

"Okay," Billy said to the two novices, "stand up and let's see you walk."

Sky and T.R. obeyed and nearly collided into each other in the process. But at Billy and Kyle's urging, they kept walking around the loft until they could do so without staggering and weaving.

"You work this gonna think—" said Sky. "I mean, you think—"

"Boy, you two are the sorriest drinkers I ever seen."

Leaning on each other, Sky and T.R. tried to protest, but they had such difficulty getting the words out that they started giggling instead, crumbling to the hay in a heap of laughter.

Billy made them keep working on it until they could feign soberness fairly well—that is, if no one looked too closely.

"Just don't draw no attention to yourselves," offered Billy.

"How we gonna have fun, then?" asked T.R.

Kyle answered, "You'll have fun 'cause you'll be able to laugh at all the dull conversation."

"And," added Billy, "now you won't be too shy to ask a girl to dance."

"Yeah," said T.R. "I feel like I could ask 'em all to dance! Why, I think I'll ask Becky Sue—"

"Uh-uh," warned Billy. "She's for me."

"Let's go an' have some fun," said Sky.

They trooped down the ladder. T.R. tripped near the bottom but Sky caught him. T.R. threw an arm around Sky.

"Now you've saved my life, too, buddy! You're some kind of redskin hero!"

Sky only laughed, high on the alcohol and on the heady sense of camaraderie he suddenly felt. He was ready for anything now.

---

It was dark when the boys rejoined the party. The dancing was just about to start. Lanterns had been strung around the yard and around a plank "dance floor" that had been set up. The musicians were tuning their instruments.

Pausing at the edge of the crowd, Sky took a deep breath. He felt good. Real good.

The musicians started with "Santy Maloney," and about half the crowd formed a circle for the dance. Since there was no strict pairing of couples for this particular dance, Sky didn't feel the least awkward in joining the circle as it skipped in rhythm to the first verse. When the second verse began, everybody was having such a good time no one noticed that Sky and his new friends were laughing louder than the rest, or that they were clumsy on their feet. By the time the song was over, everyone was warmed up and ready for more.

When the leader called, "Okay, choose a partner for 'Bow Belinda,'" everyone scurried around to obey. Billy went right for Becky Sue. Billy's example, along with the whiskey-induced boldness, impelled Sky straight toward Jenny Yates. He held out his hand to her, and she took it with a smile sweeter than the peppermint stick Sky had eaten to hide the smell of alcohol.

They formed two long lines, boys on one side and girls on the other. First the boys bowed several times to their chosen girl, then the caller instructed them to take the right hand around. As Sky took Jenny's hand he felt a tingling up his arm as if her little, soft hand had some power of its own. He had never had so much fun in his life.

———

As Bill Yates, standing on the sidelines, watched the scramble for partners, he didn't know what shocked him more—that the half-breed had the nerve to ask his daughter, or that she accepted with such a winning smile. He felt the flush of anger rush up his neck as they touched hands. His own hands were clamped into fists at his side.

How dare that dirty Injun touch his daughter! He wasn't gonna stand for it. Just as he was about to take action, a quiet voice beside him spoke.

"Listen, Bill, calm your hackles." It was Doug Lowell.

"Try and make me!"

"I ain't going to have no trouble at my party."

"You'd think different if he was dancing with your daughter."

"It's just a dance," Lowell said, "don't mean a thing. In fact, you just hold tight and I'll show you I can practice what I preach."

As soon as the dance was over, Lowell found his daughter—a pretty yellow-haired girl who had no lack of dance partners.

When the musicians announced the next tune, she went right up to Sky and asked him to dance. A few mouths dropped open— not so much that she had singled out Sky, but that a girl was asking a boy!

48

Watching, Big Bill crossed his arms, striking an ominous pose. But he held his peace. This time.

———————

Sky was giddy with exhilaration. He'd never danced with a girl before, always shying away from the possibility of rejection in the past. Now, not only had the girl of his choice accepted him, but another had actually asked him. He had never known how much fun you could have with a few swallows of whiskey. Too bad he hadn't discovered it earlier.

But he started to regret it when one of the musicians called to him as he danced near to them. "Hey, Sky, everyone needs a little rest. Sing a song for us."

"You're doing just fine," Sky said, wondering if his voice sounded completely normal.

"Come on. You can use my guitar."

Jenny came up to Sky. "Oh, Sky, won't you? I love to hear you sing."

How could he refuse that?

Accepting the guitar, he took an extra moment tuning it. His fingers felt a bit numb, and his lips seemed thick and unwieldy. He picked a lively tune so no one could notice if he made any mistakes.

*"Buffalo Gals, won't you come out tonight, come out tonight? Oh, Buffalo Gals, won't you come out tonight, and dance by the light of the moon?"*

When he finished, someone called—was it Sam's voice?—for him to sing "Red River Valley." Out of the corner of his eye, he saw Jenny clap her hands and join in with others who were also encouraging the request.

This was one of Sky's favorites, and besides a few hymns, it was one that he did especially well. But his lips were dry and his fingers seemed to fumble over the more delicate chording.

*"From this valley they say you are going. We will miss your bright eyes and sweet smile. . . ."*

He couldn't help his own eyes straying once more toward Jenny. Did she realize he was thinking of her as he sang?

*"For they say you are taking the sunshine that has brightened our pathway awhile. Come and sit by my side if you love me, do not hasten to bid me adieu. But remember the Red River Valley, and the boy that has loved you so true."*

When he started the second verse, he picked the wrong chord,

49

and with a lopsided grin of apology, he started over. But he managed to get through the rest of the song without a hitch. And when he was finished, he even enjoyed the applause which he usually hated. He noticed Big Bill Yates's scowl, and Griff's knit brow. But he ignored them. Right now, all he wanted was to bask in Jenny's praise.

# 8

# THE MORNING AFTER

Sky awoke the next morning with a start when he heard his ma's knock on his door. Outside his window he saw the sun just starting to lighten the sky. Sky had a slight headache, but nothing like the miseries some of the cowhands had after a Saturday night drunken spree.

He dressed and went out to the kitchen. Breakfast was steaming on the table and Yolanda had made her specialty, fried bread thickly sprinkled with sugar. That's when he remembered it was Sunday morning, and that Sam would be preaching at the church in Danville. His circuit allowed him one Sunday a month in Danville. On the off Sundays there was no church, though Deborah always had devotions for the family and any interested hands in her living room.

When church was in Danville, the day was nearly as hectic as a workday. Morning chores had to be done, then everyone had to be ready to depart on the three-hour drive to town so they could arrive by ten. Sam, of course, had to be the first one there to open up the church and get a fire going to warm the building. The whole family was expected to ride together to church.

This morning going to church was the last thing Sky wanted to do. He wondered if Billy, Kyle, and T.R. would be there. Maybe they could get together afterward and finish T.R.'s bottle of whiskey. But Kyle never went to church and Billy hadn't been in months. T.R. was the only regular attendee, besides Sky, in the group. Maybe Sky would go over to Billy's place and see what he was up to. But first, he had to get out of going to church.

He pretended to pick at his food. It was a hard ruse because he was hungry and Yolanda's cooking was good. But it had the desired effect.

"Sky," his mother asked, "is something wrong with you? You've hardly eaten a thing."

"My throat's a little sore," he lied. "Might be coming down with something."

"I'll fix you up with a remedy," said Yolanda.

"Yeah, I think that's what I need."

His ma laid her hand on his forehead. "Well, you don't feel warm. Maybe you just had a little too much barbecue last night."

Sky instinctively started to balk. The statement made him seem like a little kid. But in time he remembered to take advantage of it instead. "Yeah, I do have a little bellyache, too."

"Perhaps you ought to stay home today," she said.

"But, Sam, weren't you expecting me to sing?" asked Sky.

"Don't see how you can sing if your throat's ailing you."

"I hate to let you down."

"Don't you worry," said Sam with concern. "You just take care of yourself."

———————

Deborah breathed in the fresh air, still crisp with a morning chill. She was disappointed Sky hadn't come with them. It struck her how her family was beginning to dwindle. Was this just a preview of the future? Only she, Sam, and Yolanda left to carry on family traditions? She ought to be able to accept it, for it was natural for children to grow up and strike out on their own. But it wasn't easy, especially since she had always been so close to her children. Then she reprimanded herself. Sky was still young, and one missed church service didn't add up to him leaving forever.

"Too bad about Sky," Sam said, as if he knew what she was thinking.

"Oh, I'm sure it's nothing serious."

"No, he didn't look none too sick."

"Sam, do you think he was faking?"

Sam concentrated for a moment on guiding the horses over a particularly rocky stretch of road. Deborah waited patiently for his response. She had a feeling there was more on his mind than Sky's possible illness.

In a few moments he said, "I've been a little concerned over his lack of interest in church."

"But he was just with you on your circuit. You said he sang beautifully at the baptism."

"That's true, but he hadn't gone with me for a while before that. And . . . I don't know, it just seems he's more detached than usual."

"Maybe it's just normal rebellion. All kids that age go through it, so I suppose Sky's turn had to come."

Deborah sighed. Perhaps she was downplaying it too much. But Sky had always been the "easy" child. For so many years Carolyn had been the child she was forever agonizing over. Carolyn was the rebellious one, sometimes too independent for her own good, and filled with emotional anguish she usually kept bottled up. Sky, on the other hand, was far more easygoing and good-natured. He was a quiet child, but he had never given the impression of intense emotional struggles. Or, had his struggles simply been buried beneath the more overwhelming concern over Carolyn?

Were his needs just becoming more noticeable now that Carolyn was gone? Had they always been there? Perhaps Sam was just blowing things out of proportion. Sky's biggest problem had always been the bigotry of their neighbors toward him. But if last night was any proof, even that seemed to be taking a turn for the better.

"You know, Sam," Deborah said, breaking the brief silence, "I really don't think we need to worry about Sky. Last night he seemed to be having a real good time. He actually appeared to be getting along with Billy Yates. Maybe the other boys are finally accepting him."

"Sure seems to be coming from out of the blue. Wonder what brought it on."

"Could have been one of your sermons," Deborah said with a playful smile.

"I won't deny the effectiveness of my sermons, but most of the boys I saw Sky with last night haven't heard me preach since . . . I can't remember when." He paused. "And, Deborah, do you think Billy Yates is the best company for Sky? He's a wild one."

"I don't know. But if Sky is finally making some friends, it won't be easy to raise objections to them. Anyway, Sky has a good head on his shoulders. He'll use sensible judgment."

"Let's hope so."

Deborah felt slightly uncomfortable as Sam spoke. She didn't like the tone of his voice, the uncertainty she sensed in him. She decided to let the matter drop. No sense thinking up trouble where none existed.

"What did you think about that barbed wire salesman at the Lowells' last night?" she asked.

"A real slick operator," said Sam. "He's winning over several ranchers."

"It worries me, Sam."

"That fellow was right about one thing—there ain't nothing much we can do about progress."

"I suppose I'm an anachronism around here, but fencing off the open range just doesn't set well with me. I keep thinking of a dream Broken Wing had about a terrible fenced-in place. To him, it had been a nightmare about the Indian reservations. But this strikes me as similar. I've never much liked closed-in places."

"You gonna fight it, Deborah?"

"I don't want it to come to that. If it did, I could never be a party to a range war. But I might not have much of a choice. Mr. Eddings might have won some ranchers over, but he's got plenty of others up in arms. The first person who tries to put up that wire is going to meet opposition—and regardless of what Eddings says, there are enough hotheads in this county to make that opposition more than verbal."

"Speaking of hotheads," said Sam, "I heard a rumor last night that Bill Yates was working on a deal to buy some of that barbed wire."

"I'm not surprised. I sometimes wonder if he deliberately tries to be on opposite sides from me."

"This doesn't seem a good time for Sky and Billy to get friendly."

"No, it sure doesn't."

"Let's just pray our young folks don't get caught in the middle."

"I'm praying trouble can be avoided altogether."

But even as Deborah spoke the words of faith, she wondered if it could be possible. South of them in an adjacent county, there had already been trouble, and one cowboy had been killed in a gunfight. But that had been a hundred miles away. Maybe in Danville County they could learn by the mistakes of others. Yet even Deborah had to wonder how the free range advocates and the barbed wire advocates could ever find common ground. By its very nature, wire fence was going to get in someone's way.

Perhaps a friendship between Billy and Sky could turn out to be beneficial. Rather than being caught in the middle, they might serve to foster compromise. Deborah smiled to herself. It took more faith than she had to picture Billy Yates in the role of peacemaker.

# 9

# HEATED WORDS

After church the congregation gathered for coffee, lemonade, and cake. Since there was only one Sunday a month with the preacher, the people tried to make the most of it. Often weddings, baptisms, dedications and such were taken care of on that day. But on this particular Sabbath there were no weddings and only two baptisms, so the gathering was purely social.

Since most of the folks present had just been to the Lowells' barbecue and were already warmed up to one another, the flow of conversation was easy and steady. Sam circulated around, feeling more the host today. Deborah, not the social creature that Sam was, talked with a small group of ladies. But she had less in common with them than with their rancher husbands, so her attention soon wandered from the talk of recipes and fashion. She caught a snatch of conversation not far from where she stood.

"Don't think I've met you before," said a man whom Deborah did not know. He was speaking to Eddings, the fence salesman.

"Name's Dwight Eddings, and I am new to these parts. I'm a salesman from Ohio." Eddings thrust out his hand, and the other man shook it.

"Glad to meet you. I'm Arnel Slocum. From Kansas myself, but I bought a small ranch here six months ago." There was a short pause before Slocum said casually, "So, what is it you sell? Maybe it's something I need."

"I have a strict rule never to do business on the Sabbath."

"And I respect that. I'm just asking for curiosity's sake, not business."

"In that case, I sell fencing."

Deborah had a good view of Slocum, and at the moment Eddings mentioned fencing, Slocum's face changed dramatically. All the friendliness fell from it, but Deborah couldn't quite identify the emotions replacing it.

"Fencing, you say?" Slocum's voice was strained. "What kind of fencing?"

"All kinds, but I specialize in a new fencing material called barbed wire. Ever hear of it?"

"I heard of it."

"I'm so enthusiastic about it that I better not say another word or else I may start to sell it, and that would never do today. So, tell me about your ranch, Mr. Slocum."

"You got a nerve coming here to the house of God." Slocum's tone sent a chill down Deborah's spine. Others also noticed Slocum's raised voice, and heads turned.

"I . . . I don't understand." Eddings seemed genuinely confused.

"You do the devil's work! You don't belong in a church."

Sam arrived on the scene just then. "Mr. Slocum, I brought you a glass of lemonade—"

"I don't want none." Slocum was wild-eyed now, shaking with anger. "And, Reverend Killion, I don't see how you can let a man like this in your church."

"All are welcome in my church, Mr. Slocum," said Sam. "But if you got a problem with someone, I think it's best we talk together in private."

"This is something that's gonna affect everyone here." Slocum looked up at the others, who were all focused on the scene. "Don't let this man fool you. He's gonna bring us all to doom with his wire. He's gonna—"

"Mr. Slocum," Sam put an arm on Slocum's shoulder, intending to soothe him.

Slocum jerked away, and Bill Yates chose that moment to intercede. He strode toward Slocum and spoke in a tone just short of challenge. "Listen here, Slocum, you got no right spreading slander about someone you don't even know."

"I don't need to know him. His kind are all the same. They only care about making money. They don't care that what they're selling is a killer."

"I take offense at that," said Eddings. "What I represent is the wave—"

"Wave of death!" shouted Slocum. "You wanta see? I'll show you—" Slocum yanked off his jacket, then shoved the sleeve of his right arm up as high as it would go. Turning his arm toward the crowd he revealed a ragged scar, red and mean-looking, that ran from his elbow up the length of his arm, continuing under the sleeve. "And there's more of the same on my back, too. That's what comes of barbed wire! Where I come from in Kansas they got the wire. But a storm knocked down some and the grass hid the fallen wire so's I couldn't see it when I was riding. My horse panicked when she got tangled up in it. She broke her leg and had to be shot. I got so cut up it nearly killed me, too."

"An isolated accident, Mr. Slocum," said Eddings.

"You know very well it ain't isolated. There's plenty of others that's been caught in barbed wire."

"You don't know what you're talking about," said Bill Yates.

"Bill," said Sam, "why don't you let me handle this."

"You'd like that, wouldn't you, Reverend? We all know where the Wind Rider people stand on the issue."

"I don't have any stand, except for peace and harmony among the people of this county."

"There'll be peace so long as no one interferes in what a man does on his own land," countered Yates.

"Anyone who gets that wire near my land," warned Slocum, "will wish he never laid eyes on Eddings."

"All right! That's enough!" said Sam sternly. "I'll have no more such talk on the Lord's day. But I think there ought to be a meeting between all interested persons very soon. Let's say Wednesday evening at the Cattlemen's Hall."

The gathering ended on that note. No one had the heart to continue socializing after what had happened. But Deborah sensed that Slocum had stirred emotions among his listeners that had been merely simmering beneath the surface. She hoped Sam's meeting would help, but she couldn't see how if all the opposing forces were as emotionally charged as Slocum and Yates. Only trouble could come of it.

# 10

# THE PRANK

Sam's meeting was a failure. Both Yates and Slocum were absent. Those present talked back and forth for three hours and resolved nothing. Both sides viewed any compromise at all as an infringement of their rights.

Within the next couple of weeks, Bill Yates's barbed wire fence started going up. It encompassed ten square miles of range, cutting off two roads and the all-important pond.

Sky knew how his mother felt about open range, and he realized that most of her feelings about the sanctity of the wide open prairie sprang from her years with the Cheyenne. As Indian freedom had been cut off by encroaching whites eventually forcing them onto reservations, Deborah's natural inclination made her abhor even the semblance of confinement. Had Deborah's views been based on anything but her Cheyenne experience, Sky might have taken a different approach himself. But it appeared to him that if the open range somehow related to Indian principles, then fencing must basically be a white man's movement. Of course, open range proponents were also white, but they were mostly the small ranchers—renegades so to speak. Deborah was one of the few big ranchers to favor open range.

From Sky's vantage it seemed clear that the *white* thing to do was to favor barbed wire. And since he wanted so desperately to be white, he tended to side with that contingent. It was subtle at first, but his association with Billy soon began to solidify his position. And it was clear from the beginning that continued friendship with Billy meant taking his side in the fence issue. A couple of other youths, sons of small ranchers and thus opposed to barbed wire, were blackballed from Billy's circle of friends when the fence first started going up on the Yates's Flying Y Ranch.

Sky was tired of being a loner. For the first time in his life he had friends his age. The fence issue seemed a small concession to make. No one really cared what he thought, anyway.

He and Billy and T.R. could be found together almost anytime they had free time from work. Kyle joined them once or twice, but he was far less accepting of Sky's presence than the others and soon he stopped coming when Sky was there.

When the other three got together, one or the other of them always managed to have a bottle of whiskey to share. Sometimes they played poker, sometimes they performed stunts or had races on their horses, and sometimes they played practical jokes on cowboys they knew. But always they got drunk first. It just seemed that everything was more fun that way.

The three young men met up at the pond one night. Billy slapped Sky on the back when Sky produced a bottle of apple jack. "Hey, boy, where did you come up with this?"

"One of our wranglers had it. Can you believe his nerve? He's lucky I didn't turn him in for having this alcohol."

"My pa would have fired the man," said T.R.

"It's a strict rule on our place, too," said Sky. "I saved the fellow's hide by getting rid of this for him."

"Who cares if he ain't privy to your *helpfulness*."

"Go on, Sky, open it," urged T.R.

"This is brandy," said Billy. "It's rich and sweet, so you gotta go slow with it."

They went slow, but drank more than half the bottle anyway. Billy kept saying it was good stuff. It must have been, for Sky couldn't remember being drunker. He couldn't remember much about that night, least of all who had been the first to mention Reily, the Flying Y foreman. It must have been Billy who told of seeing the foreman finish a whole bottle of whiskey in one night and not even stagger afterward.

The foreman was a mountain of a man who dwarfed even Big Bill. An Australian, he had fought crocodiles bare-handed, and it was rumored he had fled Australia with a murder charge over his head. He was the toughest man Sky had ever seen, even tougher than Griff.

"The only thing I ever seen that's a match to Reily is my pa's new Galloway," Billy said. "That bull's ornerier than a polecat that's swallowed a rattler."

One thing led to another, and the boys soon concocted a plan.

They would "liberate" the bull so the cowboys would have to catch it.

They rode to the Yates ranch, their heads swimming with the strong drink. Sky nearly fell out of his saddle twice. But they finally made it, stopping a few hundred feet away to form a plan of attack.

Since the bull was new and the main pasture was not all fenced in yet, Yates was keeping the expensive animal in one of the big pens near the stable. It would be a small matter to open the gate. The problem was to open it, spread the alarm of the bull's escape, and get away before being caught by either the bull or the foreman. The boys decided that one of them should take care of the gate while another, awaiting his signal, would waken the hands in the bunkhouse; the third would guard their horses. Somehow that last, relatively safe job fell to Billy.

"Hey, it's vital our horses don't get away in all the excitement. We'd be up a creek without a paddle then," he said.

"You're the oldest," said T.R. "It's only right the most important job go to you."

No one mentioned who was getting the most *dangerous* jobs. But Sky and T.R. gave no thought at all to possible dangers. In fact, they fought over who should have the riskiest task, that of waking the bunkhouse. That person took the greatest risk, for he would be the last to make a getaway from the scene. They settled it with a coin toss, which Sky won.

It was late, and not a single light burned at the ranch. Sky and T.R. crept in as quietly as they could. T.R. went to the bullpen and nearly lost even his alcohol-induced nerve when he found the bull standing only a few feet away from the gate.

Sky hesitated, but T.R. waved him on. "When he gets out I can shut myself in the pen and get out on the other side."

Sky moved on to the bunkhouse. He could hear snores inside. He found what he was looking for at the end of the long front porch—the cook's dinner bell, which also acted as a general alarm during emergencies. A couple of clangs on that in the middle of the night, and those snoring cowhands would be falling all over each other to get outside. But Sky couldn't find the iron bar used to strike the bell. He panicked a moment, fearing he wouldn't be ready in time to position himself so he could see T.R.'s signal. He looked around frantically until he spied a broom leaning against the wall. That would do in a pinch. Taking the broom, he went to the end of the bunkhouse where he had a view of the bullpen.

T.R. was waiting until he saw him, so the moment Sky waved,

T.R. threw back the gate latch and pushed the gate wide open. The bull lazily looked at the swinging gate, then up at T.R., who was perched on top of the fence rail.

"Move it, you big hunk of lard!" T.R. urged the bull.

Sky watched, amazed that the so-called ornery bull suddenly seemed so tame. What was needed was some loud noise to get him riled up. Would T.R. think of that? Just as long as he didn't try to fire his—

But T.R. decided that firing his six-gun would be just the thing. It obviously didn't dawn on him that it would not only wake everyone up, but the men would more than likely be charging out of the bunkhouse ready for a gunfight.

T.R. raised the gun and fired. "Ya hoo!" he shouted, and fired again.

The Galloway charged through the opening, taking half the swinging gate with him. The jolt knocked T.R. off the rail, and he fell outside the pen. White with panic, T.R. scrambled to his feet, but the bull didn't notice him. T.R. ran for it.

Sky watched, momentarily stunned to stillness. Then shouts from the bunkhouse stirred his senses, and throwing down his useless broom, he also raced away from the scene. But not before a couple of cowhands fired at his retreating backside.

He had no trouble outrunning any cowboys who might choose to pursue him. But when he cast a hurried glance over his shoulder, he saw no one. Perhaps they were too occupied trying to recapture the bull. When Sky reached the horses, T.R. had just arrived himself. Billy shot questions at them but they were too breathless to answer, and there was no time for questions if they wanted to make a clean getaway.

They mounted up and galloped away.

Back at the pond, the boys dismounted and T.R. and Sky excitedly recounted their escapade to Billy.

"But what were those gunshots?" asked Billy.

"Had to wake up the bull," said T.R.

"What?"

"Nearly got me shot," complained Sky. "Those cowhands were looking for a fight."

"Didn't think of that," said T.R., a lopsided grin of apology pasted on his face.

"Well, I need a drink after all that," said Sky.

"Me, too."

They finished off the bottle of apple jack, and most of a bottle of whiskey Billy had. Any sobering effect the prank might have caused was quickly dissipated in more drink.

----

Sky got home late. He'd had a hard time staying in his saddle on the ride home. He started toward the house but a lamp was burning, so he decided against that and headed, instead, to the bunkhouse. He'd rather one of the hands catch him like this than his ma or Sam.

Aside from a brief moment of panic when the bunkhouse door made a loud creak, he slipped inside undetected. He found an empty bunk and crashed on it fully dressed. Suddenly his stomach, which had been queasy since he left the pond, finally erupted its misery. He hardly had time to turn his head. Vomit ran down his chin, onto his clothes and his blanket. Then he passed out.

----

For several weeks Sky had practiced a successful deception. No one at all knew of his frequent escapades with Billy. He had felt quite satisfied with himself and saw no reason why anyone should ever know. His ma had mentioned once or twice about him looking "peak-ed" in the morning, but she accepted his excuses that it must have been something he ate, or that he was tired from working late.

When Sky awoke the next morning, it crossed his mind that his secret was probably spoiled now, but he did not immediately care. What disturbed him most was the sunlight pouring in through the unshuttered window. Who had the nerve to open the shutters with men still sleeping?

The bright light penetrated his closed eyelids and pierced his throbbing brain. He had already experienced minor hangovers, but nothing like this. The entire top of his head felt as if it were about to explode—and he almost wished it would and end his misery. But it wasn't only his head that troubled him; his stomach was still queasy, sending waves of renewed nausea up to his throat. The stench from the previous night didn't help. He moaned, fearing his stomach would lose its contents again. He tried to get up, but movement only made it worse.

Sky barely noticed the footsteps approaching his bunk, and only the shadow blocking the horrid sunlight caught his attention. He opened his eyes to the merest of slits and saw Griff's tall figure looming over him.

"Feeling poorly, son?" Griff asked.

The voice seemed to boom in Sky's ears.

"B-bellyache," Sky answered thickly.

"Something you ate?"

"M-must be."

"I've *eaten* the same thing a time or two," said Griff.

Even in his misery Sky noted the sarcasm in Griff's tone. It began to dawn on him that he'd been found out.

"I don't care what you do to me, Griff. Just so you kill me first and end my suffering."

"That bad, huh?"

"I don't reckon it could get worse."

"I got something for you," said Griff, and for the first time Sky noticed he was holding a big tin cup. "This is the cook's special concoction. Drink every last drop."

Groaning, Sky forced himself to a sitting position on the edge of the bed. With shaking hands he took the cup.

"Ugh!" he sputtered as the brew touched his tongue. It smelled like camphor and tasted like cod liver oil and—something he couldn't identify. He turned his head away from the awful stuff.

"I said drink it!" Griff ordered, and the sharpness of his voice made Sky's head pound.

Sky choked it down, and for a moment it seemed as if it would come right back up. But that urge passed and in another moment his insides began to calm.

"What's in that stuff?"

"You don't want to know," said Griff. "Okay, now it's time for a bath."

Since he didn't feel like arguing, Sky submitted, even when Griff's idea of a bath was for Sky to go out back, strip to his longjohns, and let Griff pour several buckets of cold water over him.

When they were back in the bunkhouse and Sky had dressed in clean clothes, Griff instructed Sky to sit at the table.

"Okay, now how about talking?"

"Where is everyone?" Sky hedged.

"Working."

"They know?"

"Couldn't hide the smell, son, even if they didn't see you. Anyway, nearly every man here has at least once passed out in his own vomit, so you couldn't hide it from them."

"Anyone . . . else?"

"I ain't seen your ma yet this morning, if that's what you mean."

64

"You gonna tell her, Griff?"

"What do you think she'd do to me if she found out I kept it from her?"

"Come on, Griff!" pleaded Sky. "Help me out, just this once. Ain't a fellow allowed one mistake?"

"*One* mistake, you say?"

"Sure, it's not like I'm out every night drinking and carousing." The lie came incredibly easy. But he rationalized that it was best for his ma's sake that the whole truth be whitewashed a bit.

"Your ma would have a fit if she saw what I seen this morning. And I sure don't want to be the one to cause such a scene. But I figure all boys have to indulge at least once in their lives—and I don't personally see nothing wrong with the occasional drink or two, despite the fact that alcohol don't mix well with my own constitution. So, I'm the last one to preach at you. But, Sky, it's still a fact that your ma and pa don't believe in strong drink."

"But I'm almost a man, Griff. Ain't it my choice?"

"Sure, but is that what you're gonna choose even if it'll break your mama's heart?"

"Aw, Griff, that ain't fair!"

"There I go preaching. Guess I forgot myself for a minute."

"You gonna tell her, Griff?"

"This puts me in a bad place, Sky. But I'll tell you what bothers me more than the drinking, and that's who you been hanging around with."

"What do you mean?"

"You been with Billy Yates, right?" When Sky nodded, Griff went on, "He's always been a troublemaker. I can't see where associating with him is gonna lead to anything but trouble."

"He's my friend, and he's been nothing but okay with me."

"What brought on this sudden bout of friendship? A few months ago, we could barely keep you two from killing each other."

Sky told him briefly about the snakebite incident.

"And now he's your bosom friend?" said Griff, still skeptical.

"Why not? We finally got to know each other as people—you know, not just 'Injun' and 'white man.' "

"I don't know . . . that Yates's mean streak seems too deep to change so easily—"

"Yeah? Well, what do you know anyway?"

"I know a sight more than you, boy. And I'll give you a piece

65

of free advice. The only time you can trust a polecat is when he acts like a polecat."

"So, I guess everything Sam preaches about repentance and turning over a new leaf is just hogwash. No one can ever change."

"I ain't saying that—"

"You used to be an outlaw, Griff. I guess you're still an outlaw."

Griff smiled and rubbed his chin. "Guess you got me there, Sky." Griff paused and shook his head in defeat. "Now, about this other problem . . ."

"You gonna tell my ma?"

"You gonna do it again?"

Sky shook his head adamantly. "Are you kidding? After the way I feel? I ain't never gonna touch the stuff again."

"Then, in that case, I don't see no reason to say anything to your ma."

"Thanks, Griff."

Griff stood and started to leave, but paused at the door. "Sky, you take care of yourself, okay? I know from my own experience how life can kind of pull a fella into things before he knows what's happening. I never meant to become an outlaw, but that's just what happened. And I've regretted it ever since. I guess I don't want to see the same thing happen to you."

"Don't worry, Griff. I wouldn't let nothing like that happen."

Griff eyed Sky for an uncomfortable moment before he finally left the bunkhouse. Sky sighed with relief when the door shut. He fully believed his final affirmation to Griff, but he couldn't get out of his mind the fact that Griff didn't look very convinced.

# 11

# DINNER
# CONVERSATION

Sky drew range duty for the next three days, and he was glad to get off alone. He told himself he liked the friendships he had made, and despite the awful hangover, he'd never had more fun than when they let loose the Yates's bull.

Why, then, was the peace of being alone so soothing? Just him, his horse, the cattle, and his guitar.

He didn't ponder that question too much. And at night, when his thoughts were free to wander as he sat alone by his campfire, he reined them in by concentrating on his music.

Sky returned home to a tense atmosphere. There was talk among the Wind Rider hands of trouble over Bill Yates's new fence. No one had details, and everyone seemed to have a different version of the story. Sky got the full tale at dinner that night. Griff, who usually ate with the hands, joined the family for the evening meal. Sky supposed he was there specifically to discuss the fence.

"The Yates's fence stretches across the old Parker Road," Griff explained. "Seems Collier was taking his family into town on that road when they found it blocked. A Flying Y hand happened to be riding by, and he told them they'd have to go around. Collier refused to move and finally the hand fetched Yates. Going around would have added two hours to the trip into town from the Colliers' place. Yates said it wasn't a public road, and since it was on his place, he could do what he wanted with it. Well, Collier finally gave in and went around. He had his family with him and could hardly do more."

"And if he hadn't had his family?" asked Deborah.

"Two or three of the spreads out by Collier's place have been using that road for years, and now Yates just cuts it off," said Griff. "Seems to me the ranchers could make an issue over it."

"Will there be gunplay?" asked Sam, though he must have already known the answer to that question.

"There has been in other counties," Griff replied. "Why should we be any different? People will put up with it to a point, turn the other cheek once or twice, but Yates and the fence people are only gonna be able to push so far."

"We have enough range to weather this," said Deborah. "But the small ranchers depend on open range."

"Deborah, do you mean we'll stick our head in the sand 'cause it don't affect us?" Griff's tone carried a challenge.

"I don't believe in settling differences with violence," said Deborah.

"We fought Indians together," Griff reminded her.

"Only in self-defense."

"Ain't this the same?"

"Our lives aren't in imminent danger."

"Our *way* of life is," said Griff emphatically.

"Let me ask you something, Griff," countered Deborah. "Would you kill to protect our range?"

"People are gonna get killed, Deborah. I don't see no way around it."

"You didn't answer my question."

"Okay, you want an answer—here it is: It ain't *my* range, it's yours. I'm just the foreman. I always do what the boss tells me." Deborah smiled and Griff added, "Well, almost always." His sheepish grin was once more replaced with solemnity. "If you don't want to fight this, I won't. But then you'd better be prepared to give up the open range."

A long moment of silence followed, broken only by the hollow clanking of forks against plates. Sky could see that no one, including Griff, liked to hear in actual words just what they were facing.

Sam broke the tension. "I wish that meeting had done some good."

"You did your best, Sam," said Deborah.

"A stubborn mule like Yates ain't gonna have anything to do with meetings," said Griff.

"If only he could be made to realize there is a peaceful solu-

tion—that everyone, by compromising a little, will only gain from
it."

"But doesn't he have the right to do what he wants with his
own land?" Sky asked.

"No matter how big this land is," answered Griff, "one man's
actions are bound to touch another. A fence is a prime example of
that."

"But he put gates on the two public roads his fence crossed,"
said Sky. "Maybe the others need to compromise, too."

"Whose side are you on, boy?" said Griff.

"I'm just trying to be reasonable. Isn't that what Sam was wanting?"

"It's going to be hard for all of us not to take sides," said Deborah. "I know when I rode out yesterday and saw that fence, it
made me sick at heart. Part of me cries out to fight anyone who'd
do that to my lovely prairie. Then I remember what fighting did
for the Indian people. They were doomed to lose from the beginning."

"But they still fought," said Griff.

"Yes, and I suppose they'd do the same again."

"Even lost causes are worth fighting for if that's what you believe," said Griff.

"I won't fight," Deborah said firmly.

"The sanctity of a man's land is one of the basic human laws,"
said Griff.

"Don't that apply to Bill Yates, too?" asked Sky.

"I don't know about you, Sky," said Griff. "Maybe you been
spending too much time with them sidewinders—"

"Or, maybe I'm just not too blind to see the forest for the trees."

"Sky!" Deborah said. "Don't you speak to Griff in that way."

"You mean I don't have any say in what goes on in this ranch?"

"I didn't mean—"

"You can't have me run this place when it's convenient, then
expect me to go back to being a little kid again when it suits you.
Maybe you should take a look. I'm not a kid anymore."

"Sky," said Sam, "no matter how old you are, you won't speak
to your elders in that way, especially to your mother. You need to
apologize."

"I'm sorry," Sky said quickly, with just enough edge to his tone
to indicate he wasn't happy about it.

"Yolanda," said Deborah, "don't you have some pie for us?"

"Sí, señora. I made pecan special for when you got home, Sky."

"I ain't much hungry for pie right now," said Sky. "Maybe later." He pushed back his chair and started to rise, then he paused and looked at Sam. "May I be excused?"

Sam started to speak, and it was obvious from the look in his eyes that what he was about to say wasn't going to be simple permission. But Deborah interceded.

"Yes, Sky."

---

Sam wasn't happy with Deborah's handling of the situation with Sky. He was generally relaxed with his stepchildren, and since he'd never had children of his own, he often felt inadequate in dealing with problems of youngsters. Thus, it was natural for him to leave most matters of discipline to Deborah.

There was one area, however, in which he felt strongly, and that was the matter of respect. In the past, it had always been more of an issue with Carolyn than with Sky. But he couldn't abide disrespect, even if it was rare.

Shortly after dinner, he went into the kitchen for another cup of coffee. Yolanda and Deborah were finishing up with the dishes. He poured himself a cup, then sat at the kitchen table. He drank quietly for a while, considering if he wanted to bring up the subject of the dinner discussion. He uttered a silent prayer asking for the right words and the right opportunity. When Yolanda dried her hands and left, Sam figured there might not be a better opportunity.

"Have some coffee with me, Deborah?" he asked casually.

"Sounds good," Deborah replied. "But first, come and look at something."

He rose and went to the window where she was gazing out. It was dusk, and the sky was a mixture of fading colors and murky gray. The yard was mostly in shadows, and the figure seated on the ground, leaning against a fence post about twenty feet away, was barely visible. But the guitar cradled in his arms left no doubt it was Sky.

"I remember when we bought him that guitar," said Deborah. "He saw it in a store window when we were visiting Fort Worth."

"He was only twelve."

"Yes, but he had to have that guitar. I thought it was a whim and would end up cast aside for a new fancy, like other toys. I tried to tell him we knew no one who could teach him how to play it. But you said you'd help him learn."

70

"Pretty cocky of me, since I didn't know nothing about playing musical instruments."

"But you know music. If you were Sky's real father, I'd say he inherited his voice from you."

"I can carry a tune fair to middlin', but that boy goes way beyond me."

"But you both sat down with the book that came with the guitar and figured out all of the chords and such."

Sam smiled. Those were such pleasant memories. He had truly felt like Sky's father then, and probably had never felt closer to Deborah's son. "Well, Sky figured it out mostly by himself," said Sam. "I'm glad it worked out, though. He's got a real talent. He can play anything, even makes up his own tunes."

"It's more than that, Sam. Many times I think music is like medicine for him."

Sam just nodded and continued to watch out the window, recalling many other times when Sky would retreat just like this—and escape into his music. Sometimes his fingers would move over the guitar strings with a fury, as if demons were being released from his soul through his hands and being carried away by the music. Sometimes there would be a peace on his face while his fingers glided over the strings, as if the Spirit of God were washing over the boy's heart and soul.

Deborah spoke again. "He wouldn't have that if I hadn't listened to you back in Fort Worth." She paused. "I guess this is my roundabout way of saying I'm sorry for cutting you off the way I did at the supper table. I don't exactly know why, but sometimes I feel so protective of Sky."

"It's not been easy for him being half Indian in a county of nearly all whites. He's taken a lot of jaw from folks."

"I guess that's it. I want to make a pleasant world for him."

"No matter how hard you want to keep him safe, Deborah, you know he's gonna have to face the world someday."

"I'm afraid of losing him, Sam." Deborah stopped, took a ragged breath. She was on the verge of tears. "Losing him not only to a mean and cruel world, but also to himself. When we talked a few Sundays ago about Sky, you said something about him being more detached lately. I don't know why I didn't notice before, but since we talked, I've seen it, too. It's hard to talk to him, and when we do talk, more often than not it ends up in an argument, like at supper tonight. I feel like his enemy instead of his mother."

71

"I reckon sometimes to young folks that can be one and the same."

"Do you think he'll get over it?"

"Carolyn did."

"That's true. I suppose we just have to hang on until maturity rides the 'buck' out of him."

"I couldn't think of a better picture of being a parent," chuckled Sam.

"Let's just pray he doesn't buck us right off on our backsides."

They laughed and found the levity refreshing. Sam was glad to see the tense lines on Deborah's face relax. But that night he was on his knees for an hour in prayer for Sky.

# 12

# JENNY

After roundup, ranch work slowed down for a while, and so one day after coming in from range duty Griff gave Sky the day off. Sky wouldn't have gone out to the Yates place except, having time on his hands, he was bored. Even if Billy was now his friend, he had good reason to wonder if Big Bill would welcome him. But what was the worst he could do to Sky?

He didn't find Billy at the corral or in any of the outbuildings, and none of the hands knew where he was. At last Sky went to the house. As he was approaching, Jenny Yates waved to him from the back porch. She was holding a broom, but even with a faded old apron covering her yellow dress, and her hair carelessly pulled back in a bun with a damp strand of hair falling in her eyes, she looked like the prettiest girl Sky had ever seen.

"Texas dust," she said, giving the broom a little shake before she leaned it against the wall. "We never see the end of it."

"I always tell Yolanda she ought to give up trying."

"I know I'll never get rid of it," Jenny chuckled. "I'd just like to keep it from taking over. So, what brings you all the way out here in the middle of the morning, Sky?"

"I got the day off and I thought I'd see if Billy wanted to go riding."

"He went to town with my pa."

"Oh." Sky couldn't hide his disappointment. "Guess I'll just have to be bored alone."

"I don't know if this is as good as riding, but I just baked some cookies—"

"I best not."

"They're my ma's recipe. Before she died, they won her a blue ribbon at the county fair."

"You don't say."

"Come on, you've gotta try some."

"I don't think your pa would approve."

"My pa isn't here. But, anyway, he doesn't seem to mind your friendship with Billy, so there's no reason why we couldn't be friends."

"Okay, you've convinced me. Besides, I've got a sweet tooth that would never forgive me if I turned you down."

She opened the door. Sky stepped inside, immediately greeted by the delicious fragrance of freshly baked oatmeal cookies. He took a deep breath and forgot all about the trepidation he felt as he entered the home of his nemesis for the first time. Jenny slipped off her apron and hung it on a hook, then took a pin out of her hair and let it fall in soft curls around her shoulders.

"I look a sight for receiving company," she said, straightening her dress.

"No, you don't—not at all." Sky was glad she couldn't tell that his pulse had suddenly increased.

Jenny's cheeks flushed a bit, and she smiled shyly. The slight awkwardness they both felt was lifted when she brought a dish of cookies to the table where Sky had seated himself. She got a pitcher of lemonade from the icebox, poured them each a glass, and then sat across the table from Sky.

"These are the best cookies I ever tasted," Sky said after finishing one in two bites. "Your ma would be proud."

"I always hoped she would be. She died when I was four years old, so I can hardly remember anything about her. All the reminders I have are things like her recipe box and a trunk of clothes."

"I know how that is," said Sky. "My pa died when I was two. But I have nothing of his."

"That's too bad. I've found great comfort over the years touching my mother's things. How did his things get lost?"

"They didn't get lost." He hesitated, wishing the subject hadn't come up. He didn't like to be reminded of his Indian heritage, especially in the presence of this pretty white girl.

"What happened?" she prompted innocently. Her eyes were filled with curiosity and interest.

"It's the Cheyenne custom when a warrior dies, his lodge is taken down and all his belongings are distributed among others in his tribe."

"Oh . . . I nearly forgot that you're part Indian."

"I'm sorry . . ."

Embarrassed, Jenny tried to salvage the conversation. "Was your father really a warrior?"

"Yes. He died fighting the white man."

"Oh, my!"

"I'm sorry, Jenny. I didn't mean to shock you."

"I'm not shocked at all." She paused, then added with a sheepish grin, "Well, not much, at least."

"I'd be surprised if you weren't," said Sky. "You must have grown up hating Indians just like everyone else."

"I guess I grew up *around* it, but it just never seemed right to me to hate anyone. It's not what I learned in church."

"But your pa goes to the same church."

"It's confusing, isn't it? But no matter what my pa thinks, there's just something inside me that tells me all people are equal before God, and nobody deserves hatred just because of the color of their skin."

"That's if you think of Indians as *people*. I got a feeling your pa doesn't. And you know what? I kind of think the only way Billy can be friends with me is by ignoring my Indian half. I don't mind; I'd just as soon he ignore it, anyway."

"But you are who you are."

"And that don't bother you at all?"

Jenny sipped her lemonade thoughtfully, then looked up at Sky with earnest eyes. "No. I just can't see anything but that you are a nice person, Sky." She sighed. "I suppose if you came here all dressed in Indian clothes, I might feel a bit strange. But I hope I'd be able to see past that to the nice person inside."

"Well, Jenny Yates," Sky said grinning, "*you're* the nice person. I wish you could rub off on . . . well, on other people."

"My pa is too set in his ways for that."

"That's too bad, 'cause I wouldn't mind seeing more of you."

"And why shouldn't you?"

"Come on, Jenny. Your pa might tolerate me and Billy being friends—though even that baffles me to no end. But I don't expect he'd feel the same about you."

"My pa lets me do whatever I want."

"I wish I could be as innocent as you, Jenny. But I know how the real world is."

"Sky . . ."

She reached out and laid her hand on his. Her touch sent a thrill through Sky's body. Her fingers were so smooth compared to his calloused, work-hardened hands. And they were so white against his dark skin. Very, very white.

He tried to swallow past a lump in his throat, and he was afraid to meet her gaze. But he forced his eyes upward—anything to keep from looking at that reminder of her whiteness. Her eyes were wide, filled with an entreaty that could hardly be refused. But what did she want? Did he dare reach out to her? Yet even as the questions formed in his mind he felt silly raising them at all. He was white in every way but the stain on his skin—that flaw that was becoming more and more ugly to him.

"I'd better get going," he said at last, his words dry and forced.

"I really want to see you again."

"Sure." He pulled his hand away from hers and quickly rose.

"I'm going riding tomorrow up by the pond," she said. "Maybe you'll be riding up that way, too."

"I . . . don't know."

"I'll look for you."

# 13

# THE POND AND OTHER ENCOUNTERS

Sky couldn't help himself. The next day he rode out to the pond and met Jenny. They rode and talked for about two hours until Jenny had to get back home. Sky showed her a little out-of-the-way place up a rocky rise where the mesquite was ten feet tall and thick, offering some shade in the heat. From there you could look down on the windswept range, and no one ever came that way to bother you. He knew he'd find her there the following day, and he did. It became their special spot, perhaps even their *secret* place.

In spite of Jenny's talk about her father letting her do what she pleased, there seemed an unspoken agreement between them that they should not meet publicly. They did nothing but talk when they were together, but they knew things would get too complicated if anyone, especially Big Bill Yates, knew of their friendship.

And that friendship grew quickly. Both were starved for a deep relationship, living as they did on the lonely prairie. Sky may have found new friends in Billy and T.R., but those friendships did not even approach the level of emotional intimacy that he needed. Jenny listened without judging and didn't try to offer pat answers. And she accepted him for himself, as white, as Indian, and as a confused half-breed.

One day, she asked him to play something on his guitar. He was embarrassed at first, but soon relaxed as he began fingering the familiar strings. He sang a couple of old ballads, which she praised enthusiastically.

"Do you ever make up your own songs?" she asked.

"I guess I fool around a bit. It's kind of a challenge."

"Would you sing one for me?"

"I'd feel stupid. No one but my horse and the cows ever heard them."

"Please."

He felt such a trust toward her that it didn't take much more coaxing.

"I just made this one up," he said, then began picking out the chords of the song he made up out on the range.

> My warrior's song borne on the wind,
> Blows from the empty pale blue skies;
> Its chanting moan that has no end
> Sweeps teardrops from my heaven turned eyes:
> White eagle soars on broken wing
> For peace and glory long since gone;
> He leaves a lonely shattered dream,
> And hopes to sing his song at dawn.

"That's beautiful, Sky. But kind of sad."

"I guess I sing mostly when I'm sad. It helps me."

"I wish I had something like that for when I'm sad."

"Do you get sad, Jenny?" he asked, concerned.

"Doesn't everyone?" she replied.

"What makes you sad?"

"Missing my ma, and I suppose just plain lonesomeness. It's hard sometimes, being the only girl for miles around."

"I never thought of that. Must be as bad as being the only Indian."

"I'm glad I've got you, Sky. I can't say enough how much it means to me."

"I feel the same, Jenny." He started to strum his guitar once more. "I been thinking of another verse to my song. It's just for you." Sky's fingers sought out the previous tune, and the words flowed gently from his lips.

> I sing of hands like silky pearls
> Touching my rough and darkened skin;
> Of sunlight catching light brown curls,
> Eyes that see my thoughts within:

Sky's voice paused but he continued playing the tune, his gaze momentarily taking in Jenny's attentive countenance. A breeze blew her silky hair around her face and she reached her slim, graceful hand to brush the stray hair back. Why did he sometimes feel so troubled watching her? It was almost as if Jenny were like the breeze—powerful, yet so very hard to hold on to. Maybe that's why the words of his song had formed as they had. Maybe he feared how easily something so sweet and vital could slip through his fingers. He sang again:

> O prairie winds make our hearts blend
> And smother all our doubt and fear;
> If you should go my lovely friend,
> I'd lose the world that I hold dear.

"Don't be afraid, Sky," Jenny murmured when he finished. "I'll always be your friend."

He had a sudden tightness in his throat, as if he could weep at her words. *Always*, she said. *Always*.

———————

One afternoon after several more meetings Sky and Jenny were racing their horses, and when they came to the Mesquite Rise, as they had come to call their place, they were exhausted. Breathlessly dismounting, they lay in the grass laughing. The shade of the mesquite hardly made a difference in the summer heat.

"You ride real well for sidesaddle," said Sky.

"Ha! You had to give me nearly a quarter of a mile handicap, and even at that you beat me."

"How would you like to learn to ride astride?"

"My pa would have a fit."

"What he don't know won't hurt him."

"I guess we already know that." She smiled coyly. "You think I can do it with this skirt?"

"If you don't worry too much about being ladylike."

"Okay, I'm game."

They jumped up and went to Two-Tone, and Sky gave Jenny a few instructions. Then he gave her a leg up, and she swung into the saddle. Immediately Sky knew it had been a bad idea when Jenny's skirt hitched up above her knees. She wasn't wearing bloomers, and her bare knee and leg above her high-topped shoes were suddenly exposed.

Sky stared. He'd never seen a female's knee before—except for

79

Carolyn's when she was a lot younger, and that hardly counted. He tried to look away, but when he saw the stricken look on Jenny's face, he realized his gaze had tarried too long.

"It was too hot for them," she said, referring to her absent bloomers.

But Sky felt it was he, not her, who needed to make apologies and excuses. After all, he had stared brazenly at the revealed leg, and he had only barely restrained an urge to touch her smooth skin. Sky knew from that moment it was no good trying to claim mere friendship as their only bond. He also knew they should have ridden away from there right then.

Instead, Jenny dismounted, and soon they were seated once more in the scanty shade of the mesquite.

"Jenny, we ought to go." But Sky no more meant it than he had meant to stare at her bare leg.

"I don't want to go. Maybe I'm just a hussy—"

"Don't even say that. You are the purest, sweetest girl there ever was."

"Then why do I want nothing more than to kiss you, to feel your arms around me?"

Sky licked his dry lips. His chest and arms ached. He knew what he was going to do—it was just too late to stop.

He moved toward her, and he had barely lifted his arms before she melted into his embrace. Their lips touched. It felt so good, so sweet. He couldn't remember any reason why it might be wrong.

"I love you, Sky," Jenny murmured.

"Me, too, Jenny." He kissed her again.

Suddenly Jenny tensed. "What's that?" she said.

Sky hadn't heard a thing besides his pounding heart. But when he turned his head away from Jenny, he heard it, too. An approaching horse.

Panic filled him and made him momentarily immobile. But perhaps if they stayed still, no one could see them. Then he remembered the horses. They hadn't even tried to hide them, but they were tied to the mesquite, and so might be out of sight.

"Don't move," Sky said. He crept forward to where he could look down the slope.

He recognized the palomino right away. It was Griff's. Sky relaxed but he still didn't relish even a friendly intrusion. Sky held his breath hoping Griff would ride on by. But the palomino slowed and Griff's eyes turned toward the rise and the mesquite where the horses were tied.

Griff would recognize Two-Tone right away. Would he stop? Griff reined his mount to the right and started up the slope.

"Howdy!" he called.

Sky stood and waved. It was no use trying to hide now.

"Thought I recognized old Two-Tone," said Griff.

Griff's gaze shifted and focused over Sky's shoulder. Sky turned slightly and saw that Jenny was now standing. Her hair was mussed and bits of grass were clinging to her dress. Maybe Griff wouldn't notice.

"I was out riding," Sky said, "and happened to run into Miss Yates. She was a bit lost and asked me to escort her home."

"That was right neighborly of you, Sky." Griff looked between the two young people. Something in his eyes and in the tone of his voice told Sky that Griff didn't believe a word of his story. "I'm heading in that direction. I can take you the rest of the way, Miss Yates."

"I don't want to put you out," said Jenny.

"Like I said, I'm going right by there."

"Well, I—"

"Listen, Griff, I can do it." Sky's words were sharper than he intended. But if Griff knew what was going on, why was he playing this cat and mouse game?

"I'll take her, Sky." Sky knew that tone—it wouldn't abide argument. He looked at Jenny.

"It's okay, Sky," she said. "I think it would be better if I went with Mr. McCulloch."

Sky watched silently as they rode off, and the minute they were down the slope he kicked angrily at the dirt.

"Blast him!" Sky sputtered to himself. "He didn't have no right."

Sky jumped on his horse and headed in the other direction. He rode until he got to the Lowells' place. T.R. was sitting on the porch braiding strips of rawhide to make a quirt. He glanced up and nodded a welcome. Sky and T.R. had hit it off quite well in the last few weeks. Once, after having too much whiskey, T.R. had let it slip that he'd always liked Sky but had kept his distance before because Billy had strongly discouraged it.

"Afternoon, Sky, what brings you out this way?"

Sky dismounted. "Those doggone adults! They think they can butt into your life and push you around all they want. I'm madder than a hornet!"

"What happened?"

"Makes me too mad to talk about it."

T.R. leaned forward. "What you need is an *attitude adjuster.*"

"You got some?"

"Sure. Come with me."

T.R. laid aside his rawhide. Sky followed him across the yard and through a small pasture to a springhouse. They went around to the back and T.R. lifted a plug of grass to reveal a bottle of whiskey. They sat down and had a couple drinks.

Sky thought he felt better afterward. At least, when he got home later, he didn't vent his anger on Griff. And he was glad Griff said nothing about the incident, either.

# 14

# FOURTH OF JULY

Sky had always been a hard worker, so no one at the ranch was too bothered by his frequent absences. When one of the hands brought it up once, Longjim voiced the general feeling.

"It's about time he had a chance to be a kid," he said.

Only Griff showed some hesitancy, but he kept his doubts to himself. He had seen enough that he'd probably be within his rights to tell Deborah, yet it went against his grain to meddle in that way. If one of his cowhands was misbehaving, Griff wouldn't have gone to the fellow's mother like he was a child—he would have confronted him as a man, and that would have been that. Sky was old enough to deserve the same treatment, the same respect.

Griff *had* talked to Sky. Perhaps he would do so again if things worsened. In the meantime, maybe it was okay just to let the boy sow some wild oats.

---

Sky took full advantage of his freedom, spending more and more time with Billy and T.R.—and with Jenny. He sensed he was treading a precarious line, but there was a certain thrill in that risk that drew him rather than discouraged him.

He was so caught up in his own world that he was hardly aware of the rising tensions in the county. The Yates fence had been cut several times, and Big Bill had begun posting armed guards at intervals along its perimeter. A man who had been shot in the act of cutting, and thankfully only wounded, turned out to be Arnel Slocum's hired hand. The Lowells were beginning to put up barbed wire, as were several homesteaders. A Texas Ranger had been dispatched to the area to help keep the peace.

Then the Brazos River dried up. It was only a matter of time before thirsty cows forced the tensions to the breaking point.

The Danville Fourth of July festivities seemed to be timed perfectly to provide a healthy outlet. Rivalries could be played out in various rodeo contests, and good food and entertainment could lighten bitter spirits. Or so people hoped.

For Sky, this was the first Fourth of July he was actually looking forward to. There was to be a box social for supper. The ladies would prepare supper and the fellows, unaware of whose box was whose, would bid on them. Jenny had described her box to Sky so he could buy it and they could eat together without fear of reprisals.

There were many other activities to keep Sky entertained until then. Cowboys could display their skills in calf roping, bronc busting, and bull riding. Griff, Longjim, and the Flying Y foreman and top hand were the primary contenders in these contests.

After watching the rodeo for a while, Sky and his friends grew restless. When Billy suggested they "have some real fun," Sky and T.R. made no argument. Their first stop was to sneak behind the livery stable and share a bottle of whiskey. Emboldened by the liquor, T.R. displayed to his friends a prize no Fourth of July could be without—a pocketful of firecrackers.

"Where'd you get those?" asked Sky.

"Bought 'em at a Chinaman's store when I was in San Antonio last spring. Come on, let's light 'em and spook some horses."

"We ought to be able to do something better than that," said Billy. He rubbed his chin thoughtfully, and deviously. For all Billy's faults, he was a true leader, and no one disputed his authority.

"What you got in mind?" asked Sky.

Billy glanced toward the outhouse where there had been a steady stream of "patrons" that day. Then he showed Sky and T.R. a little trick he'd picked up. He took out his cigarette fixings, sprinkled tobacco on a paper, then took a long string of firecrackers and placed the first fuse in with the tobacco. He finished rolling the cigarette with the fuse inside.

"This'll act like a timing device," he informed his friends. "Now, let's watch the fur fly," he said, heading toward the outhouse.

Sky snickered, "If I know what you got in mind, more than fur is gonna fly."

Billy slipped into the outhouse and wedged his makeshift "bomb" under the seat. Sky and T.R. watched from a distance. After Billy rejoined them they hid behind the livery stable, where they still had a good view of the outhouse. They never expected who the next user would be, but it was too late to do anything about it when the man approached.

It was Bob Tebbel, the Texas Ranger.

The boys groaned.

Then Sky decided that he could impress his friends every bit as much as Billy could. The moment the Ranger entered and pulled the door shut behind him, Sky grabbed a loose board from the stable wall, glanced around to make sure no one was looking, and raced up to the outhouse.

Sky wedged the board between the door handle and the ground. Inside, he heard the Ranger humming: "As I walked out on the streets of Laredo . . ."

Sky returned to the stable, to the adulations of his buddies.

In another moment, the fireworks started.

Sharp explosions of gunpowder were mingled with yells and curses from the Ranger as he pounded and kicked at the jammed door. Sky, Billy, and T.R. were doubled over with laughter, especially when the outhouse collapsed with the force of the Ranger's abuse.

"What are you boys up to?"

Caught up in the moment, they hadn't heard the sheriff approach. But even now, they struggled to choke back their laughter.

Billy managed a hardly believable denial. "Nothing, Sheriff. Nothing at all."

"You boys come along with me."

He gave T.R. a shove, and Sky knew better than to resist. The sheriff nudged them toward the destroyed outhouse, where the smell alone should have been sobering. But the fury of the enraged Texas Ranger was made all the more comic by the ridiculous sight of him scurrying to yank up his drawers.

Ranger Tebbel and the sheriff had barely finished their heated tongue-lashings when Doug Lowell, Sam, and Deborah arrived on the scene, along with a couple dozen curious bystanders.

His mother and Sam took Sky off alone.

"Sky, how could you do something so irresponsible?" she asked. "Someone could have been hurt."

"Aw, I never heard of no one getting killed with a firecracker." Sky was trying hard to appear sober, but it was difficult to restrain his amusement. He kept remembering the sight of the big, tough

Texas Ranger, screaming and red-faced, with his trousers down about his ankles.

"Sky," Sam said sharply, "you'd better get serious about this. You ain't too big for me to take a board to the seat of your pants."

"I don't see what everyone is in such an uproar about. We was just having a little fun."

"You've caused the destruction of public property," said Sam. "And Bob Tebbel's clothes are ruined. You're just lucky nothing worse happened."

"I have half a mind to send you right home," Deborah added.

"Going home would be too easy for this boy," said Sam. "I used to work with Tebbel when I was a Ranger. He's my friend—and he's a good man. You're not going home. You're going to make this right!"

Sky tried to hide his relief over this. The last thing he wanted to do was miss the box social. But he wasn't so happy when he found out what Sam had in mind.

He and Billy and T.R. were set to work repairing the mess they had made—rebuilding the outhouse, washing down the soiled walls, and then, while Tebbel, the Ranger, took a bath, they had to scrub his clothes. The Ranger, though he had a change of clothes to wear, made sure the soiled and rank-smelling garments were laundered to perfection. The boys were scrubbing out stains that had been on the clothes for years.

They finished barely in time for the box social, with only a few minutes to spare—minutes they spent washing off the sweat of their labor so as to be presentable around the ladies.

# 15

# Box Social

The Cattlemen's Association Hall was decorated for the event. The money raised by auctioning off the boxed suppers was to go toward purchasing supplies for the school, so the hall was filled to capacity. Sky didn't care much about the school, but he had ten dollars in his pocket which he intended to spend. His ma would have had a fit if she had known how he planned to use his hard-earned money. But these days he didn't care much what his ma thought about things.

And Sky was determined, no matter what it cost, to buy Jenny's supper that evening.

It was hard ignoring her as he walked into the hall and saw her across the room. It was hard keeping his eyes from straying in her direction during the evening before the auction began. But no one could know about their relationship. When he bought her box, it had to seem completely innocent and coincidental.

Then he saw Kyle Evanston with Jenny. Kyle was paying an excessive amount of attention to her, and Jenny was too nice to rebuff him. Sky began to fume. He was just as good as Kyle. Why should he have to keep up this pretense, acting as if he and Jenny were strangers? It wasn't fair.

Well, in a little while it wouldn't matter. No one could do anything about it if he happened to buy her box.

Sky had planned a devious strategy for the auction. He would bid on several boxes before hers, always quitting in time to lose it to another. That way no one would suspect their prearrangement when her box came up.

When the box wrapped in lavender calico came up for bid, Sky's palms began to sweat. It was Jenny's box. He felt like everybody could see his nervousness, hear his pounding heart.

"What opening bid do I hear for this pretty little box?" asked the auctioneer.

Sky wanted to yell, "Ten dollars!" But he kept quiet. Let someone else start.

"Fifty cents!" Kyle Evanston called out.

Sky tried to recall if Kyle had bid on other boxes. It seemed this was his first bid of the evening. It had to be a coincidence.

Sky said, "One dollar."

"One dollar and fifty cents," returned Kyle.

"Two dollars," someone else put in.

"Two-fifty," said Kyle.

Could Kyle know?

Sky's heart raced. "Three dollars."

When Kyle raised it to four dollars, a murmur of excitement ran through the crowd. The highest price paid so far for a box had been five dollars.

A cowboy said, "Five dollars."

Sky didn't like to be the one to make the next significant bid and thus draw attention to himself, but as he hesitated, the auctioneer called, "Is this expensive meal going to go to this here cowboy? Going once . . . going—"

"Six dollars!" Kyle yelled.

At that moment, from the tone of Kyle's voice, Sky knew that Kyle was fully aware of whose box it was. But Sky wasn't about to be intimidated.

"Seven dollars," he countered.

"Eight dollars," said Kyle, glaring at Sky as he spoke.

The auctioneer said, "We got some mighty rich young folks in this here crowd. I doubt anyone can top your bid, Kyle. So, going once—"

"Ten dollars!" broke in Sky.

The auctioneer got an uncomfortable look on his face. He glanced at Kyle, but Kyle's face had turned to stone, dark and hard. Sky knew he had outbid Kyle. He started forward to claim his prize.

Then another voice called out, "Eleven dollars."

Sky spun around. The final bid had come from Big Bill Yates.

"Pa!" cried Jenny. "That isn't fair!"

Yates pushed his way to the front and claimed the box. "My girl ain't gonna eat with no Injun, I don't care what anybody says."

The room grew suddenly silent. For a moment it seemed as if no one would intercede. Sky felt utterly alone. He felt like something inhuman, deserving of derision, even revulsion. And in that moment he despised himself almost as much as he hated Bill Yates.

At last Sam spoke up. "Listen, Bill, it's all in fun. It don't mean nothing."

"Come on, Pa, don't ruin the party." It was Billy.

"Shut up, Billy," said Bill. "You don't have to pretend to be his friend no more. It's gone too far. He's started to think he's as good as the rest of us—"

"Listen here—" Sam began.

But Sky didn't wait to hear the rest. Elbowing his way through the crowd, not looking at a single face, he escaped the room. He didn't have to stick around and listen to this. He was just as good as the rest of them. Wasn't he?

He went to the livery stable for his horse. As he was saddling up, T.R. Lowell came in and started saddling his own mount.

"What are you doing?" asked Sky.

"I don't figure you want to be alone right now."

"Well, you're wrong. That's just what I wanta be."

"That wasn't right what happened in there."

"Oh, yeah!" fumed Sky. "It ain't me you oughta be telling."

"Come on, Sky, it ain't easy standing up to Big Bill. Besides, who would have listened to me?"

Sky tightened the last cinch, then grabbed the reins and started walking away. When he was outside, he mounted and rode off. After a few minutes, he realized T.R. was riding behind him. He kept going. He rode for half an hour, trying to lose T.R. in the moonlight, but his human shadow was persistent. Finally he turned around.

"Go away, T.R.," Sky said. "Leave me alone."

T.R. galloped forward. "You may not want people, but how about this—" He reached down in his saddlebag and took out the bottle of whiskey they had started earlier in the day.

Sky shook his head and smiled. "You sure know how to get on my good side. Come on, then." It was better not to be alone, anyway. He just kept thinking when he was alone. The diversion of a friend and a drink or two was what he needed.

They rode to the Mesquite Rise and got drunk. But before Sky got too numb with alcohol, he had to find out one thing from T.R.

"What do you know about what Big Bill said—you know, about Billy pretending to be my friend?"

"Nothing."

" 'Cause I don't need no friends, especially fakes."

"I ain't no fake. I just never had the nerve to buck Billy before. I guess I don't have as much character as you."

"Me?"

"Sure. You saved Billy, even though he'd always treated you like dirt. I liked you a sight more than I ever liked Billy, but I knew I'd be blackballed if I told Billy where to get off and did what I wanted. I didn't think I had the guts to handle having only one friend, and him an Indian. Probably if the tables had been turned, you would have done what you wanted—just because it was right."

"Well, you ain't gonna see me try to do what's right again! It just blows up in your face like a stick of dynamite. Now, gimme some more of that whiskey. I'm tired of talking."

There was only one swallow left, and when Sky had drained it, he threw the bottle aside with an angry grunt. T.R. made himself a friend for life by producing another bottle.

"Had two hid by the stable," he said. Sky practically knocked him over with enthusiastic praise.

Eventually Sky reached the point where he no longer felt the pain of rejection. He almost forgot about how sweet it would have been to have supper with Jenny, and the whiskey seemed to obliterate even the fantasies he'd had of one day marrying her and walking through town with her on his arm in front of everyone.

Almost, but not completely.

But when such thoughts did assail him, he met them with anger instead of a sense of worthlessness.

"You know, that Big . . . Big Bill Yates had a nerve. He ruined my supper," Sky said drunkenly.

"If it were me, I'd get back at him," said T.R.

"What should we do? Blow up his outhouse? That was funny."

"Is that gonna pay him back for humiliating you?"

"Never!"

"There's only one thing that means more to Big Bill than his daughter."

"What's that?"

"His fence, you dummy."

"Yeah. . .?"

"I know where to find some cutters," T.R. said.

# 16

# FOUND OUT

Sometime past midnight, Sky and T.R. sneaked into Arnel Slocum's barn and there found a pair of long-handled wire cutters.

"It's practically illegal for him to have these," T.R. said.

Sky took the cutters. "We'll save him from getting in trouble."

For the next two hours, stopping only for swigs from the bottle of whiskey, the two youths laid waste about two miles' worth of Bill Yates's fence. They made cuts every couple of feet so that it would be impossible to repair. They were never once challenged by a guard. They did not even see a guard. Everyone was probably at the Fourth of July festivities.

Hiding the cutters in a clump of mesquite, they headed for home. Sky decided to sleep in the bunkhouse that night. He would rather risk discovery by Griff than his ma. But when he came out of the stable after leaving his horse, one of the cowhands was just leaving the bunkhouse, probably on his way to use the outhouse. Maybe he was worrying too much. Besides, tomorrow morning Sky would be better off alone in his room than in a room full of men. He went to the house and slipped in through the kitchen door.

He tried to be quiet, but he was none too steady on his feet. He bumped into a kitchen chair, and it crashed to the floor before he could catch it. He stopped dead still, listened but heard nothing. Feeling more confident, he continued on to his room. Every creaking floorboard made his heart leap. At last he grasped the door latch of his room and was "home free."

"Sky?"

His mother's soft voice made him jump and crash against the door. He stood there, not turning, for a long moment, his head resting against the wood. He took a breath and, deciding he could pull this off just like always, turned.

"Hi, Ma." He tried hard to make his voice sound normal.

"Is there something wrong?"

"No . . . no, everything's fine . . . just fine." He thought he was succeeding in his ruse; after all, it was too dark for her to discern details about his appearance.

"Sky, have you been drinking?"

"Me? Oh no . . . never—"

"Don't lie to me, Sky. I can smell it. What's going on?"

For a brief instant Sky wondered if he should stick to his denial. But at the last moment, his mother's no-nonsense tone managed to penetrate his alcoholic fog.

"I just had one drink, Ma. I was so upset about what happened at the party . . . I didn't think about what I was doing."

"One drink. . . ?"

"Well," his mouth tilted in a lopsided grin, "maybe two."

"How could you, Sky? It's those boys you've been hanging around with. They're a bad influence—"

"Don't say nothing 'bout my friends, Ma."

"You didn't do things like this before they came along."

Sky's sheepishness quickly turned to ire. "They're the best friends a fellow ever had. You ain't got no right to talk 'em down. No one else cared how I was tonight, but T.R., he was there—"

"There with a bottle of whiskey, wasn't he?"

"What do you know? He was there, that's all."

"Oh, Sky, can't you see—?"

"You're just jealous," Sky fired back, ignoring his mother's shock, the tears in her eyes, evident even in the darkness, at his disrespectful tone. "You just can't stand that I've got a life—I'm not just the lonely Indian boy anymore who needs his mama. Well, I don't need you!" His voice rose. "I got friends. They'll take care—"

Suddenly a door down the hall opened. "What's going on out here?" Sam demanded.

"Nothing!" yelled Sky. "Leave me alone—all of you!"

He pushed open his bedroom door, stepped inside, and, before another word could be said, slammed the door behind him.

———

Once she and Sam were back in their room, it was a few minutes before Deborah could talk. Sam found her a handkerchief, but she couldn't wipe away the ache in her heart along with the tears. All she could think of was sweet, dear Sky, the child of love, the child of her heart, of everyone's heart. He had been a different person tonight. A stranger.

It had to be the whiskey. And his so-called friends.

Those terrible boys he was associating with were leading him astray, making him behave like a hooligan. That incident with the outhouse was proof. Sky would never have done anything like that before. And coming home drunk, talking to her the way he had—that wasn't Sky.

Deborah turned to Sam, her tears now dry, replaced with indignation. "I'm going to speak to Bill Yates and Doug Lowell tomorrow. They need to know what is going on. And I'm going to forbid Sky to see them."

"Deborah—?"

"I'm glad this happened, Sam. It has forced me to take a good look at what's going on. You voiced doubts about Sky's association with those boys, but I tried to give them the benefit of the doubt. Well, not any longer!"

"Deborah, I know you're upset—"

"You bet, I'm upset! And Sky may not like what I'm going to do, but in the long run he'll thank me. I have to look out for him, and until he can show better judgment in his choice of friends, I'm going to have to step in. If only I had done something sooner. But thank goodness it's not too late. I'm not going to let this isolated incident grow into a real problem." She paused and took a breath.

Sam quickly interceded. "Deborah, do you think it's right to blame the other boys entirely?"

"What else could it be, Sam? He's never done anything like this before."

"Are you so sure?"

"Sam—"

"He's been going off a lot with them lately—*by his choice.* I never saw anyone *drag* him away."

"Are you saying Sky is the ringleader? I can't believe it. And I would think, Sam, you would support my son instead of trying to blame him."

"I ain't blaming no one. When you say he's being cajoled along by others, it's like saying Sky has no backbone. And that is something *I* can't believe."

"Well, maybe they've deceived him in some way so he's making these choices. Remember what Bill Yates said at the party about Billy pretending to be Sky's friend."

"I don't know about that. But think what Sky will do if you try to tell him he ain't thinking for himself, that he's just a poor steer being led down the trail."

Deborah opened her mouth to argue the point, then realized what she was doing. "Oh, Sam!" Frustrated, she ran a hand through her hair.

Sam said, "It's only normal that a mother would want to defend and protect her child."

"Have I always been so blind?"

"Let's not worry about that now, dear," Sam said gently. "Let's forget about blaming and fault."

"But I don't know what else to do."

"Do you want a couple of suggestions?" When she nodded, he continued. "First, we gotta face the fact that there's more going on with Sky than bad associations. I've been seeing it more and more lately in him, and tonight I heard it in his voice. He's full of bitterness and pain, Deborah. I have a feeling our sweet Sky has been pushing it down all these years and it's finally coming to the surface. I don't know what to do about it all, Deborah, but I know who does."

"Then we better ask Him, Sam. Thanks for reminding me. For a minute I was feeling I had no place to turn."

"You don't ever need to feel that way, Deborah. Come on, let's pray."

―――――

When he awoke the next morning, Sky couldn't remember a thing about the previous night. His throbbing, aching head seemed to squeeze out anything so complex as memory. It even surprised him that he was in his own bed, in his own room. How could he have been so stupid as to come home? In the past, he'd slept it off in the bunkhouse, or, if it was really bad, in the barn, away from inquisitive eyes. No one had been the wiser. His ma had always assumed he'd risen early and gone out to the barn to do his chores.

Well, there was still no reason for anyone to know.

But as he lay in bed trying to get the nerve to open his eyes and face the bright morning light, a snatch of memory began to return. Something had happened in the hall last night. His ma—

"Oh no!" he groaned.

Now he remembered. His ma had caught him.

Still, she had no way of knowing this wasn't the first time. She was a fair person. She'd let him get away with one "mistake."

Nevertheless, he wasn't eager to get out of bed and face her. How many times had he used the "I'm sick" excuse? Could he get away with it one more time?

The knock on the door echoed painfully in his head.

"Yeah?"

"Breakfast is ready." His mother's voice sounded even and calm. Maybe it wouldn't be so bad to face her.

Then again, maybe it would.

"I'm not hungry," he said.

"I would like you to join us." Yes, her tone was calm, but he detected a certain edge to it also.

Sky knew he couldn't avoid her forever. "Okay, I'll be right there."

The first portent of doom struck him as he entered the kitchen ten minutes later. Yolanda was gone. Sam and Deborah were seated at the table, coffee cups in front of them, stony looks on their faces. This was not going to be a pleasant meal.

Sky poured himself a cup of coffee, but instead of sitting at the table, leaned against the washbasin.

"Come and sit, Sky," his mother said. She seemed to be reaching out to him.

But Sky felt too defensive to accept her conciliation. "Don't feel much like sitting." Actually, he felt very much like sitting. His head was spinning and his stomach was queasy. But he stubbornly held his ground. "I reckon I'm in trouble," he said, taking the offensive.

"What do you think?"

"Well, if you really want to know, I think a fellow deserves a second chance after just one mistake."

Then Sam turned his eyes toward Sky. His incisive gaze looked more like that of the Texas Ranger he once had been than of the country preacher he was now.

"One mistake? That's all it was, Sky? You never done nothing like this before?"

Sky shifted his eyes down, staring at the coffee cup he held. His hand was shaking. "You wouldn't believe me, no matter what I say," he mumbled.

"That's not true, Sky," Deborah said. "I want nothing more than to believe you."

Sam nodded. "You just look at us, Sky, and tell us you ain't done nothing like this before, and we'll believe you."

Sky's guilt combined explosively with his physical discomforts. "Whatever," he snapped.

95

"Sky!" his mother exclaimed. "Don't you dare talk that way to us!"

"Well, even if I did tell the truth, what good would it do? I'd still be in trouble."

"That ain't the point, Sky," Sam said. "You were raised better than to lie to your parents. That's worse than what else you might have done."

"Sky, if you have a problem, we want to help you." His mother took a breath, trying to calm herself. "Can't you talk to us?"

For good or ill, Sky was spared having to confront that question when Griff appeared at the kitchen door.

"Sorry to interrupt your breakfast," Griff said. "But there's trouble out at Arnel Slocum's place."

# 17

# TROUBLE

"It's only eight in the morning," said Sam.

"I guess bad news travels fast," shrugged Griff.

"What happened?"

"Apparently about two miles of Flying Y fence was cut to ribbons last night. Bill Yates was hopping mad. Found a pair of cutters in the bushes which he somehow linked to Slocum. That was just after dawn. He and a dozen of his hands rode out to Slocum's place."

"Oh no! Was anyone hurt?" asked Deborah.

"One man wounded that I know of. But looks like it's only just begun. They got kind of a standoff out there now. Several of the small ranchers have come to Slocum's support. Who knows what's happened since our man rode past this morning. Could be more wounded, even dead."

The moment Griff mentioned the cut fence, Sky's alcohol-clouded memory was jolted. But at the thought of people getting killed because of his prank, Sky let out a groan before he could catch himself. Sam immediately glanced in Sky's direction.

"You know anything about this, Sky?" Sam asked.

Sky felt as if his head was getting crushed beneath the weight of Sam's question. He wanted to lie, to be able to deny everything, but he knew it was too late. Besides, Sam had been right about one thing—lies simply didn't come easily to him, especially when the situation was as serious as this. His foolish actions could have started a range war!

Still, it wasn't easy to take responsibility. "I . . . I can't remember everything I did last night. I—"

"You get drunk again, boy?" erupted Griff.

"Griff. . . ?" Deborah gave him a pointed look.

"Deborah, he promised me he wouldn't never do it again, or I would have told you."

"We better not get off the track," Sam interjected. "You didn't answer my question yet, Sky."

Again Sky felt utterly alone, just as he had at the box social. But this time he'd brought it on himself. This time he had alienated those who loved him.

"I did it," Sky admitted, still not able to look at anyone as he spoke. "I was mad over what Bill Yates did to me. I got drunk and . . ." He couldn't finish; it was just too hard to listen to himself admit to such stupidity.

"Oh, Sky." He could hear his mother's disappointment in her voice.

"Maybe it ain't too late to do something about this," said Sam. "Griff, would you go out and get some of the boys to saddle up all of our horses?"

Griff nodded and left.

Turning to Sky, Sam continued, "You willing to try and set right what you done, Sky?"

"Sam, you ain't gonna make me go out there and tell everyone what I did, are you?"

"It's the only way I can think of to stop a blood bath."

"It's probably too late, anyway," Sky replied miserably.

"Let's pray to our God it ain't."

---

Two things worked in Sky's favor that day. For one thing, Arnel Slocum had learned of Bill Yates's plans to storm the Slocum ranch in time to shore up the defense of the ranch. By the time Yates arrived with about a dozen armed men, Slocum had enough guns ready to hold him off. In the initial shoot-out, one of the Flying Y cowhands had been wounded, but after that Yates and his men had to run for cover. Whenever one ventured out, Slocum's fire-power forced him back.

The second thing working for Sky was that shortly after the beginning of the altercation, Bob Tebbel, the Texas Ranger who had been the brunt of the Fourth of July prank the previous day, showed up on the scene. He was able to get both hotheads, Yates and Slocum, to agree to a truce long enough for each to tell his side of the story. This was a drawn-out process because both men refused to come out of hiding, and the ranger had to act as a middleman over quite a distance.

It also was to Sky's advantage that many years ago, when Sam had been a Texas Ranger, he had worked with Ranger Tebbel. They had saved each other's lives so many times they had lost track of who owed whom, but a lasting bond of loyalty had been formed between them.

When Sam, Deborah, Sky, and Griff rode up to the scene, Tebbel kept Bill Yates from firing on the new arrivals.

"Howdy, Sam," Tebbel said. "See you still don't carry a gun."

"None of us are armed," said Sam, "except Griff, but he ain't planning to use his gun."

"What brings you out here? This ain't exactly a picnic."

Bill Yates answered before Sam had a chance. "They're free range people. It's obvious why they're here."

"Pipe down, Yates," said Tebbel. "Go ahead, Sam. What do you got to say for yourself?"

"Arnel Slocum had nothing to do with cutting the Flying Y fence," said Sam.

"How do you know?" countered Yates. He was obviously not happy to have his anticipated vengeance interrupted.

"Because I know who did it."

Sam hesitated and inclined his head slightly toward Sky, just enough so Sky would know it was his duty to speak up.

———

Sky wanted more than anything to escape. He had to face not only Bill Yates, but also the Texas Ranger he had humiliated the day before. He looked around, wondering if he could fit under one of the nearby rocks. Then he remembered what T.R. had said last night about him having character and doing what was right. At the time he had repudiated such behavior as useless. Having character hadn't done him much good at the box social; it hadn't allowed him to have supper with Jenny.

He felt differently now with his ma and Sam and Griff watching him. Especially with Sam and Griff, two men he admired deeply and had grown up wanting to imitate. They were expecting him to be a man of character now, to show the kind of courage it took to own up to one's mistakes.

How could he turn tail with them watching?

He nudged his horse forward until he was next to Sam. Maybe it would be easier making the awful admission with him close.

"I done it, Mr. Tebbel," Sky said.

"Just you?" asked Tebbel.

"Yes, sir."

"I wouldn't expect you to say anything else." Sky thought Tebbel actually admired this hint of loyalty.

Sky had spoken too softly for Yates to hear. Yates yelled, "What'd he say?"

Tebbel answered, "The boy here cut your fence."

"The boy—? You mean that dirty Injun!"

"Simmer down, Yates."

"I ain't simmering down, no way!" Yates, with a new and just as acceptable target for his anger, strode out from his cover. "I always knew it would come to no good letting this Injun live here among decent white folks."

"Shut up, Yates. Now!" ordered Tebbel.

Yates was not intimidated even by a Texas Ranger. "I demand you arrest him. I want him locked up. What he done is a felony, and he better not get away with it. Why, this ought to be grounds to send him to the reservation where he belongs—"

Tebbel pulled his gun, aimed it at Yates's head, and cocked it. "I said shut up!"

"You gonna defend him after what he done to you yesterday?"

"Seems your boy was involved in that, too, Yates."

"Led astray by that Injun—"

"Ha!" The dry laugh came from Griff.

"First of all," Tebbel went on firmly, "I ain't defending no one. I'm here to keep the peace. And right now, it's you, Yates, that's keeping me from doing my job. I want to hear the boy out—and I don't want no interruptions." He glared at everyone, then rested his eyes on Sky. "Go on, boy, tell me what happened."

"There ain't nothing to tell," said Sky. "I did what I did, that's all. I wanted to get back at Mr. Yates for treating me like dirt at the social yesterday. I see now it was a stupid thing to do. I never figured on Mr. Slocum getting blamed."

"This is a serious thing you done."

"I know," said Sky, with real contrition. "I reckon I'll be going to jail for it."

"Bob," said Sam, "he's just a boy. Do you think jail is a bit harsh?"

"Wait a minute!" cried Yates. "I ain't gonna stand by and watch him get off scot-free."

"Don't worry," said Tebbel. "This is too serious for that. You realize that, boy? You gotta make amends for what you done."

Sky nodded, fully resigned to spending the next couple of years in jail.

"What I'm gonna order you to do," Tebbel continued, "is to make full restitution for the cost of the damaged fence. How much damage was done, Yates?"

"This is an outrage!" ranted Yates. "You're showing favoritism just because Sam used to be a ranger. It ain't right. I won't—"

"Listen, Yates, you figure I ought to lock up all the boys in this town for foolish pranks? Then you best get your boy for me."

"But—"

"Quit your arguing, or I'm liable to pull this trigger. Now—*how much?*"

Yates conceded, but not happily. "Two hundred dollars."

Sky's hope at being spared a jail sentence was suddenly dashed. Two hundred dollars, or two thousand—it would take him a lifetime to pay back that much money.

"I ain't got that kind of money," said Sky.

"Don't worry, boy, we'll find a way for you to get it." Tebbel turned and yelled toward Slocum's men, "All right, I want all of you to clear out and get back to your work." To Yates and the Wind Rider people he added, "You folks will come to town with me so's we can put an agreement down in writing."

# 18

# BILLY'S CHANGE

After considerable haggling they finally came to an agreement. Sky would have to pay twenty dollars a month until the two hundred dollars were paid off. Bill Yates wouldn't agree to anything less than full payment immediately, so Sam and Deborah agreed to pay him out of their money. Sky would then have the money, plus interest, withdrawn from his pay for working on the ranch. But worst of all, he'd have to make an initial payment of all the money he'd been saving for a new saddle—as well as the ten dollars he had put aside to buy Jenny's dinner at the box social. He was going to be very poor for quite a long time.

He should have been relieved it was no worse. Had Bill Yates had *his* way, Sky would have been lynched.

Still, a sense of gloom hung over him, and he knew it had to do with more than his punishment. He felt his parents' disappointment keenly. And he knew it was going to take a lot of work on his part to earn their pride and trust again. As much as he tried to convince himself and everyone else that he was a man, not dependent upon his parents' approval, it still hurt.

When they exited the sheriff's office and he saw T.R. down the street, he immediately wanted to excuse himself from his parents' stern presence and seek out his friend.

"Can I catch up to you in a minute?" Sky asked.

Sam saw T.R. and frowned. "There's a heap of work to do, and the day is still young."

It was two in the afternoon. By the time they returned to the ranch, it would be nearly suppertime and quitting time. Were they going to work him day and night in order to get their money back?

"I'll only be a minute."

Sam and his ma exchanged a look that Sky interpreted as, "T.R.

102

is one of his troublemaking friends, so we'd better not let Sky go with him."

Sky jumped on this before a word was spoken. "You mean I can't have friends no more?"

"We want you to stay out of trouble, Sky," Deborah said. "Can you do both?"

"I'm gonna try."

"I guess we can't ask any more than that. You can have a few minutes. We're going to get started, but we expect you to catch up."

"Thanks, Ma." Sky started to go, then paused and turned back to them. "I really mean that about trying. I'm not going to get in trouble again."

He headed down the street, where T.R. was waiting for him. By the time Sky reached T.R., his parents and Griff were riding out of town.

"You get in a lot of trouble?" asked T.R.

"Coulda been worse, I suppose."

"You never said nothing about me."

"Of course not."

"I appreciate that, Sky. What are they gonna do to you?"

"I gotta pay for the fence."

"I have a little money saved—"

"Naw, that won't work. They'll wonder where it came from. Just don't worry about it. It was because of me we did it, anyway."

A new voice interrupted them. "Well, lookee here, it's the renegade redskin." Billy sounded just like he used to, full of venom.

"Listen, Billy," Sky explained, "I was drunk. Didn't hardly know what I was doing. You know how it is."

"All's I know is that's a fine way to pay me back for all I done for you."

"It wasn't intended for you. I was trying to get back at your pa. You saw how he treated me—"

"What you do to one Yates, you do to all."

"Yeah? Well, if that's how you want it. But let's get one thing straight—you never did anything for me. It was me who saved your ornery hide. I never asked for your friendship."

"Well, you never got it! And you'll never know how sick it made me to fake it, you slimy son of a rotten savage—"

"Why you—" Sky let his fist finish his statement. He had taken enough abuse from the Yates clan that day.

Billy stumbled back with the unexpected blow. But before Sky could take aim for another strike, Billy came back with his own big fist. It landed on the side of Sky's head; his neck nearly snapped and everything went momentarily black. His knees buckled, but T.R. caught him before he hit the ground.

"Can't take it, you dirty half-breed—" jeered Billy.

Sky's head began to clear. He struggled against T.R.'s hold, in spite of the fact that it was the first time anyone had ever come to his aid in a fight.

"Come on, Sky, we better get out of here before there's more trouble," said T.R.

"Whose side are you on, T.R.?" asked Billy.

"His," said T.R. "I don't want no two-faced friends like you."

"Oh yeah?" Billy took a swing at T.R.

But Sky freed himself from T.R.'s loosened grasp and thrust himself between the two.

"I can take him," T.R. sneered gamely, despite the fact that he was four inches shorter than Billy and at least fifteen pounds lighter.

"Try it!" dared Billy. "That's how you Injun lovers like it—two against one."

The impending scrap was halted by the sudden appearance of the Texas Ranger.

"Okay, break it up! There's been enough trouble in this county for one day."

Not even Billy had the nerve to stand up to the Ranger. With a scowl and a sneer at Sky, Billy stalked off.

Although Sky was still angry inside at how Billy had turned on him so unfairly, he could not prevent a stab of regret as he watched Billy leave. It wasn't so much at the loss of a friend, because T.R. helped fill that void. But over the weeks since his association with Billy had begun, Sky had discovered some redeeming qualities in Billy. Maybe it had all been a big act, but Sky thought no one could act that well. There had to be more to Billy than that surly bigotry he presented on the surface.

Sky still had T.R., but T.R. had just admitted last night how hard it was for him to buck Billy. Sky wouldn't blame T.R. if he soon found it too hard to alienate himself further from the white community.

Sky left T.R. in the street. Maybe friends weren't worth the cost. Maybe it was his lot in life to be a loner—with just his ugly brown skin for company.

# 19

# THE WHITE STALLION

Sky worked hard for the next couple of weeks. Sam and his mother thought he was finally straightening up, becoming the old Sky again. And he let them think that. But he knew he was working mostly to distract himself.

Many times when he was riding alone on the range, he toyed with the idea that maybe he'd just keep on going. He no longer felt like he belonged anywhere. Even at home he felt awkward, unable to shake the sense of shame he felt for his previous behavior. Deep down, he knew his parents had forgiven him because it wasn't like them to hold a person's mistakes over him. But he couldn't forgive himself.

When he was at home, he almost always had his guitar in his hands, hiding behind his music. He could be with his parents and they could be enjoying his playing and singing, and they never were able to tell that he was further away from them than ever.

Sky took all the range-riding work Griff offered. It was better to be alone on the prairie than to be alone in a room full of people . . . with his own family.

One day, out on the range, Sky decided to camp on the Mesquite Rise. Maybe he was a glutton for punishment. Or maybe he hoped that by some chance he'd find Jenny there waiting for him as if nothing had ever happened. Sky didn't blame Jenny for dropping him. She was a Yates, and he wouldn't expect her to do anything but stick by her family.

In the morning Sky built a fire and put some coffee on to cook.

While he waited for it to boil, he took up his guitar and began to play.

*"Oh, bury me not on the lone prairie . . . where the coyotes howl and the wind blows free. In a narrow grave just six by three . . . Oh, bury me not on the lone prairie!"*

The mournful tune suited his mood as he sat in this place where he'd once known happiness. So did the morning sky, with dark clouds tumbling quickly across its blue expanse. A stiff wind started up, knocking over the coffeepot and emptying its contents.

Sky gave a disgusted grunt, kicked out the fire, and decided to move on. There wasn't much protection where he was. He carefully wrapped his guitar in his bedroll, loaded his gear, and was about to mount up when he heard his name.

"Sky!"

"Jenny?"

"Finally!" Jenny was walking up the rise, leading her horse. She dropped the reins and ran to Sky, throwing her arms around him. "I've been coming here nearly every day, hoping you'd come."

"You have?"

"Of course! I've been dying to see you. But I didn't dare go to your ranch or even send a note. This was the only way I could think that no one would find out about." She kissed his cheek and held him tighter.

"I thought you would hate me after what happened. I wouldn't have blamed you."

"Sky Killion!" She stood back, a hurt expression on her face. "How could you ever think that? I love you, Sky, and I always will. My pa deserved what he got—I know it wasn't right what you did to the fence, but the way he treated you at the box social wasn't right either. I'll never forgive him for that."

"But Billy said you Yateses stick together—"

"That Billy! I'm furious with him, too. The way he's been talking about you lately—I've never seen anybody stoop so low."

All at once the thunder started, followed immediately by streaks of lightning.

"We're in for a soaker," said Sky.

Another crack of thunder made Jenny's horse whinny and shy skittishly.

"Let's tie these horses up on the mesquite," said Sky. "I got a slicker we can get under to stay dry."

It started raining as they tied up the second horse. They found a small dry patch on the ground, and throwing the slicker over them, they managed to keep at least their heads and shoulders dry. The rain came down in a solid sheet, and it wasn't long before they were sitting in a puddle.

"Maybe this'll help the drought," Jenny said. "And there won't be any more trouble over the fence."

Sky doubted one rainstorm was going to help. The ground was so hard and dry that most of the water would just run right off or get evaporated when the sun came out again. But he didn't say that to Jenny. Why do anything that might spoil the unexpected surprise of Jenny's arrival? His head was still reeling pleasantly— far better than the feeling he got from whiskey—at her sweet words a moment ago.

*I love you, Sky, and I always will.*

He hardly even felt the rain; he welcomed it, in fact. The longer it rained the longer he could sit close to Jenny, his arm around her slender shoulders. They talked, and it truly did seem as if the past hadn't happened. Sky began to wonder if they could go on, just as it had been before. It didn't matter what others thought. But more importantly, it didn't matter to Jenny. Today, she proved that beyond all doubt.

Then the rain stopped and the sun parted the clouds.

"Guess it's over," said Sky regretfully.

"Does that mean you're going to have to leave?"

"I don't want to."

"Sky, I've got a wonderful idea. Let's ride up to the canyon and see if we can find those mustangs. Maybe we'll even see the white stallion."

"That's a long ride, Jenny."

"No one'll miss me today. Pa and Billy rode to Jacksboro early this morning. They won't be back till after dark."

"We could make it back long before dark. I've got food in my saddlebags and plenty of water." He paused briefly, wondering about the repercussions of taking a day off from work. Then he shrugged. How much more trouble could he get into? He grinned eagerly. "Okay, let's do it!"

———

The day turned into a magical one, a day Sky would never forget. The rain had heightened the usual intensity of the high plains. Sky and Jenny approached the gateway to the great Palo Duro Canyon, awed by its tall escarpments, vivid red rocks, and blasted

107

earth. The sky was clearing, but huge clouds dotted the blue expanse in stark relief.

Sky led the way along the narrow path where they had to ride single file. He had been here many times, but he constantly looked back to make sure Jenny was doing all right. This rough country made the rugged plains around their homes seem tame.

It was not yet noon. The ride had taken nearly three hours. Jenny was quite proficient at riding sidesaddle, but it did slow them down to some extent. Sky thought about giving her his saddle so she could ride astride; he'd have no problem riding bareback. But he decided against it after recalling the last time they had tried that. It was difficult enough being near Jenny, and feeling as if they were the only two people in the world.

If only it were true. . . .

"Look over there, Sky!" Jenny's excited voice broke into his thoughts.

His gaze followed where she pointed. He saw nothing.

"I thought I saw movement," she said.

"It's gone now. Probably just an antelope. Let's keep going."

They rode for half an hour down a steep trail Sky had used once a couple of years ago when he had spotted the herd. But today they saw nothing but dry grass and jackrabbits. Deflated, they slowly climbed back up the precarious trail. When they reached the top again, they were hot and thirsty.

"You want to head back?" Sky asked.

"Are you kidding? I came to see a white stallion, and that's what I intend to do."

Sky grinned. "I didn't know you were so stubborn."

"I have my moments," she replied coyly.

"Well, do you mind if we eat first?"

"I suppose . . ."

It was a hurried meal because they were both anxious to continue their quest. But after another hour of July heat, even Jenny was ready to give it up.

"There's one more place we can look," Sky said when they paused to have a drink from his canteen. "It's not too far. After that we need to head back if we hope to get home before dark."

They struck the ravine in fifteen minutes. A thousand years ago water flowed through here, but it had dried up so long ago that not even the Indians remembered that time. It cut between steep walls of rock, making a path about a hundred feet wide, then it opened out into a meadow where there was a natural underground spring. It was a boxed-in area, and under normal conditions the stallion would have been too smart to lead his herd in here. But this had been a dry year, and water and grass were scarce enough to warrant such a risk—if the spring wasn't also dry.

Even if they didn't find the horses, it was such a pretty place that it might redeem the day for Jenny. Then Sky saw the tracks. He put up his hand for her to stop, then dismounted and took a closer look. The rain had done a good job of obliterating most of the tracks, but a few close to the ravine walls were still clear.

"Horse tracks, all right," Sky said. "Can't be too old."

His heart was pounding excitedly as he jumped on his horse and they started again.

In a few minutes the ravine opened up into the meadow. It was a huge grassy area. Sky could barely see the surrounding canyon walls at the other end. The grass was dry, but it was more plenteous here than anyplace else up on the high plains.

Sky reined in Two-Tone as his eyes swept the area.

"There!" he breathed. About half a mile away, some thirty mustangs were grazing peacefully.

"Can we get closer?"

"Sure. But I don't want to spook them until we see if this is the White's herd—" Sky gasped suddenly as his eyes swept up toward a hill overlooking the grazing herd. "It's him!"

Why the stallion hadn't been the very first thing they saw, Sky didn't know. Sam would have spiritualized it, saying, "We miss God's wonders when we look down instead of toward heaven." But now that Sky and Jenny saw the stallion, it was as if they could see nothing else. His white coat, gleaming in the sunlight, mesmerized them.

"Come on," Sky murmured.

They rode forward quietly and slowly. It seemed to take forever to cover half the distance to the herd. They could not get closer. The grazing mares heard the intruders and loped away. The stallion snorted and stamped his hoof.

Sky could not say what suddenly possessed him. But he let out a piercing whoop, dug his heels into Two-Tone's flanks, and lurched into a gallop after the mares. The herd responded instantly, their previously cautious lope changing into a frenzied run.

The stallion reared majestically from its perch, then raced down the hill to the rescue of his mares.

Two-Tone was probably the best horse in the Wind Rider remuda—probably the best in the county, though Sky had never participated in local races to prove that fact. The black-and-white stallion had once been a wild mustang like these, with his own small harem of mares to protect. Of course, he had only been a princeling compared to the King White, but he had the strength and stamina to make quite an exhibition that afternoon.

Sky gave his mount full rein, holding nothing back. He whooped and waved his hat over his head until the wind snapped the hat from his hand. Then he just rode, keeping close on the heels of the great White. When the white stallion headed up the ravine to the safety of open country, Sky followed. He felt less as if he were chasing the White than that the White was *drawing* Sky after him.

Sky thought briefly of Jenny, but he could no more turn back to find her than he could stop his own destiny.

He dropped his reins. Two-Tone didn't need Sky's directions. Sky raised his arms over his head, closed his eyes, and laughed as he had not laughed in a very long time. There was an indescribable joy in feeling Two-Tone's raw power under him.

And the freedom.

That's what it was all about. That's what the White was taking him to find. Or maybe he had found it already, in these few minutes of true liberty.

An image flitted across Sky's mind—a Cheyenne warrior, mounted on a mighty gray stallion, galloping on the warpath. His long black hair streamed out behind him, feathered lance held aloft over his head, war cry on his lips.

Sky had no real memories of his father, but he knew the image his mind had produced was of Broken Wing, Cheyenne warrior. This was the first time he had thought of his father in months.

Then Sky felt his mount slow. He opened his eyes. The White was still running ahead of them, but Two-Tone was tiring, or perhaps he just had enough good sense to think about conserving some strength for the ride home. Sky grasped the reins once more, also trying to rein in his own inflamed emotions. He was not disappointed that the wild ride had ended. He couldn't explain how he felt, and he didn't want to ruin it by too much analyzing. But deep inside, Sky knew the White had taken him where he had intended, to a place within himself he had thought was well hidden. Whether it was blood, or heritage, or just the lingering stories from his mother, he was reminded that more existed within Sky than the image he tried to project. It took him completely by surprise.

He didn't know what to do with it.

Then he heard Jenny riding toward him. He turned, suddenly embarrassed.

She drew up beside him. "Why, Sky Killion! I never in my life have seen such riding. I'll bet you could have captured that stallion if you had kept it up."

"No." Sky dismounted and walked a few paces. Jenny also dismounted and followed. "I hope no one ever catches that white stallion," he said.

"Neither do I. I was just joking." She reached out and took his hand in hers. "Sky, you looked just as majestic out there as that stallion."

"I only wish I could be like him."

"What's wrong, Sky?"

"Nothing." He kicked at a rock. "We'd better get home."

"So soon? There's still time."

"Your pa would kill me if he found us together."

"I hate that he's so protective."

"It's not just that. He wouldn't kill Kyle Evanston."

Jenny kicked at the same rock. "It's not fair!"

"We can't do anything about it. I can't change who I am—what I am. If only I could, I'd do it for you!"

"Can't you believe me?" Jenny entreated. "I don't want you to change. I love you for who and what you are."

"Do you really love me?"

Instead of speaking, Jenny reached her hands up around Sky's neck, pulled him close to her, and kissed him passionately.

"I love you, too," Sky murmured.

They kissed again, but then Sky pulled away. Jenny was too special for him to allow his rising emotions full vent. No matter how much they loved each other, they could never be together. So why torture each other?

"Sky," Jenny said impulsively, "let's get married."

There was nothing amusing in what she said, but he found himself laughing at its complete insanity, especially considering his own feelings of hopelessness at the situation.

"I'm not joking." And indeed, he had never seen her more earnest. "We'll run away from here. It's the only way. We'll go to Mexico. No one there will care whether you're Indian and I'm white. We can be free there."

*Free.* Was it possible? Or was such a hope as fleeting as the moment of freedom he'd experienced chasing the white stallion?

111

"I don't know, Jenny."

"Do you love me?"

"I said I did."

"Then that's the only way."

Sky lifted his eyes toward the mustangs now grazing placidly some distance away. The white stallion was prancing around his herd protectively. Sky found no answers there, not that he really thought he would. This was no magical beast granting wishes like in a fairy tale.

If it were, would Jenny be the wish he'd ask for? Before he could form a mental answer to that question, a snatch of that image of Broken Wing popped into mind.

Yes, Jenny was what he wanted. Anything else was simply a dream—even more of a dream than that of a half-breed Indian marrying the white daughter of his perpetual enemy.

"Sky, we can get on our horses right now and just keep on riding." She looked up at him with imploring eyes.

How could she love him so? How could she be so different from everyone else? He was nothing but a half-breed—not good enough to be Indian, not good enough to be white. Why didn't that bother her as much as it did nearly everyone else? As much as it bothered *him*.

But why should he question it? Why not embrace her love, enjoy it? There might never be another like it, like her again.

"This is complete craziness, Jenny."

"Be crazy, Sky. Please!"

"We can't just take off now. That *would* be crazy. We need food, money—"

"Does that mean we're going to do it?"

"I reckon so."

She threw her arms around him joyously. He kissed her, lifting her off her feet and swinging her merrily around. He was finished with his debates. They could have real happiness only if they went away. And he decided then and there he wanted that more than anything.

# 20

# DAWN RENDEZVOUS

Sky and Jenny returned to the Mesquite Rise an hour before sundown. They made plans to meet there the next morning at dawn. Jenny would pack that night and take her gear out somewhere away from the ranch while everyone slept. Then when she left in the morning, should anyone see her, it would look like she was just going for a ride. Sky would have an easier time, but even he would have to be discreet in getting away from his house with enough supplies for the long journey to Mexico.

When they parted, he tried not to think about how crazy their plan was. He just thought about how much Jenny loved him—enough to leave her home and family in order to share her life with him forever. He didn't know how he deserved such love, but he didn't allow himself to dwell on that, either.

---

Billy awoke with a start. He thought a sound had awakened him, but as he came fully awake and lay still to listen, he heard nothing. He couldn't go back to sleep. He had been having a hard time sleeping lately. He wasn't sure why, but it certainly had nothing to do with a guilty conscience over Sky Killion. He had tried to be decent, way beyond any debt he owed. But that half-breed had paid him back by destroying his ranch. He owed him nothing else, especially lost sleep.

But after tossing and turning for a few minutes, he decided to get up. He had never been one to enjoy only his thoughts for company. It must be nearly dawn anyway.

113

Billy went to his window to verify the time, and the light streaks of gray in the east told him he was right. Just as he was about to turn away from the window, he saw a rider cross the yard and head toward the gate. Even in the hazy light he could see it was a female.

Jenny.

What could she be doing out at this hour? She'd had a passion for riding lately—must be her new horse—but she had never left home *this* early. She exited through the gate, which was open, went a hundred yards to the oak tree, and dismounted. She retrieved something—it looked like a carpetbag, but he couldn't be certain from that distance. She hitched the bundle to her saddle, mounted, and rode away.

What was the girl doing?

It almost looked like she was sneaking away, running off. But why? She had been upset after the box social. She had left in tears. Billy had thought it was just because their pa had embarrassed her. At the time he thought she had been overreacting and had even told her so. She had only cried more. Billy felt a little guilty that she was so upset because he'd had a part in sabotaging the affair. He had seen Jenny's box ahead of time, and because he knew Kyle was sweet on Jenny, Billy informed Kyle. Kyle had paid him a dollar for that bit of information.

When Sky started bidding on his sister's box, Billy had interfered again. Over the weeks he had come to like Sky, but there was no forgetting the fact that he was half Indian when it came to his socializing with white girls, especially if the girl happened to be his sister. Billy's father had observed a silent but meaningful exchange of looks between Billy and Kyle, and realizing there was something going on he should know about, he had quietly spoken to Billy and gotten him to reveal that the disputed box belonged to Jenny.

If it hadn't been for Billy, Jenny's evening might not have ended as it had. On second thought, Big Bill would have stepped in regardless. If he hadn't, Jenny would have ended up having dinner with an Indian.

Now Jenny was sneaking off in the darkness. Had she really been that upset?

Billy pulled on his trousers and boots, strapped on his gun, and grabbed his hat. He had to go after her and see what was going on, and hopefully try to talk some sense into her. One way or the other, he'd get her home before their father found out and really

114

raised the roof. Maybe she was just going for a ride. Maybe . . .

He smiled at the thought. Maybe that sly fox Kyle had arranged a romantic meeting with her. But why so secretly? Kyle could come anytime to court Jenny with her father's blessing. In fact, if that was Kyle's game, he was harming rather than helping his chances with Jenny by fooling around in secret. Big Bill wouldn't like that at all.

By the time Billy had saddled his horse and got started, Jenny was well out of sight. He had no trouble, however, following her trail, especially as the sun rose. He could have caught up with her easily, but curiosity made him follow at a distance for a while. If she was running away from home like a rebellious child, he'd intercept her easily. If she was meeting Kyle, he'd like to know that, too. He would never find out if he nabbed her prematurely.

Obviously, Jenny wasn't worried about being followed—or at least she was taking no precautions to prevent it. When Billy caught sight of her for the first time, he hung back but she took no notice at all of him. He followed for about an hour until he saw she was heading toward a mesquite-covered rise. It would make a fine place for a romantic tryst.

When he saw her dismount, he did the same, keeping his horse out of sight, some distance away. Billy proceeded on foot to the rise, the thick mesquite providing ideal cover. He soon heard voices, male and female. Ah, so it was Kyle!

Billy was still perplexed about all the secrecy as he crept in closer. His first view was of Jenny in a man's embrace. Only when they turned slightly did Billy realize it was not Kyle at all whom Jenny had gone to meet.

It was the half-breed!

Billy was stunned at first. He must be seeing wrong. But, no, there could be no doubt. His sister and that Indian were holding each other, kissing.

Fury replaced Billy's shock. How could she? But more to the point, how could that rotten Indian have the nerve to touch his sister?

Billy spent no more time nursing his anger. He jumped to his feet and lunged into the clearing where Jenny and Sky stood in each other's arms.

---

"You dirty Injun cur!" Billy shouted.

When Sky saw Billy's hulk intrude into the clearing, he instinc-

115

tively broke away from Jenny. He hated himself for it, but he felt guilty, as if Billy had a right to his recriminations.

"Wait a minute, Billy!" Sky retorted, trying to recapture some of the confidence he'd felt earlier when he believed he actually could marry the beautiful white girl.

"You get away from my sister."

"You don't have any right—"

"I got *every* right!"

Sky hesitated. Maybe Billy was right. Maybe he was just a dirty Indian who didn't deserve—

Suddenly Jenny stepped forward. "Billy, please don't do this to us. Can't you understand? I love him."

"You're mixed up, confused, deceived. You'll get over it."

"We love each other, and we're going to get married," she replied with a firmness that gave Sky hope again. "Don't try to stop us."

"You're lucky I found you," said Billy. "Pa would kill you both if he saw you."

"Billy, you've never denied me anything—"

"This is where I start. This is where I draw the line." Billy shook his head. "Jenny, he's an Indian, for heaven's sake!"

"He's a *man!*"

"That's what he tried to pretend. Even I almost forgot for a while. But see what comes of it? You try to be decent to his kind, treat him like an equal, and he begins to believe it. He begins to think he can have all that white men have. But Indians aren't men—they're filthy animals—"

"Take that back," Sky demanded. "You ain't no better than me."

"Only half of you is worth spit," taunted Billy. "But even that half is cow dung compared to a real white—"

Sky lunged, but Billy was ready for the attack and clipped Sky on the side of the head before Sky could touch him. Sky absorbed the blow and shook off the pain. But Billy's right fist was thrusting for another blow. Sky ducked, and before Billy could recover from the misplaced blow, Sky landed his own right on Billy's jaw.

"Stop it!" Jenny cried.

"Get away from here, Jenny!" Billy ordered as he aimed another punch at Sky.

Jenny tried to intercede but Billy pushed her away. She stumbled back, tripping on the hem of her skirt, and fell to the ground. Both young men stopped momentarily. When she scrambled un-

116

hurt back to her feet, they continued their brawl.

Angered at Billy's mistreatment of Jenny, Sky took the offensive, throwing all his weight and all his anger into a punch that knocked Billy flat on his back.

"I've taken all I'm gonna take from you!" panted Sky, ready to attack again.

But as he made his move, Billy drew his six-gun. Sky saw murder in Billy's eye, and he prepared himself to take a bullet in the chest. But Billy hesitated. Maybe Sky's previous estimation of Billy had been true. Maybe there was more to him than he let on.

"Billy, don't be crazy!" Jenny screamed.

"You get out of here right now, Killion," said Billy, ignoring his sister, "and I won't kill you."

"He's not leaving—not without me," said Jenny.

"You're a fool, girl. You don't know what you're saying."

"Come on, Sky, let's go." Jenny took Sky's arm.

"No you don't!" Billy said.

"Billy, put that away," said Jenny. "You don't want to hurt anyone."

"Oh, yeah? It's about time someone put a bullet in this Injun."

"Is that how you'd repay him for saving your life?"

"I've already paid for that," said Billy. "I ain't about to let this redskin turn my sister into a slut."

"You ain't gonna shoot no one," said Sky, trying to trust that one moment of hesitation in the other, trying not to think of the violence etched in Billy's scowl.

"You think you're gonna walk away from me this time, Injun?" Billy cocked the gun. "You've gone too far now. You've touched my sister. Heaven only knows what you've done to her."

"He never did anything to me," Jenny pleaded, "except love me."

"Just that's enough to make you unfit for decent men—"

Billy's hand shook as it continued to level the gun at Sky's heart. Sky began to sense that Billy wanted to kill, and, for the first time that day, he was honestly scared.

"Jenny, get on out of here," Sky said.

"I said I wasn't leaving without you."

"I'll come for you, don't worry."

"You ain't going nowhere, 'cause you'll be dead," yelled Billy. "But you listen to him, Jenny, and go, because I don't want you to see no killing."

"Never!" she cried defiantly.

117

"If that's the way you want it, then watch this Injun scum die!"
Billy meant it this time. His finger squeezed the trigger.

Jenny threw her arms around Sky. The gun fired.

Jenny clung so tightly to Sky that even as her body convulsed with the impact of the bullet, she did not let go.

"Jenny!" Billy screamed, dropping his gun in horror.

Sky wrapped his arms around Jenny. If only he held her, the unthinkable would not happen. Then the initial shock and horror wore off and he took up her limp form in his arms.

"Sky, don't let me go!" Jenny murmured.

He knelt down in the grass, continuing to hold her in his lap like a hurt child. Her eyes were closed now, her breathing shallow.

"Sky, are you here?" Her eyes snapped open in panic.

"I won't leave you."

"I love you so, Blue Sky, son of Broken Wing . . . my Cheyenne warrior. . . ."

"Jenny. . . ." Tears filled Sky's eyes. "I love you, too. I always will."

Billy roused himself from his shock. "What have you done?"

"Me?" Sky gasped.

Billy stumbled toward where Sky sat cradling Jenny.

"Billy . . . why . . ." Jenny's voice sounded horribly like death. "Why couldn't you let us be. . . ?"

"It was Sky's fault, Jenny. He should have left when I told him to. . . ." Billy's voice trailed away, lacking conviction.

"We've got to get her to a doctor," said Sky.

"I'll take her," said Billy.

"No!" cried Jenny. "Don't let go of me, Sky! Hold me . . ."

Then she was silent, and the hand around Sky's neck fell heavily. The rise and fall of her chest ceased. Sky thought he could almost *feel* the life float away from her, leaving only an empty shell in his helpless arms. He couldn't speak. The tears that now spilled freely from his eyes were accompanied by neither sound nor movement. He felt as lifeless as the body he held.

He hardly noticed when Billy turned and ran away.

# 21

# THE STORY

When Sky rode into town, he still held Jenny in his arms. She had told him not to let go of her, and he wouldn't.

As he came abreast of the sheriff's office, Billy, the sheriff, and Ranger Tebbel came out. Sky kept riding until he came to the doctor's office, where he stopped. He dismounted and gently eased Jenny off the horse and into his arms once more. The sheriff came over with the others close behind.

Still ignoring them, Sky pushed open the door and went in. The doctor was there with a patient. He glanced up at Sky and his burden, a sudden look of alarm on his face.

"What's this?"

"Jenny Yates," Sky said in a brittle tone.

The doctor quickly dismissed his first patient. "Put her on the examination table."

Sky held back.

"You gotta put her down for me to examine her, boy."

Still Sky did not move to obey. He had been holding her for so long he thought he might surely crumble without her. "She wants me to hold her."

Shaking his head, the doctor checked Jenny's pulse and lifted one of her eyelids. "Boy, it isn't gonna matter to her anymore," he said sadly.

"I've got to hold her," insisted Sky.

The sheriff, who had been quietly standing in the doorway, interceded. "Don't make things worse for yourself, boy."

"It's what she wanted. . . ."

"Let the doc take her now, Sky," said the sheriff.

Billy came up behind the sheriff. "Make him put her down, Sheriff. It ain't right that he should touch her."

"Let me handle this, Billy," said the sheriff.

"I don't want no Injun scum touching my sister!" Billy shouted.

"Calm down, boy," said the sheriff. He turned to Tebbel. "Keep that Yates kid in tow, Bob, while I handle this. I don't want no more trouble."

With that, the sheriff approached Sky and tried to pry the body from his arms. Sky resisted at first until the doctor also made the attempt, with a much gentler manner.

He placed his arm around Sky. "She knows you held her until the end, Sky. She doesn't expect any more from you. Lay her down here. She deserves a proper burial, don't you think?"

Sky took a breath that deteriorated quickly into a sob. "Doc, Jenny's dead. . . ."

"Let me take care of her now."

Sky eased the body down on the examination table. Blinking back more tears, he slipped his hands away but then on impulse bent down and kissed her soft cheek one last time. It was cool with death, and he instantly wished he hadn't done it. He feared the awful feel of death would obliterate his memories of her warm, vibrant life.

"Come with me, Sky," the sheriff said. "Back to my office where we can talk."

In a few moments they were in the office. The Ranger had joined them and so had Billy.

"Now, I want to hear what happened," said the sheriff.

"I told you," said Billy. "The half-breed shot my sister. I . . . I reckon it was an accident. He was trying to shoot me, but he was wild, out of control."

The lies penetrated Sky's numb senses, but his response was detached, as if he didn't care.

"I didn't shoot her, Sheriff—"

"You no good, lying Injun—!" Billy lunged toward Sky, but the Ranger held him back.

"Go on, Sky. What's your story?" said the sheriff.

"Billy wouldn't let us be together . . . that's all we wanted . . . he was gonna shoot me. Jenny . . . she stopped the bullet meant for me. Why'd she do it, Sheriff? It should have been me."

"All lies!" yelled Billy, struggling against the Ranger's firm hold.

"Thanks, Bob," said the sheriff to the Ranger. "These too have been at each other's throats for years. I don't doubt at all that one was trying to shoot the other."

"They seemed friendly enough on the Fourth," said the Ranger.

"They sure worked together to interrupt my trip to the outhouse."

"I reckon a few days of friendship wasn't enough to erase all the hate."

"So what are you gonna do?"

"I'm gonna lock 'em both up, mainly for their own protection. It's a sure bet they'll still try to kill each other if I let 'em loose. Then I'm gonna send for their parents."

"Kyle Evanston will verify my story," said Billy.

"What's this?"

"He was there. I had him hide off in the bushes in case there was trouble. He must have run away when the shooting started."

"Okay, I'll get him, too."

The sheriff put Billy and Sky in separate cells. Sky slumped down on the cot, his head bowed. He still felt the chill of death on his lips. It should have been him lying dead and cold in the doctor's office.

*Why couldn't it be me?* he cried inwardly.

No one would truly have cared if it were him lying there dead. He was a worthless half-breed. Not good enough to be white, not even good enough to be Indian. He was a speck of worthless Texas dust. Instinctively he glanced over at Billy, who was lying silently on his bunk, eyes closed, perhaps asleep—though how he could sleep, Sky could not imagine. He felt a twisted envy for Billy's whiteness, and for the fact that no matter how mean Billy was, he'd always be accepted and worth something in the eyes of others.

Sky wanted to hate Billy for what he did, for shooting Jenny. But he could not even manage that for the moment. Billy had only pulled the trigger. Sky had really killed Jenny—by loving her, by thinking he was worthy of her. From the beginning he should have told her no, to stick with her own kind. Instead he had lured her along, getting her to love him and finally sacrifice herself for him.

*Why did you do it, Jenny? I wasn't worth it!*

But he knew the reason. It was love. Her love had been so clean, so pure and sweet. She saw none of the ugliness in him, none of the flaws. She saw only the person he was beneath the brown skin and straight, black hair. He still didn't understand how that could be. He only knew he'd never know love like that again. He didn't deserve it, anyway. He deserved only the pain it caused.

He lay back on his cot and stared at the ceiling. Not thinking, not moving, just staring. He lost all track of time.

Afternoon shadows were slanting across his cell by the time he stirred. He heard voices in the next room, the office. Loud voices and sounds of a struggle.

"Gimme that gun, Yates!"

"Let me go, or I swear I'll kill you, too!"

"No, you don't—"

There was a loud crash, sounds of furniture scattering. Then the door that led to the cells burst open. Big Bill Yates stood there, red-faced, panting like an animal, wielding a Colt 45. He fired once, but his aim was wild. The bullet nicked the floor about a foot from Sky's cot.

Instinctively Sky winced and jumped up. But then he didn't move. He stood there like a target, like an invitation. Yates aimed the gun at Sky's immobile form and, saying nothing, started to squeeze the trigger. Then something rammed him from behind with such force it knocked him off his feet. The gun flew from his hand and misfired.

Sky felt only a surge of disappointment. That's how it ought to be—a life for a life. He scowled at the newcomer.

Sam.

He and Yates tussled on the floor for a moment as Big Bill tried to reach the gun.

"There ain't gonna be no more killing today, Yates," said Sam.

"Get away from me, Preacher, or I swear to God I'll kill you, too."

"God don't want any part of this, Yates."

The sheriff, sporting a swelling bruise on his cheek, slipped into the room and retrieved the gun. Only when he aimed the weapon at Yates did the grief-stricken father calm somewhat. Sam was finally able to let go and stand.

Sam went to Sky's cell. "You okay, boy?"

"Why'd you stop him, Sam? It would have been right."

"Don't talk like that, Sky."

The sheriff said, "Now, you see why it's best I keep him locked up, Sam?"

"Locking up that filthy Injun ain't gonna help him," snarled Bill Yates. "He's dead, do you hear me! He's dead."

"We still don't know who killed the girl, Yates," said the sheriff. "The gun we found at the scene was Billy's, and it was fired recently. Sky's gun hasn't been fired in days—I checked it."

"You trying to tell me Billy killed his own sister? That's hogwash. Didn't know you was an Injun lover, Sheriff."

"I ain't, by golly! But I still gotta see that justice is done."

122

Billy, who had been awakened by the melee, spoke up. "Pa, I told them Kyle would verify my story."

"And we're trying to locate Kyle," said the sheriff. "Now, I want everyone to clear out of here. And, Bill, I'm keeping this gun."

"I'll get another."

"Don't be a fool, Bill. You kill anyone in my town—on purpose—and I'll see you hang."

Yates stared aghast at the sheriff. "You trying to tell me if you decide my daughter's death is an accident, that Injun'll go free?"

"It's possible. There'll be an inquest as soon as the judge comes through here."

Yates said nothing more—the cold look of malice on his face needed no words. He turned on his heel and exited.

"Pa!" Billy called after him, the dejection in his tone evident. But Yates did not return. Billy lay back on his cot, silent again.

Sam asked to be able to see Sky for a few minutes and the sheriff let him in the cell. Sam immediately embraced Sky, but it was awkward because Sky did not return the gesture.

"Your ma's out somewhere on the range," Sam said. "I sent someone looking for her. She'll be here soon."

"Do I have to see her, Sam?"

"I know you're grieving, and you feel terrible. But don't shut out the people who love you. You may not think so, but you need us."

"You should have let Big Bill kill me."

"Did you kill the girl, Sky?"

"What does it matter?"

"You don't have to hate yourself for something you couldn't do anything about."

"Are you saying I should hate the person who did it?" Sky glanced over at Billy, who was lying down with his eyes closed again, apparently uninterested in the softly spoken conversation in the next cell.

"I ain't saying you should hate anyone. That ain't gonna do no good, no more than Bill Yates killing you will. This is a terrible tragedy. But there is absolutely nothing we can do to change it. You have to go on, Sky, if for no other reason than to be able to see what good God is gonna bring out of this terrible thing."

"Don't you see, Sam? I don't want to go on—I can't." He dropped his head and ran his hands through his hair, pulling at the dark strands as if the small pain from that might stir something in him that had died.

A few minutes later, Sky's mother came in. The sheriff let her in the cell and she rushed to Sky's side. No one spoke. The moment her arms were around her son, he laid his head on her shoulder and wept like a baby.

# 22

# THE PRECIOUS BOTTLE

An inquest took place in a week, when the circuit judge arrived in town. Billy maintained his story that, though it had been an accident, Sky had fired the shot that had killed Jenny. Kyle Evanston verified Billy's testimony; however, there were enough inconsistencies in his account to introduce an element of doubt. Thus, when Sky told his side, in spite of the fact that it lacked fervent conviction, it was impossible for the court to lay blame for the incident solidly at anyone's feet.

Jenny's death was ruled an accident. The young men were set free by the court. Their only consequences would be having to live with themselves.

Despite the decision of the court, however, a large majority of the local people were convinced that Sky was guilty. And Big Bill Yates did all he could to further inflame passions against Sky, even to spreading the word about a possible lynching.

At first, Sky hardly cared what anyone did to him. He probably would have bought the rope himself. But as time passed, his grief began to give way to anger. He was tired of his parents' gentle admonitions about forgiveness. It would have been far too easy to forgive either Billy or himself. Jenny was dead, and it would be a long time before they had suffered enough for their part in her loss.

But the more both Yates men flung their scathing recriminations at Sky, the more he began to focus his anger and hatred on them. Especially Billy.

At night when Sky could sleep—which was seldom these

days—he would relive in his dreams that awful moment when Billy pulled the trigger and Jenny slumped in Sky's arms. Many times the horrible images would recur in waking moments just by closing his eyes. But the dreams were worse in their vivid clarity. Sometimes that moment would replay itself over and over again in quick succession until he'd wake up screaming.

At times the dreams were even more twisted. Sometimes Sky would be holding the gun—just as Billy had claimed at the inquest. And Sky would fire over and over again as if his hatred was for Jenny, too, and he *wanted* to see her dead. But by far the most satisfying of these disturbing dreams was when Sky held the gun on Billy. The spectral Sky emanated sheer delight as he fired upon Billy. The satisfaction he felt frightened him more than all the other dreams together.

There was only one way Sky could think of to end the dreams. He rode into town one day and found a stranger who looked as if he would do anything for some money. Sky paid the man to buy him a bottle of whiskey at the saloon. He then rode out to the Mesquite Rise and began to drink himself into oblivion. And it worked, too. He didn't feel anything. And when he passed out in a drunken heap there on the very spot where Jenny had been slain, he did not have a single dream.

In the morning he awoke with a pounding headache and didn't feel at all rested. But at least the heavy shadows of nightmares weren't hovering over him.

He drank some more and decided that if he could stay in a state of mild inebriation, life would be much better. He played his guitar and sang—mostly loud, nonsensical songs—until he passed out again.

That's how Griff found him shortly before sundown.

"Okay, boy, it's time you went home. Your ma is beside herself with worry about you."

"Howdy, Griff, old friend," Sky said, rousing from his stupor. His voice was slurred, and his eyes saw two Griffs bent over him.

"You look a sight, Sky."

"What'd ya mean? I never felt better." He slumped back to the ground, eyes rolling back in his head.

Griff grasped him under the arms and lugged Sky to his feet. "We gotta walk some of this off."

Sky's knees buckled, but after a few minutes of Griff nearly dragging him, he began to move on his own, though he still needed Griff's support.

"Griff, I didn't have no dreams last night."

"That's good."

After they walked about for a few minutes, Griff let Sky sit again as he built a small fire and fixed coffee.

"A couple of cups of my coffee'll clear that head of yours," said Griff.

"Who says I want a clear head?"

"You want your ma to see you like this?"

Sky gave him a lopsided, drunken grin. "I don't much care when I'm drunk."

Before long Griff thrust a tin cup of hot coffee into Sky's shaking hands. "Drink it!"

It was burning hot, and Sky spit out his first scalding mouthful. "You trying to kill me, Griff?" Sky yelled.

"I said drink it!"

Still complaining, Sky drank it and also a second cup Griff forced into his hand. When he began to act a bit more lucid, Griff decided they could head home. They loaded up Sky's guitar and were about to mount when Sky stopped.

"Just a minute. Forgot something." Sky returned to where he had been sitting to retrieve the whiskey bottle which was still about a quarter full.

As he bent over to pick it up, Griff's boot shot in front of him and kicked the bottle away.

"You don't need that, Sky."

"Yes, I do."

"No, you don't. Now, let's get going."

Griff took Sky's arm, but Sky wrenched it away.

"I ain't wasting good whiskey!"

"Look here—"

"You gonna preach at me, Griff? Don't I get enough of that from Sam?"

"Having a couple of drinks is one thing, Sky, but using the stuff to escape from your problems is another."

"Don't you tell me what I shouldn't do!"

Sky shoved past Griff toward the bottle. When Griff tried to intercede again, Sky took a swing at him. Griff ducked, avoiding the blow.

"Don't start what you can't finish, boy!"

"I can take you any day, old man!"

Sky lunged again, this time clipping Griff with a hard left. Griff retaliated with a right that had downed many grizzled cowboys.

127

Sky toppled over. But as Griff stood over Sky with what appeared to be a self-satisfied look on his face, Sky leaped to his feet and bashed a fist into Griff's nose. The blow drew blood.

"If that's how you want it, Sky—" Griff took another swing.

Sky dodged the blow, then came back with a left to Griff's belly. Griff doubled over, gagging. Sky backed off a bit. It had only been a year since Griff had nearly died from a gunshot wound to the very spot Sky had struck. But Sky wasted little time on guilt. While Griff was coughing, Sky lunged for the bottle.

Just as his hand closed on it, Griff's body landed hard on top of him. Sky grunted and dropped the whiskey.

"Blast you, Griff!" He clipped the foreman hard on the side of the head.

"Don't be a fool!" Griff yelled.

"Why you doing this to me, Griff?" Sky reached back to aim for another swing, but Griff blocked the punch and landed his own blow that split Sky's lip.

" 'Cause I love you, you idiot!" said Griff.

"If you really did, you'd let me have that bottle." Sky lurched toward the bottle again. "I need it, Griff!"

Sky struggled to get past Griff, but Griff held him at bay. All at once Sky seemed to take a good look at what was happening. He was fighting Griff, his dearest friend in the world, over a bottle of whiskey—a mostly empty bottle, at that.

"Oh, Griff!" A sob broke through Sky's swollen lips. He sank to his knees in defeat, and Griff went down with him, his arms around Sky.

"It's okay."

"You don't understand." Tears welled up in Sky's eyes. "I gotta have it. I gotta forget!"

"Maybe there's some other way. Maybe Sam—"

Sky shook his head. "Sam don't know. His answers don't help."

"Maybe that's because you won't let them help."

"I've tried, Griff! It's never gonna go away. It just gets worse."

Griff grabbed the whiskey bottle. "And you think this is gonna help?"

Sky looked away, a little ashamed, but he nodded. Griff pushed the bottle at Sky's chest.

"Then take it. Ain't no use trying to stop you."

Sky looked down at the bottle. He wanted very much to open it and pour the remainder of its contents down his throat, but for the moment Griff's admonitions kept him from giving in to that urge. He tore his eyes from the bottle and looked up at Griff.

"Guess I'm ready to go home," Sky said.

"Now *I'm* gonna be in hot water with your ma for bruising you up." Griff helped Sky to his feet.

Sky touched a swelling bruise on Griff's cheek. "You don't look that great, either."

"Maybe she'll believe we was in a stampede."

"I *feel* like I was, at least."

They returned to their horses, and Sky slipped the bottle into his saddlebag. When he glanced up, he saw Griff watching him. He was grateful when the foreman made no further comment.

# 23

# DEPARTURE

Sky was more isolated after Jenny's death than ever before. In large part, it was a self-imposed isolation. But even T.R. deserted him. And the hands at the Wind Rider Ranch also kept their distance. Most folks, believing he killed Jenny, simply thought it wiser to stay clear of the volatile Indian.

He found comfort in whiskey but made a point—usually—not to drink so much that he couldn't function normally. If his family knew he was drinking, they refrained from nagging him about it. But he spared them all from uncomfortable confrontations by staying away from his parents as much as possible, rising in the morning before them and returning home after they were in bed. When he did happen to encounter them, he was detached. He was becoming quite proficient at being invisible—even in the presence of others. Often, when he couldn't literally hide from them, he'd hide behind his music, spending hours playing his guitar, making up countless tunes.

But this couldn't go on forever. Sky's parents might be willing to give him time to work out his grief and pain. Bill Yates wasn't.

About a month after the inquest, Sky rode into town one day, trying to get a fresh supply of whiskey. This was not always an easy task. No one who knew him would be party to supplying "firewater" to an Indian—especially to this particular Indian, who had already proven he had a violent temper. Sky had made two previous attempts and had come up dry. He had now been a week without anything—a week with very little sleep except what was disturbed by those terrible nightmares. He was feeling frayed and a little desperate.

In addition, Sky's funds were running short. It was a week until payday, and the little pocket money he had after paying his debt for the fence was down to one dollar. He gave it to a drifter he saw exiting the saloon.

"Buy me a bottle of whiskey," said Sky, "and you can keep the change."

The drifter shrugged, took the money and went back into the saloon, returning in a few moments with the bottle. Sky took it eagerly, then headed down the street to the livery stable.

He was almost at the stall where he had left Two-Tone when he ran into Billy and his father.

"What you doing, Injun boy?" asked Big Bill.

"None of your business."

Sky started forward, but they blocked his path.

"What's that you got?" Billy poked the bottle with his finger.

"Leave me alone." Sky glared at Billy. The image of Billy firing the bullet that killed Jenny flashed through his mind. Hatred filled him. But he knew he couldn't fight both Yates men together.

"You think we're gonna let a wild savage have firewater?" sneered Big Bill.

"Pa, I think I should take it from him."

Sky lurched away from Billy's reach but lost his grip on the bottle. Billy caught it as it slipped from Sky's hands.

"Give it to me," Sky demanded.

Billy threw it down, shattering it on the hard dirt. Enraged and no longer caring about the uneven odds, Sky charged his antagonists. He was instantly laid flat on the stable floor next to his broken bottle. Before he could recover, Big Bill drew his pistol.

"You ain't gonna kill me right out here in public," challenged Sky. The livery stable, being on the edge of town, was hardly public. And he hadn't seen anyone else in the stable since Billy and Big Bill had showed up. Was that more than a coincidence?

Yates fired into the dirt about three inches from Sky's head. Before Sky could get up, Billy, who had drawn his gun right after his father, fired at the dirt on the other side of Sky's head. Sky's ears were ringing and his eyes were burning from the flying dust and straw. But he didn't dare move, not with both guns trained on him.

"Go ahead and kill me, Yates!" sneered Sky. "But if you want to kill the person who killed your daughter, then shoot the man standing right next to you."

"You lying Injun!" Billy yelled as he fired again, his shot coming so close to Sky's shoulder it burned a hole in his sleeve and singed his skin.

Yates leveled his gun on Sky's head. His next bullet would bury itself in the middle of Sky's forehead. But Sky felt chillingly calm. By all appearances Yates had every intention of firing that shot. Yet Sky did not flinch. His eyes dared Yates to pull the trigger.

But Yates lowered his gun.

"This ain't the time or place, half-breed," he said. "You ain't worth the risk of me putting my head in a noose. When you die—and mark my words, it's gonna be soon!—there won't be a soul who can prove I was involved."

Sky jumped to his feet. "You should have taken your chance while you could, Yates. I'm starting to want a taste of revenge, too. I loved Jenny and she loved me—and Billy took her away from me when *he* killed her." Sky swung his gaze toward Billy. "But maybe I don't have to kill you, Billy. Maybe the truth is just gonna eat you up inside."

Billy licked his lips and swallowed before he looked away from Sky's venomous glare.

Finally Billy said, "Come on, Pa, let's get outta here before I do something I'll regret."

Sky watched them walk away. What he had said was only partly true. Sometimes Sky did rise out of his self-hatred long enough to hate Billy, perhaps to fantasize about killing him. But there were a hundred reasons why he wouldn't—not the least of which being that it would simply be pointless.

Still, Sky knew beyond doubt that Bill Yates's words were no mere threat. The kind of hate he felt toward Sky would only be appeased by revenge—an eye for an eye.

There was only one thing for him to do. He would leave home. He had become an outcast in his own family, alienated from those few people who still cared about him. He was making life uncomfortable for everybody. They would be happier without him around.

———

When the time came to tell his parents, there was such a look of resignation on his mother's face that Sky felt certain she had been expecting this.

"Where will you go, Sky?" she asked.

"I don't know exactly."

"You'll keep in touch?"

"Sure." Sky wondered if his mother sensed he didn't mean it. "And I'll pay you back what I owe you for that fence. Soon as I get a job somewhere."

Sam left for a minute, and when he returned he had his old, worn Bible in his hand. Sky knew Sam cherished it, not only for the truths he believed it held but also because it had been given to him by his mother when he first embarked upon the ministry.

"Take this with you, Sky," Sam said.

"I ain't gonna take your Bible, Sam."

"I want you to. I can get another."

"It'll do more good with you, Sam." Sky pushed the book back. Then he added almost apologetically, "But I appreciate the thought."

His mother started to cry. "Ma, please don't—" Sky said.

"I can't help it, Blue Sky—" It was the first time in years she'd used his Cheyenne name. "I know you must go, but it's still not easy. It was never any secret, son, that you were the child of love, the child of my heart."

"It is ironic, I guess, that it ended up to be Carolyn who made you proud, and me who shamed you—who shamed my father."

"No, Sky—"

"You know it's true. Oh, you don't love me any less for it, but I have been a disappointment. Maybe it's true what folks say about being a half-breed—that I ain't good enough to be either white or Indian."

"I've always believed, Sky, that in you dwells the *best* of both races. I pray that someday you'll realize it yourself. And, mostly, I pray you'll find where you truly belong. I know it's not easy for a young man like you in this world, but there is a place where you will feel at home. I'm sorry it couldn't be here. Maybe someday . . ."

A sob broke through her forced composure. Sky put his arms around her. He had been trying to convince himself he didn't need the emotional support his mother offered; and even as he embraced her he tried to tell himself he was doing it more for her than him. But he knew another part of him was dying as he said his final goodbye to the woman who had borne him and raised him.

———

In the morning, before sunrise, Sky tried to slip away unseen. But as he entered the kitchen, his mother was seated at the table as if she had been waiting there all night for him.

"I found something last night after you went to bed," she said. "I thought you might want it." It was the beautifully beaded collar that his uncle, Stands-in-the-River, had given him many years ago.

133

Sky was embarrassed when he said, "I . . . I lost that a couple of years ago." In reality, he had thrown it away in one of his attempts to distance himself from his Indian heritage.

"I found it," she said, adding without reproach, "in the trash."

"I'm sorry, Ma."

"I know how desperately you wanted to fit in with your white friends—at least I know now. I retrieved this, hoping that one day it would mean something to you. This may not be the right time, but something prompted me to give it to you anyway. Please take it, Sky. It is the best thing I have for you to remember me and your father by."

Sky had already hurt his mother so much he couldn't refuse her this request. He took the collar and tucked it in the saddlebag he had slung over his shoulder.

Then, with a simple, "Bye, Ma," he turned and left.

———————

That night, after Sky had traveled about sixty miles from home, he stopped to camp. He killed a jackrabbit, built a fire, and roasted the meat for his supper. While he was getting fixings for coffee from his saddlebag, he noticed something there he hadn't packed. Sam's Bible.

Sky shook his head. "That fellow doesn't know when to give up."

He took it out and thumbed through it affectionately for a moment. Stuck in the middle was a ten dollar bill. Maybe Sam thought Sky would be more likely to hang on to the book if it held something of more material value to Sky. Sky put the money in his pocket, then returned the Bible to his bag. He didn't expect ever to read it, but perhaps someday Sky would return home and be able to give it back to Sam.

Sky glanced to the south. A sudden ache in his heart made him wonder if he would ever again lay eyes on the Wind Rider Ranch or on the people he loved there.

# PART 2

# SPRING 1886

# 24

# THE WILD WEST

A choking billow of dust rose high above the racing stage-coach. The driver snapped his quirt at the rear of the galloping mules while the shotgun rider, lying on top of the coach, fired his Winchester furiously. A dozen Indian attackers closed the distance between them and the coach as it turned a sharp bend.

Savage Indian cries rose above the explosions of gunfire. They neared their target, miraculously dodging bullets.

Suddenly from the opposite direction a contingent of mounted cowboys rushed upon the scene, firing six-guns and rifles. One Indian fell, another grabbed a wounded arm, nearly losing control of his horse. Finally, perceiving their imminent defeat, the Indians gathered up their fallen and retreated.

A tumultuous cheer rose from the thousands of spectators in the stands around the arena. The attack on the Deadwood Mail Stage was without a doubt the most popular act of Buffalo Bill's Wild West Show.

Sky rode backstage with the rest of the Indians, dismounted and, removing the blanket from Two-Tone's bare back, quickly rubbed him down. They'd have to appear again in about an hour, this time attacking a settler's cabin.

Sky looked down at himself wryly. Buckskin breeches and the moccasins on his feet were his only clothing. His bare chest was liberally marked with war paint, as was his face. A rawhide band around his forehead held two eagle feathers. He looked quite the picture of an Indian brave. Not a Cheyenne, though, for his outfit had been provided by a Sioux named Red Elk. It was almost amusing to wonder what Billy Yates would think of him now. Not in the least amusing was another thought that flitted briefly through his mind—what would his father think?

But Sky tried to avoid such thoughts. A job was a job. He had been down to his last dime when he reached St. Louis the winter after he left home. He had wondered if his impulsive decision to head East had been such a good idea. But he felt like making a drastic change in his life, an attempt to try to forget the past pain. Ironically, his mother had done just the opposite, traveling West to forget the pain of her life in the East. Maybe it would work better for him.

He had wintered in St. Louis, nearly starving on the pittance he earned doing odd jobs and occasionally singing and playing his guitar in saloons. When Buffalo Bill's Wild West Show came to town in the spring, hiring new performers, Sky put in his name. He had expected to get hired on as a cowboy—that's what he was, after all. The fact that the performing cowboys were earning sixty dollars a month plus room and board made it even more appealing to Sky. After a season with the show, even after sending money home to pay his debt, he'd have more than enough left to make it on his own.

The fellow doing the hiring had other ideas. He said it was not "theatrically" sound to cast an Indian in a cowboy part—it wouldn't look right.

"But I can bust broncs, rope calves. I even know some rope tricks," Sky had insisted.

"I'll tell you your best asset," the man said. "You aren't a reservation Indian. We don't have to post a bond to get you to work for us. You want the job or not?"

"What's it pay?"

"Twenty-five a month, a roof over your head, and all you can eat."

Sky had agreed, thinking that perhaps once he was in the show, he'd be able to get the better-paying cowboy job. So far that hadn't happened. But he'd only been with them a week.

Red Elk came up to Sky, interrupting his reverie.

"You are starting to make a good Indian." Red Elk gave Sky a friendly slap on the back. They conversed in Cheyenne, since Sky didn't speak much Sioux.

Sky nodded and smiled faintly at the well-meaning, though ironic, compliment. "I guess so."

"Come. It's time for the great chief."

Sky followed Red Elk behind the huge canvas mural that formed the backdrop of the stage, near the performers' entrance. In a moment, a mounted Indian rode past them into the arena.

138

Even Sky could not help but watch in awe as the great Sioux chief, Sitting Bull, made his daily appearance in the Wild West Show. To Sky it had seemed odd that the chief hadn't been cast as the leader of the attacking Indians. But Buffalo Bill must have thought the chief could be put to the best effect in this way. And in truth there was an undeniable power in this presentation, the lone Indian circling the arena. The old chief was truly majestic; not only in his appearance, riding tall and straight in his great many-feathered bonnet, but in the fact that he maintained this proud bearing even when the crowd began to boo and hiss. To them he was Custer's killer, and it was their patriotic duty to rail at the man. An even truer measure of the man's courage was that he maintained such dignity despite the fact that he must have known that at any time someone in the crowd seeking vengeance could have taken a clear shot at him. Yet such a tragedy never occurred. No doubt the crowd, for all their catcalls and boos, could not deny the fact that this was a magnificent man, a great warrior.

Sky didn't want to be impressed by Sitting Bull or the other Indians. But the fact was, they were *real* Indians straight from the reservation. Most had actually fought the kind of battles they were reenacting on the stage. Several, including Sitting Bull, were still considered dangerous troublemakers by the government and had only been permitted to go with the show in hopes of taming them. Buffalo Bill had to post a ten thousand dollar bond in order to take them.

Sky tried to ignore all this. He did his job from day to day, trying to relate impassively to his Indian companions. He had spent most of the last several years avoiding this very image—avoiding, in fact, all association with his Indian heritage. Now he had to meet it head on. He drank a little in order to bolster his nerve to make those silly Indian attacks every day, but he did so in secret. Drinking was forbidden among performers, especially the Indians. He tried not to look at himself in that Indian "get-up," and he frequently reminded himself that this was all playacting, not real.

Of course, he could have quit at any time. But the show was achieving one positive thing for Sky—it was keeping him busy and occupied. The traveling and variety were a welcome distraction. His first week with the show had been extremely busy, filled with rehearsing when they weren't performing or traveling. In a few days they would actually be in Washington, D.C. Sky was a country boy, and the spectacle of the big cities played upon his senses like a bottle of cheap whiskey. The effect was temporary, to be sure,

139

but with enough of such fleeting moments linked together, he hoped to find escape.

As he stood around between acts, trying to look busy with his horse so he wouldn't have to talk to the Indians, Buffalo Bill approached him.

"Howdy, Sky," said the famous frontiersman.

"Hello, Mr. Cody," Sky replied with just a hint of awe; he had only spoken personally to Cody a couple of times.

"Mighty fine show we're putting on today. Weather couldn't be better."

"Yes, sir."

"I'd like to ask a little favor of you, young fellow."

"Anything, Mr. Cody."

"Some of the boys here tell me you are Cheyenne."

"Yes."

"And you speak the lingo?" When Sky nodded, Buffalo Bill continued. "Well, here's the deal. My Cheyenne interpreter had to go back to the reservation this morning. Seems his pa has took ill. I'm in a pinch now and was wondering if you'd serve as interpreter. I'd pay you an extra ten dollars a month for the job, and you wouldn't have a lot of added work. We only got half a dozen Cheyenne with the troupe, and they don't talk much."

Sky could not even consider refusing. Of course, the money was one reason, but mostly, Buffalo Bill was just not the kind of man you refused. He did a lot for others and didn't deserve some lame excuse for a refusal. And since Sky didn't wish to reveal his real reason, his refusal would seem lame, indeed.

In the days Sky had been traveling with the show, he had studiously avoided the small Cheyenne contingent. He tended to keep to himself anyway, and he hoped this avoidance might not be overtly noticeable. But the Wild West troupe, with about three hundred people, was like a very small town and privacy was a limited commodity.

After Cody and Sky spoke with the Cheyenne, taking care of a few matters of business Cody had with them, Sky turned to leave with Cody. But one of the Cheyenne spoke to Sky, stopping him.

"Before you go, Sky, could I talk to you?" the man asked in Cheyenne.

"Yeah, sure."

"My name is Little Left Hand. When I first saw you, I thought there was something familiar about you. Have you ever been to Indian Territory?"

"Never. I was raised in Texas, by whites."

"Then I could not have met you before. It is strange, isn't it?"

Sky thought about what he'd heard many whites say—that all Indians looked alike. Maybe it was true, and even Indians couldn't tell each other apart. He didn't say as much to this Indian, however. He just shrugged.

"I don't know," he said.

"Do you have a Cheyenne name?"

"Not one I've used in a long time," Sky hedged. Then he abruptly added, "Listen, it was nice meeting you, but we'd better get ready for the next act."

Little Left Hand nodded. "Perhaps we will talk again."

"Oh, sure. That'd be fine."

Sky spun around and made his escape.

# 25

# WINTER ROSE

One of Sky's duties as interpreter was to be on hand at the Indian village Buffalo Bill had created on the showgrounds. Sky was to field questions from visitors, mostly children, to the Cheyenne who "lived" in the village.

Sky found this experience more unsettling than anything in the show. The village was very authentic, for Buffalo Bill was dedicated to presenting the frontier in scrupulously realistic detail. As Sky wandered among the tepees, he felt as out of place and time as the village itself was in the midst of a big American city. The images of his own mother and father actually dwelling in such a place were hard to shake, though he tried to do so. He himself had been born in a Cheyenne village, in his father's lodge; he had toddled after the village dogs, watched his mother tan buffalo hides, and seen, though he had no real memory of it, his father ride off to war.

But Sky did not belong here.

He knew nothing about buffalo hides, constructing a tepee, or doing sacred war dances. Glancing over to where a group of cowboys were practicing rope tricks, he shook his head. Sky could do the same tricks they were doing—in fact, Griff had taught him a dandy trick that used two ropes which he hadn't seen in the show. Perhaps he would show Cody the trick, and then they'd put Sky where he belonged.

"I like to watch the cowboys perform, too."

Sky turned. A young Cheyenne woman had come up behind him.

"Oh, they're not bad," said Sky, "but I've seen better on my ma's ranch."

"That's right—you are the Indian who should be a cowboy."

142

She didn't hide the hint of mockery in her otherwise good-natured tone.

"I *am* a cowboy."

"You don't look like one." Her eyes danced playfully over his figure clad in Indian costume.

"What do you know?" Sky snapped. He did not like being the object of her amusement.

He started to go, but she laid a restraining hand on his arm. "Please. I'm sorry for having fun with you. My father would scold me for my rudeness."

"Okay." He tried once again to leave.

"That's all?"

"You want something else?"

"What I did was wrong—it was the wrong way to try to be friendly. My father says I need to think more before I wag my tongue. Is it too late to try again?"

"Why bother?"

"Then you'd rather be alone all the time?"

"If I didn't, I suppose I'd make a nuisance of myself, like you."

"I'm sorry."

"Let's forget it ever happened. Now, I've got to get to work."

"That's why I came in the first place," she said in a far more contrite tone. "An interpreter is needed."

The girl led him to one of the tepees where several white visitors, two adults and three children, had gathered. Little Left Hand was there also, with two squaws and a couple of Cheyenne children.

"What can I do for you?" Sky asked the white man.

"My boy here has some questions for you Injuns."

"We can try to answer them. What are they?"

"Go ahead, Jake. The Injun won't hurt you."

A tow-headed boy of about nine years stepped forward. The father's assurance hardly seemed necessary for this boy, who didn't appear in the least afraid of the Indians.

"I want to know if they got any scalps," said the boy.

Sky translated the question to Little Left Hand, who smiled.

"The children always want to know this," said the Cheyenne.

"And?" Sky was a bit curious himself.

Little Left Hand ducked inside the tepee and in a moment returned carrying his lance. The top of the lance was adorned with feathers and two long, black hanks of shiny hair. Sky had half ex-

143

pected to see scalps as yellow as the boy's hair and was somewhat disappointed.

So was the boy. "Them's Injun scalps."

Sky translated for Little Left Hand, who replied, "These are from great Pawnee warriors. Next to the whites, they are the Cheyenne's greatest enemies."

Sky told this to the boy, leaving out the reference to the whites. No sense riling anyone.

The white family asked a few more questions, then left to watch a beading demonstration. The Cheyenne girl Sky had spoken to earlier approached.

"Nehuo," she said to Little Left Hand, "I told you you should have taken Bull Bear's scalps when he offered them." Turning to Sky she added, "Bull Bear has some fine white scalps. They might impress even you."

"They would frighten some whites, especially the women and children," Little Left Hand said.

The girl laughed. "Not that boy who was just here. I think he's disappointed *he'll* never be able to take some scalps."

"Some of the chiefs worry about stirring up old anger."

"All that we do here could have that effect," said the girl. "I've heard Buffalo Bill is planning to reenact the Little Big Horn Battle. Imagine what that will do!"

"Enough, Rose," Little Left Hand said sharply. "A good Cheyenne girl is seen and not heard."

"When have I ever been that?" she said with a twinkle of laughter in her large doe eyes.

Little Left Hand gave a long-suffering sigh.

"This rose has a few thorns," Sky offered wryly.

Little Left Hand laughed so hard he dropped his lance and doubled over. Rose gave her head a defiant shake and folded her arms stubbornly, attempting to appear unperturbed by the barb. Then, in spite of herself, a little giggle escaped her pursed lips. In another moment she was laughing as hard as her father.

Sky also tried unsuccessfully to restrain his mirth. He smiled and even chuckled a bit.

"Ah-ha!" Rose said, noticing his response. "You can smile. I was beginning to wonder."

Just then, to Sky's relief, the dinner bell rang. "Time to eat," he said. "See you later." He started off.

Rose hurried after him. "I have to eat, too."

"It's a free country."

It was a five-minute walk across the grounds to the mess tent where all the performers dined. Sky purposefully walked fast, taking long strides. Rose kept up, though she had to double step every so often to keep pace.

After they had filled their plates, they sat together at a table. "Why are you so persistent?" Sky asked.

"I don't know. You are my age, you are a Cheyenne boy. Why not?"

"I ain't looking for a gal," he said as he dug into his dish of stew, hoping eating might distract her.

"I think young people our age are always looking. It's only natural."

"Are you calling me a liar?"

"How come you are so serious all the time, Sky?"

"Life is serious."

Rose made no response but instead concentrated on her stew. Sky watched her covertly. Even after his solemn rebuff, there seemed to be an air of amusement about her. In fact, there was always a hint of a smile in her eyes—even if not upon her lips. Her round face, high cheekbones and large, round eyes were a perfect backdrop for all that amusement. But just as she had asked about his seriousness, he wondered about her joviality. What did she find so merry about life? Why was she so happy? Maybe she was just too ignorant to know better. But that couldn't be it. Besides her merriment, she also seemed quite intelligent. Her wit was certainly quick enough.

Probably she was just naive about life. Although she was Sky's age, she no doubt had never run into the kind of difficulties Sky had known. She was probably a complete innocent, a child at heart.

Just when he thought he might be spared further conversation, Rose asked, "Sky, do you have a Cheyenne name?"

"Yeah."

"What is it?"

He wanted to tell her it was none of her business; he wanted to tell her to go away. But he didn't.

"Blue Sky."

"Is it because your eyes are the color of a summer sky?"

"I guess so."

"If you were raised by whites, how did you come by a Cheyenne name? For that matter, how did you learn to speak Cheyenne?"

"You want me to tell you my whole life story?"

"Since you're offering, I'd like that very much."

"I wasn't offering."

"Oh."

The smile in her eyes started to fade, and Sky immediately regretted his harshness. "Okay, if you must know, my mother is white and my father is—was—Cheyenne. He was killed when I was about two years old. My mother bought a ranch after that, and we've lived in Texas ever since."

"There must be more to it than that—"

"You're never satisfied, are you?"

She giggled, but he could tell she was only laughing at herself. "I suppose I can drive people to distraction. My father always says so."

"I guess it's not so bad," Sky said with more kindness. "And, by the way, you're right—about me. There is more to my life, but I don't much like talking about it."

"I'll try not to be too curious, then."

"Thanks."

"You can ask me a question if you'd like," she said.

Sky really couldn't think of anything, but it seemed heartless to be so disinterested in her. He thought until he came up with something. "Rose is a funny Indian name, isn't it?"

"My Cheyenne name is Winter Rose. I was born in winter with the snow deep around our lodge. My father said I was as pretty as a rose that blooms in winter. Later at the Indian school, my white teacher shortened it to Rose."

"You didn't mind?"

"What's in a name? 'A rose by any other name would smell as sweet,' " she quoted, then giggled. "That's what my teacher said, anyway. But I liked it. She said it came from the greatest writer who ever lived."

"Shakespeare," Sky said.

Sky's education clearly impressed Rose, and he had to admit he liked the feeling her reaction gave him.

After a short silence, Rose asked, "Can I ask one more question—not about the past?" He nodded. "How come you joined the show? It's obvious you don't want to be here."

"I thought they'd take me as a cowboy performer. That's where I belong, not—" He stopped, suddenly concerned about offending her.

"I heard some cowboys are leaving at the end of the season,"

146

she said, seeming to ignore his discomfort. "Maybe if you spoke to Mr. Cody . . ."

"I do, every chance I get. I reckon what it boils down to is that I don't belong with them, either."

"I'm sorry, Blue Sky—"

"*Sky*," he said, perhaps a little too sharply.

"Well, I am sorry. But, *Sky*, if you are going to be with the Indians, I think you could fit in. We want to accept you."

"No one has been bending over backward in my direction."

"You've made it clear you want it that way." She paused for a moment, taking on a more thoughtful expression. "I don't think you've been around Indians very much in your life. So maybe you don't know that we can be very accepting of others—not like so many whites who allow things such as skin color to dictate their judgment of a man. But there is one thing an Indian has trouble abiding—another Indian who rejects his own people, his own heritage. That is very hard for us to understand."

"My people are white, too, you know," he said defensively.

"It must be confusing for you."

"Look, can we talk about something else? For instance, why do the Indians do these shows? It seems kind of demeaning to me. And all the attacking scenes must only confirm to whites that Indians are just as savage as they always thought."

"One important reason is the money. Many families are starving on the reservation, and the money that is earned here is sent back simply to buy food. Where else could an Indian earn this much money?"

After his own experience last winter, Sky could not argue. White boys earned twice as much for the same jobs—when he could get a job at all. He had been turned down several times because the prospective employers said they couldn't trust an Indian.

"But the show is also a way for our people to learn about the whites and to see their world," Rose went on. "Perhaps if we could understand their world better, we could somehow learn to live in peace together. Sitting Bull was promised that when we get to Washington, he will meet with the White Chief."

"What about you, Rose?"

"Oh, they won't let a mere squaw meet the White Chief." Then she giggled. "I'm sorry. I can't resist a joke. I am here because my father wanted me to come. I wanted to go to the Indian school at Darlington. I went there for a few months when I was younger,

147

but my father thought they were making me too white and he made me come home."

"Didn't they teach you English when you were there?"

"Yes, but my father does not want me to speak it on tour. He thinks that will keep the whites from taking advantage of us. It's already worked, too. Once, in a store, I heard the clerks talk about raising the price of a can of tobacco my father wanted. They didn't know I could understand. My father bargained with the clerk until he lowered the price to what it should have been."

"You want to get an education?"

"What I want most is to learn to read. Gray Antelope says there are many stories in the Bible I should read for myself, and that there is much to be learned in that book."

"Gray Antelope. . . ?" The name took him by surprise.

"She is my grandmother—adopted, of course, for she had no children of her own. She is also my best friend, though she is many, many winters older than I. Can you read, Sky?"

"Of course. I was raised in a civilized home."

"Have you read the Bible?"

"Some."

"It is a very great book, is it not?"

"I . . . suppose. . . ."

"You only suppose! If you've really read it, then you would know. The God, Jesus, gives the answer to all the questions to life in it. It shows the way to the kind of real peace no man-made treaty could ever bring."

"How do you know, if you haven't read it?"

"Gray Antelope says, and she doesn't lie."

"But maybe different people could get different interpretations from it. All I've ever gotten from it is confusion. It's not all about peace and love, you know. Some of its words are hard and condemning."

"I'll just have to read it for myself."

Sky sensed his words had left her unsettled, and he felt a twinge of guilt. He wanted to offer her something encouraging to make up for his negative statements. But he couldn't think of anything.

He was becoming cynical. The realization neither surprised him nor bothered him. He needed the kind of protection cynicism offered. He had been hurt too much to want to risk placing his heart, perhaps his soul, in jeopardy again.

Rose might have been a little deflated by what he said, but she was the kind of person to bounce back quickly. Deep down she, the naive Indian girl, might be far tougher than he was.

# 26

# NIGHTMARES

Jenny!

She ran into Sky's arms, but he couldn't hold on to her. She turned into an apparition and floated from his grasp. He desperately reached for her wraithlike form, but when he drew back his hands they were empty—except for the blood. His hands were dripping with blood.

And Billy was laughing. He fired his gun at Sky—and fired and fired. The bullets tore through Sky, making gaping holes all over his body, but Sky didn't fall. He didn't die.

"Stop it, Billy! Stop killing us!"

But Billy wouldn't stop laughing, and his open mouth seemed like it would swallow Sky.

"No!" Sky screamed.

Sky's eyes shot open. The loathsome face of Billy Yates faded. It had been a nightmare. Not real, but no less terrible. No matter how often he'd had that dream, or similar ones, the impact never dulled. He was shaking, drenched with sweat.

The vibration and the droning *clackety-clack* of the moving train was comforting. The boxcar he was in was real. He looked around to see if his cries had been audible, if they had disturbed his companions, the dozen other Indians who shared the boxcar where he slept. One man was snoring, another groaned and stirred, but all were still asleep.

Why wouldn't the dreams stop? Would he never know peace?

He thought of Billy's laughing face, and how he wanted to silence that laugh. Maybe he should have tried to kill Billy back at home. Maybe that's the only way he'd have peace. Sometimes he could almost taste the delight Billy's death would bring him. Yet he knew he would no more return home to commit murder than he would take his own life. He had thought of *both* many times. But for some reason it just wasn't in him to follow through with those thoughts. Maybe he was too much of a coward for either. Or maybe he was stronger than he thought.

Whichever it was, weakness or strength, he cursed it. Because of it, his hatred just ate slowly away at him, unrequited, un-quenched.

He really could use a drink, but around here liquor was harder to get than milk from a rattlesnake. He did all right during the day when there was a lot to keep him busy. But the nights . . . he was growing to hate and fear the nights. He had to find a way to sneak some whiskey into his quarters, just so he'd be able to have a few drinks before sleep. Buffalo Bill couldn't deny a man a little some-thing to keep him alive. It was like medicine.

That gave Sky an idea. Why he hadn't thought of it sooner, he didn't know. There had been a medicine show in the last town they played. For twenty-five cents you could buy a big bottle of elixir. One of the cowboys had commented that the stuff was al-most one hundred proof alcohol. Sky was going to have to keep a lookout for another one of those shows.

———

It must have been fate. The next town they stopped in had just such a medicine show. Sky and Red Elk had some time off and were taking a look around the town, a big town called Columbus. It wasn't as big as St. Louis, and it wouldn't compare with the cities they would get to farther East, but it had some interesting diver-sions. The huckster selling bottles of "Miracle Elixir" from the back of his wagon was the town's best draw for Sky. He bought two bottles of the stuff, and Red Elk, who was convinced by the smooth sales pitch, also bought a bottle.

"I will see if it puts hair on my chest, as the man claimed," Red Elk said as they walked away with their purchases. "Then I won't need so many blankets in winter."

"It won't put *that* much hair on your chest," said Sky.

"Why did you get two bottles, Sky? You look too healthy to need medicine."

"This is for my head."

Red Elk studied Sky as if he were looking for some hidden dis-ease. "Your head doesn't look sick either."

Sky just shook his head and said no more. Sometimes these Indians were pretty dense. Sure, the white world was new to them,

151

but was it necessary for them to show their ignorance so much?

Sky and Red Elk walked in silence. Sky was thinking about his elixir, and getting anxious to get somewhere private so he could try it. Of course he had bought it for use at night, but one little taste during the day wouldn't hurt. If Red Elk hadn't been with him, he would have ducked into one of these alleys. Maybe Red Elk wanted a taste, too. . . .

About a block ahead of them, a man stepped out of a building onto the sidewalk, then turned quickly and began walking away. Sky only saw the man's profile and then his back. But it was as if Sky's nightmares had suddenly come to life. The man was big and husky, a few inches shorter than Sky—and he had short, sandy hair.

*Billy!*

Sky gasped.

"What's wrong with you?" asked Red Elk.

"Take these," Sky said, handing his companion his bottles of elixir.

Without another word Sky shot after the man. He had no idea what he was going to do when he caught him. He had often dreamed of shooting Billy, after making him grovel on his knees for mercy. Sky wasn't armed; he didn't even have a knife. But that had never stopped Sky in previous encounters with Billy. His bare fists could do some damage. Maybe he could even kill with his fists, and the thought of that gave him some pleasure. Bashing the very life out of Billy—yes, that had a nice ring to it.

Sky raced up to the man and, without a word of warning, grabbed the man and spun him around.

"This is it, Billy!" Sky yelled.

Sky was met with the horrified face of a complete stranger.

"What is the meaning of this?" the man cried, his eyes wide with terror.

It took Sky an instant to gather back his wits. Red Elk reached him by then. Sky looked at his friend, then at the man and shook his head.

"I . . . I'm sorry," Sky said. "I mistook you for someone else."

"Well . . . I never!" The fellow backed away in a sudden panic as Red Elk reached them. "Wild Indians in Columbus! What next?" He then hurried away, almost running, taking a few backward glances to confirm that it had all been real.

When they were alone again, Red Elk said, "Sky, you'll get in a heap of trouble doing things like that. What got into you?"

152

Sky was still recovering from shock at his actions. The suddenness of that burst of violence had been disturbing. He had often thought of hurting Billy, but this was the first time he had really been certain of what he might be capable. What if he did run into Billy one day? Would he really kill him? No doubt he'd have to, because more than likely Billy would also be looking for blood.

But no matter how pleasant the idea was, or how scary, Sky was still shaking with the shock of it all.

"I need some steadying," he said to Red Elk.

Red Elk placed a hand on Sky's shoulder.

"Not that kind of steadying!" Sky said impatiently. He inclined his head toward the bottles of elixir Red Elk held. "That," Sky said.

"You need medicine?"

"Yeah."

Sky looked around. They weren't far from the arena where the Wild West Show was. The closer to the arena he was, the greater the chance of being caught, so he grabbed Red Elk's arm and pulled him down a narrow side street, around a corner and into an alley.

"Give me one of those bottles, Red Elk."

When he had the elixir he quickly unscrewed the lid and brought the bottle to his lips. Despite the fact that it tasted terrible, he took a huge swallow. What else was in there besides alcohol? It tasted the way the cresylic he used on cattle smelled. He shuddered as it burned down his throat. Then he took another drink. When he finished he handed the bottle to Red Elk.

"Have some?"

Red Elk took a more cautious swig.

"Ugh!" he said. "This isn't good."

"It's medicine," said Sky, "it ain't supposed to taste good. Come on, have some more."

"I'm not sick enough to do that."

"Well, I am!" Sky grabbed back the bottle and drank from it.

When he felt it start to go to his head, he decided it was worth the awful taste. But he had to swallow three-fourths of the bottle before it had the desired effect.

"Come on, Red Elk, old pal!" slurred Sky. "What kinda Injun are you? Loosen up. Have some fun."

"Sky, I think we were deceived. This elixir seems to have the same effect as firewater."

"You bet!"

"This is what you want?"

Sky took another swig. "Desperately."

"We are not allowed to drink. Long Hair will fire us for it."

"Buffalo Bill is drunk most of the time himself."

"But he's white."

"Well, I'm half white, so I'm entitled to get *half* drunk." Sky had another swig, as if to prove his point.

"Firewater isn't good for Indians."

"Is that what you think? That white men are better'n Indians? Stronger? Don't ya think Indians can take it?"

"I don't know, but I've seen only bad come of it for my people."

"You're just a stick—" Suddenly Sky's stomach began to churn. He was assailed not with mere waves of nausea, but with a sudden, wrenching of his entire insides. In a single, violent heave, everything inside him, or so it seemed, was ejected out onto the street. Sky staggered back. Red Elk caught him before he crumpled to the ground.

"Oh, boy!" said Sky. "This is powerful stuff!"

"Bad stuff," said Red Elk.

Sky lifted the bottle to his lips again.

"What are you doing?" Red Elk attempted to take the bottle from him.

Sky pushed him away. "The worst is over. I'm used to it now . . ."

He drank.

"Let's go home, Sky."

But Sky ignored his companion's pleas.

————

Red Elk didn't know what to do. He couldn't very well drag Sky back against his will. But even if he convinced Sky to return to their tent at the arena, the boy was already so drunk he could get into big trouble if he was caught. But Sky was not going to go back willingly. Even though it made him sick, he still drank the terrible elixir.

Did he want to hurt himself? Did he want to get into trouble, and perhaps lose his job with the show?

This half-blood boy was a confusing human being. Most of the time he was sad and serious, and he kept his distance from the other Indians. Now the firewater elixir made him seem happy. At least he was friendly and had a grin on his now-greenish face. How could he be happy and sick at the same time? But when he looked healthy, he was so sad.

Red Elk shrugged to himself. This wasn't a good time to try to figure out the half-blood's odd moods. Sky needed help, not figuring. But what to do?

Maybe Red Elk should carry Sky back to camp and say he had suddenly taken sick. But then a doctor might come and reveal what was really wrong with Sky. Still, it seemed the best solution. Red Elk tried to get Sky in his arms to lift him, but Sky struggled so much they both crashed to the ground.

"You tryin' to kill me, or somethin'?" Sky yelled.

Red Elk was too small, and the half-blood was too big. Carrying him just wouldn't work. Red Elk decided he needed help. But he needed to find someone he could trust, someone who could keep a secret. Little Left Hand was fond of the half-blood. He would help and not say anything that would get the boy in trouble.

Red Elk jumped up. "I'll be back, Sky. Stay right here."

"No place to go," said Sky cheerfully.

Red Elk hurried away. Only after he was several blocks away did he realize he had only one bottle of Elixir tucked in his belt. The other one must have fallen out when he had tried to lift Sky. Hopefully it had broken, but he would waste too much time trying to go back after it. Maybe the boy wouldn't be stupid enough to drink more of that poison.

Even though he had tried not to draw attention to himself by going in too much haste, Red Elk was sweating and out of breath when he reached the arena. The show would not be starting for a couple of hours, but the arena bustled with activity. Performers were rehearsing and helping other workers to set up scenery, visitors were roaming the grounds trying to get a preview of the show, and a few hawkers were selling souvenirs. Red Elk looked all over for Little Left Hand without success. Some of the show people, like Red Elk and Sky, had taken advantage of the time off to see the town.

Red Elk debated about taking another Indian into his confidence. But Sky had not made himself well liked among the others. Red Elk wasn't even certain why *he* had befriended the morose half-breed; he supposed he just felt sorry for him. A few times he had heard the boy cry out in his sleep as if demons were after him. He needed a friend, even if he didn't act as if he did. That was probably what Little Left Hand thought, too.

When Red Elk met Rose, he didn't think she could be of much

155

help. What did she know about helping a drunk man? And if they had to carry Sky, how could she help? But he knew she could be trusted—he'd seen the way she sometimes looked at the half-blood and he thought she was sweet on him. Anyway, she was a smart girl, so maybe she would have some ideas on what to do.

# 27

# GIVING A LITTLE

When Rose found Sky sprawled in the alley, clutching a half-empty bottle in his hand, another empty bottle lying beside him, she thought he was dead. From Red Elk's description, it sounded as though he could have been poisoned.

"Sky!" She dropped on her knees, clamped his face between her hands, and rubbed up and down.

His moan was a ghastly sound, but no less a relief. He was alive.

"Red Elk," she scolded, "how could you let this happen?"

"I tried to stop him," Red Elk said defensively.

Rose slipped the bottle from Sky's hand and smelled the contents, wrinkling her nose with disgust. How could anyone drink something that smelled so awful?

"Will he live?" asked Red Elk.

"I hope so." Rose saw the genuine concern on the man's face and immediately regretted her rebuke. "Red Elk, forget what I said. You did all you could."

But now what would *she* do? Her mind scrambled for a solution—anything to get Sky on his feet again.

"Red Elk, we passed a tavern on our way here. Go buy some coffee—as much as you can carry. Perhaps they will let you take the whole pot; buy the pot, too, if you have to. I'll pay you back."

After Red Elk had departed, Rose tried again to get Sky to move. "You must get up, Sky. They say it helps to walk it off." Her father didn't get drunk, but she'd heard from others that this approach sometimes helped. If he was poisoned . . . well, she didn't know what to do about that.

"Where's my bottle. . . ?" Sky muttered.

157

"Forget about the bottle," she said sternly. "You have to try to stand."

"Okay . . . one more drink, first . . ."

"Come on." Rose maneuvered behind Sky, put her arms around him, and tried to pull him up. "You have to help me, Sky."

He tried to move, then cried out with alarm, "My legs are gone!"

She let go of him and tried to rub the feeling back into his legs. In the meantime, Red Elk returned with a big ceramic jug and a tin cup. As Rose continued to work on Sky's legs, Red Elk began pouring coffee down Sky's throat. Sky doubled over a couple of times as if he was going to be sick again, but nothing came, and after about three cups of coffee he started to get his normal color back. With Red Elk's help, Rose was finally able to get Sky to his feet.

Sky tried to slide back to ground. "I gotta sit."

"No you don't," said Rose.

For a while they walked Sky up and down the length of the alley as if he were a giant puppet. But eventually his legs began to work on their own. They paused every so often to pour more coffee into him, and soon he was fairly lucid.

"Wha' happened?" Sky asked, looking back and forth between Rose and Red Elk as if he'd never seen them before.

"That elixir no good!" Red Elk said emphatically.

"Oh, yeah . . . I remember . . ." Sky looked at Rose. "Where'd you come from?"

She heard resentment in his tone, and it angered her. "Red Elk got me."

"Why'd he do that?"

"He thought you were dying," she said impatiently. "And maybe you were. What kind of foolish thing was that to do, drinking all that stuff?" She bent and picked up a bottle. "What does this label say?"

He squinted. " 'One tablespoon a day.' "

"So, you *can* read! Then why on earth—"

Sky grabbed his head. "Please! Do you have to shout at me? And who do you think you are, anyway, my mother? Why should you care?"

"I'm not sure," Rose said softly. "I was just scared for you." She sighed and shook her head. "Do you think you can get back to the arena?"

Sky nodded, and they started back, Red Elk and Rose holding his arms firmly. Rose wondered about Sky's question. Why *did* she

158

care? What was it about this mixed-up half-blood that kept pulling at her heart? She thought she was too sensible to be drawn just by his good looks. But she had to admit he was handsome, and his strong, muscular body was—Well, it was hard *not* to notice!

Still, she knew there was more to it. Perhaps it was that sad, lost look in those blue eyes. His words and the hard set of his mouth might try to convince people he was tough and invincible, but those eyes told a different story. They were in constant conflict with an unseen adversary. The depth she saw in Sky, the tender vulnerability he tried to cover with that hard outer shell of his, attracted her more than his physical appearance. Rose wanted more than anything to discover the mystery of Sky, the half-blood who so wanted to be white. For some reason—Gray Antelope would probably call it *faith*—she instinctively believed that a great treasure was hidden beneath the debris life had thrown his way.

———

Sky awoke in a cold sweat. The nightmare had returned, only it wasn't night at all. The muted light penetrating the cracks in the tent indicated it must be late afternoon, probably near sunset. Slowly, as he pushed aside the awful images of his recurrent nightmare, his memory began to return. He had gotten drunk on that poisonous elixir. Red Elk had helped him get back here . . . and Rose. He remembered tender hands nudging him onto his cot. The last thing he remembered was Rose coming back into his tent, assuring him that she had taken care of everything. She told him to sleep, for he had been given the day off.

He had been an idiot. What had he been trying to prove? That he wasn't afraid to die? Or that he was willing to do anything to bring on death?

The only thing he had achieved was making himself look like an utter fool. It certainly hadn't ended his nightmares. But maybe being sick had brought them on. He'd never had the dreams on whiskey.

The elixir had been a bad idea. And now Rose, who didn't have a high opinion of him in the first place, probably thought he was a complete loser.

Sky swung his feet off the cot and inched up into a sitting position. Now that he was awake, he couldn't just lie there. For one thing, he might fall asleep again, and the nightmares might return. He was feeling shaky, but he thought the best thing was to get up, maybe get some fresh air. He reached under his cot for his guitar and, using the instrument as a prop, struggled to his feet.

When he stopped swaying and felt fairly certain he wouldn't fall down, he left the tent. The grounds around the tent were quiet and deserted. Glancing up at the sky he saw that it was almost sundown. The show had already begun.

The warm late spring day had begun to cool. A slight breeze brought stable odors to Sky's nose. Sky walked in the opposite direction, avoiding not only the smelly animal areas, but the main arena also. He walked some distance to the mess tent and went around behind it, hoping to find a place to sit. He found nothing but dirt and empty crates and a couple of garbage containers. He walked a little farther, up a hill, but still found only a barren, ugly field. There wasn't even a redeeming patch of grass. He had seen prettier places on the dry plains.

How appropriate, he thought acidly as he plopped down in the dirt.

But Sky forgot about his surroundings as he focused on his music. He suddenly felt very thankful for his guitar. God had done at least one thing right, giving him music to—what was that saying?— "Soothe the savage beast."

For a few minutes he forgot his troubles, his aching head, his sore stomach, his seared heart. All that existed were the chords— the comforting, deep resonance of the minor notes, and the high, lilting, glad sounds as his fingers traveled up the scale. It was a challenge to combine the various sounds into one cohesive tune. He worked at it for some time until he came up with something he liked, then, because the challenge was in the creating, he changed a few things here and there until he had a new sound.

Before long his fingers had found an old tune, the one he had made up out on the prairie. It seemed ages ago that he had written it, but it had only been a year. He didn't often sing the song, and he certainly had never done so in public. Jenny had been the only other person ever to hear it.

*"My warrior's song, borne on the wind . . . blows from the empty pale blue skies . . . Its chanting moan that has no end—"*

He heard a noise and stopped suddenly. His head jerked up, and he saw Rose standing to one side.

"I'm sorry," she said. "I didn't mean to make you stop."

He was a bit peeved, as if she had intruded on him and Jenny during a private moment. "You should have said something."

"It was so beautiful, I didn't want to interrupt."

"Well—" He was about to give another testy response but

160

stopped himself in time. "Never mind," he said. "I mean, it's okay. It was nothing important."

"Would you mind my company for a while?"

"Sure. Come and sit down."

Her smile made him glad he had checked his attitude. She sat in the dirt next to him with her arms hugging her knees as she stared out on the fairgrounds below.

"Are you feeling better?" she asked.

"A little queasy still, but I'll live—thanks to you and Red Elk."

"I'm glad I could help." She gave him a sidelong glance, then skittishly looked back at the view. "I didn't know you had such a talent for music. Maybe that's how you can quit being an Indian in the show."

"I'm not that good. It's just something to take my mind off . . . things."

"That is a good way to do it."

"It doesn't always work. It doesn't help when I sleep." He paused. "I thought the elixir might help."

"What is it that disturbs your sleep?"

"Nightmares—" He appraised her intently—her large, wide eyes, that open innocence. He shook his head. "You've probably never lost a night's sleep in your life."

"Maybe you'd be surprised," she said with just a hint of challenge in her tone.

"Tell me, what troubles could a good Cheyenne girl like yourself have ever known?"

"If I told you my troubles, then you might have to tell me some of yours," she rejoined.

"Ouch!" he said. "There I go getting stuck by one of your thorns again." He smiled.

She laughed merrily. "I will be honest, Sky," she said, reining her amusement, "I do sleep well most of the time. My troubles must not be as big as yours. I used to have nightmares when my little sisters died, but they stopped after a while."

"How did your sisters die?"

"In a measles epidemic after we came to live on the reservation. They were young and I was like a mama to them."

"You mentioned before about people being hungry on the reservation. Is it a bad life?"

"The old folks say so. I have hardly known anything else, so I can't compare it to much. I think it's hardest on the men. They've been forced to change their whole purpose in life. But children

161

and old people suffer, too. They aren't strong enough to bear the hardships."

"So, Rose, what have you got to be so happy about all the time? Is it because you got away from all that by joining the show?"

"I am only with the show in the summer." Rose picked up a rock from the ground and turned it over thoughtfully in her hand. "I guess I think it is better to laugh at life than to cry." She paused as if hesitant to continue. "That's not all," she said finally. "My faith in God keeps me from despair and puts a smile on my face as well."

"God, huh?"

"I can tell that you don't have a very high opinion of Him."

"Do you mean God or the Great Spirit? Well, it doesn't matter. I don't know much about the Great Spirit, except what my ma has told me. But I know a lot about God—the white man's God. I was brought up on God. My stepfather is a preacher. As far as my opinion goes . . . I suppose God was okay for my parents, but, to tell the truth, I just can't see what good religion is. I don't know what is worse—to believe in God and despise Him; to believe He doesn't exist at all; or simply not to care about any of it."

"I think the first is the worst condition," answered Rose. "Hate is a very hard thing to heal."

"Well, I think the last one is where I am—I just don't care anymore. It never did much for me." He tried hard to sound casual and convincing. Down deep he feared he might hate God, but he could hardly admit that to himself, much less to Rose who had such an innocent view of faith. "Say, I missed supper," Sky said abruptly. "I wonder if I can scrounge up something in the mess tent."

"Let's go see," said Rose, jumping up.

She didn't try to return to their earlier discussion, and after that Sky made it a point to keep their conversation light and trivial.

# 28

# BIBLES AND BUFFALO HUNTS

The show was so successful throughout the summer that Buffalo Bill decided to take the Wild West to England the following spring. Sky decided to stay with the show. He might not like dressing up like an Indian and performing those silly attacks, but an opportunity to go to Europe might not come again.

The Indians returned to the reservation for the winter. Sitting Bull would not travel again with the show, but the others would regroup in the spring. After the last show in New York City, Rose invited Sky to come to the reservation for the winter, but he declined. He said he wanted to stay and see some of the sights. But in truth, the glitter of the big cities had already begun to wear off. The noise and the crowds of people, all in a hurry, were bewildering for a fellow who had spent his whole life on the open prairies. Yet remaining in the city seemed a better prospect than the reservation. Among the Cheyenne, the past was bound to greet him—not the recent past and the tragedy of Jenny's death, but rather the more distant past involving his mother and father. He already knew from Rose that his mother's old friend Gray Antelope would be there. No doubt he'd find his uncle, too, if he was still alive.

Sky continued to fight his heritage. But his association with the Indians in the show was making it harder and harder. They were good people. Rose was a delight—or could have been, if Sky had let himself enjoy her. Little Left Hand was a wise, sensitive man. In spite of Sky's reserve, which often bordered on outright rejection, Little Left Hand continued to reach out to him. Most of the other Indians had given up on Sky and left him alone.

Their reactions distressed Sky more than he wanted to admit. He was not the hardened loner he tried to project to others. But he couldn't bring himself to let down his walls and let them in.

He said goodbye to Rose and the others with disturbingly mixed emotions.

"Well, I'll see you come spring," Sky said to Rose, embarrassed by the hint of hopefulness he heard in his tone.

"I hope so."

"You're not sure you're coming back?"

"I want to. Imagine, seeing such a faraway place as England! But my father isn't sure he wants me to return to the show. To placate me, he hinted I might be able to return to school. I guess that would be the next best thing."

"You'll learn to read."

"Yes, but . . ." She let her words trail away, saying no more.

Sky wondered what she had been about to say, and for a moment there was a slight awkwardness. Then he said, "I'll miss you, Rose."

"Will you, Sky?"

"You've been like a friend to me."

"Like?"

"I guess you have been a friend. It's just that . . ." He couldn't finish. He couldn't tell her he was a dangerous friend to have. And he couldn't admit that he was afraid of friendships. Maybe it was best if she didn't come back. "Wait here a minute, Rose. I'll be right back."

Sky went to his quarters and rummaged through his saddlebags until he found Sam's Bible. He hadn't touched it since leaving home, except to shove it aside to get to other things in the bag. Sam would be disappointed. It might make up for that if Sky passed the book on to someone who might really make use of it. Besides, it only weighed down his gear. He tried not to think that if Rose had the Bible it might encourage her to stay on the reservation and continue her schooling.

When he returned to where Rose was still waiting, he handed the Bible to her.

"What is this?"

"My stepfather's Bible. Take it, okay?"

"I couldn't, Sky. It seems so special."

"It ain't doing me no good," Sky said carelessly. "Sam would want to know it was appreciated by someone."

164

"Well . . ."

"Go on. I never properly thanked you for saving my hide back in Columbus. Take it."

"All right, but if you ever want it back, you may have it. Perhaps by the next time I see you, I will be able to read something to you from it."

"Sure." He would have preferred hearing her read something from Shakespeare, but he couldn't tell her that.

She reached out to hug him. It was only an impulsive, friendly hug, and he didn't mind too much, but he backed away from her as quickly as he could without being too abrupt. Didn't it bother her at all to take such risks with people? Wasn't she afraid of being hurt?

"I'll miss you, Sky," she said. "If I don't come back to the show, come visit me."

———————

It was not a good winter for Sky. Added to his loneliness were the discomforts of poverty. In the big city he quickly used up the little money he had been able to save during the season. The one good thing in the city was that when he was dressed in his regular clothes, no one gave a second thought to selling him liquor in the taverns. A lot of his money went in this direction, but it was so cold, and whiskey helped warm him on those freezing winter days, so he rationalized the expense.

Through the coldest part of winter, he was homeless and hungry. He tried to earn money playing his guitar, but the pennies he earned did not carry him from day to day. The competition on the streets was stiff, for he wasn't the only hungry person in the city. Then, at his most desperate moment, he struck upon the idea of performing in his Indian costume. The sight of an Indian standing on a corner playing a guitar and singing "Down in the Valley" was so unique to passersby that Sky generated enough income to make it through the winter.

He was glad when spring came and he could rejoin the Wild West Show. When the troupe assembled in New York City to embark for England, he eagerly sought out Little Left Hand. The Cheyenne warrior was there; his daughter Rose was not.

"I did not want her to cross the Great Water," explained Little Left Hand. "Some of our people say much woe will befall the Indians who do this."

"Why, that's nonsense, Little Left Hand," said Sky. "It's a perfectly safe thing to do."

On the Atlantic crossing, however, many of the Indians, who sailed in steerage, gained a greater respect for Indian superstition. Some of them thought their awful sickness was indeed a punishment from the Wise One Above. Sky, who was not spared from seasickness, almost agreed. But in sickness he experienced a new camaraderie with the other Indians. At last he seemed to have something in common with them.

By the time they arrived in London, Sky's attitude was beginning to soften. He no longer pined constantly over the fact that he wasn't with the cowboys. He spent more time with the Indians. He listened to their stories and even had them teach him how to be a more realistic Indian in the show. And when a couple of the younger boys asked if he could teach them to play guitar, he gave them a few lessons.

Little Left Hand loved it. "Long Hair should see this. Maybe he will make an act called 'The Singing Indians'!"

But that would have been a novelty act which would never have fit into the "authentic" milieu of the show. And there was no sense tampering with success. Indeed, Buffalo Bill's Wild West British tour was a complete triumph. They played to over thirty thousand people a day. Even Queen Victoria attended, and she had almost never appeared in public since the death of her husband twenty-five years before. In fact, she liked the show so much she requested another command performance to which she invited royalty from all over Europe.

The buffalo hunt was a popular segment of the Wild West Show. Buffalo Bill always went on the hunt, sometimes assisted by the cowboys, sometimes by the Indians, and sometimes just by himself. Sky had never participated because there were enough other Indians whose skills in this activity were far better than his. But in their spare time Little Left Hand worked with Sky to teach him this skill. Cody's real buffalo were too valuable to spare for use in these instruction sessions, but Little Left Hand had improvised by throwing a hide over his shoulders, then acting the part of a stampeding buffalo as Sky, riding Two-Tone, attacked. Sky hadn't laughed so hard in years, but afterward he was beset with guilt. It wasn't fair to Jenny for him to be happy. And if his guilt didn't rob him of happiness, his continuing nightmares would.

It took a couple months before Sky was deemed proficient enough to appear in the arena. He could hardly wait until it came time for the Indians to hunt in the show. It was the one activity in the show Sky felt was worthy of the Indians' dignity.

When the day came for the Indians to hunt, Little Left Hand gave up his place to Sky. He also gave Sky his special lance, the one with the Pawnee scalps.

The act opened with Buffalo Bill riding out to the large water tank set in the middle of the arena. Always the showman, Cody dismounted with great exaggeration, dipped his hat into the water, had a long drink, then gave a drink to his horse. He then mounted again and rode some distance away from the tank to await the buffalo. In a few minutes about half a dozen buffalo were sent into the arena. The animals seemed to instinctively find their way to the water tank where they drank and then milled about.

Suddenly Cody fired his gun. On this signal the Indians charged into the arena and, with Cody in the lead, began chasing the aroused animals. The frightened buffalo didn't know the bullets zinging overhead were blanks. And even if they sensed, after countless repetitions, that they were in no real danger, the noise and powder burns were enough to stir them into looking the part of hunted, stampeding beasts.

Sky allowed himself to get caught up in the thrill of the breakneck chase. He let out a fierce war cry, firing his rifle furiously. Then he took up Little Left Hand's lance and waved it dangerously over his head.

Sky galloped up next to one of the charging buffalo, and as Little Left Hand had taught him, he thrust his lance at the beast. He let the tip touch the beast harmlessly; had he wanted to, Sky knew he could have taken the animal down. He'd never before felt such a rush of sheer pleasure.

At the last minute, Sky jerked the lance away before it did any damage. With another war cry on his lips, he waved the lance once more.

The crowd cheered.

And the "hunters" chased their prey out of the arena.

When Buffalo Bill rode up to Sky backstage, not even giving anyone a chance to dismount, Sky feared the worst.

"Dog my cats, boy!" exclaimed Cody. "You nearly scared my lunch out of me. Do you know how much one of them bison are worth?"

"I'm sorry, sir, I guess I got carried away," said Sky, trying to sound contrite, though he was still tingling with excitement over the experience.

"Think you can do that again?"

"Sure."

"Maybe I'll keep it in the show."

Cody rode off, and Sky dismounted, walking Two-Tone to the stable. Little Left Hand ran up to him.

"Was Long Hair unhappy? Do you still have a job?"

"No, and yes," said Sky. "He might have me do it again."

"Good. You learn well, Sky."

"Who knows," said Sky wistfully, "maybe Cody will finally appreciate my talents enough to put me with the cowboys." He only vaguely realized that he said this with far less yearning than usual.

"Blue Sky," said Little Left Hand.

Sky stopped short. He had told his Cheyenne name only to Rose. There was no reason why she might not have told her father, of course, but he had never before now used it. Something told Sky this was no coincidence.

"Yes. . . ?" Sky said cautiously.

"You are Blue Sky, then?"

"Did Rose tell you?"

"No."

Sky frowned.

"Let's take our horses to the corral, then we will talk," said Little Left Hand.

Behind one of the concession tents, they found a scraggly elm tree and a few tufts of dry grass. Sky and Little Left Hand sat together under the tree.

"I have thought for a long time that I had known you before," the older Cheyenne began. "I knew it could not be possible, and yet the puzzle would not leave me. My daughter told me you had a white mother and a Cheyenne father, and that your father had been killed. I did not question you about this because it was plain you did not wish to speak of these things. We do not speak of the dead. But maybe I have been around whites too much. I could not shake my wondering. It would come back to me at odd times when I might catch a particular look on your face that was strangely familiar.

"When you were hunting today, I thought, 'I have hunted buffalo with this man.' But that was also not possible, for the buffalo were exterminated before you were old enough to hunt. Then, Blue Sky, my old mind put together the pieces of the puzzle. And I am ashamed that it took me so long to recognize the son of the man who died to save my life."

Sky couldn't speak. He stared at Little Left Hand as if he were facing a ghost—the very specter of all he was trying to escape. Finally he heard himself say in a dry voice, a harsh whisper, "Don't speak the name of the dead, Little Left Hand."

"I know that is the Cheyenne custom," said Little Left Hand, "but do you say this out of respect, Blue Sky, or out of fear?"

Agitated, Sky jumped up and walked a few paces away. He could have kept going. The old Indian would not press him if he refused to talk. But if he had wanted so desperately to get away, he could have done so many times in the last year and a half since joining the show. If he truly despised the Indian in him, the last thing he needed was to take a job where he had to be faced with it every day.

Something was drawing him to the very thing he wanted to shun. Something inside Sky kept him here in spite of the rebellion he projected on the surface. All this time he thought he was running from his heritage. But was it possible he was *seeking* it, too?

He turned back to his Cheyenne friend. "It is I who should be ashamed," he said.

"Sit with me," said Little Left Hand.

"Can you tell me who I am, Little Left Hand?" implored Sky with a sudden rush of emotion.

The old Indian shook his head. "Only the Wise One Above can do that."

"Tell me about my father."

# 29

# A NEW PATH

Sky was alone under the elm tree. Little Left Hand had gone, leaving Sky to his thoughts.

He couldn't identify most of the emotions bombarding him. His bitterness was definitely still there. It was easy to remember Billy Yates and his betrayal, and the loss of Jenny. The resentments, the hostility, the pain—they were there, undiminished with the passing of time. They would never go away. And neither would the deep sense inside Sky that all the bigotry against him over the years had instilled in him—the sense that he was worthless, perhaps even less than human.

The truth was, Sky didn't want to let go of these things. As long as people would hate him for something he could not help, he then would return that hatred. No matter what Sam preached, forgiveness was simply not an option.

Sky's talk with Little Left Hand presented him with a new dilemma. All his life he had heard stories of the noble Broken Wing. In recent years he had distanced himself from these glowing tales, as he had shunned all he could about his Indian heritage.

But today he came face-to-face with who he was. Son of a great Cheyenne warrior. This basic truth seemed bent on haunting him.

Little Left Hand had opened the door to Sky's history. He told of how he had fallen in battle, trapped beneath his injured horse. A large force of cavalry was bearing down upon the small band of retreating Cheyenne, and Little Left Hand prepared his heart to die. But Broken Wing and Stands-in-the-River returned to rescue him. Even then it was doubtful they would have gotten away safely had Broken Wing not paused to provide cover for his comrade's getaway. Broken Wing took a fatal bullet, a bullet that Little Left Hand knew should have been his.

The old Cheyenne warrior left no doubt as he imparted the story to Sky that Broken Wing had sacrificed himself for his brothers. Sky had reason to be proud.

"I cannot tell you who you are, Blue Sky," said Little Left Hand, "but there is greatness in your blood. And the father who gave you half the blood in your body deserves much honor."

Sky had done his father an injustice in rejecting his Cheyenne heritage. But could Sky be expected to choose a life that brought him only derision? Is that why his father died, so his son could live as an object of scorn and ridicule?

Did he have a choice?

He had already seen that he couldn't fit into the white man's world outside the protective walls of his mother's ranch. There were whites out there, Sky was certain, who would accept him. Buffalo Bill treated the Indians with respect. Yet even Cody had his limits—he paid his Indian performers, who worked just as hard, half of what he paid his whites; and the traveling accommodations were not nearly as luxurious. Everything in the white man's culture seemed to emphasize the belief that Indians were not as good as whites. Sky had tried hard to pretend these barriers didn't exist for him because of his white blood. Tried and failed. He didn't belong in the white world.

But did he belong with the Indians? Wouldn't his white blood be a stumbling block? Besides, he knew only the white world. He knew little of the Cheyenne way his mother had loved so much.

He looked down at himself, still in costume from the buffalo hunt, and felt as if he were looking at another person. Could he ever really be part of his father's world?

Sky rose, trying to shake away the dilemma he could not answer. He returned to his lodgings, a big dormitory where the Indians stayed. There was no one around; the show was still going on. Little Left Hand said he'd make excuses for Sky's absence. Sky sat on his bed, took up his guitar, and lost himself in his music.

*My warrior's song borne on the wind . . .*

The sad words flowed softly from his lips. It was odd that, of all the songs he'd made up over the years, this one came back to him in moments of distress and confusion. And this was his only song that gave even the slightest recognition of his Indian blood. Maybe he was destined to take on the Cheyenne mantle. But he wasn't sure he wanted to follow a path just because destiny dictated it. He didn't want to become a Cheyenne because he had no other choice.

Yet what else was there for him?

_____

The Wild West Show finished its British tour and returned to the States in the spring of 1888. Sky's questions continued to plague him. He talked to Little Left Hand and the other Indians, but no one would, or could, provide the answers he wanted. As the ship arrived in New York, Sky sensed that he was coming to a crossroads in his life.

Sky hounded Little Left Hand so much the man finally gave Sky his opinion.

"It is not good for me to tell you what to do with your life," said the older Cheyenne. "But you will give me no peace until I speak my heart to you."

"I'm sorry, Little Left Hand. If I could figure this out for myself, I wouldn't bother you."

"It is not a bother. I am honored you value my opinion. But I must know that you will hear what I have to say, then make your own decision."

"Yes, I will."

"Blue Sky, you once asked me to tell you who you are. I still can't do that, but I think that before you do anything else in this life, you must discover that answer. Find out who you are."

"But how?"

"You must gather together all the information you need. You already know your white half. . . ." Little Left Hand paused, giving Sky a pointed look that was obviously asking him to figure out the rest for himself.

"So, I should find out about my Cheyenne half? But haven't I been doing that already, here with you and the others in the show?"

"That is like saying you know how the white man's sweet candy tastes by looking at a picture. What you see here is not real. Even I am not real when I am here. Long Hair wants to show people the real West, but he presents only a very small part, the part that tells of the glory. There is more to being an Indian, to being a Cheyenne, than the buffalo hunt or the battles. If it were not so, then we would truly be a dead people, because all those things are gone."

"What more is there?"

"You must discover that for yourself—each of us must. And those who find the answer will know true contentment. Those

172

who don't . . ." He shook his head sadly. "I have seen Cheyenne men who cannot—or will not—find that answer. And I can only say, Blue Sky, that you *must* find the answer. Don't quit until you do."

"Can I return to the reservation with you?"

"That would be a good place to start your search."

"Is my uncle still alive, Little Left Hand? Will I find Stands-in-the-River there?"

"Yes." Little Left Hand frowned slightly. "You will find much there. I will not lie to you, Blue Sky. You will find answers there, but you will also find more questions."

Sky joined the Indians as Buffalo Bill took them back to the reservation. First, they went north to the Pine Ridge Reservation in South Dakota to return the Sioux, who made up the largest contingent of Indians. Here Buffalo Bill took his leave of the group and went on to his ranch in Wyoming. One of Cody's managers would take the small remnant of Cheyenne south to the reservation in Indian Territory.

On the way they met three Arapaho who were returning to Indian Territory from a momentous journey of hundreds of miles. These men had been to Nevada and were bringing back with them a tale of fantastic proportions. Sky listened with the others in varying degrees of disbelief and awe.

"There is a man in that faraway place," one of the Arapaho reported, "who brings a wonderful message of hope to Indians. He is indeed the Messiah who will save the Indian people."

"What is his message?" Little Left Hand asked with some skepticism in his voice.

"Our people will rise again." The Arapaho paused, glancing at the whites who were standing apart from the Indians, then he lowered his voice. "We will return to our former glory. We will be proud warriors again."

"How will this be?"

"If we dance the Ghost Dance the Messiah taught us, it will come to pass."

"You can't really believe that," said Sky. "Things like that just don't happen."

"All we know is what we have seen and heard. Go and see for yourself. Speak face-to-face with this messiah. He is a Paiute named Wovoka. We'll tell you how to find him."

Sky looked at Little Left Hand. "What do you think?"

"The Arapaho are our close brothers," Little Left Hand replied.

"But they are more spiritual than the Cheyenne. Maybe they know more of these things than I. Yet, how can a Paiute hundreds of miles away know what a Cheyenne should do?"

"This is a message for all Indians, Little Left Hand," one of the Arapaho messengers said excitedly. "And I have seen the truth of it myself. While I was dancing I had a vision. I saw my dead father and he said he would return with others, and the buffalo would follow them. He told me the Cheyenne and the Arapaho would be a great nation again." He paused, looking around at his listeners, finally settling his gaze on Little Left Hand. "You know me well, Little Left Hand. Am I a liar?"

"I never thought so, Seven Bulls."

"A new day is coming for our people!"

The man's words kept Sky awake that night long after the others were snoring. Sam would probably have had a fit if he'd heard the Arapaho. After all, calling a Paiute visionary a "messiah" more than hinted at false prophecy—Sam would call it outright blasphemy.

Still, Jesus was supposed to return to earth. The Second Coming. Wasn't it possible that His return would be for the Indians? Of all peoples they seemed to be the most deserving, and the most needy. They had been treated with such gross injustice that it seemed only fair that Christ would return to deliver them.

But why did this have to have something to do with Christianity to be valid? What good had Christianity ever done for Sky, anyway? All the things he had learned from his parents hadn't helped him much lately. They certainly hadn't saved poor Jenny.

Aside from all that, Sky had made a commitment to learn what it meant to be Cheyenne. If he was searching out his Indian roots, could he ignore what Seven Bulls had to say? He spoke a message of hope to the Indian peoples as a whole. Might it not also convey hope to Sky personally? What if the dead did come back?

*His father . . .*

Could it be possible? Might he actually be able to *speak* to Broken Wing? *Learn* from him? *Hear* all the words Broken Wing had longed to tell his son?

If Sky was trying to find answers, trying to discover who he was as a man and as a Cheyenne, didn't he owe it to himself to investigate these things Seven Bulls and the other Arapaho spoke of? Even the wise and level-headed Little Left Hand could not denounce the tales out-of-hand.

Sky knew if he did not speak personally to this Paiute, Wovoka, he would always wonder.

In the morning he told Little Left Hand of a change in his plans.

"I'm going to Nevada to see this 'messiah' fellow," Sky said.

"You will not come to the reservation?" The old man was clearly dismayed.

"I'll get there eventually."

"Rose will be looking for you now. She will be disappointed."

"Rose? But why?"

"Blue Sky, I would give my blessing for you to marry my daughter."

"Marry? I've never indicated such intentions, Little Left Hand."

"It seemed to me that it was meant to be."

"I hope Rose isn't under some false assumptions. In my mind we were only friends. I doubt I will ever marry."

"Not marry? But you are so young and can yet produce many sons to carry on your father's blood."

"My heart belongs to another. It wouldn't be right to marry a woman I didn't love."

"I didn't know you had a woman. She must miss you sorely."

"She's dead."

"Ah . . ." Little Left Hand nodded thoughtfully. "That is the hardest kind of love. But don't you think one day your heart will want to reach out to another? I have buried three wives; and I loved the last as much as the first, who was my Rose's mother."

"No . . . I couldn't."

"Would she be angry if you found happiness with another?"

"It's just different, that's all. I'd rather not talk about it. But you'd better encourage Rose to marry another Cheyenne man—I'm sure there are many who would have her."

"Rose has her own mind."

Sky smiled at his own memories of Rose. The pretty dancing eyes, the ready grin, her endearing and annoying wit. She'd find a husband easily. But it wouldn't be Sky. He wasn't about to betray Jenny like that—he owed her too much. If it hadn't been for him, she'd be alive now.

"Little Left Hand, I'm going to Nevada. I don't know when I'll return. You'll make Rose understand, won't you? I have to do this, but even if I didn't, even if I went with you now, she could never have a future with me."

"Go, Blue Sky. Rose will understand. Maybe she will be able to explain it all to me." Little Left Hand smiled, but his eyes were sad. He embraced Sky. "I had hoped you would be a son to me."

"That honors me more than I deserve. But I wouldn't make you a very good son. Goodbye, Little Left Hand. I will see you again."

"My lodge will always be open to you, Blue Sky."

Sky didn't look back as he rode away. He felt a great sense of loss, but he knew he was worthless to anyone as he was now. Perhaps one day . . .

In the meantime, the path ahead might hold some answers for him. He might even find reason to hope.

# 30

# THE PROPHET

The first signs of winter were touching the prairies of Nevada as Sky, riding his old companion Two-Tone, made his way across the broken, dry land. Over his Levi's and cotton shirt, Sky wore a heavy buckskin coat ornamented with long, beaded fringe. After months on the trail, his skin was as brown as it had ever been. He was glad he had decided to travel on horseback. The train for both he and Two-Tone would have been too expensive. Besides, he hadn't been in a big hurry, and it had been good to see some of the country.

During the intervening months some of his zeal and anticipation had worn off. In Colorado he had almost stopped for good after a rancher offered him a job. That part of the country was so breathtakingly beautiful, with mountains that dwarfed even the tallest Texas hill. He worked on the ranch for a month, and although some of the men accepted him, there were always those who made him feel worthless for his dark skin. His nightmares continued to haunt him, too. He'd had to cut way back on his drinking; the rancher happened to be a very religious teetotaler who was known to fire cowboys if they got drunk even on their days off. When his nightmares were at their worst, Sky couldn't handle them cold sober. So, he quit his job and moved on.

For a time he drifted from town to town with a growing sense of purposelessness. He wondered why he kept butting his head against the walls of the white world. He would never amount to anything in that world. Why was he so reluctant to give the Cheyenne world a try? Maybe he was afraid he'd fail there, too. But could it possibly be any worse than it was now?

Little Left Hand was a smart Indian, and what he'd said made a lot of sense. Sky would never know unless he tried. As far as this business in Nevada went—well, he was almost there anyway. Why not see it through? At least it would give him some purpose in life. He hated drifting around. He was drinking too much. He needed a diversion, if nothing else.

Now that he was finally nearing the end of his journey, he began to grow excited and impatient. He had reached the Walker River Reservation in Nevada last night. In the morning he spoke to the agent at the reservation, but the man hadn't heard of anyone named Wovoka. Sky asked around, but the Indians he met seemed reluctant to give information to a stranger. Finally a white ranch hand said he knew the Paiute, who also went by the name of Jack Wilson. The hand had worked with him on a couple of local ranches. The fellow didn't know how to find him, but he directed Sky to a man named Charlie Sheep, Wovoka's uncle.

Charlie Sheep was an old Paiute, half blind and difficult to understand even though he spoke some English. It wasn't easy for Sky to convince the man he could be trusted. He finally won him over with an autographed photograph of Sitting Bull.

"If you are friends with this great warrior, then you must be okay!" declared Charlie Sheep.

Sky let it go at that. He might not be a close friend of the Sioux Chief, but they had spoken on several occasions while on tour together, and he thought Sitting Bull would probably remember him should they ever meet again. Anyway, it was enough to impress Charlie and to get Sky on his way to his anticipated destination.

Accompanied by Charlie, Sky set out early the next morning on the final leg of his journey. Wovoka lived a good forty miles northwest of the reservation. At Charlie's insistence they took the train to the settlement in Mason Valley. At the Mason Valley station they got Sky's horse from the freight car, hired a horse for Charlie at the settlement, and set out on the twenty-mile trek across the sage-covered prairie.

In the best of seasons, it was barren country, flat and treeless, covered with brown sagebrush. Now, in early winter, it was that much worse, with cold, dry winds blowing across the expanse. In the distance, mountains encircled the valley, providing some dimension, but no relief to the long, monotonous ride.

Night had fallen before they found the camp, guided there more by the rising embers of a campfire than by Charlie's poor memory and failing eyesight. Four wickiups stood in a circle—rounded huts of thatched tule rushes over poles, with a hole in the roof for smoke to escape. A barking dog warned the camp of the approach of strangers.

"It's your Uncle Charlie," the old man called.

A man came out of one of the wickiups and looked over the new arrivals. "You've brought a companion, Charlie."

"He's all right. He's a Cheyenne from the East. And a friend of Sitting Bull."

Sky stepped forward. "My name is Blue Sky. I've come to meet Wovoka."

After Charlie interpreted, the man said, "Wait here," and ducked back into another wickiup, returning in a few minutes.

"It's late, but Wovoka understands you've traveled a long way, so he will see you for a few minutes before he sleeps. Come with me."

They entered a wickiup where a bright fire was burning, giving enough light for Sky to make out his surroundings. It was a poor hovel, containing only a few essential rude household supplies. A child was asleep in a corner, lying on a thin blanket spread over the dirt floor. There were no furnishings of any kind.

A man and a woman sat in front of the fire. They were introduced as Wovoka and his wife. The guests were invited to sit, and in the light of the fire Sky had his first good look at the Paiute prophet.

He was a plain man, almost homely, and looked more like a simple farmer than a great prophet. His hair was blunt-cut at his chin line and gave his broad face an open, boyish look. Thickly built and with broad shoulders, he was about six feet tall. The Paiute was in his early thirties. His attire consisted of white man's clothes—a white cotton shirt, dark vest, and denim trousers. He spoke good English because of his years of association with whites. They conversed in English because Wovoka did not speak Cheyenne and Sky knew no Paiute.

"So, you are Blue Sky of the Cheyenne," said Wovoka. "Some of your people were here one month ago." Wovoka continued. "You have come too quickly to have been sent by them."

"I'm not from the reservation," said Sky. "Like you, I was raised by whites—by my white mother, on a ranch in Texas. I've never lived among the Cheyenne."

"Why have you come here, then?"

"I don't belong among the whites. I came here hoping to find where I belong. I want to learn of the Cheyenne ways, and it might be that if this religion you teach is real, then I could learn from my father who died many years ago."

"You want your father to come back?"

"I . . . I guess I've always wanted that. Is it possible?"

"I can't say what things are possible, but with God are not all things possible?"

"You believe in God, then?"

"Yes. My message came from God, the Great Spirit, himself."

"Will you tell me your message? Will you teach me your dance?"

Sky's open entreaty must have warmed Wovoka. He smiled, and although it was a slight smile, it was filled with kindness and benevolence. Sky saw where the man's charisma came from—not from power or forcefulness of character, but from a sincere heart. He liked Wovoka instantly and knew he had chosen the right path.

---

Sky slept that night on the ground in the wickiup with Wovoka's family. He breakfasted with them in the morning on dried fish and bread made from ground piñon nuts.

"My people are called 'fish-eaters,' " said Wovoka. "Later today we will see if there is fresh fish in the lake for supper."

Wovoka played for a while with his son, a chubby little toddler. The Paiute prophet was a gentle, attentive father who seemed to enjoy interacting with his child. But when the meal was cleared away, the child and his mother left the hut. A few minutes later, half a dozen Paiute men, including Charlie Sheep, entered the wickiup and sat around the fire pit, which held a bright blaze against the chilly November day.

"I will tell you now about my vision," said Wovoka. "My brothers here will tell what they have experienced."

Everyone looked toward the prophet with an air of respect and expectation. Some of the men in the group were much older than Wovoka, but they seemed to look up to him no less.

"One day about a year ago," Wovoka began, "the sun died and I fell asleep and was taken up into a different place than where I was. In this new world I saw people I knew who had died and there were also many I did not know, but whom I thought had been dead a very long time because they were engaged in activities that our people only did in the old times. It was a rich land, full of game, and everyone was happy and well-fed.

"Here the Great Spirit first spoke to me and gave me a message to take back to my people, and all the Indian peoples. He told me we must not give up hope, but that we must continue to be good and to love all peoples—and especially that we must live in peace with the whites. The Great Spirit told me that if we lived according to the ways he taught, we would one day be reunited with our friends and brothers who have traveled to the other world. And he gave me a dance that, if faithfully performed, would hasten these events."

"Will you teach me the dance?" asked Sky.

"Do you wish to live according to the message of the Great Spirit? Do you wish to live in peace with the whites?"

That was a hard question. Sky thought of all the years he had given to living in peace with whites, how he had tried to belong in that world, and how miserably he had failed. When he left the Wild West Show he had decided to seek his Indian roots, essentially giving up the desire to be white. That desire had proved itself more futile than ever during his months of drifting. Was he ready to give up completely on whites? If so, his family must be placed in a category by themselves, along with that half of him that was white.

Wovoka's question, however, didn't ask him to give up on whites. It asked him to live in *peace* with them. That was a far harder choice to make. The part of him that had been wounded by bigotry *wanted* to hang on to his bitter resentments—the white race as a whole deserved this. Yet what of Wovoka's message, so obviously aimed at peace?

Sky didn't want to lie to the Paiute prophet. He answered with the only truth he could. "I want to be at peace with myself, Wovoka, and I am half white."

The man nodded, seeming to understand. "We will dance the Ghost Dance in three days. Join us, and perhaps God will show you the path that leads to the peace you seek."

# 31

# THE DANCE

The Great Spirit had instructed Wovoka to dance for five consecutive days, each time bringing closer the time of fulfillment of the promise of the prophecy. Sky had heard from his mother how the Cheyenne would fast before important ceremonies in order to draw them closer to the Wise One Above, so he prepared himself by fasting for the three days before the gathering of Wovoka's people for the dance.

By the morning before the night of the first dance, Sky felt nothing but tired and hungry. He didn't feel close to the Great Spirit or God or anyone. Wovoka suggested he walk alone in the countryside.

"Go toward the great mountains," said the prophet. "The Paiute believe that at the top where the snow never melts is the road to the Milky Way—you call it the Hanging Road. The closer you are to that road, perhaps the closer you will be to God."

Sky was getting bored anyway, and he thought, if nothing else, he could take his rifle along and hunt.

For all the barrenness of the valley, there was a certain beauty in the setting, with its distant fringe of pines topped by the snow-capped peaks of the Sierras. It gave a sense of security, but also a feeling that there must be something greater "out there," something—or someone—who could form such majestic mountains.

Could it be God?

Yet, if there was really a God who was loving and caring as his parents always told him, why had He deserted Sky? Why had He allowed Jenny to die? And, if the God of Christianity really did exist and had allowed such things to happen, was that the kind of God Sky wanted to follow? He remembered the choices he had mentioned to Rose, and he felt certain that he would indeed hate such a God if He truly lived. But maybe the whites had perverted the Truth to suit their own purposes. Maybe they had perverted God himself.

What if Wovoka had met the true God? Sky couldn't give up the idea of God altogether. Part of him yearned for something greater than himself, something that could instill peace in him, quell his inner battles. He was too aware of his own weaknesses to believe he could find such things by himself. Thus, he was driven to find that something—driven because he couldn't stand the emptiness he otherwise felt.

He walked ten miles that day, reaching the pine-laced foothills. The peaks looming over him made him feel small indeed, small and empty and needy.

He desperately wanted *something*.

When he returned to camp at sunset, he was exhausted from the hike and from his days of fasting. Yet he felt good. He felt as if all resistance had been squeezed from him along with his physical strength. He was ready to be filled, ready to find what he was seeking.

About fifty Paiutes had begun to gather at the open field just outside the camp where the dance would be held, along with a handful of Indians from other tribes, who had arrived while Sky had been on his walk. He was anxious to meet them, but Wovoka drew him aside the moment he arrived back in camp.

There were certain preparations Sky had to make before the Dance, and Wovoka and a Paiute named Josephus assisted him. With a cake of red paint, made of clay from nearby Mount Grant, which was considered sacred to the Paiutes, they painted Sky's face and bare upper body. Josephus gave Sky two feathers from the sacred magpie to tie on his head. Sky added his uncle's beaded collar, hoping it might lend a good spirit to the ceremony.

The dance area was flat and had been cleared of all rocks and sagebrush. A fire had been built, not in the center of the circle, but off to the side near a thatched lean-to. The dancers made a rather odd group. Almost all were dressed in white man's clothes except for the sacred red paint and a few native adornments such as feathers. Sky took his place in the circle feeling a bit nervous, but expectant.

When all were assembled, Wovoka made his appearance, walking into the midst of the circle. He wore a white and black striped coat over his usual white man's clothes. He raised his hands in greeting, and something in this gesture, along with the deep solemnity on his face, fostered the impression of holiness about the man.

"I'm glad you have come, my children," he intoned. "Listen to my message. Listen to the words of the Great Spirit. He has sent me to teach you his ways and to show you the way to peace. My father, the Great Spirit, told me the earth was getting old, worn out, and the people were too bad. My father sent me to renew the world and make it a better place. I am to prepare you for a better world, so those we love who have died can join us. He will make the world big enough so it can hold everyone. He will take away our sickness, and we will live forever. I will talk more to you later, but now we must prepare ourselves for these things by performing the dance the Great Spirit told me to teach you."

The Prophet moved through the circle to the outside, went to the lean-to, and sat on a blanket. The glow of the fire cast an ethereal light upon his face as he closed his eyes and began to chant a vibrant, beseeching tune. The dancers moved in cadence with the solitary voice of the Paiute prophet. Some held their hands high toward the star-studded sky; some folded their hands against their hearts as if in prayer; others grasped hands with friends and loved ones.

Around they went until late in the night, their plodding feet stirring clouds of dust. One or two of the older participants collapsed from exhaustion and, at one point, Sky almost felt as if he might join them. He felt a bit foolish dancing like a savage, just as he had in the Wild West Show—only this was supposed to be real. Wouldn't the folks in Danville County get a good laugh if they saw him now?

When the dance ended that night, he was ready to quit for good. He was a civilized man—how could he ever fall for Wovoka's ramblings?

But that night his fitful sleep was filled with disturbing dreams, dominated by the specter of Billy Yates. Billy tormented him ghoulishly, as always in his nightmares, and Billy's gloating laughter continued to ring in Sky's ears long after he had awakened the next morning.

Thoughts of Billy Yates made Sky think again about his attitude the previous night. Was he extolling as "civilized behavior" the kind of treatment he had received from the Yateses and other whites? Were their actions not more savage than the dance of peace and love that Wovoka taught? By comparison, the dance was beautiful and heroic. And Sky knew that if he quit dancing, he'd

184

be forced to accept the white man's world in all its hypocrisy and bigotry as his only choice. If he considered himself too good for the Indian ways, too civilized, he was doomed to a world where he was an outcast.

He *had* to give the dance its full chance.

So he continued dancing that night and the next.

———

On the third night, Sky was deflated because he had been dancing for about four hours with no results. Then, near the end, something began to happen. He felt a subtle, unidentifiable change within him. He had been focusing on Wovoka's chant, though more with his musical ear than any spiritual sense. He began to feel lightheaded, as if his brain were detached from his feet. Was it just the effects of going without food—and whiskey—for several days? That first day of his fast he'd had a rough night with shakes and sweats, but since then there had been no further effects. His head had been very clear.

What he was feeling now was nothing like that. It felt good, uplifting. And instead of merely hearing the chant he felt as if he were *part* of it, as he sometimes did when he was involved with his own music.

Then suddenly Wovoka ended his rich chant and told the people it was time to go to sleep. For the first time since the dancing had begun, Sky's mind had started to lift from his all-encompassing awareness of his physical discomforts and his self-conscious awkwardness. He had begun to glimpse a possibility of something more, a tiny flicker of light in the dark, moonless night.

He left the circle dejected, fearing he had missed his opportunity. But for the first night since he could remember, he slept soundly, and his dreams, though he had forgotten specifics by morning, were pure.

When he joined the circle on the fourth night, he experienced a momentary panic as a rush of mundane thoughts assailed him. The lifting of the spirit he had felt the previous night was gone. He could only think about his sore feet, and he was keenly aware of his growling stomach and how the paint on his face was starting to itch.

Was he doomed, then, to never be lifted from the miseries of life? Must he live forever with that terrible emptiness inside, a longing worse than hunger?

Then, as before, a snatch of Wovoka's chant seemed to grab

him. Its sudden intensity almost made Sky catch his breath. He couldn't understand the Paiute words, but he didn't need to. All the meaning he needed was in the tone, the depth, the timbre. The song spoke of peace, of hope, and of all the beautiful things Sky had learned as a child about the Cheyenne way. The chant seemed to transcend tribal differences.

Suddenly, Sky thought Wovoka was singing in Cheyenne. He began to understand every word. The cadence of the chant, even the tune, seemed vaguely familiar to Sky, almost like the one he had made up out on the prairie. And the words were as personal as if they had risen from his own heart. He became so caught up with the chant that he wasn't certain at all who the words were coming from. Wovoka seemed farther and farther away, as did the dancers surrounding him.

> I sing of winding
>    haunted trails
> Where snow-capped mountains
>    touch the stars
> Through days of fasting,
>    nights of prayer
> To lift my spirit,
>    fill my heart;
> Come, Father, heal
>    my broken song
> Wrapped in your arms
>    where I belong;
> Dance in my soul
>    to sweet release,
> Your arrows point
>    the way, the way to peace.

Not only did the song draw Sky away from his companions, it also began to draw Sky away from himself, away from the mundane. His very soul was lifted up as if it would touch the Milky Way itself. An unseen presence washed over him.

*Come, my son.*

Father. . . ?

*I have waited so long for you, my son.*

Nehuo? Broken Wing. . . ?

*Yes. At last we are together.*

Sky reached out his hands, and for the first time in a very long time that emptiness in his heart was filled. That yearning of a little boy for his father was stilled. The distance dulled by death was bridged, and in his spirit, Sky felt himself walk over that bridge and into the waiting arms of his nehuo.

Sky did not remember going to bed that night. He must have, for when morning came he was in the wickiup lying on a blanket. Could the previous night have been a dream?

But when he closed his eyes against the bright light of morning penetrating the wickiup walls, he remembered it all. Every word of the chant returned clearly to him, and when he told it to Wovoka, the Prophet showed no recognition of it.

But more than all else, Sky's father had been *real*. Sky looked at his hand and could still feel the tingle of his father's loving touch. Even the smallest detail of what they had done together was engraved in Sky's mind.

*They were surrounded by a Cheyenne camp, many lodges scattered along a lazy little creek. All the men were gathered beneath a bright autumn sun. Not a female could be seen in the entire camp. In the midst of the men stood a tall pole on which was attached a quiver of arrows. Sky had no doubt these were Sacred Arrows. Medicine Arrows. Some of the arrows were pointed up toward the sky and some were pointed down—just one of the details that stood out to Sky and seemed somehow significant.*

*All the gathered men began to file past the arrows. The air was charged with reverence, solemnity, and fierce pride. In these arrows lay the very survival of the Cheyenne people. As Sky and his father paused before the arrows to gaze upon them, they saw the very soul of their people.*

*And Broken Wing said to his son, "You are* Tsistsistas, *my Blue Sky. Be proud. Your way of life is worth fighting for. But I hope, for your sake, victory will come by peace and not war."*

*Gazing up into his father's eyes, Sky felt like an innocent baby, able to wrap himself up in that voice, that touch, to feel secure, protected, strong again.*

The fifth day of Wovoka's Ghost Dance was that morning. They danced in daylight. No more doubts clouded Sky's perceptions. The dance filled him up, gave him peace, hope. He knew he had found the way he was seeking, as certain as he had been that he'd met his nehuo and been touched by him.

# PART 3

# SPRING 1889

# 32

# JOURNEY HOME

Sky spent the next six months in Mason Valley. Not only did he want to learn all he could from Wovoka, but he wanted to be sure his experiences were real. He began to feel more certain than ever that one day soon he would return to the Cheyenne reservation, but if he did, he wanted it to be as a man who was worthy to be called the son of a great Cheyenne warrior.

The Ghost Dance instilled confidence in him, especially as his experiences were confirmed frequently by repetition. The most significant confirmation, however, came after two months. He awoke from a sound sleep and realized he had not had a single nightmare since he had begun to dance. And he hadn't given even a passing thought to drinking, either.

Even Wovoka noticed a change in Sky. He commented one day, "When you first came I saw many storms in you, my son. But I can see they are over. You said you wished to be at peace with yourself. You have found that, haven't you?"

"For the first time in my life, Wovoka."

"What will you do now?"

"I've asked myself that many times. I think I know the answer but I'm just not sure if it is time."

"You will return to your Cheyenne people?"

"Yes."

"I was hoping you would. You will be the best emissary I could have to spread the message of the Ghost Dance. Will you do this?"

"I couldn't do otherwise. The Cheyenne people need the hope the dance offers. I want them to know the peace I have discovered."

Not long after that, a Cheyenne and an Arapaho came to the Paiute camp seeking to learn about the Ghost Dance, and to see

191

if all they had been hearing was true. They were Porcupine and Black Coyote. After participating in the dance and hearing of many amazing experiences, including those of Sky, the two newcomers were won over to the religion. They were eager to return home to tell their people.

Sky decided to go with them, but first he asked them if they could teach him the Cheyenne Way. He convinced them to travel back by horseback rather than train. He wanted to use the time on the trail to learn all he could.

The months in Nevada had changed Sky. He had shed his white man's clothes. Now he wore buckskin breeches and moccasins which he had made himself from the hides of two deer he had killed. The only hint of white attire he kept was a cotton shirt he wore under his buckskin vest, and he removed it when the chilly days passed into the warm month of May. His hair, now grown to the middle of his back, was braided and wrapped in animal fur, and he always had the magpie feathers tucked into the leather band he tied around his head. He also wore his uncle's beaded collar. Anyone seeing him would assume he was a "wild" Indian fresh from the reservation. He did nothing to dispel that impression. He spoke English only when absolutely necessary, shying away from whites whenever possible. He used his Cheyenne name exclusively.

But perhaps the most defining sign of his transition from Sky Killion, cowboy, to Blue Sky, Cheyenne brave, was the day he sold his guitar.

The drum and the chant were the music of the Ghost Dance. Although one of his first supernatural experiences during a dance had been hearing a song in the Cheyenne tongue, a song which had sounded oddly like the tune he had once made up in Texas, Sky did not often turn to his music in the way he once had. His voice raised in a haunting Ghost Dance chant was even more magnificent than Wovoka's, but that was the extent of his music these days.

Traveling with his Cheyenne friends, Sky soon found a worthy use for the neglected guitar. In Utah, he discovered a beautiful bow with arrows in a fine deerskin quiver. The clerk said it was Sioux, and after an exacting examination, Black Coyote verified this. Sky wanted the bow, but he didn't have near enough to buy it—especially since he made his desire too clear, and the clerk raised the price.

Upon seeing the guitar, well-worn but still valuable, the clerk agreed to make an even trade. But as Sky handed over the guitar, a sudden attack of reluctance struck him. He thought of when his ma and Sam had bought it for him in Fort Worth, and he remembered the great comfort it had been to him over the years. He might as well trade Two-Tone for a can of beans. The instrument was certainly as close a companion, if not friend, as his horse. Yet the bow was no can of beans. Wasn't it more like a symbol of the new direction of his life? Wasn't the guitar an emblem of the past?

As he had shed his white man's clothes, shouldn't he shed all connection to that world? For Sky, the only way he could fully embrace his Cheyenne people was to completely let go of the past. He had never been one to do things halfheartedly. If he did something, he usually jumped in with both feet. When he had learned to play the guitar, he hadn't been satisfied with the simple songs Sam and he had figured out; he had driven himself to master the instrument. When Little Left Hand had taught Sky the buffalo hunt in the Wild West Show, Sky had worked until he could perform it better than any of the others.

What he was now embarking upon was far more important than any of those other things. The Ghost Dance was life and hope to him. It had changed him. It deserved no less than a devoted response from him, as did his embracing of the Cheyenne people.

The guitar was a white man's instrument. Let the white man have it. Blue Sky would make for himself a drum from the hide of the first deer he killed with his new bow. That was the Cheyenne Way.

When the three Indians left the store and Sky strung the bow over his bare shoulder, Porcupine joked that Blue Sky looked more Cheyenne than any man Porcupine had ever known.

Nevertheless, Sky intensely felt his inadequacies. As much as he mirrored a Cheyenne warrior on the outside, he knew it would be clearly apparent to his Cheyenne people that he had not had the benefit of growing up with the ways of his ancestors. What was naturally ingrained in Porcupine and Black Coyote, Sky had to learn in a few weeks. It was impossible, he knew, but he was determined to make the attempt.

Whether the encounter with his father at the arrow renewal ceremony was a dream or real, Sky would never know for certain. But the memory was no less fresh, no less acute. It had imparted to him a pride in who he was.

Thus, Sky was an eager student. Throughout the months of their journey, his Indian companions taught him how to hunt with the new bow. And Black Coyote, who was an Arapaho medicine man, fashioned for Sky several good arrows which he said would be blessed with strong medicine. The two men, both older than Sky, had lived as free Indians before the time of the reservation, and thus were experienced warriors. They showed him how to track his prey over the most impossible terrain. In the evenings, when they made camp, Sky learned how to smoke the pipe and the various ceremonies related to it. He listened attentively to all the stories the two men had the patience to tell—both ancient legends and more recent history.

Porcupine was from a different band than Sky's relatives, so he could not relate much detail about Broken Wing or Stands-in-the-River, but Sky was willing to wait for this until he saw his uncle in person.

And that day grew ever closer.

In October, they crossed into Indian Territory. Almost unconsciously, Sky began to ride at a faster pace. He couldn't sleep when they camped that first night on the Cheyenne and Arapaho Reservation. After learning where Stands-in-the-River's camp was, it took them another day of riding before they crested a hill and viewed their first lodges. Sky reined Two-Tone to a halt.

Two dozen tepees dotted a flat plain at the bottom of the rise where Sky and his companions had stopped. The peaceful Cheyenne camp, where dogs barked and children romped, looked like a scene from Sky's dreams, or from his mother's many stories. Whether he was stepping back into history, or into the future, he did not know. He was here, ready to claim whatever awaited him.

Glancing quickly at Porcupine and Black Coyote, Sky let out a whoop and charged down the hill.

# 33

# FRIENDSHIPS RENEWED

It had been many years since the Cheyenne residents of this sleepy camp had seen such a spectacle. Many stopped their activities and stared with curiosity, reminding Sky of the spectators at the Wild West Show.

Then some of the onlookers recognized Porcupine, and the surprise turned into cheerful welcomes and excited greetings. Much to Sky's disappointment, his anticipated reunion with his uncle was delayed once more. Stands-in-the-River was away, gone to Darlington with his family to trade with the whites. But Sky was greeted warmly by Little Left Hand.

"Look at you, Sky! This is no costume you wear, is it?" The old Cheyenne grinned his approval.

"No, my friend. You were right when you directed me to follow the path of my father's people. I've finally found where I belong. You may now call me by my Cheyenne name—I wear it proudly."

"Blue Sky, come into my lodge. Tell me what you found in the far West."

Sky, Porcupine, and Black Coyote entered Little Left Hand's tepee. Sky noted immediately how much it differed from Wovoka's poor and sparsely furnished wickiup. The hides forming the walls were old and worn, of course, for it was impossible to replace buffalo hides. But there were beds and seats and many pots and utensils and two or three chests for storage—and many of the furnishings were from the white man's shops.

Little Left Hand's hospitality, however, was very Cheyenne. They passed the pipe.

"The whites want to wipe out the Indian ways," said Little Left Hand, taking a long draw off the pipe, "but they will not do so quickly."

He passed the pipe to Sky, who tried to match his friend's deep draw. He was glad he'd had some experience with smoking on the trail, for Little Left Hand's tobacco was very strong and would have choked a novice.

When the ceremony of smoking was done, Sky and his traveling companions launched into an account of their time in Nevada. Little Left Hand plied them with questions, then finally rubbed his chin and fell silent for a long moment, as if trying to absorb the remarkable things he'd heard. At length, he asked, "Blue Sky, do you believe this Ghost Dance is for our people?"

"Yes," Sky responded without hesitation. "I have no doubt because it changed me. Not only in the ways you see, but also on the *inside*. It changed my heart. It gave me peace and hope. And I believe it can do the same for all my people."

Sky could not speak the words "my people" without a thrill of pride and a sense of earnest wonder. There was no longer any question in him that his people were brown, not white.

"You will teach this dance, this religion, to the Cheyenne?" asked Little Left Hand.

"If they desire to learn—and I believe they will."

"The government Indian agents will not like this."

"Should I allow that to stop me? Would you stop, Little Left Hand, if you knew of a way that would give your people hope?"

Little Left Hand shook his head in reply, but his eyes held more resignation than assent.

The conversation halted abruptly when the tepee flap suddenly parted.

Rose entered and grinned, her eyes dancing.

"I knew you would return," she said. "I knew any path you chose would eventually lead back here. But I'm very unhappy with you for not at least stopping to say hello when you were on your way west."

"I thought it was the best thing to do," Sky said, returning her smile. Despite his attempts to forget Rose, he had to admit his pleasure in seeing her again.

"Rose," interjected Little Left Hand, "where are your manners? You have interrupted an important powwow."

"I was afraid if I didn't hurry he might escape again."

"I think I'm here for a while," said Sky.

196

"Good! Then you'll have plenty of time to talk to my father and the other men. Now, you can walk and talk with me."

Little Left Hand rolled his eyes. "How have I raised such a daughter?"

"You raised me to be a chief, Nehuo," Rose said. "Since I am only a girl and can't be a chief, I must be obnoxious instead."

Sky restrained a chuckle. Her vivacious zest was infectious, but he still felt the nagging need to protect himself around her.

"Instead of taking my guest away," said Little Left Hand, "you should be fixing us dinner."

"It's too early for dinner."

"Blue Sky is hungry after a long journey, is that not so, Blue Sky?"

"Well, I—"

"Nehuo," Rose quickly interceded, "I promise to fix a fine meal. But can't I *please* visit with Sky for a few minutes?"

"Ah, some manners at last!" exclaimed Little Left Hand, his affection evident. "If our guest wishes . . ."

Sky vacillated between wanting to run away and wanting nothing more than to be with Rose. A quick glance into her wide, expressive eyes helped him decide.

"We will talk again tonight, Little Left Hand," he said. "Perhaps others in the camp would wish to pass the pipe and hear what I have to say."

"I'm certain my lodge will be full."

———

Sky and Rose strolled down to a creek that ran through the northern end of the Cheyenne camp. The water meandered sluggishly over the rocky bottom. A few cottonwoods along the bank gave some shelter from the cool, stiff autumn breeze blowing over the surface of the water.

"Was I too pushy, dragging you away from my father's lodge like that?" said Rose.

"I guess I don't mind, not really."

"Sky—"

"Please, Rose, I prefer to be called Blue Sky now."

"Oh . . . that's very interesting." She paused thoughtfully.

"It's been a long time," said Sky, struggling to fill the silence. "What have you been up to? Did you go to school?"

"I went for a semester, then I was needed back at home. I still have so much to learn. Many of the words in your stepfather's

Bible are still too big for me. Would it be all right if I kept it longer?"

"It's yours."

"Thank you." Rose lowered her eyes. "Blue Sky, I was so glad when I heard you had returned. And someone else was glad, too. I ran down immediately and told her, and she, too, was impatient to see you. I told her I would bring you right away, if you would come."

"Who is that?"

"Surely you must know that Gray Antelope Woman is in this camp. This *is* the same Cheyenne band with whom your mother lived many years ago."

"You know about my mother?"

"I asked Gray Antelope. I hope you don't mind."

"What did she tell you?"

"Not a lot. She said that was your story to tell if you wanted to."

"Maybe someday I will tell you what I know," said Sky. "But tell me one thing. Are all the people here the same people my mother lived with?"

"Many are. Of course there have been changes over the years—deaths, marriages, births. Moving to the reservation has disrupted some bands, and many deaths have forced other bands to join together."

"Then you have been here, too, all your life?"

"I date my birth from the winter before the Washita massacre."

"I was about two at the time."

"It makes a person think, doesn't it? You and I were together then; we lived through that terrible experience together. My mother was killed at Washita."

"I'm sorry, Rose."

"I have no memory of that time."

"I'm sure you must miss her sometimes."

"Sometimes, yes. But I have many 'mothers' here in camp who have cared for me and loved me. Gray Antelope is one."

"You're lucky, then."

"I don't know if I'd call it luck."

Sky frowned slightly. He had often heard Sam say that very thing, but he didn't know how to respond. He decided to change the subject.

"Rose, someday soon our loved ones will return. You will be able to see your mother, talk to her. I will be able to hunt with my father. There will be buffalo again. The Cheyenne people will be strong as we once were when we were the most feared tribe on the plains. The white men will go back across the sea to where they came from. This land will belong to us as it was meant to."

"You truly believe this, Blue Sky?"

"When I danced the Ghost Dance, my eyes were opened, and my heart was filled with hope."

"You don't think it could be a little wishful thinking?"

"That's what I thought when I heard others speak of these things—until I experienced for myself extraordinary wonders. I saw my father and he showed me things that I could not have known about before—Cheyenne traditions that not even my mother had told me about. The Prophet, Wovoka, has truly been sent by the Wise One Above. By his power he brought rain one day, and fog another."

"It does sound incredible. But do you think it's wise to continue to seek past glory? Wouldn't it be better for our people to accept the ways of the whites, to take advantage of the progress their civilization has to offer?"

"You can accept them all you want, Rose, but they will never accept you." Sky didn't bother to hide his bitterness. "You can speak their language, wear their clothes, go to their schools—but you will never be equal to them. Never. Not in their eyes."

Rose glanced at Sky, and he saw an odd look in her eyes. Was it pity? But why should she pity him? He had finally found what he had always been seeking—a place to belong and real hope.

She was silent for a moment before speaking again. "When we were with the Wild West Show, I felt bad because you were striving so to be white and it was making you miserable. Now you are striving to be Cheyenne—"

"I *am* Cheyenne."

"That's true. And I do not wish to dampen the great hope in your heart."

"Don't worry about doing that, Rose. I am so convinced this is the way that nothing could shake me."

"I do miss you speaking Cheyenne with that funny Texas drawl." She smiled, trying to lighten their mood.

"I still have it some."

"You are very, very Cheyenne, Blue Sky, there is no denying it. Do you still play your guitar and sing? It would be too bad if you gave that up."

"I traded my guitar for a bow. I don't need it to sing Cheyenne songs."

"Oh, Blue Sky . . ."

"It's a very fine bow," he said defensively. "Made by a Sioux war chief during a Sun Dance. It has strong medicine."

"I thought your music had strong medicine."

"Come sometime and hear my new music. I'm sure there will be a Ghost Dance performed here soon."

They walked for a while in silence, then Rose said, "We are almost at Gray Antelope's lodge. Would you like to see her?"

Sky couldn't understand his hesitation. Of course he wanted to see her. Gray Antelope was like a grandmother to him, though he hardly knew her. She had come to the ranch once when he was a boy, but his memories of that visit were vague. His mother had gone once to the reservation, but up until five years ago when she had been acquitted of the murder charges against her, she had been forced to be rather reclusive. Any travel outside the ranch had been risky. Yet the close bonds between Deborah and Gray Antelope had never weakened, and Deborah spoke of her Cheyenne "mother" as if it had been only days, not years, since they had seen each other.

Sky pushed his uneasiness aside. "We should have time before your father expects us back."

———

They followed the creek for about a quarter of a mile, leaving behind the last of the tepees of the Cheyenne camp. They continued to follow the creek into an area wooded with a few oaks and more cottonwoods. Rose said in spring the creek usually encouraged some green growth and it was pleasant and cool, but now the dry imprint of summer was still evident.

The cabin set in the middle of this growth seemed to fit in naturally with the setting. Its logs were roughhewn and its frame was not perfectly square, but rather leaned with the slight slope on which it sat. A yapping dog greeted them as they approached the walkway leading up to the cabin door.

Sky was surprised Gray Antelope lived in a cabin and not a tepee.

"She says she has moved around enough in her long life and likes the feel of solid walls," Rose explained. "She took this patch of land as her allotment."

"Isn't she too far from the others? She must be pretty old."

"She does well on her own."

The cabin door was standing open, and a voice called from inside the house.

"Rose, is that you? And you are not alone."

"Hello, Nahkoa. You're right, I'm not alone. I have a surprise for you." Rose turned and grinned excitedly at Sky, then hurried up to the cabin.

"Come in, child," said the woman.

Sky followed Rose into the cabin. The light inside was dim, but Sky's sharp eyes quickly adjusted. The cabin was only one room, no bigger than ten feet square. There were none of the furnishings that one might expect in a prairie cabin—no table or chairs or beds. A mat covered with several layers of government-issue blankets lay in one corner and obviously served as a bed. Two crudely built wooden chests—probably for cooking utensils—were shoved against one wall under the only window in the cabin. A couple of pottery bowls sat on the dirt floor near the chests. Sky saw no lamps or candle holders but thought that perhaps the fire in the stone hearth might provide all the light that would be needed at night. The fire had burned low, even though the afternoon was getting chilly.

"Nahkoa," said Rose, "I have brought an old friend to see you."

"I am the old one," said Gray Antelope. "I think my friend is still very young." She looked in his direction and reached out her hand, smiling. She remained seated on a thick hide laid out near the hearth.

Sky stepped toward her and took her hand.

"Gray Antelope Woman," he said reverently, as if he were encountering an awesome object of legend and myth. "I am honored to meet you again. I am—"

"I know who you are. Your voice is familiar to me—I feel as if it were only yesterday when I last heard that voice joyfully announce the birth of his son. You have your father's voice. Come, Blue Sky, sit next to me."

Sky quickly complied. Rose stoked up the fire and then sat on the other side. Gray Antelope took Sky's hands and held them in a surprisingly firm grasp. She turned her face toward him once more. She was still smiling, and Sky saw more clearly how aged she was. Her skin was brown and heavily creased like old leather. Her braided hair was liberally streaked with gray, and her head jutted forward from a slightly hunched back. Her large-boned frame was quite thin, and Sky wondered if she ate properly.

"You have grown into a man, haven't you?" she asked. "Are you as tall as your father was?"

"My mother says so."

"And do you favor him in other ways?"

"I don't know. What do you think?"

"Rose, did you not tell Blue Sky about my malady?"

"No, I'm sorry, Nahkoa," said Rose. "But, to tell the truth, I didn't even think about it."

"You are used to it, but Blue Sky is not." Gray Antelope faced Sky again. "You see, Blue Sky, about seven winters ago a disease took away my eyesight. I am blind now."

"I'm sorry, Gray Antelope," said Sky. "I didn't know. My mother never said anything."

"Why would I trouble her with my burdens? She has burdens enough of her own."

"Does my mother write to you about all her burdens?"

"No, I don't think she does. She probably wishes to spare me, as I do her."

Sky said no more. He wondered if his mother had written to her about his troubles, but he didn't have the courage to ask. If Gray Antelope asked, he wouldn't lie, but otherwise, he'd rather leave everything unsaid.

"Well," Gray Antelope sighed, "it isn't important who you resemble. I suppose it is just the need of an old woman to recapture the happy days of her past. But you are a fine man, I can see that even without sight, and that is all that matters."

"I hope that I am a fine Cheyenne man, or one day will be."

"God will grant your every hope, my little Blue Sky. He will see your deepest desires and, with pleasure, give them to you, His child."

"That is what I was just trying to tell Rose. The Wise One Above knows that my greatest wish and that of my people is to rise again to our former glory, to be a mighty nation again."

"That sounds like the warrior in you, Blue Sky."

"I want peace, Nahkoa."

"That is a good thing to desire. The Book of Jesus says God will keep him in perfect peace whose mind is stayed on Him."

"You quote Scripture like a white person."

"Is that a bad thing?"

Sky felt suddenly uncomfortable. Not only had he been rude to an old, blind woman, but as he had spoken his defensive words, the faces of his mother and Sam had flashed before his eyes. Thus

202

he replied in a more contrite tone.

"No, not at all." Then he added, avoiding her eyes as if she could see, "We must be wearing you out, Nahkoa. Perhaps we should be leaving."

Gray Antelope's lips twitched with a slight smile. "You will come again to see me, Blue Sky? I will make a meal and serve you as I used to do when you were little."

"Yes, Nahkoa. Thank you."

Sky exited the cabin quickly. The fresh air outside was a welcome relief. Old people's homes were always so stuffy and dark. But he supposed he would go see her again. He owed her that much.

# 34

# ROSE'S CONFUSION

The next day Rose visited Gray Antelope again—alone, this time.

"I have come to fix you something to eat," she said, setting the basket she carried on one of the chests.

"I suppose I must submit to your kindness, daughter, but it's hard to admit I am such a useless old woman."

"You've spent your life serving others, Nahkoa. Now you can give the rest of us the chance to be blessed as you have been blessed." Rose began to build up the embers in the hearth. "And you're hardly useless. That's another reason why I've come. I want to talk with you."

"I will accept the trade. What is on your mind?"

"Blue Sky."

"Ah, yes. I'm not surprised."

Rose opened one of the chests and shook her head. "Nahkoa, have you been giving your rations away again?"

"I am an old woman; I don't need as much as the young ones."

"Well, you're lucky this time. I've brought some food with me."

Gray Antelope chuckled. "See, it's a good thing that I have given away my food. Now you can have the good feeling of giving. We both end up feeling good."

"Then, thank you very much." Rose grinned affectionately at the dear old woman.

Rose took a jar of milk from her basket, which she poured into a pan and set near the fire. Then she added chocolate powder and sugar. While the milk warmed, she sliced bread and cheese and laid them on a dish. When the milk was steaming, she poured two cups and brought them to where the older woman sat.

"It's hot," Rose said, sitting on the hide beside her.

"Is it chocolate I smell?"

"Yes. I don't know anyone who likes chocolate as much as you, Nahkoa."

"We should have saved it for a special occasion."

"There's a little more left. I will put it in the chest near the window and you can have it later."

Gray Antelope sipped the warm drink. She closed her eyes in delight as she savored it. That alone made Rose's sacrifice of the precious commodity worth it.

"Now, Rose, let's talk about Blue Sky." Gray Antelope picked up a slice of bread.

"He is so confusing to me, Nahkoa."

"I'm not surprised. Blue Sky isn't a simple young man. Perhaps he could have been had his father not died and had the Indian way of life not changed so much. He could have fit easily into the ways of a Cheyenne warrior. Instead, he was thrown into a world that refused to accept him for the fine man he is at heart. And that world set off his inner battles, forcing him to choose between the two peoples he loves."

"But now he has chosen the Cheyenne people," said Rose. "What must that do to his inner battles? I dreamed last night that he was screaming in agony, even though he had no wounds that I could see. I can't tend his inner wounds, Nahkoa. I have tried. When we were in the Wild West Show, I tried to tell him about my Jesus, but he wouldn't listen. I gave up because I didn't want my words to force him away as a friend. Maybe I should have tried harder. I think I let God down because Blue Sky went off and found answers from that Paiute in Nevada. I'm not sure if they are the best answers."

"You and I know the only true answer for Blue Sky."

"Then I let him down, and God, too, for not making him listen."

"Was that your responsibility?"

"Isn't it?"

"Ah, Rose . . . our Blue Sky is God's responsibility. Let God deal with him."

"But shouldn't I show Blue Sky the way? Isn't that what I'm supposed to do as a Christian?"

"I think the only thing you are *supposed* to do is trust God. That is plenty for most of us to do."

"I don't understand."

Gray Antelope sipped her chocolate. Rose was frustrated and wanted to press the older woman for answers to her confusion. But, though it wasn't easy, she remained silent.

After a few moments Gray Antelope said, "Blue Sky knows all about Jesus. His stepfather, Sam Killion, first showed me the way to Jesus. His mother is a faithful believer also. Blue Sky grew up in the presence of our Lord."

"Why, then, did he wander away? Why does he seem so bitter about God?"

"I think it has to do with his inner battles. He sees God as the white man's God. In the Ghost Dance perhaps he believes that he has found the Cheyenne God."

"Aren't they the same?"

"There is only one God. Whether the god Blue Sky has found is the same as the true Living God, I don't know. As the book of Jesus says, we will know by its fruits."

"Should I let him continue as he is—just in case Blue Sky has found another path to God?"

"The Words of Jesus say there is only one Way to God—Jesus himself."

"Then what should I do?" Rose's voice shuddered with her frustration.

"Dear daughter, we should pray for Blue Sky, and let God do what He will do."

"I guess that's better than nothing."

"That is better than *anything*!"

---

When Rose left Gray Antelope's cabin she did not go directly home. She wanted to pray, as Gray Antelope had suggested. But she wondered what exactly to pray *for*. She began by praying for Sky, that he would find his way back to Jesus. But as she walked along the creek bank, mentally listing Sky's needs, she began to feel her own inadequacies.

Gray Antelope was probably right in saying Sky was no one's responsibility but God's. Yet Rose was not the type of person to sit back either humbly or quietly. It was hard for her to admit to helplessness, and she suspected that when she was as old as Gray Antelope, she would not be as gracious about it. Gray Antelope was always talking about trusting God and placing burdens in His hands. But sometimes that was impossible for Rose to do. She had been raised to be strong. Though her father had remarried less than a year after her mother had died, this second wife had died giving birth to her second child when Rose was only five. Little Left Hand had waited many years after that to find his third wife, and so it had fallen to Rose at a young age to assume the womanly duties of her father's lodge. For the next nine years she was a mama to her two half sisters until both died in the measles outbreak.

By fourteen, Winter Rose had known her share of grief, and it had started to harden her heart. Gray Antelope helped her overcome this by introducing her to Jesus Christ. For that reason, it seemed odd then that Gray Antelope would tell Rose not to help Sky. What if Gray Antelope hadn't told *her* about Jesus?

It was confusing.

Rose wanted Sky to find the peace she had discovered five years ago during that awful time of grief. In fact, she was determined to *make* it happen.

"Dear Jesus, you've got to give me a chance to help Blue Sky. Why else have you brought us together? Give me the right things to say to him. Don't let Blue Sky get away without—"

Rose stopped and almost smiled. Her father always told her she was bossy, and she did sound a bit like she was trying to boss God.

"Forgive me, Jesus. I just don't know any other way."

She walked on a little farther, remembering yesterday when she had heard that Sky had returned. The sun had suddenly risen upon her world. It had been almost two years since she had last seen him, two very unsettling years. She had not been able to forget him.

When other young men had tried to court her, she was disinterested. None of them sparked within her the intense feelings Sky had.

She had probably begun to love Sky when she first saw him gaze so longingly at the cowboys in the show. Her heart had gone out to him in that moment, and she had never been able to retrieve it. For two years she never stopped hoping he would return. Her father had once asked her how long she would wait. But she could do nothing *except* wait until the love ceased to burn in her heart.

Now Sky *had* returned. But he still showed no romantic inclinations toward her. All his devotion was directed at that new religion of his.

Could it be that her desire for him to meet her God stemmed from a kind of jealousy? If they shared the same faith, perhaps he would be more likely to fall in love with her. She didn't want to be so selfish. If God changed Sky's heart it would, she was sure, bring him closer to her. But if God didn't wish for her and Sky to be together, she would still want Sky to know the peace and love of her Jesus.

Perhaps she should have said more to Gray Antelope. But it was hard for Rose to admit the deepest extent of her feelings. Gray Antelope had probably already guessed, anyway.

"Maybe I will talk to her later," Rose told herself.

She returned to her lodge feeling some peace. She would probably still interfere a little in God's work, but she also knew God would not let her make too big a mess of things. He had made her as she was—He understood her, knew her heart and that her intentions were pure. He wouldn't let either her or Sky down.

# 35

# STANDS-IN-THE-RIVER

Sky spent the next two days hunting with his bow. He bagged several jackrabbits and a deer and returned with the sense that he was growing more and more proficient in the ways of his fathers.

He had strayed quite a distance from camp, but Little Left Hand had given him detailed instructions on the boundaries of the reservation, warning him to be careful not to hunt outside those boundaries. Sky thought he was adhering strictly to the instructions.

He had a deer in his sights and was about to draw back on the bowstring when a settler's rattling, creaking wagon crested a rise, frightening the deer away. Sky had been down on one knee and rose, turning toward the wagon. At that moment the passengers of the wagon spotted him.

"Indians!" the woman screamed.

The driver reined the wagon to a halt. "Gimme my rifle, Nell," he yelled.

As the woman fumbled for the rifle, Sky dashed to where Two-Tone was grazing peacefully a few yards away. He jumped on the horse's back, bow still in hand, and raced away. He didn't figure it would be wise to tarry and try to reason with a rifle-toting settler.

But rather than being disturbed by the experience, Sky was oddly thrilled. He counted it a high compliment to be taken for a dangerous savage.

Back at the camp he gave the meat from his hunt to Rose, who had already agreed to skin and dress whatever Sky might bring back. He was about to relate to her his experience with the settlers when a man's voice called his name.

Sky turned, and though it had been years since he'd last seen his uncle, he recognized Stands-in-the-River immediately. His uncle placed his hands on Sky's shoulders in as close to an embrace as the stoic man would ever give.

Stands-in-the-River was taller than Sky, a thick-chested, imposing man. His broad face was lined by the years, especially at the corners of his eyes from constantly squinting at the sun. His thin lips twitched into a reserved smile, but the joy of this meeting was clearly evident in his eyes.

"Blue Sky! I knew one day you'd return to your home."

"Uncle, you don't know how glad I am to finally see you."

"Then you must not call me uncle. Years ago I told you you are my son, and I am your Nehuo."

"Thank you . . . Nehuo. Nothing gives me greater honor or pleasure."

"Come to my lodge. We will smoke and talk."

Sky turned to Rose. "Do you mind if I take a couple of those rabbits?"

She handed him two of the biggest ones, which Sky offered to his uncle.

"Many thanks, Blue Sky," said Stands-in-the-River. "We can always use meat."

Before entering his uncle's lodge, Sky deposited the rabbits with Stands-in-the-River's wife, Stone Teeth Woman. They were barely seated when the tepee flap opened and a young man entered.

"Ah, Tall Bull," said Stands-in-the-River, "I'm glad you've come. Meet your new brother." Stands-in-the-River turned to Sky. "This is my blood son. He is about a year younger than you, Blue Sky, but I have always known what you might be like through him. And look at both of you! No one would doubt by your resemblance that you are brothers."

Except for being an inch or two shorter than Sky, they did indeed share many similar features. Tall Bull's eyes, however, were deep brown, not blue.

As his father readied the pipe, Tall Bull sat and spoke to Sky. "My older brother was killed at Washita. I was too young to know him, but I always thought I missed something in not having a big brother. I welcome you."

"Thank you, Tall Bull. I never had a brother either."

The two sized each other up for a brief moment. And, as

quickly as they became brothers, they also became friends.

Stands-in-the-River had the pipe ready, and they smoked for several minutes. Then he called to his wife, who quickly entered the tepee.

"Wife, where is that bottle I brought back from the white man's village?"

Rummaging through a bundle, she produced a bottle of whiskey. She poured out three cups, handing them around. Then, leaving the bottle with her husband, she departed again.

"I made good trades in the town." Stands-in-the-River grinned proudly. "This is white man's whiskey, not the cheap stuff they usually sell to Indians."

Sky hadn't had alcohol since going to Nevada. He had been so consumed with his new life that he'd hardly even thought about it. But he couldn't refuse his uncle's hospitality. He accepted the cup and drank with his new father and brother.

For the next two hours they talked and drank and smoked again. Stands-in-the-River wanted to know all about Sky's life, so Sky told him about his mother and the ranch and the Wild West Show, omitting only the more personal aspects. But Sky did relate every detail of his experiences in Nevada.

"And you believe all this?" asked Stands-in-the-River.

"When I danced, Nehuo, I felt such fulfillment. I was a whole man again. And I know my father came to me in a vision. When I told Porcupine about my vision, he said I had described a Cheyenne arrow renewal ceremony. I had never seen such a ceremony, and my mother had never described one to me."

"She could not have. Women were not part of the ceremony."

"And this Paiute prophet says if we dance this dance, we will return to our former power?" Tall Bull asked.

"It will happen very soon, some say next year."

"The buffalo will return?"

"That is what he said."

Tall Bull nodded his head dreamily. "I have always wished to hunt buffalo as my father once did."

"What will happen to the white man?" asked Stands-in-the-River.

"I think they will be pushed back across the sea, back to where they came from. The land will be ours again, as it was meant to be."

"There will be war?"

"Wovoka talks only of peace, not war."

211

"I do not think the whites will be moved without a fight. But if all the dead warriors like your father returned, we would have an army that could do such a thing." Stands-in-the-River refilled the cups, then took a long drink before continuing. "You know, Blue Sky, I was at the Little Big Horn. I fought beside Sitting Bull and Crazy Horse. What a glorious day that was for our people. I remember the last white man I killed. Of course at the time I didn't realize that would be my last coup in battle. We felt so strong and powerful when the last of Yellow Hair's soldiers were dead. We thought we could defeat them all in time. But for that one small victory, the whites crushed us so that we could never fight again."

"Do you still want to kill whites?" Sky asked.

"Sometimes. But it wouldn't help. There are too many of them. They would just lock me up again—and that I could not stand. But with an army such as you describe, perhaps we will have another chance."

Sky was uncomfortable with this talk of war and killing whites. But for the first time, as he listened to his uncle, he believed he could fight the whites if he had to. It was becoming much easier to detach himself and his connection to his family. "Whites" were becoming just a faceless enemy.

"I don't know about all that," said Sky, "but I do know that great things are in store for our people if we are faithful to Wovoka's teachings."

"It would have to be better than what we have now." Stands-in-the-River shook his head bitterly. "So many of our people have died since we've come to the reservation. The old ones were ready for the Hanging Road, but the babies, the children . . . my own daughter died of the smallpox. What can we do without our children? We are a dying people." He drank more whiskey. "There is disease and starvation. We are at their mercy—except that they have no mercy. I sent my son to the Indian school. What did you learn there, Tall Bull?"

"They taught me reading and ciphering. They taught me how to be a farmer. I tried all the things they taught me and could not raise enough food for my family, much less to sell and make a living."

"If they wanted us to be farmers," rasped Stands-in-the-River, "they should have given us land that *could* be farmed. Still the whites are not satisfied. Now they want to take back even this rotten land. Last spring thousands of white settlers rushed into the so-called 'unassigned lands' to stake claims. I heard in Darlington that another rush will begin again here in the West. The whites are as hungry for land as we are for bread."

In the days since Sky had arrived in Indian Territory, he had begun to see some of the conditions his uncle described. But he had tried not to look too closely, for he didn't want to believe that the people he had finally returned to, the Cheyennes to whom he had at last given his allegiance, were dying.

This made him more determined than ever to believe in the powers of the Ghost Dance. It was their only hope.

"Nehuo," Sky said, "Tall Bull . . . will you dance, then?"

Both answered without hesitation.

"Yes."

# 36

# BLUE SKY, CHEYENNE WARRIOR

The Ghost Dance religion spread quickly among the Plains Indians. Sky was not the only native person seeking hope, looking for a way out of the dismal prospect life had become. Hundreds attended the dances.

Coming as it did on the heels of the great Oklahoma land rush, it wasn't surprising that many of the new white settlers grew alarmed. The Indian wars, not too far in the past, were still vividly remembered. These white settlers well knew, or should have known, that they had gained their homesteads at the expense of the Indians. Rumors began to spread among the settlers about the Ghost Dance. War dances and scalping parties were reported seen. Fear spread. White citizens cried out for troop reinforcements.

In spite of all this, Sky was experiencing some of the best days of his life. He quickly fit into the life of the Cheyenne camp. He found acceptance and camaraderie among the men. And as the son of a great warrior, he was given much respect.

As winter closed in upon the Cheyenne camp, Sky did not grow as restless as the other young men. He spent all the time he could with the older men like Stands-in-the-River and Little Left Hand, plying them with questions, learning everything he could about the Cheyenne and his father. Not only did he listen to them talk, but he also had them teach him skills. He learned to make his own bow and arrows. He learned from the medicine man, Red Feather, about potions for healing and magic, and he made a medicine bundle in which he carried a sample of the sacred red paint from Wovoka, a piñon nut and a broken eagle's feather he found while hunting. Red Feather examined the treasures and gave his approval.

Sky moved into Stands-in-the-River's lodge. Little Left Hand would have offered his lodge to Sky when he had first arrived, but both men had mutually agreed that Rose's presence would have made that arrangement awkward at best. Sky did, however, spend a lot of time with Rose. At first he didn't notice that she was almost always the one to seek him out. He was flattered by the attention and interest she showed in him. But he eventually realized she felt more than friendship for him.

He didn't know what to do about it or what to say, but since she had never actually *said* anything to him, he decided to let it slide. Sooner or later she would realize he was interested in nothing beyond friendship with her, and she would turn to someone else. In the meantime, life was too exciting and new for him to dwell too long on Rose's infatuation with him.

As the spring of 1890 came, Blue Sky felt as vibrant and alive as the newly budded plants. He could begin to use more of the skills he had learned. Blue Sky and Tall Bull became inseparable.

Stands-in-the-River had given up on farming, but he did have a small herd of cattle which Tall Bull managed. Sky lifted his ban on things *white* a bit, imparting to Tall Bull all the ranching experience he had gained over the years. But one day, the two did something Sky had never done on the Wind Rider Ranch.

Bored, Sky and Tall Bull lay under a cottonwood by the creek, trying to stay cool under the warm sun. The cattle were grazing some distance away, just within sight.

"Never thought I'd be baby-sitting cows again," said Sky.

"You said you enjoyed ranch work," said Tall Bull. "To me it's dull, almost as bad as farming."

"Nothing's as bad as farming."

"Some of our people say it would be best for us to give up the old ways and be ranchers and farmers like the whites."

"I'm not giving up something I just found," Sky said firmly. "But if I had to choose one, it would be ranching. This country would be good for that. I expect you could make a living at it at least."

"You are entitled to an allotment, Blue Sky, if you want to ranch. All you would have to do is prove you are Cheyenne. My

215

father and Little Left Hand would vouch for you."

"It's not going to come to that, Tall Bull. We're not going to have to settle for some allotment that the government could take back at any time they liked."

"And we won't need to tend cattle because the buffalo will return."

"Yes." Sky's voice trailed away as a new, and somewhat disturbing, thought came to him. "Tall Bull, when all this happens, do you think we will naturally know what to do? I mean, I've learned some of the Cheyenne ways, but I know I am not the Cheyenne my father was. Little Left Hand tried to teach me how to hunt buffalo in the Wild West Show, but after hearing stories from men who really hunted them, what I did in the show is pretty laughable. Do you know how to hunt buffalo?"

"How could I? The only buffalo I've ever seen have been in shows like you spoke of. My father has taught me some techniques, but I've never really practiced them."

Sky inclined his head toward the placidly grazing herd. "What would you do if they were buffalo?"

"I wouldn't be sitting here in the sun, that's for certain."

"Someday soon, Tall Bull, we will wake up and the hills will be black with buffalo just as in the old times."

"And we won't even know what to do."

Sky jumped up. "I won't accept that!" He ran toward Two-Tone and leaped on his back. He lifted his bow, then he strung his quiver over his shoulder.

"What are you doing, Blue Sky?"

"I'm going to hunt buffalo."

"You're crazy. How are you going to do that?"

"Come with me. I'll show you."

He rode away. In a moment, Tall Bull was mounted and riding next to him, bow in hand.

Sky let out his most blood-curdling yell, then spurred his mount into a gallop—straight toward the herd of cattle.

Tall Bull did the same and before long, the charging riders with their shouts and whoops stirred up the cows. It didn't take long for the animals to stampede. Sky and Tall Bull kept pace with the racing herd. Sky set an arrow to his bow, but he had never tried shooting at this speed and on the jarring back of a horse. It was one thing to shoot a moving target, but this was an entirely different challenge. He gained a whole new respect for his Cheyenne ancestors for whom this was their means of survival.

216

Ahead of him, Tall Bull was taking aim. His shot went wide by several feet. Sky tried a shot, but it, too, went wide. Another was short, and yet another was overshot. The supply of arrows would not last forever and the cattle would soon tire.

Sky set another arrow to his string. He eyed a big bull. Remembering some of the things Little Left Hand had told him, he kept pace with the bull, letting it get just a little ahead. He waited until he and the bull were in nearly perfect rhythm. Raising his bow, he took careful aim. But he did not shoot right away. He waited, gauging his ups and downs with those of the bull's.

"Patience," Little Left Hand had once said, "is your best weapon."

Sky waited. He let his breathing relax. There would come a moment when he would sense a certain oneness with the bull, a moment when they were not hunter and hunted, but rather a team, working together to bring prosperity to his people. The buffalo and the Indian were not enemies. They were brothers.

Sky sent the arrow flying.

It penetrated the bull's thick hide. The animal stumbled and fell.

Taking heart from Sky's victory, Tall Bull took aim again. He, too, remembered about being one with the hunted animal. But just as he was ready to release the arrow, his horse stepped into a hole. Tall Bull and his mount went down in the path of the still stampeding cows.

Sky wheeled Two-Tone around, grabbed his rifle and fired three shots over the heads of the oncoming herd. The effect was immediate. The cows were tired anyway. The shots made enough of them turn so that the others were also forced to slow or turn. Tall Bull quickly rolled out of harm's way. His horse also made it to safety.

"That was close," Tall Bull said as Sky hurried up to him.

Sky dismounted. "Are you all right?"

"Only my Cheyenne pride is injured."

"You almost had him. It wasn't your fault your horse stumbled."

They walked over to the fallen bull. The rest of the herd was milling some distance away.

Sky shook his head. "It was a foolish thing to do. It could have gotten us killed."

"Yes, Blue Sky, but every day our fathers and their fathers took the same risks to survive."

"But it loses something when all you've got to show for it is a dumb bull." Sky gave the carcass a kick.

Stands-in-the-River was drunk when Sky and Tall Bull returned to camp with the butchered carcass. He laughed heartily at the tale of the ridiculous "buffalo hunt." Sky's fears that his uncle would be upset over the waste of a valuable animal were unfounded.

"We will have good meat for a few days," said Stands-in-the-River. "That will be a change from the paltry government rations."

The next day a man from the Indian agent's office visited the camp.

"We got complaints from some settlers that your people are hunting cattle," the man said to the small gathering of Cheyennes.

Stands-in-the-River, who was still a little drunk, said, "Oh, just some youngsters having fun."

"Well, it ain't humane."

"It was only a cow."

"You just keep those young bucks of yours under control. Makes folks nervous."

Sky listened with a mixture of amusement and anger. As he did during his encounter with the settlers, he enjoyed the idea of making white people nervous. They deserved it for taking Indian land. Yet he was furious that the Cheyenne were not free to do what they pleased on their own reservation, and with their own cattle. If they had been killing people or stealing or breaking other natural and reasonable laws, that would be different. But this interference by the agency was too much. No wonder Stands-in-the-River was drunk all the time. This kind of control undermined a person's very self-respect.

Sky became more certain than ever that the Ghost Dance was the only hope for the Cheyenne people to defeat the oppression laid upon them.

# 37

# THE SUN DANCE

At the beginning of summer the tribe began making preparations for the annual Sun Dance ceremony. The whole tribe was expected to attend. Some who had taken up farming and other white ways were reluctant, but Dog Soldiers were on hand to encourage them, forcefully if necessary, to participate.

The agency frowned on all Indian ceremonies, though they had not totally banned them. The Sun Dance, with its rite of torture, made them particularly uneasy, because they understood its great significance to the Plains Indians. Still it was permitted every year, in spite of protests from nervous settlers.

Sky was not one of the reluctant participants. He was so enthusiastic, in fact, that he made a vow to endure the rites of torture in order to bring prosperity to his people. He prepared himself by fasting for a week beforehand and going up into the hills. He spent those days in prayer to the Great Spirit, opening up his heart and soul, entreating his god to visit him. When he wasn't in prayer he would hike around in the broken, craggy hills, which were now swathed in wildflowers.

Sky remembered that the success of his "hunt" with Tall Bull had been a result of his becoming one with his prey. This oneness was an intrinsic element of the Cheyenne Way. Not only in hunting, but in life, the value of nature was extolled, venerated. The very life of his people had been in the buffalo, in the earth on which they dwelt. When that lifeblood was taken from them, his people had begun to die. The white man had broken the beautiful circle of Cheyenne life, and Blue Sky prayed for it to be restored.

As the days of his pilgrimage passed and nothing happened, Sky became discouraged. He had hoped for visions and prophetic dreams, as he had experienced in Nevada. So, the last two days

219

before he had to return to camp for the Sun Dance, Sky demanded more of himself, denying himself not only food, but also water. The prairie sun was hot, even in June, and it didn't take long for him to become dehydrated. Inviting suffering, he lay under the hot sun until he nearly passed out from a combination of heat exposure and hunger. He had been praying continually to the Wise One Above, and for all those days he thought of little else. By the last day he felt weaker than he ever had in his life. Yet, at the same time, he felt primed and sharp—if not physically, then spiritually.

Expectant. Ready.

His zeal ran high as he rejoined the camp and the Sun Dance rites began.

Stands-in-the-River and Tall Bull had also been fasting in support of Sky. And they, with Sky, initiated the first day of dancing. They danced for hours each night, then each went off alone during the day seeking some spiritual experience.

The final day of dancing was devoted to physical sacrifice. This was the dance Sky had been preparing himself for. This would be the fulfillment of his vow. Stands-in-the-River was given the task of driving the wooden skewers through Sky's skin, four on the front and four on the back. Pain coursed through Sky's body, yet he was oddly detached from it. He felt as if he had stepped out of his pain-wracked body and was observing from another plane. It was as if he were moving between two worlds—not the world of white man versus Indian, but between the earth of flesh and blood and some netherland, perhaps the land beyond the Milky Way. He could feel a cool, gentle breeze floating over him, carried up from a gurgling, dancing stream. A sweet fragrance—

But a sharp pain forced him into awareness of the fleshly world—the inside of the Medicine Lodge, hot and stuffy, and the circle of chanting, dancing Cheyennes. Ropes, tied to the Sun Dance pole, had been attached to the skewers in Sky's skin. Several of the dancers had taken the ropes and were pulling them. Tall Bull and Stands-in-the-River were pulling. And Sky felt his body rise from the ground. For a moment, it was pure agony.

A voice screamed. It was his.

Then blackness followed.

He awoke to more pain. Such pain!

*Yea, though I walk through the valley of the shadow of death . . .*

No, that's not right. Another world . . . not my world. . . .

*Come to me, Great Spirit!*

220

As if in answer to his cry, the faces of his Cheyenne brothers came into sudden focus. Painted faces, chanting, moving around him in a circle. The circle of life. In them was his soul, his reason for being.

*I am a Cheyenne.*

*Have mercy upon me, O God. Cast me not away from Your presence. . . .*

No. Not the white man's god.

Sky lost all track of time and reality. The painted faces turned into other faces from his past. His mother, Sam, Carolyn . . . they were calling to him.

*"Don't wander from us, Sky."*

*"I go to my people."*

*"We are—"*

*No!*

*I am Cheyenne.*

Oblivion overwhelmed Sky again. Would his sufferings be for nothing? Would he die a half-breed, belonging nowhere?

*Oh, Wise One Above! Wovoka, show me the way.*

Darkness edged in around him. Terror enveloped him. There was no peace. There was no hope.

Then the darkness grew lighter. Faces surrounded him, but not the painted countenances of Sun dancers. They were the faces of children.

And Sky, in the midst of those youthful faces, was a great warrior like his father, returning from the hunt, the carcass of a huge buffalo bull in tow. The children ran out to him, calling, "Nehuo! Nehuo!"

They were *his* children. Many children.

They were strong, round and healthy. Not like the sickly, starving children he had seen on the reservation. Blue Sky's children were not reservation children. They were free.

Then he saw a woman at work by his lodge. He saw only her back at first, but she was dressed in calico and the hair tumbling down around her shoulders was light brown and curly. . . .

"Jenny!" he cried.

Then the woman turned, and it was Rose's face, framed in Jenny's curls.

"They are *my* children," Rose said. "*Our* children."

And suddenly the hair and the calico were transformed until the true image of Winter Rose stood before him. She glowed with a beauty that made Sky ache inside.

221

The children ran up to her, wrapping their arms around her. "Nahkoa!"

Blue Sky wept with joy and took Rose's hand.

———————

The next face Sky beheld was that of Stands-in-the-River, bending over him, a look of fear and concern in the stoic eyes.

"You have done well, my son."

"Is it . . . over?"

Sky was no longer in the big Medicine Lodge of the Sun Dance. Stone Teeth Woman approached. She did something to Sky's chest that sent sharp pain through his body.

"Your wounds are clean," she said. "But now you must drink and eat." She put a cup to his lips.

The cool water hurt his sun-cracked lips and burned his raw throat, but he forced it down. He was a Cheyenne warrior, and he was too strong to succumb to suffering.

By the next morning he was strong enough to eat a little something, and he was rested enough to ponder his experience.

He had prayed for a vision. Had he received it? The dream of the children and Rose was still vivid in his mind. What could it mean? Rose had been the last thing on his mind. He had been so wrapped up in the preparations for the ceremony, he had hardly seen her in two weeks.

"Nehuo," he called to Stands-in-the-River, "did the Great Spirit come to me?"

"It seemed to me he did," said Stands-in-the-River. "I thought I saw you touching him."

"I've never felt closer to my people, Nehuo," Sky said. "Inside, I truly feel Cheyenne."

"Then it must be that the Wise One Above came."

"I think so, too. But I don't understand it all. Can I tell you what happened?"

"I am not a medicine man, Blue Sky. I'll get Red Feather, he will know."

Before long, Stands-in-the-River returned with Red Feather, the Cheyenne shaman. Sky sat up. He was still in pain, but he refused to bow to this weakness. Tall Bull joined them, and the four passed the pipe, then Sky told them about his dream.

"The Wise One Above has spoken well to you, Blue Sky," said Red Feather. "He has shown you the way to step fully into your heritage as a Cheyenne warrior. He has told you to carry on the blood of your father. In so doing you will shed the last of the white man's ways. You must take a Cheyenne wife. It would please the Great Spirit if Winter Rose were that wife."

Jenny's death had put such a hard shell around Sky's heart that he felt certain he could never love anyone else. He was afraid to open himself up that way again, to invite more pain. He had long been aware of Rose's beauty and endearing spirit, but he had been careful to appreciate her only at arm's length. It was too risky to get close.

He looked at Red Feather and shook his head in confusion. "Marriage? I . . . I don't know. . . ."

"Surely you knew you would marry one day."

"I guess I tried not to think of that. The girl . . . the other girl in my dream . . . she was special to me. I think she still owns a big part of my heart."

"The dead white girl?"

"Yes."

"Is it she who owns your heart, or the white world she represents?"

"I—" Sky started to defend himself, then stopped. Was that what it boiled down to, then? In clinging to Jenny, was he also grasping her world, the world he had once longed to be part of? That world had hurt him, despised him, rejected him. How could he still want it?

After the ritual of torture, he felt he had at last attained the coveted goal of being a true Cheyenne. What he had endured had put him in a special class. Not every Cheyenne warrior had made that sacrifice. It elevated him to a place of respect among the Cheyenne. He thought that would be enough.

"I am a Cheyenne," Sky said plaintively.

"Then embrace your people with your *whole* heart."

# 38

# THE PROPOSAL

Red Feather told Sky that he should marry Rose while the Medicine Lodge still stood so that good medicine would bless their lives together.

Sky wasted no time. He didn't want to lose his nerve. He tried not to think of the fact that he didn't love Rose. Instead, he convinced himself that this arrangement was the best way. Neither could be hurt if they didn't love each other. They liked each other, and he would care for her as a husband should.

Besides, he wasn't about to force her into anything. He would present himself honestly to her. She would only marry him if she wanted to.

He was still quite weak, but he set out to find her regardless. She was with a group of women gathering herbs near the creek. He watched her for a moment before he made his presence known. She was laughing and talking with her companions in that easy manner of hers. The warmth of her smile, her eyes, was almost palatable like summer heat waves.

Yes, he could care for her easily.

"Rose," he called.

The group looked up at the sound of his voice. Some of the women giggled and gave her friendly nudges toward him. Rose responded with a perplexed look. Then she waved and smiled, and walked to him.

"I'm glad to see you're feeling better," she said.

"I'm still a little weak, but nothing to speak of."

"I saw the ceremony, Blue Sky. It took great courage."

He shrugged. "I only did what the Great Spirit required of me." Sky wished he could just blurt out what he wanted and have done with it. He was beginning to wonder if he should go through with it. But he knew it would not be right to be too blunt. He might not love Rose, but he was certain she would want some ceremony surrounding the proposal. And he did want her to say yes. If he had to marry someone, he preferred it was her.

"Would you walk with me for a few minutes?" he asked.

They walked along the creek away from the group of women. Sky's mind was in a turmoil over choosing the appropriate words. He thought of the time with Jenny. That had happened so easily and naturally. Love had made a difference, he supposed. And she had brought the subject up to him.

It wasn't going to be so easy this time. Rose obviously had no idea what was on his mind.

He let the conversation follow trivial paths for a while, hoping one would naturally lead to what was on his mind. When he saw that tack was getting him nowhere, he decided to forge ahead the best way he could.

"Rose, during the ceremony, the Wise One Above spoke to me."

"That's what you wanted, wasn't it?"

"Yes, but I didn't expect what he told me."

"What was that?"

"That I should take a wife."

"Oh?"

He told her about his dream. "You are his choice for me, Rose."

"I know I should be honored."

"You are not?"

"I have thought for a long time that you are God's choice for me, Blue Sky. Does that surprise you?"

"It does, but I'm also glad to hear it. Then you understand what I'm talking about."

"I do a little. But, Blue Sky, my God gave me something else to accompany the feeling that you are His choice. He gave me love—for you. Has the Great Spirit given you the same thing—for me?"

Sky licked his lips; they were still parched and sore. "I can't lie to you, Rose. I don't have the same feelings for you. In a way, it would be easier if you didn't have them, either."

"But I do."

"I'm sorry."

She managed a slight smile. "I suppose I never thought a relationship between us would be normal."

"I wish I had more to offer you, Rose. Perhaps in time such

feelings would grow. But in the meantime, I will care for you faithfully and be a good Cheyenne husband."

She stopped walking, turned, and looked at him so closely that he grew uncomfortable. What did she see? Did she really love him as she said? It gave him an odd feeling—almost as if he were stealing from her. And he would have dropped the whole thing at that moment except he recalled a snatch of his dream, where, weeping with joy, he had taken her hand in his.

Was such joy really possible, or did it only exist in dreams and visions? But, if this were from the Great Spirit . . .

Rose spoke, "Blue Sky, I will give you my answer tomorrow. If it is acceptable to me, my father will bring gifts to your lodge—in the Cheyenne Way."

---

Rose had never been as interested in marriage as most girls her age. It hadn't been easy losing her little sisters, and that made her reluctant to bear children and risk more such loss. And this was not an idle fear, for there was much death among little children on the reservation.

But another aspect added to her reluctance. For much of her life she had been tied to the responsibilities of caring for a family. As grievous as the loss was, when it happened and she found herself freed of the burden, she had wanted to enjoy it for a while. She wanted to enjoy something she'd had so little of—her youth. In the last five years she had turned down several marriage proposals. She wasn't certain exactly when she'd be ready, but she had trusted God that He would let her know.

And from the first moment she had met Sky at the Wild West Show, she had *known*. He was the one for whom she was ready to offer her freedom. Yes, *offer*, for it would be no sacrifice with him. And to bear his children, she would risk the pain of loss.

If only he felt the same way. Perhaps in time, as he had said, that would happen. But it might never happen. Could she stand giving her love and never having it returned? Worse than that, could she bear seeing him married to another? She had no doubt that if she refused him, he *would* find another.

Rose went to visit Gray Antelope. As usual the old woman didn't give any answers. She just quietly listened as Rose poured out her heart. Then they prayed together.

An hour later, as Rose was about to leave, she said, "I still don't know what to do."

226

"You don't?" Gray Antelope smiled. "I think you knew the minute you walked into my lodge."

———

Sky was sitting outside sharpening arrowheads when Little Left Hand approached with an armload of gifts—blankets, a good hide, a hunting knife.

"I have come to speak with your father, Stands-in-the-River." He tried to maintain a certain formality, but Sky saw the edges of his lips twitch upward.

"He's inside."

Sky followed Little Left Hand into the lodge.

Little Left Hand said, "Stands-in-the-River, I wish to accept your son Blue Sky's proposal of marriage to my daughter. Here are gifts. They are small compared to my happiness." He glanced at Sky and finally let his lips relax into a full grin. "This is a good day for my lodge."

"We accept your gifts," said Stands-in-the-River. "Come smoke with us to seal the bargain."

The marriage ceremony was performed the next day while the Medicine Lodge still stood. Because of the short notice, Rose did not have a wedding dress—not that her father could have afforded one. But all the women in camp contributed what finery they had, and Rose ended up looking lovely on her wedding day. A fine new shawl from one woman, a cotton skirt and crinoline from another, a beaded buckskin blouse from another, jewelry from others, and a new pair of moccasins from Gray Antelope.

When Sky first saw her as she entered the Medicine Lodge, he wondered what was wrong with him that he didn't love her. He was truly unworthy of her, and this feeling deepened as the glow of her love focused on him. He wanted to be happy, yet a pall hung over him, weighing him like a burden. Another thought also disturbed him. His mother was not present for his wedding day. She didn't even know about it.

He reminded himself over and over that this is what the Wise One Above wanted. In marriage to a Cheyenne woman he was entering fully into the life of his people, leaving the past behind completely.

But he still found it hard to look Rose in the eyes—those eyes so filled with love.

227

# 39

# OUT OF STEP

Changes were coming to the reservation. That first influx of white settlers east of the reservation was but a harbinger of things to come. Shortly after the Sun Dance, more pressure was applied to the government to open up land on the Cheyenne and Arapaho reservation to settlers. The Cheyenne were presented with a plan whereby each individual Indian would be given an allotment of his own, along with a cash payment for reservation lands given to homesteaders.

Some Indians already had allotments and were trying to farm, though more often than not they were unsuccessful given the unfriendly geography of the area. But the traditional Indians who wanted to maintain the old ways tried to fight the government claims on their reservation.

Little Left Hand was among a delegation of Cheyennes and Arapahoes that attempted to persuade the government officials of their wishes.

"The Great Spirit gave all this land to the Indians," he told them. "He does not want us to sell this land. Though I am a poor man, money means nothing to me. My wealth is the land. The land is what we want. We do not want to sell it."

But the officials applied pressure, resorting to many empty promises. When that didn't appear to be working, they threatened to cut back on rations which were already scandalously skimpy.

Bargaining went back and forth all summer. Sky attended some of the sessions, and even he, with his knowledge of English, was often confused. It was obvious to him that the agents were purposely distorting the issues so that the Indians would never be clear on what they were agreeing to—if they agreed.

Besides this, Sky was also busy with his Ghost Dance devotion.

It seemed when he wasn't in Darlington listening to land negotiations, he was participating in dance ceremonies. He spent very little time with his new wife.

———

Rose tried to be patient. Blue Sky was young, only twenty-two, and it was understandable that settling down wasn't easy. He was nice to her when he was around, but even that was a bit disturbing. He was almost *too* nice. They had been much more comfortable around each other before they were married. Now politeness existed between them, but little else. Rose had hoped that in the physical duties of marriage, she might somehow win Sky's love, but thus far even that had not been successful.

Rose was doubting herself more every day. When they had been married a month, Gray Antelope took note.

"I hear the sadness in your voice, Rose."

"It's harder than I thought it would be."

"Marriage was never an easy thing."

"Nahkoa, I'm afraid my love will grow cold if it's not returned."

"There is a verse in the Bible," said Gray Antelope. "I memorized it before my sight left me. It says that love 'bears all things, believes all things, hopes all things, and endures all things.' "

"Yes, Nahkoa, I remember those words. They are some that I wanted to learn to read for myself."

"I wish I could teach you, dear one." Gray Antelope stopped and scratched her head thoughtfully. "Rose, didn't you learn your letters at the school before your father had you come home?"

"I learned what the letters were and the sounds they make, and I read something the teacher called the First Primer. Well, I read part of it—not enough to help me understand the words in the Bible."

"I've just had an idea," said Gray Antelope. "I think that if you got the proper books, you could teach yourself to read. I've heard of others doing that, and you are a smart girl. I think you'd be able to easily."

"Teach myself? What an idea, Nahkoa! A crazy idea, but I love it! I'll do it!"

While Gray Antelope might not have imparted to Rose any astounding spiritual answers, she had done the next best thing. She gave Rose something to take her mind off her troubles. And in the process, Rose would also gain the means by which she could strengthen her own spiritual walk.

Rose rode to Darlington with Sky the next time he went. She found her old teacher at the Indian school and convinced her to loan her a couple of primers. Supplies were limited at the school and she was reluctant, but in the end she couldn't refuse such an eager student. Two of her regular students could share books for a while.

This new project consumed Rose, and she became much more content with her relationship with Sky—or, rather, their lack of relationship. She pored over the books every day, but it was still a slow process. Sky seemed to approve of her endeavor; maybe he liked the fact that it kept her too busy to pine over him.

One day she heard Sky approach. She was eager to read him something from the Bible she had finally figured out. But he wasn't in a good mood, and she put the Bible away.

Sky was carrying a gunnysack, which he carefully dropped on the ground in the tepee.

"Our monthly rations," he said.

"Good. We were running out of a few things."

"I should be bringing home meat instead of this rotten stuff." He poked his toe at the bag.

"When we get our allotments, we could raise cattle and have meat all the time. With ours and my father's together, we could have a nice ranch."

"I didn't rejoin my people to be a rancher."

"It may be our only choice."

"If you don't believe in the Ghost Dance, that is." There was a slight edge to his voice. This wasn't the first time the subject had arisen between them.

Rose tried to be diplomatic. "I'd like to."

"Then why don't you come with me to a dance?"

She had gone to one dance and hadn't liked it much. All she could think of was that all those people were putting so much hope in something that seemed pretty farfetched to her. She had left the ceremony depressed, even oppressed. She'd made excuses for not going the other times Sky had asked her. He didn't ask often. Perhaps he liked the opportunity to get away from her.

"Maybe I will," she said.

"There's one tonight."

Rose went off to prepare the evening meal. But that night she joined Sky at the ceremony.

About a hundred Cheyennes and Arapahoes gathered in a cleared glade five miles from Rose's camp. She wondered how many other dances were going on at that same time and just how widespread the religion was. There were several chiefs and Dog Soldiers present, and Little Left Hand was there. Apparently her father had overcome his initial skepticism.

Rose had hoped to remain an observer, but when Sky offered to put some of the sacred paint on her, she couldn't refuse him. This meant so much to him, and their marriage was shaky enough without her balking at something so important. She joined the large circle, and when the drums began their steady cadence, she moved with the group. Several of the men were wearing the special Ghost Shirts. Sky had one, as did Tall Bull and Stands-in-the-River. Wearing the shirts was mostly a Sioux practice, but the idea had caught on, though on a smaller scale, in the south. It was said the shirts were impervious to bullets. Rose didn't like the practice, for it hinted at violence, and most of the Ghost Dancers insisted the religion was completely peaceful.

The only thing Rose enjoyed about the dance that night was listening to Sky sing. Actually it was more of a chant, and his usual tenor was an octave lower, but each note he uttered was clear like the starry night, haunting like the images of the past he prayed for. But even listening to Sky's beautiful voice brought heartache. Rose thought about the lovely songs he used to sing while playing his guitar. His music had meant so much to him at one time. It seemed such a loss.

She stole a glance at Sky and saw the rapture on his face. He, at least, had no regrets. He had found his way. Who was she to judge him or what he was doing?

*Oh, God of Jesus*, Rose silently prayed, *I am so confused. How can I tell my husband he is wrong when I'm not sure myself? If only I knew more of what your Book said. I know the answers are there.*

At that moment a woman in the group let out a yell as she stumbled into the middle of the circle. Moaning and crying, she sank to the ground and lay flat, face down. Her prostrate body jerked a couple of times, then was perfectly still. Alarmed, Rose started toward the woman who didn't even seem to be breathing. But before Rose got too far, the fallen woman let out a monotonous moan that turned into a chant.

> I see my father, he comes down to me . . .
> Down to me, down to me . . .
> "You are a daughter of a magpie," he says to me.

231

The woman chanted for a few more minutes and then lay still again. This time Rose made no move toward her. This is why everyone came to the dance, hoping for a vision. Everyone except Rose. She didn't want a vision. She only wanted peace and security, and to be happy with her husband.

# 40

# MOMENT OF LOVE

Sky wanted to be a good husband—he simply had no understanding of what that meant. He had grown up with a very good example in Sam, but in his present state of mind, he was trying so hard *not* to think of Sam that the past didn't do him much good. Nevertheless, common sense, instinct, and his own deeply ingrained sense of humanity told him to be kind to Rose, gentle when he touched her, and considerate. These principles, however, were not always easy to practice, especially when they interfered with his own needs and desires. The peculiar relationship he had with Rose also confused the matter.

Once when he thought he was being a model husband, polite and solicitous, she burst into unaccountable tears. He couldn't get her to tell him what the problem was, and he ended up getting frustrated and angry and walking out. He actually began to wonder if she perhaps preferred him to be gone. Thus, he rationalized his frequent absences.

When he wasn't in Darlington or at some ceremony, he went hunting. Game was not as plentiful on the reservation as it once had been, and he often came home empty-handed. Still, he enjoyed riding or hiking over the countryside, and Tall Bull, who often accompanied him, was a far easier companion than his wife.

One day, after unsuccessfully stalking a big eight-point buck, he and Tall Bull lay in the grass resting. A little breeze kept the hot sun from completely baking them, and the pleasant fragrance of prairie grass wafted over them.

"Tell me something, Blue Sky," Tall Bull asked. "Are you glad you married Rose?"

Sky was surprised at the question. He and Tall Bull were not often given to philosophical conversations.

233

"I guess so."

"I've been thinking of taking a wife, too." Tall Bull brushed at a bee buzzing near his face.

"Who's the lucky girl?"

"I went to school with her. Martha Buffalo Horns. She is in Porcupine's camp."

"Do you love her?"

"We've loved each other since school, but I had hoped I'd have more to offer her when we married. But if I wait any longer, we'll probably die of old age. When the agent gives out allotments, we'll be able to get ours together and have over three hundred acres—even more if we can combine our parents' allotments. We ought to be able to do something with that much land."

"Don't forget, Tall Bull," said Sky emphatically, "it will never come to that. Wovoka's prophecies will come true long before the government doles out its skimpy allotments. We'll have the whole country again."

"Oh, of course. But aren't you going to sign up for your allotment?"

"Rose keeps nagging me about it."

"Our father will sign up, as will many other believers in the Ghost Dance. It will appease the government agents and keep them off guard for what is coming."

"There is merit in that way of thinking."

"And we must be prepared for the possibility—"

"Don't say it, Tall Bull!" snapped Sky. "We will not fail!"

"I wish I could have your faith."

"When we go to the next dance," said Sky, "I will pray for you that you will have the kind of experience I've had—then you won't doubt anymore."

They fell silent. Sky plucked up a long blade of grass and chewed on it. He thought about the time in Nevada—how close he had been to the Great Spirit, and how real his encounter with his father had been. Since then, except for the Sun Dance vision, he had not had an experience of the same magnitude. More and more, he clung to those earlier episodes, depending upon them for his faith. And just as his stock of faith ran low, some token experience would bolster him again—perhaps an inspired dream, or simply a sudden deep sense of camaraderie and belonging as he danced with his brothers. No matter what, Sky had too much invested in this way to give up on it.

Tall Bull's voice broke the silence. "Blue Sky, we got off the subject. I wanted to ask you for advice about marriage."

Sky let out a dry, humorless laugh. "You must be pretty desperate to ask me. I wouldn't be hunting with you all the time or off somewhere else if I were doing a better job of being a husband. Why don't you ask Nehuo?"

"I have. He says a man must show his wife early who is boss and rule her with a strong hand. He says a beating every now and then is good for a woman."

Sky considered the words. Stone Teeth Woman and Stands-in-the-River had been married some thirty years, and Stands-in-the-River had never taken any other wives, so it might be his methods were successful. But when Sky thought of Rose, he said, "I doubt that would work with my wife. I think if I tried to hit her, she'd hit me back."

"I think the same thing about Martha. And, if you want to know the truth, my father's ways might keep control of a wife, but they don't make for a happy home. Still, I don't think just loving a wife is enough either."

"I thought that might be all that was needed. If I could love Rose, it would make everything all right."

"I don't see how you can't love her, Blue Sky. She's a beautiful woman."

"And she has many other good qualities."

"So. . . ?"

Sky shrugged. "I must be crazy."

He didn't know why he couldn't love her, why he was . . . afraid. Had the loss of Jenny affected him so deeply that he'd never be able to love again? He thought of his mother and how deeply she had loved his father, yet as time passed she had been able to love again. She now had a deep love for Sam.

Maybe he just wasn't trying hard enough. Maybe there was still part of him trying to maintain a hold on the white man's world. Maybe if he loved his Cheyenne wife too completely, he'd have to relinquish just as completely that other world.

That evening as he returned home, his thoughts were still churning within him. But he felt a new determination to shake the shackles of the white world once and for all.

He asked Little Left Hand to spend the evening at a neighbor's lodge, to which his father-in-law agreed with a twinkle in his eyes. Then Sky gathered a bouquet of late-blooming wild daisies. They weren't much to look at, but he was fortunate to find anything surviving in the summer heat.

When he entered the lodge, Rose was busy preparing the evening meal. Smiling, he held out the flowers.

"I found these on my way home and thought you might enjoy them," he said.

Her surprise was obvious. "That was thoughtful of you, Blue Sky. I'll put them in water right away." Taking the bouquet, she filled an empty tin can with water from a skin, placed the flowers in the can, and set it by the center pole of the tepee.

"Our meal is almost ready," she said.

"Your father won't be here. He said he is going to Red Feather's lodge."

"To eat?"

"Yes, I think so."

"Then it will be just you and me."

"That's what it looks like."

A slight smile twitched on her lips, then she returned to her work. As Sky watched her, he realized more than ever what a fool he was. She was as poised and graceful as any woman he had seen—even Queen Victoria and the titled ladies who had attended the Wild West Show in England. She was intelligent, with just enough spirit to make her interesting. For the first time since he had known Rose, Sky allowed himself to enjoy her many attributes. And before he realized it, strong feelings were surging through him.

He got up from where he was sitting and laid his hand on her shoulder. She started a bit, and as she turned to face him, he put his arms around her and kissed her passionately. She in no way resisted his advances. They kissed again, and she dropped the spoon she was holding.

"Rose, I am so lucky to be your husband."

"It's about time you realized it," she said lightly.

"You are so beautiful. . . ."

"Oh, Blue Sky, how I've longed . . ."

But he didn't let her finish. With his lips on hers, he gently nudged her to the hide they used as a bed.

"Oh, my sweet wife," he murmured, embracing her. Holding her close, he could feel the throb of her heartbeat against his own chest. For the first time in their marriage, he felt no sense of duty or obligation. Her nearness was a delight to him.

———

Later, Sky's arms were still around Rose as if he were afraid to let go and break the spell. Her eyes were closed, but there was such joy on her face.

Rose opened her eyes. "Are you watching me?" she asked in a dreamy, contented voice.

"It pleases me to see you so happy."

"How could I not be happy, Blue Sky? I have loved you so deeply for so long, what else would I feel to have that love finally returned? All my dreams have come true, my husband."

*Dreams . . .*

Sky thought of his dreams and realized Rose had never been part of them.

"Only one thing is lacking," she said, turning and laying a loving hand on his cheek. "To hear the words from your sweet lips, my love."

"Rose, I do care for you."

"But love. . . ?"

A knot formed in Sky's throat. Why couldn't he say the words? They were so simple, and they were all she wanted to hear. Even if he wasn't sure he meant them, what harm would it do to say the words? But he hesitated too long.

"I'm sorry, Blue Sky. I shouldn't have pressed you. I should have been satisfied."

"You have a right—"

"No! I don't want your love out of *right* or *duty*. I knew what the situation was when we married."

"I feel as if I deceived you tonight."

"Why? Because of a moment of weakness? I understand how it is with men."

"I did feel something—"

"Good. That's a start then, isn't it?"

Her voice was too even, the good nature too forced. Sky pulled away from her and sat up. "You would be within your rights to divorce me," he said.

"How could you even suggest such a thing? I married you fully aware of how it was."

"But I've seen your sadness, and I've heard you weep at night when you thought I was asleep. I've seen the longing in your eyes."

"Well, maybe I did have some expectations. Maybe I hoped things might change." She paused, and when she spoke again a kind of panic filled her voice. "Maybe you would like to divorce me?"

That would be so easy. Maybe Red Feather had misinterpreted the Sun Dance vision. Maybe this whole thing had been a mistake. Yet it was done; he and Rose were married. Though divorce was a much simpler matter among the Cheyenne than with the whites, such an act would still disgrace Rose. And even aside from the disgrace, Sky still knew he couldn't do it. Perhaps by doing such a thing he'd be admitting his own failure as a Cheyenne. Perhaps, too . . .

He stole a glance at Rose. Perhaps there had been something to those feelings he'd had earlier.

"I won't do that, Rose, not unless you want it."

She shook her head. "I'm not ready to give up. The hope I have, Blue Sky, is still strong. I suppose it's a lot like the hope you have in the Ghost Dance."

"Oh, Rose, I don't deserve you!"

Rose stood. "You must be hungry. Let's eat and rest from these serious matters for a while."

Sky was more than willing to comply, but he sensed innately that it would be only a short reprieve. Sooner or later their problems would catch up with him again.

# 41

# BROTHERS

Sky went to Darlington with several other Cheyenne to observe the continuing debates over the Dawes Act, the proposal to break up the reservation. All summer they had haggled with the government and now, as summer waned and autumn began showing its golden colors, it seemed an agreement was close.

Sky, Little Left Hand, Stands-in-the-River, and other traditionalists backed the powerful Cheyenne chief, Old Crow, arguing against the allotment plan, desiring the reservation to remain intact. But the more compliant Arapaho leader, Cloud Chief, was gaining ground in his support of the agreement. Many Arapaho also supported the plan, especially after their chief had induced the government to agree to a larger settlement. The eighty acres originally proposed by the government was increased to one hundred and sixty for each Indian—man, woman, and child.

"If you accept this deal," one of the commissioners said, "you'll be richer than any white man."

When the Indians tried to get more money for the unallotted lands, the commissioner told them, "Do you realize you'll be getting five hundred dollars up front? That's more silver than you can fit in your pockets. You'll need to fill up your saddlebags to carry it home."

It was, certainly, a tempting offer. And if they didn't consent to the Dawes Act, it could be invoked forcefully, and the Indians would end up getting nothing.

When the talks resumed in October after a break of several weeks, Old Crow and his followers attempted to boycott the meetings. A rumor was spread that the first Indian signer of the agreement would be killed. Nevertheless, the Arapaho chief finally signed the document.

Old Crow's contingent refused to sign. When Sky and Tall Bull attempted to intimidate some signers, they were taken into custody and were only released when Old Crow promised not to stand in the way of signers again.

It took a month before the required names were gathered—seventy-five percent of the adult male members of the two tribes—though it was never certain just how legitimate the end result was. There was certainly some stretching of the meaning of the word *adult*, and there were accusations that some women had signed. Besides that, the actual number of names required seemed too low to represent seventy-five percent. But there was never any proof of these inconsistencies, and certainly the government officials never challenged the end result.

But long before the Dawes Act became law, trouble arose from an entirely different avenue.

In the north, problems were arising among the Sioux. They, too, had been suffering for years at the hand of the white man. Their reservation had been cut in half, then large tracts given to white settlers. In the process, their annuities had been cut back, leaving many hungry and some starving. The previous spring, outbreaks of influenza, measles, and whooping cough had killed many Sioux, especially the children and the aged.

They were ripe for the teachings of Wovoka. And, unlike the more peacefully inclined southern tribes, the Ghost Dance religion among the Sioux took a more militant form. They began to use the Ghost Shirt, with its supposed magical protection against bullets. The Sioux were ready for battle.

Rumors of the situation up north had been filtering down south all summer. Stands-in-the-River had said several times that he was going up there to see for himself what was happening. He had fought side by side with many of these Sioux; they were friends and brothers to him. But because the situation at home was shaky, too, with the government commissioners trying to rob more land, he stayed home.

One evening in early December, Stands-in-the-River had been missing all day. The weather was turning cold, and his sons had grown concerned. They found him in Darlington sitting in an alley, a half-empty bottle of cheap whiskey in his hand. He was with another Cheyenne named Little Elk.

"My sons! My sons!" Stands-in-the-River said in a drunken slur. "Look at them, Little Elk, aren't they cause for pride?"

"I haven't seen better," said the man, who was about Stands-in-the-River's age. It was difficult to tell which man was drunker.

"Come on, Nehuo, it's time to come home." Tall Bull put an arm around his father.

"Home? Not now, my son. I'm going north—"

"Someday, Nehuo."

"No. I mean it this time. I'm going. Can't do nothin' more here. Our land's been signed away. I'm gonna help my brother, Sitting Bull. They're gonna arrest him. He's too powerful and the whites want to kill him. Tell them, Little Elk. Tell them what you told me."

Little Elk explained that he had just returned from a trip north to visit his wife's relatives; his wife was a Minneconjous Sioux from Big Foot's band. "Many soldiers have come to the Sioux reservations—as many as were once in a herd of buffalo. Many Indians became afraid and fled to the Badlands where the soldiers could not find them. Two . . . three thousand are there hiding. But the soldier chief has called them hostiles."

"Why did the soldiers come?" asked Tall Bull.

"Many Indians have taken up the Ghost Dance. Maybe the whites are worried. Most of the big chiefs are in hiding—except Sitting Bull and Big Foot, of my wife's people. Even before I left, there were rumors that Sitting Bull was going to be arrested."

"Why doesn't Sitting Bull join the others in hiding?" asked Sky. "Surely he must realize his danger."

"Maybe he believes stronger than the rest in the power of his shirt."

Sky had heard that Sitting Bull had wholeheartedly embraced the Ghost Dance religion, and that despite his stint with Buffalo Bill and so-called civilization, the government still considered him a dangerous man, with a powerful hold on his people.

"He knows," Stands-in-the-River continued, "that there is only one way to be rid of the whites."

"But how do you expect to help him, Nehuo?" Sky reasoned. "By the time you got there, it would probably be too late."

"I must try."

"We need you here, Nehuo," said Tall Bull.

"Sitting Bull needs me. I fought with him at the Little Big Horn. We killed many white soldiers together—" Stands-in-the-River grinned with relish. "I saw Yellow Hair fall dead! And many other bluecoats, all dead. I, myself, counted many coup for my dead son. And I killed some for your father, Blue Sky—he was not forgotten. There was never a better time. We were punished strongly for it, but I still think it was worth it." Then he thrust his head very close

241

to the two young men, as if he had some great secret to tell them. "We will fight again, one last time. I feel it coming. The Great Spirit tells me."

"We won't have to fight," Sky said patiently. "When the whites see all our dead return—many millions of them!—they will flee across the ocean."

"Will you fight next to me, Blue Sky?"

"We won't—" Sky tried to reason again, but his uncle wasn't listening.

"A Cheyenne man is nothing if he is not a warrior!" Stands-in-the-River declared. "Will you fight? Or are you too white?"

"Nehuo—"

"Don't let a double heart kill you as it did your father!" Stands-in-the-River cried. "Remember, Broken Wing, it is a good thing not to live to be an old man!" Stands-in-the-River hadn't even realized he had called Sky by his father's name. Maybe, in his drunken stupor, he thought it was twenty years ago and he was a young warrior again.

"Let's go home," urged Tall Bull.

"I go north in the morning when the firewater wears off," Stands-in-the-River insisted. "I fight!"

———

The next morning, Sky awoke earlier than usual. He crept out of his bed, careful not to wake Rose or her father, and went outside. It was cold and frosty out, and he tugged a blanket tightly around his shoulders. He liked the quiet peace of the early morning hours, before the world woke with all its troubles and woes. It was a hopeful time. A new day still lay ahead; anything could happen.

But Sky's peace lasted only a moment. A hundred yards away, at Stands-in-the-River's lodge, Sky saw movement. He then remembered how his uncle had insisted he was going north that very morning. Sky hurried toward the lodge.

Tall Bull and Stands-in-the-River were arguing, and, though their voices were low, they were harsh with intensity.

"Don't be a fool, Nehuo," said Tall Bull. "You can't save Sitting Bull."

"He is my brother. I owe him my loyalty."

"Is it your duty to risk your life?"

"Of course. What else is there?"

Tall Bull glanced up and saw Sky approach. "Blue Sky, maybe

you can talk some sense into him."

Ignoring both of them, Stands-in-the-River threw a halter around his horse, getting him ready to ride.

"Nehuo," Sky said in a patient, reasonable tone, "what do you think you can do to help?"

"Please," groaned Stands-in-the-River, "I don't want to hear white man's logic. Both my sons have been around white men too much. Tall Bull, I was afraid that school would ruin you. But when they threatened to cut off our rations if I didn't let you go, what could I do? And you, Blue Sky . . . well, you can't be blamed entirely for the way you are. Perhaps I must accept that my sons will never understand what it means to be a Cheyenne. For that I blame only the whites. They have robbed you of what you are, just as they have robbed us of our land." He was more sober now than he had been a few hours earlier, and he clearly knew exactly what he was doing and saying.

"Nehuo," Sky pleaded, "I want to understand. You know I want that more than anything!"

Stands-in-the-River sighed. "Ah, Blue Sky . . ." he said affectionately. "A Cheyenne warrior does not fear death, especially death in battle. We say 'nothing lives long, only the mountains and the trees.' I have lived to be an old man, but I am not as blessed as your father who died in glory. That is what it means to be a Cheyenne. I have lived too long, I think. My hair is too gray and my teeth are falling out. Would you deny my dying like a warrior?"

"No," breathed Sky, caught in the intensity of the older man's speech.

"Blue Sky, don't encourage him," said Tall Bull.

Sky ignored Tall Bull. "Nehuo, is that what I must do to be a Cheyenne warrior?"

"My son, you must *fight* like a warrior. Let the Wise One Above decide about the dying."

"Will you wait for me to ready my horse and say goodbye to my wife?" asked Sky.

"I will wait as long as it takes." Stands-in-the-River grinned at Sky. "You are your father's son. I feel as if I am with him once again. Thank you, Blue Sky. I feel—" A shadow seemed to darken his countenance. He closed his eyes, past pain suddenly etched on his face. Just as quickly as the shadow appeared, he shook it away. "Your father has returned from the dead, just as the prophecies said." Then he added, almost as if he were trying to convince himself, "This is a good thing."

Tall Bull turned to Sky. "You're not really going to do this?"

"Let's ride together like true brothers, Tall Bull."

"This is craziness."

Sky turned and, facing Tall Bull, placed his hands on his shoulders. "It probably is. But if there is a last fight, a last stand against the whites, I don't want to be in my lodge when it happens. I'll die like my father if I must. I am a Cheyenne warrior, Tall Bull, and so are you."

"I hate this world we are in," said Tall Bull. "Nothing is simple."

"Ride with me, Tall Bull. You are my best friend, my brother."

And between men and warriors it could not get simpler than that.

"I'll go," Tall Bull said with resignation, "if only to keep you two out of trouble."

# 42

# ROSE'S NEWS

Traversing six hundred miles at that time of year was no small feat. Stands-in-the-River pushed them to their limits. Each of them had an extra horse, and so they were able to cover much ground in a day. But that wasn't good enough for the old Cheyenne warrior. It had taken Little Elk a week to reach them, and he had been able to travel part of the way by train because he'd had permission to leave the reservation. Stands-in-the-River, Sky, and Tall Bull were away from the reservation illegally. They couldn't take the train because of risk of capture. Even on the forced march Stands-in-the-River was leading, it might take as many as ten days for the travelers to reach the Sioux reservation, and in that time anything could have happened to Sitting Bull. In their favor was the fact that the government moved slowly and often inefficiently.

"The whites will wait until the weather turns bad," Stands-in-the-River said, "when the ponies are weak, and when movement is difficult. They don't want to risk Sitting Bull fleeing to the Badlands with the others."

Snow began falling when they crossed the Platte River, but they were more than halfway there and their spirits were high. The weather was still fairly mild, and in some places the new snow melted as quickly as it hit the ground. The travelers' biggest problem was food. They had brought only the barest minimum so as not to deprive their families, and game was sparse. But Stands-in-the-River had no qualms about raiding settlers' farms along the way.

Only once did they almost get caught. Tall Bull had tripped over a fallen wire fence, waking the farm dogs who raised such a racket one might have thought a whole tribe of Indians was attacking instead of three stealing a few tidbits from a smokehouse.

The farmer fired a couple of shots, but Sky was positive the farmer never got a good look at them. The last thing they needed was an alarm to be raised over marauding Indians.

Sky was thoroughly enjoying himself. Each day on the trail was an adventure in survival. Sky's delight in the challenge almost—but not quite—made him forget the scene with Rose before he left.

"How can you go away now?" she had said. "Winter is the worst time of year, when you are most needed."

"You've gotten along without me before this," argued Sky. "You'll have your father."

She quickly changed her tactic in the face of his logic. "And why must *you* go? There are enough Sioux to care for themselves. Why would a great warrior like Sitting Bull need a few Cheyenne to come to his rescue?"

"I'm not going to stand around and argue with you about it."

"Your uncle is looking for a fight, isn't he?"

"I don't know."

"Is that what you want, Blue Sky?"

"No one wants to fight."

There was a moment of silence, and Sky realized his statement was not true. But what if he *did* want to fight? He was a warrior. It was his destiny.

"Please, Blue Sky, don't go." Rose changed her tone to entreaty, almost pleading. "I'm afraid for you. If there are soldiers there—"

"It means nothing. Just white man threats," he assured her in a gentler tone.

"Then they won't need you."

"Stands-in-the-River and Tall Bull are going no matter what. Don't you understand that I can't desert them?"

"I understand." She sighed. "It's just that—" She paused, hesitant.

"Rose, I have to go. I'll be careful."

"Blue Sky, I must tell you something then before you go. . . ."

"What?" He was growing impatient. His uncle was waiting.

"I wanted to wait until I was certain. But . . . it may be that I am expecting your child."

The announcement hit Sky like a blow. It shouldn't have surprised him—after all, it was bound to happen. Yet it had been the furthest thing from his thoughts—not only at that moment, but for a long time. His Sun Dance vision aside, he simply never thought of himself as a father.

246

But why did it have to happen now? He wasn't ready for it, and it made his leaving that much more difficult.

"Are you sure? It seems rather convenient for it to happen right now." The accusation went against all his instincts about his wife, and all reasonable assessment of her character. But he was anxious for an excuse.

"What are you saying, Blue Sky? That I'm lying?"

"Well . . . it's just that . . ."

"How dare you!" she railed. "If you think I'd lie about such a thing just to keep you here—Oh, what arrogance! I wouldn't want to keep you here if you were the last man on earth. Go! Go on your stupid quest. You're right, I was taking care of myself long before you ever came along—and I can keep on doing so—"

"Rose, I'm sorry—"

"Sorry? Ha! You're only sorry you got married and acquired a millstone around your neck."

"Won't you let me make it right? Won't you forgive me?"

"You'd like that, wouldn't you? Well, I refuse to make it so easy on you. Go to your friends. I've given all I can to you."

"All right!" he yelled back. "If that's how you want it. No one can say I didn't try." He stalked out of the tepee.

She called his name as he left, but even the desperation in her voice didn't stop him. She was better off without him anyway.

He stayed angry and defensive until he was many miles away and it was too late for him to go back to her. Maybe he wouldn't go back at all. What good did it do? She obviously was happier without him. He recalled clearly that irrepressible smile in her eyes and her buoyant good humor at the Wild West Show—qualities that had been almost entirely absent since they had married.

He was no good for her, maybe no good for any woman. He had ruined Jenny's life, finally causing her death. Would he lead Rose to her death, too? Yes, he should go far away from her. It was better—

Then he remembered what she had told him. Was she really going to have a child?

At the thought, Sky's stomach knotted so badly he felt sick. How could he ever have his own child? He was nothing but a lost child himself sometimes. How could he be a . . . father?

"Blue Sky, is something wrong?" asked Tall Bull as he rode beside Sky.

Sky blinked, startled. "No . . ."

"You looked as if you might fall off your horse."

247

"I was just thinking about something Rose told me before she left."

"She wasn't happy with you, eh?"

"That's only part of it." Sky looked to where Stands-in-the-River was riding about thirty yards ahead. "I don't want anyone to know about this," he inclined his head specifically toward his uncle. "Not until it's certain, all right?" Tall Bull nodded. "She told me she might be with child."

Tall Bull grinned instantly. "Now I see why you almost fell off your horse. I'm glad you're going to go through it first. You can tell me all about it."

"I'm not looking forward to it."

"I can imagine. More frightening than facing a thousand blue-coats alone."

"I've been hoping it's not true. I've even thought—" Sky stopped, unable to speak what he was feeling.

"Don't say it, Blue Sky. The Wise One Above will give you strength for this. Remember, you withstood torture in the Sun Dance and you were given a vision of your children. Didn't you say there were *many* children?"

"Don't remind me!"

"Well, my brother, it's too early to start worrying now, anyway. There are many months before it is born. Let's just worry about what lies ahead of us in the Dakotas."

"Gladly!"

But in their wildest hopes or nightmares, neither Sky nor Tall Bull could begin to imagine what they might be riding into. Stands-in-the-River, a seasoned veteran of the Indian Wars, had a much better idea, but all he talked about were past glories. Victories had been few and very far between for the Plains Tribes, but Stands-in-the-River managed to get a great deal of mileage out of them, especially now that his companions had nothing to do each night when they camped but listen to him. He made it all sound so grand that as they approached the Dakota border, even Tall Bull was gaining enthusiasm.

# 43

# WITH THE SIOUX

As they entered the reservation, the travelers decided to find Big Foot's band, the people of Little Elk's wife. They hoped to get information on what had been happening. Big Foot's village, on the Cheyenne River, was on the way to the Standing Rock Reservation, where Sitting Bull would be.

When the travelers arrived at the site of Big Foot's camp, they found it had moved from where Little Elk had been several weeks ago. It was close to the usual time of the arrival of government goods, so they reasoned the band might have gone to the agency to pick up annuities. They headed in that direction.

After ten miles, they were suddenly challenged by a Sioux sentry. A good number of Indians worked for the whites as scouts and Indian police, Sky knew—in some cases against their own people. He grew apprehensive when the sentry leveled a rifle at them.

"We're Cheyenne from the south," Stands-in-the-River said. "Big Foot knows me. I fought next to him many times. My friend Little Elk told me there was trouble here, and I came to stand with my friends the Sioux."

At the mention of Little Elk, the sentry lowered his rifle. "Little Elk's wife is my cousin. My name is Spotted Eagle." The man glanced toward the surrounding hills and scattered trees. "The bluecoats are watching our camp. Let's hope they didn't see you. Come, I'll take you to the camp."

They were taken to the chief's lodge. Big Foot was a middle-aged man with some streaks of gray in his long, dark hair. Sky could not easily judge the man's true size, for he remained lying on the ground during their entire visit. He coughed frequently and spoke with a rattle in his voice.

"Ah, my brother, Stands-in-the-River," said Big Foot, "you

haven't come at a good time. The soldiers are after us, and I am sick like an old man."

"That is exactly why I have come, to support my Sioux brothers."

"If only it would help! But my hope is almost as cold as the ice on the ground." He coughed. "Let us smoke together, then we will talk."

Smoking the pipe was hardly advisable for the sick chief. Sky suspected that the man might have pneumonia. After they passed the pipe, Big Foot coughed so much they had to wait some time before he could speak.

Finally he said, "Do you want to hear our troubles?"

"That's why we have come," said Stands-in-the-River. "Are the soldiers still here? Where is Sitting Bull? We heard he was to be arrested."

"Our brother Sitting Bull has taken the Hanging Road."

Stands-in-the-River groaned. "That can't be!"

"Yes, he is gone from us."

"What happened?"

"The soldiers came to arrest him. When he resisted, he was shot twice—killed by his own people, by the Indian Police."

"At least he died as a warrior," said Stands-in-the-River.

"The white man had left him nothing but bitter memories and hatred."

"What of you and your people? Are you in danger?"

Big Foot gave a weary sigh. "I have tried to take the white man's hand and follow their rules. But that is not enough for them. They want to take away my honor as a man and a Human Being. Several days ago refugees from Sitting Bull's band came to my camp for help. They were starving and nearly frozen because they had no blankets. Should I turn them away, my own people? I could not do this, so I took them in. For that the soldiers declared I was hostile and would have arrested me. Even then I would have gone with them. The white chief Sumner is my friend, and he promised me safety. But when we saw more soldiers arrive, my people became afraid, and so we stole away in the night."

"Then the soldiers are now pursuing you?"

"Yes."

"I hope we haven't led them to you. But we were careful. For our own reasons we were constantly on the lookout for soldiers. Where will you go, Big Foot?"

"We will join the others in the Badlands. What about you?"

Stands-in-the-River glanced at his sons. "We will stay for a while, at least until it seems the danger is passed."

Sky didn't object to staying. He didn't look forward to going home. If they stayed awhile, maybe Rose would cool down, and then she might actually want to see him. At any rate, he was content where he was.

It was about a hundred-mile journey south to the Badlands. The band, about three hundred and fifty in all, traveled as quickly as they could. But many were sick and weak, especially those from Sitting Bull's band, and Big Foot himself got progressively worse. Most were women and children—widows who had joined Big Foot because he believed in the Ghost Dance. The women hoped to bring back their dead husbands.

Finding enough food was a constant problem for the large group, but they made no raids of settlers' homesteads as they traveled. Big Foot wanted only to get to the safety of the stronghold and take no unnecessary risks.

When the band was close to its destination, Big Foot sent scouts into the Badlands to attempt to make contact with the Sioux who were in hiding. Stands-in-the-River had been growing restless, and he volunteered to go with these scouts. The band had been traveling as quickly as possible, but it was slow going with so many women, children, and sick. Besides, he confided to Sky, he was sure Big Foot was ready to surrender to the soldiers at first opportunity. At the pace they were going, they would never outrun the army. The bands in the Badlands might be getting up a war party. He could only hope.

Sky was almost inclined to join his uncle. Yet the Ghost Dancing in Big Foot's camp was as intense as Sky had experienced outside of Wovoka's camp in Nevada. Sky believed, or hoped, that such dancing would soon bring results. Thus he stayed with Big Foot, and Tall Bull remained also.

The scouts had been gone only a day when the soldiers finally caught up with Big Foot's band.

———

Custer was long dead, and the Seventh Cavalry had a new leader. But a handful of officers who had been dispatched to other flanks while the fateful two hundred had been surrounded and killed at Little Big Horn were still with the regiment.

Among them was a man named Godfrey, once a lieutenant, now a captain. He had once had some sympathy for the Indian cause. He had helped save a poor white squaw woman and her fine gray stallion. He had given her a gift of a good bow because she had lost so much at the terrible Washita massacre. But Godfrey hadn't thought of Deborah Graham in years. Twenty-two years, to be exact.

At Little Big Horn Godfrey saw the slaughtered bodies of his comrades. He had looked upon the slain and naked body of his commander, General Custer, lying on a grim hill. It didn't matter that there were no mutilations as had been reported. It didn't matter that Little Big Horn was not a massacre involving women and children. What mattered was that Indians had murdered Godfrey's friends, his comrades, his leader. For that there could be no forgiveness.

So, as several troops of the Seventh Cavalry bore down upon Big Foot's camp, mercy was not foremost on their minds. But neither was battle, for that matter. Like most of the others, Godfrey didn't anticipate a fight. Other than the few seasoned veterans, most of the soldiers in the unit were new recruits who had never been in combat of any kind. They were under orders simply to detain the band, disarm them, and take them to Fort Bennett. Godfrey had no great love for Indians, but after all these years he didn't plan to take out his malice on this band at this particular time.

Still, Big Foot had already slipped away from the army once, causing no end of trouble. The commander of the Seventh Cavalry was not disposed to be as trusting as Sumner had been. Big Foot's white flag was ignored and the commander refused to parley. He would accept only unconditional surrender. There were only about a hundred warriors in Big Foot's band, and they were cold and hungry and tired—not much of a threat.

Godfrey was surprised when the regimental commander, Colonel Forsyth, arrived and actually sent his own surgeon to tend the sick chief. Forsyth even gave Big Foot a tent with a stove in it. What was the world coming to? These were hostiles, for heaven's sake!

But their orders were to escort the band back to their reservation. In the meantime, the Indians were to be disarmed and kept under close watch.

The captives had to be moved to where the remainder of the Seventh was camped. The addition of four more units, bringing the total to four hundred and seventy troops and four Hotchkiss light artillery guns, made certain that the Indians didn't slip away again.

In spite of their weakened physical condition, the Indians were herded together and moved once more—to a place called Wounded Knee Creek.

# 44
# THE LAST DEFEAT

The morning after Big Foot's band made camp near Wounded Knee Creek, a detachment of soldiers surrounded the camp. Others entered the camp in order to disarm the Indians.

Sky watched how the troops were deployed. Obviously, the soldiers were not anticipating any trouble. If they had been, the commander would not have placed his troops in such a way that they'd be vulnerable to gunfire from their own comrades.

The Indian camp had been set up on a flat plain backing a dry ravine that ran into the Wounded Knee Creek. The soldiers made their camp north of the Indian camp about a stone's throw away. Between the Indian camp and the army camp, Forsyth had pitched three or four army tents to house those among the Indians who had no shelter. One of these was the tent with the stove for Big Foot and his family.

The Hotchkiss guns sat on a hill overlooking the bivouac area to the northwest.

After the army distributed rations to the hungry Indians, the warriors, numbering only about a hundred and twenty, were ordered to gather in a cleared square in front of Big Foot's army tent. Big Foot was carried out of his tent on a stretcher and set down among the other warriors.

It worried Sky that the soldiers were separating the warriors from the women and children. Tensions increased, both among the whites and the Indians. Sky felt as if he had truly stepped back into history. It hardly seemed possible that he, who had lived his whole life among white men, was now facing the bluecoat soldiers of his own country, of the United States. His enemies.

When Sky was told that this was the Seventh Cavalry, his blood raced. These were the very men who had killed his father and left his family homeless and destitute. One of these very men might have pulled the trigger that had robbed Blue Sky of the life and love of his father.

Suddenly Sky felt more Cheyenne than he ever had in his life. Memories of a white mother who had loved him faded. The scars of his Sun Dance wounds throbbed, reminding him that he was a Cheyenne warrior, and that at long last he might be blessed with the honor of counting coup upon his enemies.

The soldiers bullied their way into the center of the gathered warriors.

"All right," ordered a captain through an interpreter, "we're here to collect your weapons. I want about twenty of you at a time to go into your tepees and bring out all—y'hear, *all!*—your weapons."

Several soldiers pushed at the first group of Indians, Sky among them. When one of the bluecoats gave him a hard shove, Sky lurched toward him, fire in his eyes. But Tall Bull, who was nearby, restrained Sky.

"Don't be crazy, Blue Sky. We don't have a chance against all these soldiers."

Sky took a deep, shuddering breath, swallowing his ire like poison. So, was he the only one ready to defend himself? Were the others all talk and bluster? They had talked big during the Ghost ceremonies. Had they lost their nerve in the face of the bluecoat show of force? But Sky did as he was told. He wasn't the chief, and even Big Foot was complying.

The Indians returned from the tepees with only two guns. This seemed to enrage the soldiers. A detail moved in to search the tepees. They were like looters with no order or discipline, ransacking the lodges. From inside the lodges came the screams of women and cries of children.

The warriors grew restive, not knowing what might be happening to their wives, sisters, and children. Then, amid the confusion, came the voice of the medicine man, Yellow Bird.

"Remember, my brothers, you need not fear the bluecoats; you wear the magic shirts that will stop the soldiers' bullets. Resist them! Don't let them hurt our wives and children!"

Yellow Bird walked among the warriors blowing his eagle-bone whistle.

"The time of the fulfilling of the prophecies is now! The Great Spirit is with us. If we fight, he will send back our dead as he promised. We have been faithful to his dance, and now we will be rewarded. Your shirt will protect you. Resist!"

Sky listened, entranced. Was his year of devotion to the Ghost Dance about to pay off? Was this the time? Wovoka had said it would be soon. Why not now?

Sky gathered renewed confidence as he remembered the promises of Wovoka. He *felt* the strength of the Ghost Shirt he wore under his blanket. And, as he looked around, he saw in the eyes of his brothers the same confidence. The white man's day in glory was coming to a close. The native peoples would rise again.

The time was now!

---

The soldiers returned from their lengthy search, and, angered at the results, dumped a pile of weapons into the dirt. There were only forty rifles, old pieces that had been used by their grandfathers. They had also gathered anything that even remotely resembled a weapon—axes, cooking knives, even tent stakes. What did the soldiers expect? Sky wondered. Are they disappointed because they had done their job of subjugating the Indians too well?

What the soldiers suspected, but what Sky well knew, was that not all the weapons were in that pile. Many of the warriors carried knives beneath their blankets. Sky felt his own knife resting hard and comfortably beneath his Ghost Shirt. Sky had also seen a few guns, being hidden under shirts and blankets.

"We are strong!" chanted Yellow Bird. "The dead will take up arms with us. Our shirts will protect us."

"Shut that man up!" yelled the captain. Though he couldn't understand Sioux, he was obviously getting unnerved by the medicine man's chanting and that insidious whistle.

A soldier moved toward Yellow Bird, who defiantly kept up his chanting. Just before the soldier reached him, the medicine man grabbed a handful of dirt and threw it into the air as if it were a magic potion.

At that moment, as if Yellow Bird had sent a signal, a young Sioux warrior made his move. He drew the pistol hidden under his blanket and fired.

A soldier fell.

In an instant, the troops guarding the square retaliated with weapons that were not antiques, and which hit their marks with deadly accuracy. They fired into the group of warriors at a range too close to miss. In that first volley of shots no less than half the warriors were killed instantly. The rest of the warriors withdrew

256

their knives to make what defense they could. The odds were tremendously against them, especially when the outer cordon of troops surrounding the camp moved in. But with the soldiers and Indians grappling at such close range, the soldiers' guns were for the most part useless. If they fired, they could hit their own men.

Sky wielded his hunting knife like an extension of his hatred—slashing, thrusting, drawing as much white blood as he could. Soldiers fell around him, but through the sweat dripping in his eyes, he saw that warriors were falling, too. Out of the corner of his eye he saw Tall Bull tussling in the snow-covered ground with a bluecoat.

Sky had no time to think about his brother's safety. He could not even think of survival—that was an impossibility. How could any Indian survive this carnage? Where was the magic of the Ghost Shirts? Why had the dead not come to aid them? But Sky forced even despair from his mind. He must think only of taking as many bluecoats with him as he could.

*"It is not a good thing to live to be an old man!"*

What irony that Stands-in-the-River was not here! He had wanted a fight more than anyone. Sky couldn't be glad that his uncle was safe. The man would be tortured that he had not been there to fight beside his sons, to die with his sons.

But Sky drove all but one thing from his mind.

Revenge! It was the Cheyenne Way, too. And at last Sky could make his father's killers pay.

A soldier had drawn his Colt and was trying to maneuver it so he could fire. Sky grabbed his wrist and brandished his knife. As he backed up, he nearly tripped over something—Big Foot's stretcher. In that moment of imbalance, the soldier was able to position his finger on the Colt's trigger. Sky lost his footing and fell to his knees just as the gun fired. The bullet whizzed over his head, then the soldier fell, knocking Sky to the ground. Tall Bull stood over the soldier, a blood-smeared knife in his hand.

"Thank you, my brother," Sky said as he scrambled to his feet.

He paused for a brief moment to assess Big Foot's condition. The chief had been killed in that first round of gunfire. He, more than anyone, had wanted peace with the whites. He had surrendered and was ready to go with them. Now he had taken the Hanging Road . . . as they all would.

Suddenly, as if the present nightmare were not bad enough, the Hotchkiss guns, planted on a hill overlooking the camp, opened fire. Spitting death at nearly fifty shots a minute, they rained fiery sleet upon the camp. More warriors fell, but many bluecoats fell, too, victims of friendly fire. The bullets ripped into the canvas and hides of the tepees in the Indian camp, killing women and children who were inside. Some fled the tepees and headed toward the ravine in hopes of finding shelter there. But the artillery fire swept the length of the ravine also.

Sky and Tall Bull had been fighting side by side. Tall Bull was wrestling with a soldier, then Sky was driven away by another attack and lost sight of his brother. Fending off soldiers in fierce hand-to-hand combat, Sky tried to locate Tall Bull. At last he saw him, fighting alongside a small group of the remaining warriors. They were trying to break through the line of bluecoats to get to the camp and protect the women and children.

Then suddenly a barrage of artillery struck Tall Bull several times. His body jerked grotesquely, and finally he fell in a bloody pool in the snow.

Sky faltered momentarily. He had wanted to fight side by side with his friend, but he hadn't considered how it might end. He had seen only the glory. Now all he saw was the sight of Tall Bull ripped apart by the deadly gun. It filled his vision like a stain. And in that instant Sky saw everything—the field of death, the fallen bodies, the slaughter.

*O Great Spirit! Come to us. We need you. Save—*

Sky's silent prayer was cut off by bluecoat gunfire. Like an answer, one bullet exploded in Sky's back, spinning him around. Another creased his skull, bringing darkness and oblivion.

# 45

# AFTERMATH

An Indian ran up the side of the ravine, dodging the rapid-fire artillery. Godfrey raised his rifle and fired. The Indian jerked back, then tumbled to the bottom of the ravine. As the body rolled down, the Indian's blanket fell away. A woman.

Godfrey gasped. How many other women had he killed? It was so hard to tell when they were wrapped in their blankets. But would it have mattered? The men had to know they were not just killing warriors. *He* should have known. And what of the children? They certainly could not have been mistaken for warriors.

But in the confusion and passion of battle, sometimes—

No! There was no excuse for what was happening here today. Like the others, Godfrey had gotten carried away. He had allowed too much bitterness to build up after Little Big Horn. He had allowed that single defeat to make him forget all the other army victories. He had forgotten Washita. And because of that he, like his comrades, was allowing another Washita to happen. Suddenly he remembered the old saying: *He who forgets history is doomed to repeat it.*

Doomed, indeed.

Godfrey turned in his saddle as three soldiers were about to fire on a retreating trio of Indians.

"Stop!" he shouted. "Those are civilians."

The soldiers gave him dumbfounded looks. When did that start to matter?

In spite of the sick ache in his stomach, Godfrey felt a little better. He had found his humanity at last in all the slaughter. But it was too late. The massacre was nearly over. Already the gunfire was diminishing. All that could be done now was to salvage what they could, find the wounded and get them tended to.

He glanced up at the sky. Ominous clouds were banking up. Bad weather was on its way. If there were survivors, they would surely die if they were not found. So, even as some soldiers were still hunting down and killing fleeing Indians, Godfrey began the dreadful task of examining bodies, looking for wounded.

Snow started to fall as wagons were loaded with survivors. Thirty-one dead soldiers were found and loaded to be buried later. The Indians were harder to count, for many wounded had probably crawled away, hoping to hide until the soldiers left. But in so doing they sealed their own fate. They would die in the blizzard that was coming. Only fifty-one Indian survivors, all wounded, were found by the soldiers that day. Fifty-one out of three hundred and seventy. And only a handful of these were warriors.

———

Sky briefly regained consciousness and tried to move. He lifted his head off the icy ground, but the pain was too great for any more movement. He fell back into the snow.

Suddenly he saw the blurred image of a bluecoat hovering over him.

Where was his knife?

"Here's one that's alive!" the bluecoat shouted.

Sky groped about on the ground with his hand. He touched something cold—the blade of his knife! But his hands were frozen and would not obey his mind's command to grasp the weapon. He could do nothing when two bluecoats grabbed him, one taking his feet and the other grasping him under the armpits. They hoisted him up from the ground as if he were a side of beef. Then they dumped him in the back of a wagon, and darkness closed in again.

When he next woke he was—

No, he must be dreaming. A huge cross filled his vision, glowing like an apparition, taunting him, reminding him of his folly. He closed his eyes. If this was reality, he couldn't stand it. If it was a dream, it was but a prelude to a nightmare.

Much later he opened his eyes again. The dreamlike quality was removed by sunlight streaming in through windows. He saw the image he had seen before, and it was no apparition at all, but a large wooden cross on a table with a lamp sitting beneath it. Two of the windows on either side of the cross were stained glass.

He was in a church.

Sky's gaze swept the room. Several pews had been pushed back against the walls, and straw had been scattered over the open area. Blankets had been put down to receive the wounded. He estimated about forty Indians lying on the makeshift beds. Most were women and a few children.

Groaning, Sky shut his eyes, but he couldn't shut out the persistent images of the terrible battle—not only the slaughter of his friends, his people, but his own killing as well. How many coup had he counted in the fight? Somehow it didn't seem to matter anymore. There had been no thrill in it, no glory. Some white men were no doubt dead by his hand, yet it had done no good. It hadn't brought back his father—none of the old Cheyenne had come to the rescue as promised.

And the only true friend Sky had ever known was gone. *Oh, Tall Bull, we should have listened to you!* he thought. *Yours was the only voice of reason. Instead, I lead you to your death.*

Sky's thoughts were interrupted when a woman came to tend his wounds. They weren't serious, she said. A bullet had gone clean through the fleshy part of his back. Another had struck him in the head. It had probably proved his salvation, because it had knocked him unconscious, removing him from the battle before another bullet had the chance to kill him.

Sky wasn't grateful.

So, he was spared. For what? What did he have left? Human Beings had not been the only casualties in that fight. They had also lost the last hope of the Indian people. That's what came of putting your faith in—in anything. Sky still had his Ghost Shirt on, split in half from where someone had tended his wounds. It was covered with blood, and he looked down and saw the hole in the front where one of the bullets had exited.

There was no God. There was no Great Spirit. If there was, he must be the cruelest or weakest entity in the world. But he couldn't blame God. *He* was the one who had been foolish enough to believe.

Never again!

But what was left, then? He was too worthless to believe in himself. Why believe in anything? The answer to that question came quickly, for Sky had grown up in a home filled with faith. Belief brought hope.

But it didn't matter. He no longer cared.

--------

The next day when Stands-in-the-River found him, Sky was a far different young man than the one who had eagerly ridden north seeking to be a Cheyenne warrior.

Sky's uncle was a different man, too. He was as completely broken as a bag of useless bones. His proud shoulders were slumped, his once fierce eyes were glazed.

Stands-in-the-River could not even muster much enthusiasm when he said, "Blue Sky, I found you."

Sky's tone was just as lacking in effect. "I'm glad."

"All my children are dead except you, Blue Sky."

I wish I were dead, too, Sky thought. The only thing that can possibly bring joy to my life would be traveling the Hanging Road. But I can't even believe in that anymore.

Sky lifted haunted eyes toward his uncle. "Nothing lives long, only—" But the rest of the Cheyenne dirge caught in his throat.

Stands-in-the-River dropped to his knees by Sky's bed, laid his head across Sky's chest, and wept.

*Nothing lives long, only the mountains and the trees. Joy is dead, purpose is dead, hope is dead. But the trees still reach tall and strong up to the Milky Way. The mountains, with rock-hard security, stand imperturbable.*

If only I could be a strong tree or a hard mountain! Sky cried inwardly. I would bend with the wind and not break, I would deflect the pelting rain, and the ice of winter would melt off my stalwart back.

*But I am only a man. I have crumbled and eroded. I have broken like straw.*

# 46

# DEBORAH
# AND SKY

Rose jerked awake, hearing awful, shuddering sounds. Cries of distress. Sky's cries.

Looking across the lodge to where her husband lay, she saw him toss and turn violently in his bed.

"Go away!" he moaned. "Don't kill us!" Then, in a desperate shout, "No!"

He sat up in his bed, panting as if he had been running. Rose threw back her covers and rushed to him.

"Blue Sky," she whispered softly, soothingly. She put an arm around him, and though it was deep winter outside, he was drenched with sweat, and trembling. "It's only a dream," she murmured.

He looked at her with wide eyes as if he feared it wasn't true. Then he slumped against her. "They've come back! The nightmares! Billy!"

He wept in her arms—the first time she had ever seen him cry, and she was certain the first time he had cried since Wounded Knee.

Rose embraced Sky with all the love and concern in her heart. Word of the massacre at Wounded Knee had preceded Sky's arrival. She expected there would be pain in his blue eyes, both from the physical wounds and the emotional. She was prepared to comfort a mourning man. Nothing could have prepared her for the empty shell that greeted her.

Bitterness, anger, hatred, tears—all would have been preferable. But except during his nightmares, he gave no indication of his deep grief.

"Rose," Sky had said when he had greeted her upon arriving home, "it's been a long journey. I'm starved. Is dinner ready?"

In the days that followed, she tried everything to get him to talk, to express his grief. But he said nothing, talking only when required. It was as if Wounded Knee had never happened. In a way, Rose welcomed the nightmares. She feared he might explode by holding so much in. At least at night he was able to release something, though he never mentioned the nightmares or thanked her for her comfort in the night.

She talked to Gray Antelope about it. After all, the old Cheyenne woman had been through her share of battles and massacres.

"It's different for women," Gray Antelope said. "We are grateful if we have escaped and if our loved ones have escaped. If they don't, we naturally grieve. But the warriors who survive must live with the shame that they didn't die with their brothers. In the old days, the hope of revenge roused them from their shame. There was always another battle to be fought. But Blue Sky and his uncle do not even have that hope to spur them on. There will be no more battles, no more victories, no more chance of revenge. They lost everything a Cheyenne warrior has on that Wounded Knee battlefield."

"What can be done, then, Nahkoa?"

"Pray for him."

"I have, but it doesn't seem to help."

"Give God time, little one."

———————

An outbreak of influenza that winter deterred Rose from her prayers. She became very ill with the sickness and lost her unborn baby.

Sky was not at her side when her fever finally broke and she recovered from the state of delirium that had held her for a week. His absence was almost more despairing than the loss of her child. She could have other babies, but not if her husband truly did not love her, did not even care enough to stand vigil at her bedside.

When he finally did return to the lodge, he was drunk.

"You look better," Sky said with as much concern as his slurred voice could contain.

"I lost our baby."

"Good. This is no world to bring a kid into."

"Oh, Blue Sky!" Tears streamed down Rose's face. "I would have loved him because he was yours."

"Him?"

She nodded. For the first time since he had returned from the Dakotas, Rose saw something akin to emotion flicker across her husband's face.

"Oh, God . . ." he whispered. Then he shook his head bitterly. "What am I saying? This is proof that there is no God."

"I'm sorry, Blue Sky."

"Don't be sorry. I'm glad, do you understand? I want no sons. I want no children. You don't have to worry about me touching you again."

He left the tepee, and she didn't see him for two days. He was drunk again. And from then on, he seemed always to be in some stage of inebriation. She came close to real hatred toward Stands-in-the-River. He usually supplied Sky with whiskey, and he often went out drinking with Sky.

Many of the Cheyenne continued with their Ghost Dancing. These had never believed in the immediate fulfillment of the prophecies. To them the ceremony represented a hope for the future, not unlike the Christian's hope of Heaven. But Sky never again joined the Ghost Dancers.

Rose had never much liked the dancing, but at least then Sky had been vital, a man of purpose and meaning. Now, if he found hope anywhere, it seemed to be in a bottle of whiskey.

She tried to get him to attend church with her, but he'd have absolutely none of that. And because Gray Antelope advised that it might not be good to press him too much, Rose eventually stopped asking him. Sometimes it seemed as if her prayers were only making things worse. The preacher at the church in Darlington talked about giving thanks to God in everything, but Rose had a very hard time being thankful for Sky's emptiness, his purposelessness, his drunkenness.

One day as the spring of 1891 began to appear, Rose was visiting with Gray Antelope, talking about the old times. Gray Antelope wasn't one to dwell on the past, but she did enjoy telling youngsters of her life and experiences. She was relating a story of something that had happened when Sky's mother had lived with the Cheyenne.

"We were picking berries in a grove of cottonwoods," Gray Antelope said. "It was summer, and the berries were sweet and big. Wind Rider made the great discovery first. Hidden in the tangle of berry bushes and grass, we found a baby mountain lion. I said we must hurry away because the mother might come back and attack us, but Wind Rider said it looked just like a kitten she had when she was a little girl on her farm in Virginia. She wanted to take it for a pet. I had never heard of such a thing. Dogs were good pets—if you had to, you could eat them, and they were useful in warning of the approach of danger. But what could a cat do?

"Anyway, I convinced her to leave the animal alone. But the next day—we couldn't help ourselves—we looked in the place again. The animal was still there. I was sure then that its mother would not return. Since the poor baby was probably starving, I said it would be a good thing to take it. Wind Rider took as good care of that animal as she did her own babies. Then, when it was strong enough, she let it go back to the wild, and we wept at its release. Imagine, growing so fond of a cat! The creature was completely useless, but somehow it made us feel good."

"I saw a cat in New York City," said Rose, "when I was with the Wild West Show. It was in an alley, and I could see it had no home. It let me get close enough to touch its fur and hear its purring sound. Then it darted away and I never saw it again. Strange animals."

"Maybe now that I have a house with walls and will move around no more, I will find one of these creatures Wind Rider called kittens."

Rose smiled. "You know what I liked best about your story, Nahkoa? I liked to hear of the peaceful times of long ago. Too often we count the passing of time by battles and death. The everyday times are the ones I like best."

"There were more of those than the others—too bad we don't remember them as well."

They were silent for a while, and Rose thought of what she knew of Sky and his mother and father. There had been many months of happy times between the battles, although Sky seemed to have no memory of these.

Then an idea struck Rose. "Nahkoa, you won't believe what I thought of. I think it's really possible, too. It wouldn't take much. A letter, perhaps. Of course, a telegram would be faster. I wonder how much such a thing costs—"

"Hold on, child!" Gray Antelope laughed. "What are you talking about?"

"Nahkoa, I know what Blue Sky needs. She who could tame a mountain lion cub could bring hope to my husband's heart."

266

"You speak of Wind Rider?"

"Yes! If we wrote to her, I know she would come to see her son."

"He has made it clear he wants no one to know where he is."

"Once he sees his mother, he will thank me. Oh, Nahkoa, I think it's worth the risk. Can you tell me she wouldn't give him the love and comfort he needs?"

Gray Antelope shook her head. "I can think of no one who could do it better."

"I'll write her a letter today. I think I've learned enough to spell the words properly."

"A letter is too slow. I have a little money put away; you can use it for a telegram."

The next day Rose went to Darlington, and the clerk at the telegraph office helped her with the words she couldn't spell. The telegram was sent, then the waiting began. But Sky's mother must have wasted no time in making her reply, for Rose received an answer in three days. Deborah Killion would arrive in Darlington by train in another three days. She must have left home while her response was still en route.

Rose wanted to surprise Sky, but he happened to be in Darlington with his drinking friends, and when the telegram from Deborah arrived, the clerk gave it to him. He was furious.

"How could you? You know how I feel about this!"

"But, Blue Sky, you must want to see your mother. It's been many years—"

"I'll decide what I want!"

He left the camp that day and didn't return.

————

Sky spent the next two weeks in the hills, living off game and whatever roots and wild berries he could find. It had been nearly six years since he last saw his mother, but she had never been far from his thoughts.

Even a grown man needs a mother's love, and many times Sky wished he were a little boy again and could rest in her embrace and receive her love and comfort. He would have given almost anything to see her and talk to her again. Anything but his pride.

He simply could not let her see what he had become. He knew she would love and accept him, but his reticence sprang from his own inadequacies. Twice while Deborah was in the camp, he crept close in hopes of getting a look at her. Once, he saw Deborah and Rose strolling along the bank of the creek, talking. Even from a distance he could see an easy amiability between them. He wondered if they were talking about him. Surely they must be—if not then, at some time. What had Rose told his mother?

So much for his pride. His wife had probably revealed his darkest side. But still, he could not face her.

On the day she was scheduled to leave, Sky went to Darlington. After being bolstered by a few drinks, he went to the train station to look for her. She arrived on horseback with Rose, and he watched covertly as they dismounted, checked in Deborah's carpetbag, and sat on a bench to await the train. At last he found within himself a speck of courage and made his way toward them, shambling and swaying a bit.

"Hi, Ma," he said sheepishly.

"Sky!" Deborah jumped up and would have embraced him, but he stepped back and took her hand instead.

He could not accept the love she had to offer. Besides, if she got too close she'd probably be able to smell the alcohol on his breath.

"Sorry I missed your visit," he said.

"I was disappointed."

"Well, there was just things to do, you know how it is."

She nodded, but he could tell she didn't understand at all. Even he didn't understand, and he wished now he had stayed away completely.

"There's so much we need to catch up on," Deborah said.

"That's okay. I'll write you a letter." They both knew he would never do that.

"I can stay a few more days."

"Naw. Sam's probably expecting you. It's my fault. I don't—" He stopped. He had been about to say he didn't deserve for her to change her plans for him. But that was getting too personal, too revealing. "No, you get on your train. I just thought the least I could do is say hi."

"Sky, I came to see you, to spend time with you. I've missed you, son."

"It's been a long time, huh?"

"Too long."

"We'll try to get down your way sometime," he said. It was so easy to make false promises.

Then the train whistle blasted as the big engine roared into the station. For a moment the noise of its arrival dominated every-thing.

When it quieted down, Deborah said, "I don't have to go."

"Yeah, Ma, you do. It's best that way. You can't do me no good."

"I don't believe that, Sky."

"You better get aboard."

"Well, I'm not leaving until you give me a hug!"

She took a step toward him, and Sky backed off.

"I can already tell you've been drinking, Sky," Deborah said. "It doesn't matter to me. I just have to touch you. You're my son. I love you!"

He couldn't deny her that; he had already been cruel and self-ish enough. But he couldn't tarry as long in her tender, accepting embrace as he would have liked. The emotion that had been so close to the surface during the entire encounter was about to get out of control.

The moment she dropped her arms, he said a quick, choked goodbye, then stumbled away. He turned once before he was out of sight and saw her board the train. He heard the train rumble away. And as the sound of his mother's departure echoed in his ears, tears spilled from his eyes.

# 47

# FIREWATER

Sky found the man who sold the Indians firewater and paid his last coins for a bottle. He went off to a place just outside town where some boulders made a secluded spot and drank alone. He hoped the liquor would numb the awful desolation he felt. But instead it just seemed to make him angry and sullen. He was angry at his mother for coming and making him feel this way. He was angry at Rose for interfering. He was angry at himself for—everything else.

He was glad when he saw his uncle ride by. This wasn't a good time for him to drink alone.

"Hey, Nehuo!" Sky called, rising from his hiding place. He held up the bottle as an invitation.

"Just what I was looking for," Stands-in-the-River replied as he dismounted.

They shared the bottle as they talked.

"So, the white squaw woman is gone," said Stands-in-the-River.

"Yeah. Did you see her?"

"Once. But like you, I stayed away when I could."

"What'd she say when you saw her?"

Stands-in-the-River screwed up his face in deep thought, then scratched his head. "I can't remember. I was drunk."

"Oh, well, she probably just would have preached at us—all that God-talk. I don't need that."

Sky's uncle shook his head. "That's not why I stayed away." He took a swig off the bottle. "Wind Rider Woman has strong medicine. She always did."

"What do you mean?"

"I think she walks side by side with the Great Spirit. I think she is part of the great circle of life. And maybe if we hold her hand the circle that the white man broke will somehow be mended."

"You're talking foolishness, Nehuo. Have another drink."

They finished the bottle. It had been a small bottle for which the peddler had charged as much as for a big bottle. Sky and his uncle mounted their horses and returned to town for more.

After they completed their transaction with the peddler, Sky said, "I'm hungry. You got anything to eat with you, Nehuo?"

Stands-in-the-River shook his head. "But I got more money."

"Where'd you get all that money, Nehuo?"

"A white man saw my Ghost Shirt. Said he'd pay me good for it. It was good for nothing, so I took it off and gave it to him. Got me five dollars for it."

"Wish I'd known. They took mine off at the hospital and kept it." A shadow momentarily darkened Sky's face. "It was all bloody anyway."

"Come on, son, we will get some food at the store."

Shopping at the store wasn't a common occurrence for the Cheyenne on the reservation. They seldom had money for such a luxury. Most of their goods they received from the agency. However, two other Indians were already in the store—a man and his wife—plus a white man and two white women.

Sky was browsing around, looking at the big barrels by the counter. One barrel was filled with apples, another with pickles, and yet another with hard biscuits. A meal fit for a king. His attention, however, was diverted to a scene at the counter. The two Indians had come up to the counter with their purchase—an iron kettle with a handle. The clerk looked right at them, then continued with some paperwork he was doing. The Indians waited patiently. Then a white woman came up with some items.

"Howdy, ma'am," the clerk said with a smile. He took the items. "Anything else for you?"

"Yes, I want a length of calico. The green one, the second bolt from the top."

"Right away, ma'am."

Sky couldn't believe how patiently the Indians were accepting this. "Hey!" Sky said. "Those Indians were next, you know."

"I beg your pardon?" The clerk was clearly annoyed.

"You looked right at 'em and ignored them."

"I'll thank you not to tell me how to run my store." The clerk turned to get the fabric.

The Cheyenne man looked at Sky and silently shook his head.

His eyes said, *Please, don't start trouble.*

Sky shrugged and returned to his browsing. The white woman paid for her purchases. Then, with deliberate slowness, the clerk gave his attention to the Indians.

The man put the kettle on the counter.

"That'll be one dollar," said the clerk.

Sky thought that was an exorbitant amount. He glanced toward the shelf where the kettles were kept. Sure enough, a card by the kettles read "thirty-five cents."

Since Wounded Knee, Sky had paid little or no attention to the injustices on the reservation. It was more his surly mood than any sense of righteous indignation that made him speak up.

"Hey! Those kettles don't cost that much," Sky said.

"Listen here, no Injun is going to talk to me that way," warned the clerk. "You keep in your place or I'll eject you from my store."

The clerk stepped out from behind his counter. Sky thought he was about to be thrown out, but the clerk, who was half a foot shorter than Sky and twenty pounds lighter, didn't dare. Instead, the clerk went to the kettle shelf and took down the sign.

"Those kettles were on sale," said the clerk. "I forgot to take down the sign."

It was obvious the faded sign had been in place for months, maybe years.

Sky started toward the man, but Stands-in-the-River sidled up to him and laid a restraining hand on his arm.

"Let's go," he said. "I'm not hungry anymore."

Sky wrenched his arm free with more force than was necessary. Suddenly he wanted to hurt a white man, and this clerk seemed to stand for all Sky despised. He stalked toward the hapless man and grabbed his starched collar.

"You're a dirty cheat!" Sky yelled.

By now the other white man in the store was aware of the trouble. He hurried to the clerk's aid. Sky wanted to laugh in their white faces. If he had a weapon he could have easily killed them both. As it was, he was perfectly ready to take them on with his fists.

Stands-in-the-River and the other Cheyenne man tried to pull Sky back. He struggled against their restraint.

"Leave me alone!" he shouted. "I can take 'em."

In the meantime, the clerk grabbed a broom and struck Sky with the handle. He also told one of the white women to fetch the sheriff.

"Please," the Cheyenne man begged the clerk. "We get him out and there be no more trouble. He is young—you know how that is."

"I'll see all you dirty Injuns thrown in jail!"

When the sheriff arrived and got to the bottom of the situation, Sky was led off to jail, where he spent three days.

When the sheriff released him, he gave Sky a stern warning. "You get in trouble again and you'll get more than three days, understand? And the same if I find you drunk again."

Sky just scowled at the sheriff and sulked away. He had just spent three of the most miserable days of his life. Three days without whiskey. All he could think of was where to get some—fast.

He couldn't find the whiskey peddler. He didn't have any money, but he hoped he might get some on credit. But the fellow had been discovered and driven out of town. That's usually how it was. The whites ignored the illegal whiskey peddling because of the profit it brought. But when there was the least bit of trouble in which an Indian was involved, the citizens got on a righteous bandwagon to rid the town of evil firewater.

Sky returned to camp. He hadn't seen his wife in days, but it was Stands-in-the-River who he sought first. The last time he had seen his uncle, he had a new bottle of whiskey. Maybe there was some left.

Sky was lucky. The incident in town had shaken Stands-in-the-River enough to go on the wagon for a while. More than half a bottle was left.

"You sure you want this, Blue Sky? The white man's prison must not have been too bad, then."

"The white's man jail was miserable. But they ain't gonna take away the only pleasure I got left. Gimme the bottle."

Stands-in-the-River couldn't argue with that. Sky was right. What else did they have left? He handed over the whiskey, and Sky took the bottle into the woods by the creek and made up for lost time.

# 48

# THE GIFT

As summer approached, Rose became more and more excited about the changes coming to the reservation. There were still some Cheyenne who opposed the allotments. Old Crow and a few of his followers still refused to sign the enrollment. Rose had nothing against tradition, but there was something to be said for progress, too. And, regardless of how anyone felt, progress was going to come. The Indian people had to accept the inevitable if they wanted to succeed.

The communal life of the village was all she had ever known, and it was a good life. But in order to survive and live well in the white man's world, she had to adjust to the white man's ways. She could cling to the old ways if she wanted to stay hungry and poor, but Rose wanted a better life than that. Perhaps she had been among the whites too much, but she thought some of their ways were good, too. Like Gray Antelope, she was drawn to the idea of a home with walls that stayed where they were placed. She liked the prospect of having a little garden next to that house. She liked the fact that it would be all hers, and that by *her* labor it could prosper or fail.

She wasn't surprised that Sky showed no interest in any of it. He no longer opposed it—he just didn't care. But he didn't care about anything these days, except that his supply of whiskey didn't run out. Rose was successful in getting him to enroll for his allotment. He had been drunk that day and didn't know what he was signing. He'd heard there was money involved, and that sounded good because he needed money to buy whiskey.

Rose could not find Sky when the agents came to take them to pick out their land. It was just as well. He would have chosen a tract near the closest supply of firewater. Rose and Little Left Hand

274

chose the land, a pretty piece in the valley of the Washita River. With the three allotments—hers, Sky's, and Little Left Hand's—they would have four hundred eighty acres, part crop land, part grazing. Much to Rose's surprise, Stands-in-the-River chose his and his wife's allotments adjacent to theirs.

"When I die, Blue Sky will have my land. It is the right thing, for he is my only living child."

Rose was sad for the broken old man who had lost so much. But she couldn't help calculating the total of the combined allotments—eight hundred acres! If they worked hard, they could make a truly good life for themselves.

If only she could get Sky to rise out of his terrible depression and take an interest in life. To make anything of this land she needed him. Stands-in-the-River and Little Left Hand were too old to put in the kind of labor it would take to make it prosper.

In July, the first of the money for the unalloted reservation lands was distributed among the Indians. Rose had never seen so much money in her life—over two hundred dollars, counting hers and Sky's and Little Left Hand's. Most of the money she put into the bank to save for the day when they would need to buy seed and livestock for their land. Some of her friends thought her crazy for using the bank—just giving her money back to the white man! But she had learned about banks while on tour with the Wild West Show and already had a little stashed away. For putting her money in the bank, the white banker would give her extra money back, which he called interest. And then the temptation of squandering the money would be gone. So many of the other Cheyenne had gone out and spent their money foolishly. Some had been cheated by unscrupulous merchants. Rose wasn't going to let that happen with her money.

And she wouldn't allow Sky to get his hands on the money and spend it on firewater. She did have one extravagant purchase she wanted to make, though. When she discussed it with her father, he said it was a wise idea.

"It may be like buying medicine for your unhappy husband," he told her. "A potion that might fix his damaged heart."

She went to Darlington and ordered it from a catalog. It would take a long time to arrive, and Rose was not very patient. She checked at the store every time she went to town. But she told the storekeeper that under no circumstances was he to give it to Sky when it arrived. It was to be a surprise.

Two months after she placed her order, the package arrived.

She took it home, then waited anxiously the rest of the day for Sky to get home. That morning he had left saying he was going hunting. She hoped he was telling the truth and that he came home sober.

Unfortunately, the men on the reservation could no longer support their families by hunting. Since game was so scarce, hunting was merely a diversion. Farming was considered women's work and demeaning for a warrior. So many of the men just collected their annuities, drank firewater, and stewed over the past glory days. She had yet to get Sky to take an interest in the allotment. The government had offered to loan the use of plows and other tools for the first couple of seasons. But nothing had been done beyond a small patch Little Left Hand had planted with her help.

Rose hoped that her surprise would give Sky something more to occupy himself with, at least until he got a desire to work the land. He needed something meaningful to take his mind off whiskey. She prayed God would use her gift like a healing potion for her husband.

Sky came home that evening empty-handed. He dropped his bow carelessly in a corner of the lodge. If he had gone hunting, he had not stayed at that task the entire day. He reeked strongly of alcohol.

Rose considered waiting for a better day to present her surprise, but she had been waiting so long already. Besides, she had discovered from Deborah that Sky's twenty-fourth birthday would be soon, and she thought it would make her presentation that much more meaningful. Most of all, she couldn't wait simply because she was counting on this gift being what Sky needed to make him feel better, to make him happy again. So, despite an inner urge for caution, she rushed forward.

"Hello, Blue Sky. I'm glad you're home early. I have a special meal planned."

"Well, don't expect meat."

"We have fish from the creek."

"You goin' out fishing now? Is that what it's come to?"

She tried to ignore his slurred, harsh voice. "One of the boys caught some and gave it to us."

"I see . . . takin' handouts."

"Come and sit down, Blue Sky." She nudged him gently to a place on the hide.

Sky looked around. "Where's your father?"

"He is visiting neighbors."

Sky's eyes narrowed. Was he thinking she was going to seduce him as he had seduced her once before when Little Left Hand had gone to visit neighbors? Rose restrained a smile. How she would like that! To feel his embrace and his love, or at least his affection, as she had felt that other time. But it wouldn't be the same, not with him so drunk he probably would have no idea what he was doing.

"Blue Sky, I have something for you."

"Yeah, what?"

She retrieved the package, so large she had to carry it in both arms. She set it down next to him and grinned as if her gift had already done its good work and her life was as she hoped and dreamed it would be.

"Go ahead, open it," she urged.

"I don't have nothin' for you," he said. "I never gave you a gift."

"You gave me Sam's Bible."

"That doesn't count; it was just some old thing I wanted to get rid of."

"Well, it doesn't matter. Someday I'm sure you will give me something. Now, open it up before I burst."

"Where'd you get the money—?"

"Blue Sky, I have heard the saying, 'Never look a gift horse in the mouth.' Just open it."

She stooped down and helped the process along by cutting away the string and loosening the paper. When he still did nothing, she opened it entirely herself and gazed proudly at the contents.

The black case was more sleek than in the catalog. She unbuckled the clasps and lifted the lid. She took her own eyes off the polished new guitar inside just long enough to observe Sky's reaction.

At first he stared blankly, then he frowned slightly. "What is this, woman?"

"I'm sure it hasn't been so long that you have forgotten. I thought it might bring happiness to you as it used to do in the past."

"This must've cost a fortune."

"I would pay anything for you to be happy again." From a table she picked up something else and handed it to him. It was a beaded strap she had been working on in secret since the day she ordered the guitar.

Sky gave her a pained expression as if her caring had hurt him, as if the thought of happiness hurt. He didn't take the strap, but he did reach down briefly and touch the shiny finish of the instrument.

Suddenly he jumped up. If there had been any magic in the moment, it was now lost. He glared at her with accusation in his eyes.

"Where'd you get the money to buy something like this?" he said, his voice rising. "We're starving, and you're squandering our money foolishly!"

"Foolishly?"

"That's right. But why not? Everyone else does. You're just another Injun who doesn't know no better than to buy stupid white man trinkets."

"You don't need to speak that way to me, Blue Sky. I was trying to do something special for you." Her lip quivered as she spoke.

"With this?" He kicked at the case. "I coulda found better things to do with the money."

*To buy whiskey?* she wanted to say, but she held her tongue. She also bit back her rising tears.

"Well, it's done now," she said stoically.

"I still want to know where the money came from," he demanded.

"What does it matter?"

"I'm still the husband in this lodge! The whites can't take all my manhood from me. I'm still in charge of you—and you can't—"

"I just wanted to do something good."

"Well, you did something stupid instead. Now, where did it come from?"

"Some of our money from the government came—"

"And you spent it on this!"

"Only some. The rest is put away."

"Oh, yeah! Who gave you the right to do that?" He was yelling now. The sound made Rose wince.

But even as she tried to defend her actions she realized he was probably right. She had taken over his husbandly duties. She had never thought how that might make him feel. He had lost so much already, and now she had taken something else from him. She had wanted to help, but instead she had only made things worse.

"I'm sorry, Blue Sky. I didn't think."

"Well, you're a bossy, stupid woman, and I'm sick of it!"

"Blue Sky . . ." The rest of her words choked on a sob.

"Don't think crying will help you now."

278

Her tears spilled unchecked. "Please—"

"Stop that. It ain't gonna help."

"I'm . . . I'm . . . trying. . . ." But she could not control it. All the pain and repressed emotions of her unhappy marriage flooded out in bitter weeping.

"I said stop!" he screamed.

Then he struck her.

Rose stumbled back with the force of the blow. When she lifted her hand to her lip, she felt blood. She stared with horror at her husband. But Sky was as shocked as she was, perhaps even more so. He looked at his hand as if it held a smoking gun.

Then he turned and fled the lodge.

# 49

# TWO LOVES

Sky spent the night in the hills, sleeping on the grass. When he awoke the next morning, sweating under the sweltering September sun, the events of the previous night were hazy. Unfortunately, they weren't hazy enough.

Had he actually hit Rose? He looked at his hand, and it seemed as if it still stung with the horrible deed. What kind of man would do such a thing?

A drunken fool.

He tried to think of excuses. After all, he'd been through a lot in his life. Rejection and failure and disappointment and loss. Especially loss . . . starting with his father. What man would be strong enough to take the raw deal that had been handed to him? He was bound to break. It had started happening long before Wounded Knee. Maybe it had begun the minute he had let himself believe in the Ghost Dance and hope. Maybe even before then, with Jenny's death. Or when Carolyn had left him friendless and alone, desperate to do anything to be accepted.

Or the day he had been born, marked with blue eyes and dark, ugly skin of a soul that belonged nowhere. His mother should have known better. Or did her own selfish fulfillment mean more to her than the shame of spawning a worthless half-breed?

His mother . . .

Thinking that way only confirmed his complete depravity. There was not a nobler woman. She had always made it clear that he had been the product of love—complete and pure and total. The kind of love he would never experience. With thoughts of his mother, all his excuses fell apart. Few people had known more pain and loss than she. Yet rather than destroying her, it had ennobled her. How had that happened?

She'd say it was her faith.

"Ma, I'm just not good enough for that kind of faith. I don't have it in me. I've tried to believe, but it never works. Maybe God isn't for half-breeds."

He licked his lips, parched from the hot sun.

"I'll tell you, God, if you did care about me, you'd make a bottle of whiskey appear now."

That's all he believed in anymore.

"I'd sell my soul for a drink of firewater."

He thought about riding to town. He didn't have much money, but with a little resourcefulness he could get what he wanted somehow. Then he remembered Rose and what had happened last night. Like a sharp goad, the memory of her bloodied lip pricked him again. She was too good for him. Not so much for what he had done to her, but because he knew he wouldn't change—he *couldn't* change. The clarity with which he saw things now—and he had only been a few hours without alcohol—was too frightening to want to face more of it. He needed the numbing blur that whiskey gave him. He simply could not survive without it. He couldn't give it up.

And because of that Sky feared a repeat of what he had done to Rose. He didn't want to hurt her, but he was desperate to hurt someone, to make someone pay for all his pain. She was a convenient target.

He knew what he had to do.

———

It was late afternoon as Sky came down from the hills and approached the camp. He paused and looked at the tepees, about thirty of them, scattered up and down the banks of the creek. On the surface it looked peaceful—children playing, dogs romping, women about their household tasks. But Sky knew it was not always as it appeared. Not only for him, but for all the Cheyenne people he had so wanted to be part of.

The Cheyenne camp was dying a slow death. Soon it would be no more, memorialized romantically only by the likes of Buffalo Bill Cody. The Cheyenne would be moving to their allotments, and the community would be dead. That's what the whites had wanted—the individualization of the native peoples, and thus the demise of a society. Give them land ownership and they would become just as self-serving, selfish, and greedy as their pale benefactors.

The American dream achieved.

But what did he care? He had tried both ways and had been chewed up and spit out, not once but twice. Let the camp break up and die. It was nothing to him. He was leaving.

He walked to Little Left Hand's lodge, abruptly pushing aside the tent flap. He was greeted by the startled faces of his wife and father-in-law. Rose's red and puffy eyes told him that she had been crying. He ignored the ache that the sight of her inflicted on him.

"I have come to say goodbye," he said without fanfare.

The startled expressions remained.

"I'll pack a few things," he went on, "and be out of your way quickly."

"Out of our way. . . ?" Rose was making a gallant effort to recover from the shock of this sudden announcement. "You can't do that."

"It's the best way. The only way." Sky found his saddlebags and began loading them with his few belongings.

"Are you doing this because of what happened last night?" Rose asked. "I understand that you . . . weren't yourself. I know it won't happen again."

Sky paused as he placed some tin goods in the bag. "How can you know that? I don't even know. In fact, I'm almost certain it *will* happen again."

"But you don't have to run away. All you have to do is fix the problem that caused it to happen. Don't drink any more firewater."

*All I have to do* . . . She had no concept of what she was asking. She had no idea that she was asking him to stop doing the only thing that was keeping him alive. "Be thankful, Rose, for what I'm doing. You could end up like Stone Teeth Woman."

"Oh, Blue Sky . . ." She bit her trembling lip.

Sky couldn't face her; he turned to his father-in-law instead. "Thank you for everything, Nehuo. I wish I could have done more for you."

"You have been the son I did not have."

"I guess I should consider myself lucky for all the fathers I've had." Sky's voice was dry, lacking any appreciation at all.

Little Left Hand embraced Sky. "I don't like to see you go. You are an important part of the circle of our lives."

"The circle is broken, Nehuo. I think it has been broken for a long time."

"Goodbye, my son. I will leave so you can be alone with Rose."

The old man moved quickly and was gone before Sky could

protest. The last thing he wanted was to be alone with Rose. He finished packing, avoiding her as much as possible in that small space. But in too short a time his saddlebags were full.

"Blue Sky," Rose said finally, "you left your home once and it didn't help. How do you think it will help this time?"

"I didn't say it would help."

"Then why are you doing it?"

"You know why. Don't torture yourself anymore with silly questions."

"I know only that you are my husband, Blue Sky—"

"Don't call me Blue Sky—I'm not worthy of a Cheyenne name."

"I'm afraid you can't change wives like you do names."

Sky did not respond, quietly cinching up the saddlebags. He slung them over his shoulder.

As he attempted to exit, Rose moved in front of him. "Don't go," she pleaded.

He sighed. Why did she have to make this difficult? "You are right about one thing, Rose. I can't leave like this. It wouldn't be right. So, I am divorcing you now."

"What? You can't do it, just like that, without even a witness."

"All right."

Sky left the tepee. Since Little Left Hand was nowhere to be seen, Sky grabbed the nearest man he could find. When they returned to the tepee, he said, "Three Fingers, will you witness the fact that I am divorcing Rose?"

"This is a sad thing," said Three Fingers.

"It's all my fault." Sky felt he had to explain. "She is a good wife. I'm just no good for her."

"I will bear witness then."

Usually, in Cheyenne tradition, a divorce was announced by some token ceremony, often by the husband in the company of his warrior friends. In lieu of that, Sky did the best he could to give it as much veracity as possible. He'd seen only one divorce since he joined the tribe, so he copied what he'd seen. He took a piece of kindling lying by the fire pit, held it up briefly, then threw it into the pit.

"That is my wife," he said. "I throw her away. Any man who wishes to take that stick can have her."

Three Fingers sighed with pity and said to Rose, "Sometimes these things just don't work out." Then he left the tepee.

"Go ahead, then, Sky," Rose said when they were alone. "Run

away. But I will always be your wife."

"Find yourself a husband who is worthy of you."

"I already have."

He shook his head and prepared to leave.

"Wait," said Rose. The guitar lay in the same place he had left it the other night. She picked it up and held it out to him. "Take this with you."

"You keep it and sell it. You can use the money."

"It's not mine, it's yours. Take it."

"I would just sell it to buy whiskey."

"I don't care what you do with it. It belongs to you."

Sky took it. He couldn't bear to hurt her any more than he already had.

Then the time for parting had come. He was glad his hands were full, for he had an almost overwhelming urge to embrace Rose, to hold her one more time, to feel her strong love, a love he knew he'd never feel again. If only he had been able to love her in return. If only that empty ache he felt at the prospect of leaving her was love. But it couldn't be. He wasn't capable of loving anything as much as he loved whiskey.

# PART 4

# WINTER 1893

# 50

# WANDERER

Sky couldn't remember the name of this town. Even if his mind hadn't been clouded with alcohol, he had been to so many towns they had all begun to blur together.

If oblivion was what he had been seeking when he left the reservation a year and a half ago, he had reached his goal. Whiskey simply numbed the despair that constantly dogged him. The perpetual stupor kept him from thinking about what his life had become. He drifted from town to town, earning just enough money to buy whiskey and the barest minimum of food and shelter to keep alive. Always alone, never fitting in, often the brunt of hate and bigotry. He couldn't remember the last time he'd had a real conversation with someone, or received a kind word or a gentle touch.

Winter was the worst time. Sky had been both a Cheyenne warrior and a Texas cowboy, and he knew how to take care of himself. He could hunt, and he knew how to make a good camp, even in the snow. He had learned from experts how to survive in the wilds. But no one had ever taught him how to get whiskey from nature.

That first winter he had managed fairly well. But as drinking became more and more important to him, he cared less about anything else. Finally, he had resigned himself to staying close to civilization, where there was access to liquor.

The present winter was proving harder than he expected. His health had deteriorated, and his spirits were low. He hadn't been able to hold down a job longer than a week, and the jobs he did find were hardly worth the effort—sweeping out stables and saloons, mostly. A couple of times he worked as a mercantile stockboy, and he often played his guitar for pennies.

When the cold weather came on, he tried to be more responsible, mainly for his own survival. One job, sweeping a general store and loading and unloading merchandise, he had held for two weeks. He had cut back on his drinking, only getting drunk two or three evenings a week. Then he got involved in a card game, gambled away all his money, and ended up breaking into the store, where he stole fifty cents for some whiskey. He was caught trying to exit the store. His boss felt sorry for him and didn't press charges, but he made Sky leave town.

Winter was no lark in Nebraska where his travels had now taken him. He traveled on foot through knee-deep snow, his moccasined feet as numb as his brain. He had been out in the weather for two days trying to find a place to settle for a while. He had been run out of the last town he came to—for no other reason than that he looked like trouble. When he stole a drink from a jug he found on a farm, the farmer had chased him off his property at gunpoint. Another farmer had given him a loaf of bread before shooing him away. One night a homesteader had let him sleep in his barn. The second night, when the temperature had fallen below zero and Sky wondered if he was going to have to spend that freezing night out in the open, a Mennonite family had actually let him stay in their home.

But no one would give him whiskey.

It was a freezing March evening when he walked into Riverbend. He no longer had a horse. Poor Two-Tone had nearly frozen to death last winter, and out of sympathy and humanity Sky had sold the animal to someone he hoped would care for it better than he. That had dampened any thoughts Sky might have had of traveling to more distant parts. It wasn't like the old days when he had been young and eager and able to hitch up with the likes of Bill Cody. No one wanted anything to do with a drunken Indian. He was only twenty-five, but he felt like a hopeless old man with more of his life behind him than ahead.

The Saturday night crowd at the Riverbend Saloon was boisterous. One of the local farmhands was getting married, and he and several of his buddies were kicking up their heels before the big day. The saloon girls were busy, the gambling tables were full, and the beer and whiskey were flowing freely.

The bartender was a balding man in his fifties, tall, with a once-muscular frame that was quickly turning to flab. Sweat beaded on his forehead as he worked briskly to keep up with the trade.

"I'm looking for work," said Sky.

"What kind of work?"

288

Sky had chosen this particular saloon because it had been the only one of the four or five in town that hadn't had the sound of music drifting out its door.

"I can sweep." He gestured at his guitar. "And I can entertain."

"Hey, Bob," one of the saloon girls called. "That's just what this place needs."

"I can't afford to hire someone else," Bob said. From the appearance of the run-down saloon, Sky didn't doubt his word.

"You don't have to pay me anything," said Sky. "Just let me put out my hat and get tips for my music."

"Tips, eh? You make much that way?"

"Depends."

"Might be I'd be doing you a favor letting you play in here." Bob scratched his protruding belly. "I'll let you do it, but I want ten percent of your take—consider it rent for using my place."

There was one small matter Sky had to make sure of before he agreed. "You have anything against me spending my money in your place?"

Bob chuckled. "Shoot, I ain't never turned money down from no one, even Indians. Long as you don't cause no trouble, you can spend all you want here."

---

Sky was concentrating on his music. Even the noise in the room had faded into the background. He could have been alone.

*"My warrior's song borne on the wind . . . Blows from the empty pale blue skies . . ."*

Sky had to be pretty drunk to sing the song he had made up so many years ago, but the tune and the words never stopped haunting him. He sang only the first part, though, and had to change that a bit to suit his despondency. "He leaves a lonely, shattered dream, and *never* sings his song at dawn." How right it seemed to change the word "hope" in the final line to "never." Sometimes when he was particularly inebriated, he'd sing the song over and over again as if he enjoyed torturing himself.

He paused, reaching for a nearby glass of whiskey.

"That's a mighty pretty song," a voice called. "But don't it have a happy ending?"

Sky looked up, realizing for the first time that he had an audience. A saloon girl sat at a nearby table, her chin resting in her hands. "No, it don't," he answered abruptly.

"All stories should have a happy ending."

"You'll have to find yourself another musician for that."

"I've been listening to you for two days now, Sky," the saloon girl said, "and I still can't figure out where all that sadness in you comes from."

"All Indians are singing their death songs. Why shouldn't I?"

"You're different from most Indians I've seen. Except for the way you dress, I almost start to forget you are an Indian." She paused and studied him for a minute with a very frank appraisal.

Sky shifted uncomfortably and swallowed more of his whiskey. No doubt his attire proclaimed his inner turmoils louder than any words could. His buckskin breeches and the moccasins on his feet were the same ones he'd worn when he lived on the reservation. He no longer had the same shirt, although he couldn't remember how he'd lost it. It had been replaced with a white cotton shirt, now stained and dirty, which he had stolen from a clothesline. Over that was a burgundy brocade waistcoat he had won in a card game. It once had been an expensive item that had gone with a cashmere suit. Sky hadn't been lucky enough to win the whole suit, but that was just as well. It probably would have ended up as worn and frayed as the waistcoat now was. Covering the whole odd ensemble, at least on cold days such as this, was the blanket he had worn in the Cheyenne camp. It had once been beautiful, with rust and brown colors woven into a geometrical pattern, but now it was all faded to a mousy brown. Sky's hair was long, but he no longer bothered to braid it or wrap it carefully in strips of leather. It hung straight and tangled under a dusty, tattered wide-brimmed hat.

Ironically, he still wore his uncle's beaded collar and the magpie feathers in his hat. He was a man who had essentially given up trying to be anything in particular. He didn't dress for effect—in fact, he put no thought at all in what he wore. Everything he owned was on his back—except for his saddlebags, which he kept in the little shed he occupied behind the town's livery stable.

He couldn't say why he hadn't sold the guitar. In the West a man's horse was supposed to be his most important possession, yet Sky had kept the guitar and sold Two-Tone. But every man had his priorities, and to Sky whiskey was his only true friend now. The guitar was simply a means to buy more whiskey. Wandering from saloon to saloon, he was usually able to earn enough money to keep the daily supply of firewater flowing. Even in the West, the novelty of a guitar-playing Indian was good for something. Bob, the saloonkeeper, was making out pretty well in his deal with Sky.

Not only did he get his ten percent, but most of the rest also found its way into Bob's pockets to pay Sky's bar bill.

The saloon girl shook her head with a regretful expression on her face.

"You're a good-looking buck—I mean under all that dirt and them awful clothes. You got a squaw or anything?"

"No," Sky said.

"Well, I ain't gonna be busy later. . . ."

Sky shrugged. "You don't wanta get mixed up with me. I'm bad medicine, especially to women."

"Maybe you just ain't found the right woman yet."

She was probably right. Jenny and Rose had been far too special for him. Each, in her own way, had been a treasure, a pearl of great price. Then they had fallen into his worthless hands, and he had destroyed them—well, Jenny at least. Maybe he had gotten away in time to spare Rose.

Sky deserved no better than a cheap saloon girl. She was thirty years old, although she looked forty. She might have been pretty once, but she had given herself to far too many broken-down losers—like him. There was a scar above her right eyebrow where one of her past customers had vented his anger on her. Maybe she was just drawn to such men. She had taken an interest in Sky from the minute he had come into the saloon. Perhaps she thought she could help men like him; or maybe she thought as little of herself as Sky thought of himself.

Maybe she *was* the right woman.

But Sky wasn't looking for a woman at all—unless, of course, she had free whiskey to offer.

"Hey, you, Injun!" a voice yelled from across the room. "Let's have a tune."

"I got customers that want to hear music," Bob added. "So quit yammering with Lyla and get over here."

"Gotta go." Sky paused to toss back the rest of his drink.

"My offer still stands."

Sky shrugged silently, then went over to the knot of cowboys who were hankering for music.

"None of that funeral music you was playing before," said one of the cowhands. "We want something lively."

Sky had once been able to play hymns without thinking or feeling. Now he could do the same with anything else. His playing of "Clementine" and "She'll Be Coming Round the Mountain" had his listeners clapping, stamping their feet, and singing along. Some of the men took the girls and began dancing. Everyone was laughing. Coins rattled together as they dropped into Sky's up-turned hat. No one noticed—or cared—that the musician sang without a smile, or that his eyes were hollow and empty.

The first chance Sky got, he turned over some of the coins to Bob for a shot of whiskey. Bob had no qualms about selling liquor to Indians. Too few passed through Riverbend for the authorities to worry themselves over. By two in the morning, Sky's hat was empty and he could barely see the strings on his guitar much less finger a recognizable tune. Bob didn't care; most of his customers were gone by then anyway.

Sky tried to get one last drink.

"You ain't got nothing to pay for it with," said Bob.

"Aw, come on. I'll pay ya back t'morrow."

"No credit."

Lyla sidled up to where Bob and Sky were talking.

"This one's on me," she said.

"You're a real sap," said Bob.

"But a fine . . . fine sap," said Sky expansively. "A better frien' I never had."

She drew close to Sky. "Well, honey, that's what I want to be to you, a friend."

Bob offered a snide laugh.

"What do you see in that broken-down old Injun?" asked Bob.

"He ain't old," said Lyla, "and he ain't completely broken-down—not yet, anyway."

"I'm tryin', though!" slurred Sky.

"That'd be a real waste." Lyla ran her hand over his shoulder. "You're as much a man as any of them cowboys that were in here."

Sky laughed without humor. "Why, I *am* a cowboy, didn't ya know?"

"Okay, you two," said Bob, "if you want to carry on, do it on your own time. I'm closing up for the night."

Outside it was snowing and the wind was blowing, but the icy blast did nothing to sober Sky up. He swayed on his feet, and Lyla put an arm around him to hold him steady. She didn't let go even after he had gained some control.

"I better see that you get home okay."

"Home. . . ?" he laughed dryly. "That'll never happen."

"Come on."

"You're going to get all wet."

"I've been wet before."

"Lemme see then . . . which way. . . ?" Sky rubbed his eyes, hoping to rub some of the fog out of his brain as well. He had lived in so many places, in so many towns in the last two years.

"Tell me where you live, and I'll do the rest."

"Ah . . . the livery stable, that's it. Behind it."

The livery stood at the opposite end of town, and before they had gone even half the distance, the storm accelerated into a full-blown blizzard.

At last they reached the shed. Lyla flung open the door and shook her head. "How can anyone live here?"

The shack was less than seven feet square. Sky could barely stretch out full length in it, but that was a minor problem compared to the cracks in the siding and the thin roof that rattled and creaked dangerously with every gust of wind. The owner had put a little stove in the corner. Sky wouldn't have survived there otherwise.

"It's a rotten pit," Sky said with a lopsided grin, "but it's home."

"We should have gone to my place," Lyla mumbled. "But we'll just have to make the most of it. I ain't going back out in that storm."

"You're stayin'. . . ?"

"I thought I might."

"Did I invite you?" The question was entirely innocent. Sky truly couldn't remember.

Lyla quickly built a fire in the stove, then stripped off her wet coat and laid it in front of the stove. This done, she turned her attention to Sky. She eased him down to the bed, which was nothing more than a blanket over the straw-covered floor.

"Let's get them wet duds off you."

"They ain't so wet." Sky was only vaguely aware of what was happening or of what this woman's designs might be. He certainly wasn't in a state of mind to care.

She took his blanket from his shoulders and laid it beside the stove, then removed his vest and shirt. Holding them distastefully by two fingers she also dropped them on the floor near the blanket. She paused and admired Sky's chest.

"A bit scrawny, but with a couple of good meals you'd turn into something." She touched his shoulders again, then noticed the scars on his chest. "What are these?" she asked as she fingered them.

"The marks of my foolishness," said Sky.

When Lyla began to unbutton her own dress, Sky forced himself back into focus.

"What're you doing?" he said.

"What do you think?"

"I'm not sure . . . I've had a awful lot t' drink. . . ."

She smiled.

"Listen . . . ah . . . Lyla, I thought I said I didn't want no woman."

"And I said—"

"You don't understan'—I'm like poison. I'm no good—" He stopped suddenly. Lyla was getting fuzzy before his eyes. When she leaned close to him, all he saw were her two eyes and a big, toothy grin. When she spoke, her voice seemed to be coming from a long distance away.

"Come on, Sky, let me show how the right woman can be," she was saying—at least that's what he thought she was saying. He couldn't tell for sure. Her voice kept changing from loud to soft, and at times didn't even seem to be coming from her mouth. He knew he was about to pass out.

Lyla seemed oblivious. She was smiling and cooing and kissing him.

Sky shook his head but he couldn't tell if she saw. "You gotta understan', Lyla, I ain't even good enough for a cheap saloon girl."

"So, I'm cheap, am I?" Lyla jerked back. "Why, you filthy Injun! I was starting to feel sorry for you. I was going to be nice to you, treat you like a person. You ain't nothing but a—"

Sky never heard the rest of her tirade. He passed out, but as consciousness slipped away from him he vaguely heard screams and felt a gust of cold air as the door flew open.

# 51

# OUT IN THE COLD

Sky awoke in a daze. Hadn't he been living in a shed? But this was no shed.

It wasn't much better, but the walls were solid brick. He was lying on a thin mattress on a cot—probably the most comfortable bed he'd had in months. He turned to get a better view of his surroundings, and his head spun with shock and pain.

The fourth wall in the room wasn't a wall at all, but a set of bars. He was in jail.

How had he gotten here? He shut his eyes and screwed up his face, trying to think. He remembered singing for the cowboys last night. Everyone was having a good time. He hadn't done anything that could have landed him in jail. And no matter how hard he tried, he couldn't think of another thing after that. It was an awful feeling, but it wasn't a new sensation. It had happened a couple of times before. Once he had lost three days, and the most frightening part of it was that he had been conscious most of the time. Later, people had recounted to him things he had done, but he had no memory of any of it. But never before had he ended up in jail.

The situation might have been more disturbing to Sky if he hadn't been so warm and comfortable. Maybe he might even get some food soon. He hadn't had a decent meal in a long time. But there was something more important than food—something which he was very unlikely to get in jail.

He jumped up from the cot. "Hey! Is anyone out there?" he yelled. The sound of his own voice made his head throb, but he kept on. When no answer came, he yelled again and again.

"Pipe down in there!" someone finally called from the outer room.

In a moment the door separating the cells from the main part of the jail opened. "What do you want?" the sheriff snapped.

"What's going on?" said Sky. "Why am I here?"

"I ain't surprised you don't remember. You was drunker than a skunk when I brought you in here."

"All I remember is I was singing in the saloon last night—"

"You been in jail for *two* nights, you crazy Injun."

"What happened?"

"Lyla at the saloon said you lured her back to your place and . . . you know, tried to have your way with her."

"No!"

"Well, by the looks of you when I brought you in, I figured you were too drunk to have your way with anyone. But she was screaming and raising such a ruckus that I had to do something."

"You can let me go now, then."

"Ain't that simple. She says she's gonna press charges as soon as she recovers."

"Recovers. . . ? Was she hurt?"

"Nah. Not a scratch on her. Just shaken up, or so she says. But I don't know why she's in such a dither. What more can she expect from the business she's in?"

"If you know I didn't do nothing, then why can't you let me go?"

"It's her word against yours, and I'd lose my job for sure if I took an Injun's word over a white woman's, even if she is just a saloon girl."

Sky couldn't argue with that. He decided to broach a more important issue. "Sheriff, I ain't feeling so good. You don't suppose I could have a little whiskey—you know, for my stomach?"

The sheriff laughed. "You got nerve, boy, I'll say that! You're already in trouble because of drinking, and now you want more?"

"It's just that . . . my stomach . . . you know . . . ."

"Sorry, fella."

"Please!"

"No can do. But I'll get you some grub."

The sheriff left, and Sky paced back and forth in the cell. After a while the walls began to close in on him like a trap. He began to sweat, and his heart was racing. An hour passed and he felt like he was going to jump out of his own skin. According to the sheriff he had been two days without a drink. No wonder he wanted to scream.

The sheriff brought in a tray of food, but Sky was no longer interested in eating. He could only think about one thing, and the more he thought about it, the worse it got.

"Sheriff!" he called. "Get me a drink—please! I'm begging you."

The sheriff opened the door and came back in. He looked at Sky and shook his head. "You poor drunken Indian. I feel sorry for you, really I do, but I gotta uphold the law even if no one else around here does."

"Just one!" Sky pleaded. "That's all I need. I'm gonna be sick if I don't get something."

"Try and eat. Maybe that'll help."

"Eat! What good will that do?"

"Just try."

"I don't want to eat!" Sky swung at the tray, sending dishes and food everywhere.

"Doggone it! Look at the mess you've made! What's wrong with you, boy?"

"I'm gonna die if you keep me locked up like this."

The sheriff, clearly finished with the discussion, left without further comment. Sky yelled at him a few more times; when that had no effect, he gave up and continued to pace. It wasn't right for them to do this to him. It had to be cruel and unusual punishment. He ought to have a lawyer. He had some rights, even if he was only an Indian.

After a while he picked up a chunk of bread that was still on the floor and began to eat it, hoping to divert his mind from what he really wanted. It didn't help.

He lost track of time. The high, barred window in his cell must have looked out on an alley, for it didn't let in enough light for him to tell where the sun was. It seemed as if hours, even days, passed before the sheriff returned.

"That woman from the saloon is here to see you."

"What does she want?"

"I don't know. You don't have to see her. Probably be better if you didn't."

"I don't want to see anyone."

The sheriff left, but returned in a few moments with Lyla close at his heels. He turned toward her. "I told you to wait."

"I figured I could convince him better myself," she said.

The sheriff looked at Sky. He shrugged. He was past caring.

"Okay," said the sheriff. "I'll give you five minutes, Lyla. And he's real agitated, so don't do nothing to make it worse."

When the sheriff left, Lyla came close to the cell.

"What do you want?" Sky snarled.

"I don't feel right about getting you locked up."

" 'Cause you know I didn't do nothing."

"I ain't never had a man turn me down, much less an Indian."

Sky rankled at the derision in her tone, but he choked back his ire. If she was trying to apologize and get him released, he didn't want to do anything to spoil her intentions.

She went on, "I just got mad at the things you said. Before I knew it, I was trying to get back at you. I'd had a lot to drink, too."

"Yeah. . . ?"

"I don't want you to rot in jail."

"Neither do I. You gonna get the sheriff to release me?"

"I'd like to. But . . . well, I just can't do that without losing face."

"I'm dying in here," Sky said. "I gotta get out."

"Look, all you have to do is apologize to me, in front of the sheriff. Tell him you was drunk and didn't know what you were doing, and that you'll never do it again. I'll say I believe you and that I'm not going to press charges. He'll release you then."

"You want me to admit to attacking you?"

"It's either that or sitting in jail. You're an Indian; you could get a few years in prison for what you done."

"I didn't do anything!"

"No one'll believe you." She tried to look sympathetic, but not too successfully. "Look, I've lost five jobs in the last three months. I can't afford to lose another. I ain't a young girl anymore. The Riverbend Saloon might be the bottom of the barrel, but if I lose it in the middle of winter, I don't know what I'll do. It's either you or me."

Sky could muster little sympathy for the woman's plight. All he could think of was himself and his terrible thirst. The thought of another minute locked up was enough to drive him insane, much less another year or more. In the end his need for a drink, rather than sympathy, motivated him.

"Get the sheriff in here," he said.

He wondered if he could possibly sink lower than when he looked the sheriff in the eye and confessed to Lyla's accusations.

When the sheriff said, "You sure about this?"

Sky said emphatically. "Yeah, I'm sure! But I ain't gonna do it again—ever!"

The sheriff said to Lyla, "And you want to drop your charges?"

"I guess he deserves another chance. I think he's gonna quit drinking because of all this."

———

Sky couldn't remember anything that felt as good as the fresh, free air. He gulped it in, but it only momentarily appeased his basic hunger. He wondered if he still had his job at the Riverbend Saloon. He should have asked Lyla to put in a good word for him. But he had already groveled enough for that day. He decided to get his guitar, which he hoped was still in the shed, and try another place.

When he got to the livery stable, the owner met him as he was heading around back. The man handed Sky his guitar and saddlebags.

"You can't stay here no more," he said. "I don't want no troublemakers around here."

Considering the icy winds howling around him and the heavy clouds threatening a fresh snowfall, Sky took his sudden homelessness in stride. All he could think of was getting a drink. But word had already begun to circulate around town, at least among the saloons, of what Sky had supposedly done. They all turned Sky away. He even offered to trade his guitar and saddlebags for a drink. One bartender finally conceded but was firm in giving Sky only one shot in exchange. Sky drank it so fast it was like having nothing at all. He tried to get more, but he had nothing left to pay with but the worthless clothes on his back. The bartender kicked him out.

Riverbend was a town of eight or nine thousand. There must be somewhere else besides the five saloons where a man could get a drink. It was after six in the evening, and the two stores in the town were closed. The thought of breaking into the stores briefly crossed his mind, but he didn't dare risk getting thrown into jail again.

Trudging through the snow, Sky headed toward the residential part of town. Perhaps someone there would have mercy on him. But no doors were opened to a ragged Indian. He was starting to shake all over, and he knew it wasn't just from the cold. His feet felt numb through his worn moccasins. He got sick on the street once and a passerby crossed on the other side to avoid him.

He'd get arrested for sure if he stayed in these respectable parts, so he returned to the main street. It was dark and late. Nothing was open now but the saloons. He went back to the Riverbend Saloon and found Lyla.

"Lyla, you gotta help me," he said.

"I already helped you by getting you out of jail."

"What good is that, if I'm gonna die anyway?"

"You still got a place to stay, don't you?"

"I got kicked out."

"I guess you could stay at my place, but—"

She was cut off by Bob. "Hey, you no-good Injun! I thought I told you to get out of here."

"I—" Sky tried to defend himself, but the bartender cut him off.

"And, you, Lyla—are you encouraging him? I don't want him around here. If you want to keep your job, you better steer clear of him."

Lyla looked at Sky and shrugged. "I gotta look out for myself." She turned on her heel and walked away.

Sky wandered around for another hour until his legs were too weak and frozen to hold him up. He nearly collapsed in the street, but he staggered to the side of a building—not an alley, but a wall with an open field on the other side. He must have made his way to the edge of town. Sky wished for a more sheltered space, but he didn't have the strength to go any farther. At least he was out of the wind, and the eaves of the roof hung out enough to keep the snow from falling directly on him. Shivering, he clutched at his thin blanket.

"It is a good day to die," he mumbled. Then he laid his head against the wall and closed his eyes.

# 52

# RESCUE THE PERISHING

"Dear God, please let him be alive!"

The man bent over the Indian and listened for a heartbeat. He could hear nothing.

"Maybe I should have become a doctor instead of a minister," he murmured to himself.

He placed his hands against the Indian's icy face and rubbed gently, hoping and praying for some response.

"Come on, man, I don't want to start my morning off with a corpse."

Then he saw a faint movement of the man's chest. He was alive, though just barely. The minister attempted to lift him, but the Indian's limp, unconscious body was unwieldy. By degrees, and with considerable effort, he got the Indian up over his shoulder and, with a mighty lurch, heaved to his feet. The rising sun shifted slightly so that the shadow of a church steeple fell across the Indian's unconscious form.

The minister looked up and smiled.

"Whoever you are, I think you are a lucky man indeed to have passed out next to my church. Luck. . . ? Well, more than that, I trust. Let's go before my back breaks."

He carried the Indian past the church to a house fifty feet away—a quaint little place with a white picket fence around a small front yard, now perfectly blanketed with snow. A wisp of smoke rose from the chimney. When the minister opened the front door, he was greeted by a homey warmth.

301

"Reverend Harris, look what I've found!" the minister called as he entered.

"Remember, you're to call me George, now," came the reply from another room. In a moment the speaker appeared, wiping his hands on a cloth. He was a man of about sixty, about three decades older than the first man, with thin gray hair and kind brown eyes. "So, what have we here?"

"I found him next to the church."

"Is he alive?"

"Barely. I'll put him in my room."

The younger minister carried the Indian down a short hallway to a small bedroom. He pulled back the covers on the bed and laid him on the clean white sheets.

"An Indian, isn't he?" said Reverend Harris.

The younger minister grinned. "I believe so."

"Just what you've been looking for, eh, William?" Reverend Harris asked, coming up behind him.

"Can you guess what I was praying for this morning?"

"No doubt what you pray for every day as you take your morning walk. Ah, the impatience of youth. Five times you've requested an assignment to a reservation, and every time the president of the mission board tells you the same thing—"

"I have to complete my internship." The young minister frowned.

"You will have your certificate in a month."

"So, it shouldn't hurt to start praying now."

Harris smiled affectionately. "I'm going to go fetch the doctor. See if you can scrape some of the filth off your Indian. And you know where the spare blankets are, don't you?"

"I'll manage. Make sure the doctor hurries."

"I won't tell him his patient is just a drunken Indian." Harris wrinkled his nose.

It hadn't been so noticeable outside, but now, in such close quarters, the smell of alcohol was nauseatingly evident, along with other odors William did not care to define.

"I don't care what he is," the young minister said. "He needs our help, and that's all that matters."

Harris hurried away, mumbling something about "the idealism of youth."

William got several spare blankets and laid them over the still form, then went to the kitchen to prepare a hot brick to put at his feet.

When the brick was in place, the minister stood back and gave his patient a brief appraisal. Already the warmth was doing some good. The man's breathing was a bit more even, and the frost had begun to melt off his eyebrows. William was gratified to find only a small patch of frostbite on the man's cheek. He had known of cases where men lost their entire noses to frostbite. But there was something perplexing about this Indian, something vaguely familiar. Of course, he had seen Indians pass through town before, but Riverbend was far enough away from any reservation that, much to his dismay, he had little contact with Indians.

William was distracted from these thoughts as the man stirred.

"Hello, there. Are you coming to?" But there was no response to his question.

He continued his inspection of the Indian's extremities. The fingers were intact, but as he removed the moccasins that had more holes than leather, he noticed that the feet didn't look as good. William had little knowledge of medicine, but he thought he detected some signs of frostbite. He said a quick prayer that the fellow's feet would be saved.

The doctor arrived just as William was putting a fresh brick under the covers.

"So, you've found yourself a half-dead Indian." The doctor sniffed as he drew near the patient. "Well, maybe all that alcohol running through his veins saved his life. But it might be the thing that'll kill him, too." The doctor felt the pulse in the man's neck, then examined his extremities. "He's going to lose a couple of toes, that's for certain. But that seems the extent of the damage so far."

"He'll be okay, then?"

"Too soon to tell. Any number of things can still kill him. He obviously wasn't in good shape even before he ended up on your doorstep. But one thing at a time, I always say. First let's try to save his feet. Take away those bricks. I know you meant well, lad, and I'll need them later, but for now I want you to immerse those feet in cool water. As soon as the circulation returns, we can put the bricks back. You can also concentrate on cleaning him up—I hope he doesn't crumble when we wash away all the dirt."

The doctor helped to get things started, but soon he had to leave to tend other patients. Two ministers, he said, could do everything he was able to do. He left some tincture of iodine to paint on the feet once the circulation was restored. And he instructed them to give the patient as much tea and broth as he could tolerate once he regained consciousness.

Harris went to prepare breakfast and a kettle of broth while William tended the patient. In about an hour the Indian's feet were turning pink again. The ends of two toes on his right foot, however, remained discolored. William painted on the iodine, murmuring another prayer as he did so. Then he got a bowl of hot water from the kitchen and began the process of cleaning up the patient.

He had only begun when the man stirred again, opening his eyes and quickly shutting them against the morning light. Strange eyes for an Indian . . . blue eyes.

"Where . . . where am I?"

"You're in my home. I was about to give you a bath and some clean clothes."

"How . . . long?" The Indian began coughing.

The minister answered when the coughing had stopped. "I found you this morning. You weren't by the church yesterday, so I assume you were only there one night."

"Church?"

"Yes. Pretty fortunate, eh?"

The man shook his head slowly, whether out of denial or disbelief the minister couldn't tell.

"What's your name?" asked William.

"Who cares?"

"Well, I'd like to call you something. You may be here for a while."

"A while?" Pause. "You got any . . . thing to drink?"

"I'll get you some tea—"

"Ugh! Nothin' else?"

The minister rubbed his chin thoughtfully. Something was nagging at him. "What is your name?"

Again the Indian didn't respond.

"Well, maybe you'll feel more sociable once you're cleaned up."

William began scrubbing at the man's face, and after several rinses the water in the bowl was brown. But he stopped when the first layer of grime was gone. He couldn't believe it. He just couldn't believe it! But even the voice had sounded familiar. And those haunting blue eyes. . . .

———

At first the warm water on Sky's cold face felt good. But then

304

the scrubbing had begun, and the soap stung when some got in his eyes. Wasn't it enough that this person had robbed him of death? Did he have to torture him as well?

Sky tried to move away, but the hands attacking him were strong. When was the last time he'd had a bath? He had taken a swim in a creek last summer. No soap, though. He'd had more important things to buy with the little money he had.

At the thought of whiskey, every nerve in Sky's body began to ache. He needed a drink—now. He started shaking again.

The man hovered over him like a nursemaid. "Are you cold?"

"A glass of whiskey would warm me up real good," Sky said.

"I'm afraid you've come to the wrong place for that," the man said, almost apologetically. "This is a parsonage. Reverend Harris and I are ministers."

Sky tried to open his eyes again. But the light was still too bright, and now they were also burning from the soap. He squinted against the pain.

"Let me shut the curtains," said the minister.

As the light dimmed, Sky attempted to look around. Everything was still fuzzy, but he was in a room with white painted walls and simple furnishings of some dark wood. The minister still stood facing the window as he finished closing the drapes. He was of husky build and probably only a few inches shorter than Sky. From the back he vaguely reminded Sky of Sam—big and muscular, the kind of physique you didn't usually associate with a minister. The stranger, however, was younger than Sam, with blond hair.

Sky rubbed his face and eyes. His hands were trembling, even though he was much warmer. His eyes fixed on a vent above the door that must be letting in adequate heat from a stove somewhere else in the house. Still, his feet were throbbing with pain, his stomach hurt, and his chest ached every time he tried to take a breath. He kept coughing, too, and the shaking just would not stop.

Why had this man bothered to save him? He was better off dead.

Then the man turned, a slight smile on his face. It was such a broad, friendly face. There was a gentleness in it and—

Sky shook his head and rubbed his eyes. He must be seeing things. It wouldn't be the first time he had become delirious when he had gone without alcohol. But he had never seen anything like this before.

He must be going crazy. He needed a drink more than ever.

"What is it?" asked the minister.

"Go away," said Sky. "Leave me alone."

"I didn't plan this to happen."

"What do you mean?"

"I think you know."

Sky forced his eyes open.

"It can't be you! This is another nightmare."

"I hope I'll not be part of your nightmares ever again."

Sky groaned. "Billy . . . Yates?"

The minister smiled and extended a hand. "Reverend William Yates," he said. "Also known as Billy."

# 53

# BLAME

It wasn't a nightmare. It was worse—worse than anything his mind had ever created to torture him. Sky threw off his covers.

"What are you doing?" asked Billy.

"I'm leaving."

"You're not well enough for that."

"I can take care of myself."

Sky swung his feet out of bed and tried to sit up. His head swam, and as his feet touched the cold floor, pain shot up from them to meet the pain shooting down from his chest. The blood drained from his head, and he realized how weak he was. But he forced himself to stand. Immediately his knees buckled.

Billy rushed to him and caught him before he crumbled to the floor. Sky tried to wrench himself away, but Billy's huge, strong hands held firm.

"Leave me alone!" Sky yelled.

"Let me help you, Sky," Billy pleaded.

"I don't need your help," spat Sky, still struggling to free himself, though he hardly had the strength even to stand. He finally broke free, only to fall hard on the floor.

Billy knelt beside Sky and lifted him again in his arms.

"You know how much I hate you?" said Sky. Physical struggle was useless, but fury still seethed inside him.

Billy simply nodded as he laid Sky back in the bed. Gently, like a mother caring for a child, he pulled the covers back over Sky.

"I guess it won't help," Billy said, "but I've changed, Sky. I'm not the same man I was."

Sky looked at him coldly. "Neither am I."

"Oh, God . . . what have I done?" Billy said mournfully. Then he turned to a bureau, opened some drawers, and removed a few

307

items of clothes. "The doctor says we ought to get you cleaned up."

"Don't touch me! I ain't gonna be beholden to you."

"Sky, I could lay down my very life for you and you still wouldn't owe me anything. But if you prefer, I'll have Reverend Harris come in and help. Either way, you have to get out of those dirty, damp clothes. You'll catch your death."

Sky laughed dryly. Did Billy really think he cared if he caught a cold or not?

Billy didn't wait for a reply. He turned and left the room.

Again Sky tried to get out of bed, but the exertion made him cough so hard he spit up blood. Frustrated and disgusted, he fell back against the pillow, stewing about his misery.

Why couldn't he have died out there in the snow? Why couldn't his worthless life just end? And why, of all people, did it have to be Billy Yates who found him? That old snake! And, to make matters worse, the scoundrel looked so clean and pure and—of all things!—innocent. It wasn't right. It wasn't . . . fair. It was Billy's fault in the first place that Sky was where he was. All Sky ever wanted in life was to be a rancher, to be accepted and have friends like everyone else. Yet Billy had always been there goading him, demeaning him, hating him, and, in the end, teaching Sky how to hate. How many times had Billy Yates made Sky feel less than human, the worthless half-breed? And then Billy had finally killed the one person who had accepted Sky as he was, who had loved Sky. Jenny had never seen the half-breed; she had never seen the Indian, or even the white boy trying desperately to hide that despised half. She had loved him for his heart, his soul.

He was glad she couldn't see that heart now—it was black and stained. And his soul . . . did he even have one anymore?

Tears suddenly sprang to Sky's eyes. Cursing, he wiped them away with his hand. That was the worst part—he had enough of a soul left to realize the depths to which he had sunk, but not enough to desire to do anything about it. It was too late for him. He was better off dead.

The bedroom door opened again. This time it was an older man.

"I'm Reverend Harris," the man said.

Sky said nothing.

"We must get these clothes off you."

"I want to go to a hospital," Sky said.

"There is no hospital in Riverbend. The nearest would be Omaha."

"So, am I a prisoner here?"

"You are free to go whenever you wish." Reverend Harris stepped back accommodatingly.

Defiantly, Sky tried to rise again, but collapsed back onto the pillow, coughing and shaking.

Without saying another word, Harris began removing Sky's clothes. Sky couldn't fight it, but he scowled the entire time. It took about an hour to get his body washed. They were both silent the entire time. When the task was finished, Sky would not admit how good it felt to be dry and clean, nor how soft and nice the clean white flannel nightshirt felt. He was probably wearing Billy's nightshirt, and that fact only made him testy.

Harris picked up Sky's clothes, his face twisted in obvious distaste. "I'll try to wash these since they appear to be your only belongings, but don't blame me if all I can do for them is burn them." Harris turned to leave.

"Hey!" Sky called as Harris reached the door.

"I'd appreciate being called by my name, young man. Reverend Harris."

"Yeah . . . well, you can see I'm a sick man."

"We do agree on something."

"I need a tonic—for my cough. I've known some doctors who'll give whiskey or something similar if there is no tonic available. I gotta have something."

"For medicinal reasons only?" Harris lifted one eyebrow.

"Come on . . . please."

Shaking his head sadly, Harris left.

Billy must have been waiting outside the door. The conversation between Billy and Harris drifted in to Sky.

"I think we ought to give him some whiskey," Billy said.

"I'll not have the devil's brew in my house."

"I think he needs whiskey—I mean *really* needs it."

"I've known people like that before, William. It doesn't help to contribute to their habit."

"But, George, he's got so many other problems right now. That cough sounds like more than a mere cold. And he's shaking so much and so agitated. Maybe if he had just a little whiskey, it might calm him and make him easier to help."

"William, I don't mean to be harsh with you, but don't forget what you told me in the kitchen. You gave him his first whiskey, and now you have the opportunity to see that he has his last."

"For that very reason, I can't stand to see him suffering. It's all my fault!"

"Yeah, Billy, it is all your fault," Sky yelled. "And if I die 'cause I don't get any whiskey, that'll be your fault, too."

Harris opened the door. "It's useless to lay blame, young man," he said to Sky. "But one thing is certain. No matter what anyone else did, *you* always had a choice in your own destiny."

"Did you tell him everything, Billy?" Sky called. "Did you tell him how you betrayed me? How you killed your sister?"

If Sky had meant to torture Billy, to plunge a knife into his heart and twist it cruelly, he had been successful. But Billy didn't wait to hear more. With an agonized expression on his face, he turned and fled like a desperate fugitive.

Harris turned back to Sky. "If I weren't bound by God, I'd throw you back out in the cold."

"You'd be doing me a favor," Sky retorted.

They left him alone for a while after that, except once when Harris came in with a cup of hot broth. Sky offered no thanks— the sanctimonious minister knew he didn't want *soup*. Sky's thirst for alcohol grew worse with each passing minute. It had never been this bad before. He wept, he yelled and screamed, and he begged—but no one was listening. They were probably off somewhere praying for his eternal soul. They were probably in church, the hypocrites.

He tossed and turned in bed, although movement only made him feel worse. The nightshirt was quickly soaked with sweat. He was burning hot one minute, and then the next he thought he would freeze. He began seeing things. A bat flew into his face, and Sky tried to fend it off with his hands, only to find he was beating at thin air. A rat crawled up on his bed.

Sky screamed.

A hand reached over and touched his forehead with a cool cloth, but Sky could no longer tell if this were real or illusion. The hand was large but so gentle. Perhaps it was attached to some kind person, not a monster who would deprive him of what he needed most.

"Gimme a drink. Please!"

A voice spoke as if from the opposite end of a tunnel. "God, fill him with the water of life."

"You dirty betrayer!"

"I know I am guilty." The voice was broken with sobs.

310

"Help me. I'll forgive you, if only you'll help me."

"Lord Jesus, what shall I do?"

"Have mercy!" Sky begged as if he had the answer to the man's prayers.

But instead of mercy, Sky received another attack from the horrible bats—several of them now, diving at his face, over and over again so that he couldn't fend them off. He could see their eyes, their ugly, beady eyes, and they were laughing at him.

"You poor excuse for a Human Being. You crazy Injun."

"Leave me alone!"

"You stinking half-breed."

"Help me!"

# 54

# BEAUTY FOR ASHES

Billy sat beside Sky's bed all night. He knew it wasn't right to think of himself when Sky was suffering, yet he could not stop feeling as tortured as Sky looked. Despite what Reverend Harris's voice of reason tried to say about the uselessness of laying blame. Billy knew that what had happened to Sky was truly his fault. Even when they were young and he had ridiculed Sky and aimed his hatred at him, Billy had realized that Sky was a basically decent person. Even when they had come to blows, Billy had known he was fighting an honorable opponent. Sky had done nothing to deserve the hostility aimed at him. His only fault—which of course was no fault at all—was that he was born half white, half Indian. But Billy had pushed Sky far more than any other man could have taken. And what had Sky done in return? He had saved Billy's life.

And he had repaid that act of honor by pretending to be Sky's friend. He knew now he hadn't been pretending. He had liked Sky's company. If only . . .

If only I hadn't been such a weasel back then, Billy told himself. He glanced over at Sky's restless, struggling, half-conscious form. Maybe there was a moment along the line where Sky *had* chosen his own path, but that didn't exonerate Billy.

I pushed him toward that path, thought Billy, not only by giving him his first whiskey, but by making him feel like dirt.

"Help me!" Sky pleaded.

"I'm trying!" Billy didn't know if Sky heard. He had been begging for whiskey all night between his screams. For the most part it had been the incoherent voice of delirium. But Billy was having

312

a hard time ignoring those plaintive cries.

He had never felt so helpless in his life, and never had he wanted to help more.

He sat next to Sky's bed for hours, crying more than he ever had in his life. Once, Sky had fallen out of bed, and another time when he made another attempt to get up, Billy had to hold him down for several minutes until Sky returned to some semblance of calm. Finally, around midnight, Billy's nerves were nearly shot and Reverend Harris insisted he get some rest.

Harris had offered his bed to Billy, but instead he put on his boots and winter coat and left the house. He went across town to an area he had never visited. Though most of the town was closed up and deserted at that hour, this section was lit and busy by comparison. A few people were outside, but most of the activity was coming from the several saloons. He entered the first saloon he came to. Music was wafting out from it to the street. It reminded Billy of when he had been younger and thought such places were fun. It reminded him of his drinking days, but those were not fond memories. He had gladly left that life behind him.

No one registered any surprise at his presence in the saloon. Unfortunately, few of the customers came to church often enough to recognize him. Billy went up to the bar.

"I'd like to buy a bottle of whiskey," he said.

"You want a glass, too?" asked the bartender.

"Just the bottle."

Billy put some coins on the counter, took the bottle, and exited as quickly as possible. He tried not to question what he was doing, whether it would do more harm than good. If he wavered at all in his decision, he only had to conjure in his mind a picture of poor Sky, writhing in his bed, screaming, delirious. He could not stand another minute of Sky's suffering. And giving Sky whiskey was the only thing he could think of that might help. It would only be temporary relief, of course, but it seemed to Billy that Sky could not possibly survive both the abstinence from alcohol and the physical sickness that was assailing him. If it hadn't been so late, he might have sought the doctor's advice. Yet, down deep, he feared the doctor would agree with Reverend Harris.

Maybe I'm too weak, Billy thought, but I can't let him go on any longer like that.

When he returned to the house, he found Reverend Harris dozed off in the chair next to Sky's bed. Sky was quiet. Before wak-

313

ing Harris, Billy hid the whiskey. Maybe he wouldn't need it after all.

"Has it been that long?" asked Harris, in a bit of a daze after Billy awakened him from a sleep he greatly needed.

"I couldn't sleep." It wasn't really a lie; he wouldn't have been able to sleep had he tried. "Go on to bed. I'll take over."

"Oh, lad, I'm sure it won't matter if we both sleep."

"No, I won't leave him alone."

Harris patted him affectionately on the shoulder before leaving. Billy dropped into the chair. Sky was asleep, but obviously not at peace. He was still shaking violently, and moaning, and his breathing was terribly labored and rattling loudly.

Just as Billy thought the crisis might have passed, Sky came awake screaming.

"The dead, the dead! They want me. . . . It's my fault . . . I stopped dancing."

Billy jumped up and laid what he hoped was a comforting, calming hand on Sky's arm. "It's okay, Sky. You're safe."

"The arrows . . . I broke them . . . I destroyed them. . . ."

Billy touched Sky's forehead. It was burning hot. His bedclothes were soaked, and blood was splattered on his pillow from his coughing. Billy changed Sky's blankets and took his wet nightshirt off completely. He also examined Sky's feet. One toe was purple to the first joint, another was discolored only on the tip.

"I'm dying!" Sky cried.

"No you're not," said Billy. It was an order, not a statement.

Sky grabbed Billy's shirt and yanked him close. "You're killing me!"

Billy pried Sky's fingers away from his shirt and, before he had time to reconsider, retrieved the bottle of whiskey from behind a dresser. He poured a little in a water glass.

"Here," said Billy, holding the glass to Sky's lips.

The unexpectedness of the strong liquid made Sky cough at first, but when he realized what it was, he quickly adapted.

"Oh, God! Thank you!"

"Don't thank God," Billy said. "I doubt this is what He'd want for you."

"No, you're wrong." Sky gulped down the rest of the drink. "God gives us the desires of our hearts. Sam always said so . . ."

When Billy started to move away, Sky grabbed his hand. "Another. . . ?"

"I don't know."

314

"One more . . . just to make the nightmares go away."

Billy poured another. He couldn't say no; he'd already hurt Sky so much. But as he was holding it to Sky's lips, the bedroom door opened.

"I thought you might like some tea—" Reverend Harris stopped abruptly as he took in what was happening. "Oh, William!"

Billy guiltily jerked the glass away.

"Hey!" cried Sky. "You can't do that." He grabbed at the glass but snagged Billy's sleeve instead, making him drop the glass. "Now look what you've done!" Sky caught the glass as it tumbled on top of his covers and brought it to his lips. Desperately he licked what few remaining drops he could from the glass.

Billy looked at Reverend Harris. "I'm sorry," he said miserably. "I couldn't stand it. I just couldn't stand it! I could think of no other way to help him."

"To help *him*?" he countered. "Or yourself?"

Billy shook his head in confusion.

---

Billy liked the church best when it was quiet and peaceful and vacant. The single candle reflected odd shadows across the wooden altar and filtered through the sanctuary. He was usually uncomfortable when the place was filled on Sundays, especially on those days when he had to preach. Preaching was never the reason he had gotten into the ministry in the first place, and no matter how often people told him his speaking was inspired, he would never feel completely right in that role.

Who was he, after all, to preach to others? Harris might insist on calling him "William," but he was Billy and always would be. It seemed right that he shouldn't forget that fact.

He had made a complete botch of his life, and he knew better than anyone it was by grace he had come to the place he was today. In God's eyes he had been totally forgiven for all his mistakes, yet no amount of forgiveness could completely erase the pain he felt. Jenny would never come back, and the fact that she had died by his hand would never be changed. And now it seemed he had destroyed Sky's life as well.

Billy fell to his knees in front of the altar. "Isn't it bad enough I have done this to Sky? But, Lord, why bring him to me of all people? He'll never let me help him—and I don't blame him. You

315

should have had someone else find him, someone he might respect."

*But I brought him to you, Billy.*

Billy lifted his head. The sanctuary was still silent; he had heard no voice except the unmistakable one in his heart.

"Why, God?" he pleaded. "You can see I'm no good for him. I certainly can't preach to him."

*I don't want you to preach to him.*

Billy was glad of that, for he had already decided that the last thing he would do was preach at Sky. But he began to run out of other valid excuses. "I am just too guilty," he said with a lame sigh.

*I tell you again, Billy, I died to heal you of that guilt.*

Billy had been over this ground so many times before that he wondered why God didn't tire of it. But every time, God seemed to take his hand like that of a child and walk him carefully through his doubt. He would be reminded through Scripture, or from another Christian, or in prayer, as now, that he had been set free from his past—if not from its pain, at least from its bondage.

Billy smiled slightly as he remembered conversations with Sam Killion. Many times Sam had told him, "If the Son makes you free, Billy, you shall be free indeed!"

"Oh, Sam, I wish you were here now," Billy murmured. "You'd know what to do." George Harris was a good man, but he'd led a fairly mundane life, raised as a minister's son, always walking the straight and narrow. His worst sin had been when he was ten years old and he stole a coin from the offering plate.

But Sam had once been filled with hate and rebellion; and he had killed because of it. It steadied Billy to remember Sam and their first meaningful encounter seven years ago. Billy had suffered terribly after Jenny's death. At first he had hid it by heaping blame on Sky. The whole county had come to despise Sky, and if he had stayed around, there would certainly have been a lynching. But it turned out that Billy Yates did have a conscience, and it assailed him even while he was accusing and threatening Sky. First, there were the nightmares until he stopped sleeping completely. He couldn't close his eyes, even while awake, without the ghostly image of his sister appearing before him, pointing an accusing finger. He started drinking a lot, but it didn't help. Jenny's dead, white face was always there haunting him.

When Sky left, Billy's father decided to go after him. He got together a dozen riders—not a hard thing to do considering the hostile attitudes toward Sky. Billy went. In his twisted mind he

316

thought that maybe killing Sky would help end his torment.

The "posse" rode to the place where Jenny had been killed. Maybe Sky might have gone there. Killers always return to the scene of their crime. Billy hadn't been there since the day of Jenny's death. He was so frayed and haggard from his lack of sleep and great distress that when he saw the place again, something snapped inside him. He fell to his knees and wept like a baby.

Kyle Evanston, also with the posse, asked, "What's wrong with him?"

"That's right where she was killed," Big Bill answered. "You ought to know that, Kyle . . . if you were there."

"Oh . . . uh . . . yeah, that's right. I just forgot for a minute."

Big Bill looked incisively at Kyle. "How could you forget something like that?"

Kyle shrugged. "I don't know."

Billy had always relied on the fact that his father *wanted* to believe Sky was guilty. What he didn't realize about his father was that, for all his meanness and bigotry, Big Bill Yates had never killed a man unjustly—at least by his own measure of justice. So Billy was shocked when his father accosted him there on the spot where Jenny had died.

"I want to hear the truth about that day, boy," Bill demanded.

"You know the truth. That no-good half-breed—"

Bill grabbed his son by the collar and yanked him to his feet. "Don't you lie to me!" He shook Billy violently.

"I tell you—"

Big Bill threw his fist into his son's face. Blood spurted from Billy's nose. Big Bill hit him again.

"What happened?"

"It . . . was an accident," cried Billy. "I didn't mean to . . ."

Big Bill dropped his son like a pile of diseased rags.

After that day, Billy's misery was compounded. Living with the secret had been bad enough; living with his father's hatred was more than he could take. He had spent his life trying to please his father and win his approval. Now, in Bill Yates's eyes, his son was no better than that half-breed. Billy considered running away like Sky had done, but down deep he knew he deserved his father's derision. He deserved all the punishment that could be piled on him for what he had done.

Finally he was driven to the ultimate punishment. Killing himself was the only way he'd ever have peace. But he failed even at that. He tried to hang himself in the barn, but the rope he had at-

317

tached to a rafter snapped with his weight and he broke not his neck but only his leg.

While he was laid up in bed, Sam Killion came to see him. Billy couldn't believe that Sky's stepfather would come to him after all he'd done over the years to hurt Sky. Even more amazing was the fact that Sam did not lay recriminations on Billy—he never once mentioned Billy's guilt. Rather, Sam told Billy of a loving, forgiving God. He shared the Gospel, and Billy listened as if he'd never heard it before. And, in a sense, he really hadn't, even though he had gone to church all his life. He had never before listened with his heart.

Billy finally turned his life, his mistakes, even his pain, over to God. Sam rejoiced—he had lost his beloved adopted son, but God had given him a new brother in Billy. Then Billy first heard the words that would become the abiding theme of his life.

Sam said, "Listen to this, Billy. This is the kind of God we have—" He opened his Bible to Isaiah, " 'The Spirit of the Lord God is upon me; because the Lord hath anointed me to preach good tidings unto the meek; he hath sent me to bind up the brokenhearted, to proclaim liberty to the captives, and the opening of the prison to them that are bound; to proclaim the acceptable year of the Lord, and the day of vengeance of our God; to comfort all that mourn; to appoint unto them that mourn in Zion, to give unto them beauty for ashes, the oil of joy for mourning, the garment of praise for the spirit of heaviness; that they might be called trees of righteousness, the planting of the Lord, that he might be glorified.' "

Billy Yates's life had been in ashes—maybe it had always been a pile of ashes. But God had cleaned up those ashes, replacing them with the beauty of love and forgiveness.

Couldn't God do the same for Sky now? Billy had no doubt about that. Where his doubt lay was in the instrument God had chosen to use. How could *he* tell Sky about God's love? Why should Sky listen to him?

*He will see, not hear.*

"God," Billy prayed, "the only thing worth seeing is you. You are the 'beauty'—I'm only the ashes."

But God reminded Billy that the beauty now dwelt within him as well. To deny that would be to repudiate the last seven years of his life. Billy Yates was by no means perfect. Only a resoundingly flawed man would try to pour whiskey down a drunkard's throat. Yet he still had something vital to offer Sky. He had the sincere heart God had given him; he had the deepest desire to please God. But most of all, Billy loved Sky Killion as only one flawed heap of ashes could love another.

Perhaps that would suffice. Billy prayed—as he had never prayed before—that God would somehow give Sky the ability to see past everything else and focus only on the light of love.

# 55

# HOSTILITY

Gradually Sky's physical craving for alcohol diminished, but not his desire. The terrible shakes and hallucinations ceased. He began to eat and put on a little weight. But he was not happy. He nearly exploded when he found out Billy had dumped out the rest of that bottle of whiskey.

"You don't need it," Billy said.

"I'll decide what I need, you sanctimonious hypocrite!"

He would have left immediately, except that his legs were so weak he could hardly stand. The doctor had been forced to amputate one of his toes, and the pain was intense. At last Sky resigned himself to his plight. He told himself that he might as well use these people while he could and get his strength back. It was, after all, still winter. In his weakened condition, he'd never make it on his own. Oddly, the desire to die diminished also. Sky was too proud to give Billy Yates the satisfaction.

But he made life as hard on Billy and Reverend Harris as he could. He showed no appreciation. He grumbled about everything. He complained about the food—although in reality he thought Reverend Harris was a great cook. And when they attempted to preach at him, he shut them down harshly. Billy never actually preached at him, never even talked about God much to him. It was mostly Harris.

"Christ died for your sins, young man," Harris told him. "Repent, turn your life over to Him. The wages of sin is death but the gift of God is eternal life!"

"Don't waste your breath, Harris. I've heard it all."

"I'll let God decide when I'm wasting my breath."

"Fine. Talk all you want. I ain't listening." Sky rolled over in his bed and yanked a pillow over his head.

Harris must have thought that if he was going to have this heathen Indian in his house, he was going to make sure the Gospel got hammered into him. Billy was more subtle—and more frustrating.

"Are you curious at all about what has been happening at home since you left?" Billy asked one day as he brought Sky his lunch.

"No," Sky said flatly. But he was in fact very curious.

"T.R.—do you remember him?—married Leeann Martin. Last I heard, they have a couple of kids. Kyle Evanston and Becky Sue Weaver ran off together to California. Now, there's a match I'll bet wasn't made in heaven." Sky had a hard time restraining a smile at the thought of the town "bad girl" and that weasel Kyle together. Unfortunately, Billy must have taken this as encouragement for he kept going. "Just about everyone's got barbed wire now, even Arnel Slocum. Your ma still keeps a big herd of Longhorns, but she also has some of the best breeding stock in the county."

Sky let him go on for a minute or two more before he said testily, "I said I wasn't interested."

"Oh, I'm sorry. Forgive me for boring you." There was a touch of sarcasm in Billy's tone that matched the amusement in his eyes. "I reckon, then, you're not interested in what happened to me."

"That's the last thing I want to know."

"Okay, then, I'll leave you to your meal." Billy turned to go.

"Oh, all right, if you must tell me . . ." Sky couldn't help himself, though he knew the answer was probably going to be some religious testimony. But it was hard to ignore the surprise of discovering that Billy Yates had gone from a bigoted reprobate to a minister. "You love all Indians now, or is it just me?"

"I love all *people* now, Sky. I just couldn't help but love people once I came to realize the extent of God's love for others and especially for me. You know who helped me along the way? This'll shock you—it was Sam."

"Sam?"

"Yeah. Pretty incredible, isn't it? After all I did to you, he reached out to me and loved me anyway."

"Well, Sam was always that way." Sky said it lightly, as if dismissing the man.

"You are lucky to have him for a stepfather."

Sky shrugged silently, then turned his attention to his food. He had to eat if he was going to get strong enough to leave this place. But the mention of Sam nagged at Sky even after Billy left the

321

room. He thought of how sincere Sam was, and how crushed he'd be if he saw Sky now talking about God with such cynicism and even outright hostility.

He wondered how he could hang on to those angry attitudes in light of all Sam had taught him. But the minute Sky realized he was starting to sound sympathetic toward God, he got mad at Billy. It was pretty low-down for Billy to bring up Sam. He didn't have the guts to preach at Sky himself, so he tried to use Sam. Well, Sam was a good man, and his religion was fine—for Sam. It had been a disaster for Sky.

Later Billy told Sky how he hoped soon to be assigned to a mission on a reservation. "That your way of doing penance for what you done to me?" Sky baited Billy.

"In a way, yes. But it's not a duty. It's something I want to do, that I'm excited about doing."

"Well, no Indian is gonna want you to preach at 'em, or tell them what sinners they are unless they turn from their heathen ways."

"Are they hostile to religion?"

"To the white man's religion."

"But Christ is for all men."

"Only if they go to the white man's church and give up their traditions. Those missionaries don't want to Christianize Indians for the good of their souls. They want to crush the Indian people's souls and spirits so Indians don't give them any more trouble."

"Is this belief widespread among the Indian peoples?"

Sky shrugged and fell silent. He had said more than he wanted, indicated too much interest. He wanted to avoid talk of religion, not encourage it.

"Please, Sky," Billy said eagerly. "I would love to hear what you have to say about these things and what your people are thinking. There is so much I need to learn."

"Learn it from someone else. I'm not interested."

When Billy left, trying to hide his dejection, Sky tried not to feel guilty. He had a right to hate Billy, and he shouldn't have to feel guilty over anything he said or did to Billy. But he found he had to work hard to hate the man Billy had become. He was so sincere and kind it was almost sickening, but there was no doubt it was real, even natural. How could that be? Billy had been the meanest, most ornery person Sky had ever known.

In the end, it was his confusion that drove Sky to leave the minister's home long before he should have.

After ten days Sky was getting out of bed and walking around his room. His legs were shaky, and he still had a bad cough and congestion in his chest. He knew he hardly stood a chance outside on his own, but he was tired of Harris's preaching and Billy's maddening sincerity. Maybe he could stand it if he had a drink or two.

On Wednesday evening both ministers went to a prayer meeting at church. Sky remembered Sam's midweek prayer meetings. They could go on for a couple of hours. He had plenty of time to slip out, go to a saloon, get a couple of drinks, and slip back in. Only two obstacles hindered him. One was the old problem of the saloons refusing to sell him liquor. But there was always a stranger willing, for a little extra money, to buy the whiskey for him. That idea, of course, led to Sky's other problem—lack of money.

He got out of bed and dressed in some of Billy's clothes, which sagged badly on him. Billy's boots, however, actually fit quite nicely. Then he began rummaging through drawers for money.

Having no success in Billy's room, Sky went to Harris's bedroom. He found two bits—that was a good start. Next, he headed to the kitchen—his ma always hid what she called "pin money" in a sugar bowl. There was only sugar in Billy's sugar bowl. But Sky found fifty cents in a Mason jar. He pocketed the money, only vaguely aware that he was stealing from the people who had saved his life. They were such saps they probably would have given him the money had he asked.

Outside, fresh snow was falling and a cold north wind was blowing. He had a hard time negotiating his way over the icy streets, slipping several times and landing on his backside in the wet snow. He was exhausted after traversing only a block. He had to hang on to walls and fences and whatever he could find to brace himself. It took him half an hour to cross town. He was wet and cold and shivering when he came to his destination—the biggest, busiest saloon in town.

He didn't go in, but rather waited outside a few steps from the door. They might still recognize him and throw him out if he tried to enter. He watched customers come and go for a few minutes until one satisfied him—a man who looked like he'd do anything for a few cents. Of course, the fellow might also steal from an Indian, but Sky couldn't very well ask an honest man to help him. He had to take the risk.

Sky gave him the entire seventy-five cents and told him he could keep the change after purchasing the whiskey. Sky waited so long he began to fear all was lost. The thief might have slipped out the back way. But at last the man appeared and handed Sky a bottle only three quarters full.

"Had to have a drink or two," explained the man. "Didn't want no one to get suspicious."

Sky grabbed the bottle, glaring at the man, then took off to find a warm and dry place where he could enjoy himself. But now that he actually had the precious bottle in his hands, he was too impatient to be choosy. He went behind the saloon to an alley, walked a short distance to the back of another building where there was a recessed, locked doorway. Snuggling in there, he was out of the direct assault of the snow and wind, but it was still freezing.

He uncorked the bottle and brought it to his lips, savoring that first drink like a pleasant memory.

# 56

# THE LOST SHEEP

Billy found Sky in that same doorway the next morning. After the prayer meeting, Billy had discovered Sky was missing. He looked for him in the saloons and even looked in some of the alleys, then at last gave up the search as futile.

When the owner of the feed and grain store went to work at seven in the morning, he found Sky passed out. The man, a member of Billy's church, had heard about his Indian houseguest. And there were few enough Indians in Riverbend to make the man wonder if this could be Reverend Yates's Indian. He had immediately sent for the minister.

"Too bad, Reverend," said the storekeeper, "after all you done for him."

"We're all entitled to a few blunders," Billy said as he bent to lift Sky into his arms.

"You gonna take him back?"

"Of course. I'm not finished with him yet—and neither is God."

"I wouldn't trust him. Them Indians will rob you blind, especially if they got the whiskey habit."

"I have nothing worth stealing, but everything to give."

The storekeeper shook his head, but he helped Billy get Sky into Reverend Harris's wagon.

Back at the parsonage, Billy put Sky between the clean sheets of his own bed and cleaned him up again. Even he was amazed at his patience, and at the love that was pouring out of him. And it was not all springing from guilt and shame. The best way he could describe it was that it derived from a sense of kinship. He had been where Sky now was, if not physically then definitely emotionally. He had known Sky's pain and hopelessness. He had suffered. He and Sky might not yet be brothers in the Spirit, but they *were* brothers in loss and pain. And so Billy's feelings went beyond sympathy to empathy.

"Not you again!" Sky groaned when he regained consciousness. "Ain't I dead yet?"

"Guess I'm like a bad penny, Sky. You're not going to get rid of me that easy. And you're not going to die as long as I have any say in it."

"Well, you don't." Sky struggled to get out of bed, but the effort brought on a coughing fit which landed him on his back again.

"Give yourself one night to rest up, Sky. If you feel better in the morning, then leave."

"Oh, I'm leaving in the morning! You can count on it."

But by late that afternoon, Sky's fever had shot up and he was hardly able to sit up to drink the broth and tea Billy tried to get into him. The chances of him rising in the morning and walking away became more remote as the day wore into night.

"Looks like God is going to keep him here one way or another," Reverend Harris commented dryly.

"Maybe, but He's sure doing it the hard way."

"Some people seem to know no other way."

Sky's health did not improve—in fact, he became much worse over the next few days. Billy hardly left his side at all. He slept in the chair next to the bed, ate his meals there, and—most of all—prayed there. When Reverend Harris begged him to take a rest he refused. He was going to be the first face Sky saw when he woke from the raving semiconsciousness which the fever had brought on. If Billy had anything to do with it, the first sensation Sky would have was that of Christ's love reflected through Billy's vigil.

*If* Sky woke up.

Each time the doctor examined Sky, he shook his head hopelessly.

"He's got too much stacked against him," the doctor said. "The pneumonia is just a symptom of everything else."

But Billy would not accept that diagnosis. "Well, Doc, he's got me *for* him—and God."

"I hope you're a fighter, Reverend Yates, because that's what this man needs more than anything."

Billy smiled ironically. "One thing you can say for me, Doc, is that I'm a fighter. I guess I fought this fellow more than anyone."

"Well, the tables are sure turned now."

Billy did not only fight in prayer by Sky's bed. He cared for all of Sky's physical needs. He washed him, keeping him as clean as

326

a mother would her newborn baby, and like a baby, he fed him broth and tea whenever Sky was conscious enough to take it. Billy dug snow from the yard and packed it on Sky's body to reduce the raging fever. He read Scriptures to Sky until his throat was raw and sore. Sometimes he would sing hymns to Sky, remembering how Sky used to like singing in Sam's services. However, Billy's off-key voice never compared to the beauty of Sky's.

Billy wondered if Sky would ever again sing such praises to God. Even if he lived, would his heart heal enough to make music again? But when he was in prayer, he couldn't shake the assurance that Sky would live and that he would raise his voice in praise again. Billy clung to that hope through the long hours and days that followed. Billy knew that Reverend Harris was trying to prepare him for the worst. He was concerned that Billy's relatively young faith would be shaken if Sky died after all.

But Billy's confidence didn't waiver. At first he had been upset that God had directed Sky to him, but he eventually came to see God's greater purpose. Sky could have collapsed and died on anyone's doorstep, but he had ended up here. It was no coincidence. God had a reason for all this, and Billy was convinced that God didn't intend for Sky Killion to die.

For over a week Sky teetered on the edge of life and death. Most of the time he was raving hysterically—partly due to the fever, partly because of his alcohol habit. Then one night Sky's fever rose so high it brought on convulsions. Billy and Reverend Harris hauled in snow all through the night to pack Sky's body, and they cleaned up the melting puddles until their backs ached. The doctor came once and proclaimed they were doing all they could but not to expect Sky to last through the night. He also ordered Harris, who was coughing and sneezing from the overwork and lack of rest, to get to bed before they had another case of pneumonia on their hands.

Billy had no time then to get on his knees to pray, but there was always a prayer in his heart. Yet he began to wonder if Sky's coming had only been intended as a way to close a painful chapter in Billy's life. With Sky's death perhaps the past could finally rest in peace and Billy could move on. Why he had to move on, and to what, he couldn't guess. Maybe this final act of ministry to Sky would help relieve some of Billy's guilt. Maybe Sky would make some deathbed repentance, and in that same breath forgive Billy.

But Sky was too sick to confess or forgive anything. *Why, Lord?* Billy pleaded with God even as he labored over Sky.

Just before dawn, Sky's fever broke. The crisis was over. Sweat poured from his body, mingling with the melting snow. It took a Herculean effort to clear away the remains of the snow and change the wet bedclothes before another chill set in. When it was done, Billy fell into the chair exhausted. It was a few minutes before he realized that Sky was sleeping more peacefully than he had since his arrival.

Billy dozed off, awakened an hour later by the arrival of the doctor.

"I see he made it through the night," said the doctor, not a little surprised.

"A true miracle."

"Helped in no small part by you, Reverend Yates."

"He'll make it then?"

"He has a better chance today than any time since he got here."

Billy looked at the sleeping form, amazed how peaceful he looked. "He's hardly moved a muscle since the fever broke."

"He has been through a lot. He needs rest. I wouldn't be surprised if he didn't slip into a coma as the body's way of healing itself."

"A coma? That doesn't sound good to me. How will he eat or drink?"

"Hopefully it won't last long. And he may slip in and out. It will be up to you to be there when he's conscious and get what liquids you can into him."

Billy had no problem with this, though Reverend Harris hinted more than once that he had been neglecting all his other duties. In the nearly three weeks since Sky had arrived, Billy had, indeed, let all his other responsibilities go. Harris tried to be patient and understanding, but doing the work of two was wearing him down. Harris hadn't said anything outright, but Billy got the message: the needs of one drunken Indian didn't stack up against the needs of a hundred members of their flock.

Billy thought of the parable of the Lost Sheep, but he didn't mention it. Yet he knew innately that *his* calling was to the one lost sheep—not only Sky, but others like Sky in the world. That's why he was seeking to minister to the Indian people. There would always be someone to minister to the hundred. He would take the less appealing path, down mountainsides, through briars, into gullies and across raging rivers after the lost and forgotten ones. He might only save one drunken Indian in his lifetime compared to the hundreds Reverend Harris ministered to, but God's heavenly host would rejoice no less over that one.

328

# 57

# A VISITOR

One afternoon Billy was in his usual place by Sky's bed. As the doctor had predicted, Sky was in a kind of comatose state. He slept a great deal, though his sleep was often beset with moaning and incoherent cries. Occasionally Sky came to, but he was never fully aware of his surroundings. During these times Billy tried to coax nourishment into him—which he sometimes accepted, but sometimes fought. It was almost as if Sky himself wasn't sure whether he wanted to live or die.

Billy grew more discouraged than ever before. He constantly had to remind himself of his initial assurance that Sky would recover. After an especially difficult night, Sky had finally fallen into a quiet sleep. Billy tried to use the time to pray but he, too, was exhausted. Not long after his eyes closed in prayer, he was sound asleep.

When Reverend Harris knocked quietly fifteen minutes later, Billy jerked awake harshly. He had been dreaming his recurrent nightmare, where he was running across a huge plateau like those he'd known in west Texas. Jenny and Sky were chasing him. When he came to the edge of the plateau, they reached out their hands to prevent his fall, but he refused their help and stepped off the edge. He always woke before he hit bottom. This time he was jarred awake just as he took the fateful first step off the edge.

"I'm so sorry to have to awaken you, William—and just when it appears as if things have quieted down a bit."

"For now," Billy said in a sleep-thickened voice. He was not in his most optimistic mood. "I wonder how much longer it will continue."

"It's in God's hands, my boy. Can you leave your patient for a minute? There is someone here I think you ought to see."

"Who's that?"

"A visitor for our patient."

Billy cocked a curious eyebrow but, saying no more, rose and followed Reverend Harris to the small foyer of the house.

"Good afternoon." Billy extended a hand to the woman waiting there.

"Hello," she said. "Please forgive my intrusion, but I was told I might find someone here that I know."

"Who might that be?"

"His name is Blue Sky, or perhaps he might be known as Sky Killion."

"Yes, he is here."

The way her eyes suddenly sparked with joy was touching. Billy wondered vaguely how Sky could have degenerated so, with someone like this woman who obviously cared for him.

"May I see him?" she asked.

"Well . . ." Billy hesitated. "Miss—I'm sorry, I don't know your name and I didn't properly introduce myself. I am Reverend William Yates."

"My name is Rose, sir. I am Blue Sky's wife."

Billy's jaw went suddenly slack. He stared at this attractive Indian woman, trying unsuccessfully to figure out how Sky could have been separated from her. Billy quickly regained his composure—he would need it more than ever in order to tell this woman of her husband's serious condition.

"Mrs. Killion," Billy said, "you most certainly can see Sky, but first could I speak with you for a few minutes?"

When she nodded, he led her to the parlor. Reverend Harris went to prepare some tea.

Rose sat on the threadbare couch while Billy took a high-backed upholstered chair opposite her. Again he studied her until he saw that it made her uncomfortable, then he became apologetic.

"I can't help thinking you are a Godsend," he said. "Perhaps even the answer to my prayers, if you don't mind my saying so."

"And it may be you are the answer to my prayers," said Rose. "But before we go on, will you tell me if Sky is all right? I have lived so long with the fear that he might be dead. Can you ease my fears?"

"He is alive."

"Thank God!"

Billy smiled. Was it possible Sky had married a Christian Indian?

330

Or had she become a Christian after his departure? Well, God did work in mysterious ways.

"Mrs. Killion—"

"Please, Reverend Yates, it might be best if you just called me Rose. I never had the name Mrs. Killion. Sky did not wish it. It may upset him to hear it now."

"I'd be happy to oblige, Rose. And now I must tell you that, though Sky is alive, he is a very sick man. The doctor doesn't hold out much hope for him, but I believe with all my heart that God will spare him."

"What do you mean, 'sick'? Is it the whiskey?"

"That, but much more, I'm afraid. He contracted pneumonia—a very serious case. He has been here three weeks. At first he was improving, then he . . . well, he went out into the weather and that made him worse. A week ago his fever broke, but he's still frequently delirious and in and out of consciousness."

"He has been here a long time."

Billy nodded.

"I might never have found him otherwise," Rose commented thoughtfully. "I'm sorry Sky had to get sick in order for me to find him, but I see now what Jesus meant when He said to be thankful in everything."

"How long have you been looking for Sky?"

"Almost two years. I can't say I have been looking that entire time. The first few months I went all around asking about him, but it was a fruitless search. This is a big country to find one lost Indian in, especially when that Indian doesn't want to be found. Eventually I had to decide whether to use up all of the little money I had on a futile search or to go back home and make sure there would be a home for Sky to return to. Gray Antelope told me it was best to leave Sky in God's hands. For, even if I did find him, would I be able to convince him to come home? It seems leaving him to God was the right thing."

"Yes, and what you've said bolsters my faith all the more that God is definitely after Sky and won't let him go."

Reverend Harris brought in tea and poured three cups.

As they had their tea, Billy asked Rose, "What brought you here, Rose?"

"About two weeks ago a man came into Darlington with a guitar," Rose answered. "A friend of mine recognized it as one I bought for Sky. It still had the strap I made with beadwork. My friend found out that the man had gotten the guitar in Riverbend.

I prayed about if I should come. Would it be another wild goose chase? I decided that if I found the man with the guitar again and could get details that satisfied me, then I'd go. I found the man, but all he could tell me was that he bought the guitar from a bartender. He'd heard of no half-blood Indian named Blue Sky." She smiled, slightly embarrassed. "I'm afraid I ignored my own decision. But I couldn't let it go. I had to come to Riverbend. For once my stubbornness turned out to be a good thing."

"It sure has, Rose. I think you are just what Sky needs to bring him out of his illness."

"I hope so, but if he was running away from me—"

"I don't believe that for a minute. Sky has been running from many things over the years, but my heart tells me you weren't one of them."

"Can I see him?"

"Let's go," Billy said. "But just prepare yourself. He's been sick for a long time—"

She shook her head. "He's alive—that's what matters."

# 58

# THE VIGIL

Rose was still moved to tears when she looked down at Sky. She remembered the proud Cheyenne warrior filled with hope from his experience with the Paiute in Nevada. She remembered the vigor and enthusiasm with which he had danced the hapless Ghost Dance. But even the broken man after Wounded Knee was better than the wraith that lay shrouded in the white sheets of the large four-poster bed. Indeed, he looked like one of the very ghosts he had once hoped would save his people.

She went to his side and lifted his thin, bony hand. How strong that hand had once been, stringing his bow for the hunt or strumming a tune on his guitar! She did not dare think of his touch, or how she longed for that again—it only reminded her of the fact that Sky had never touched her out of love, and maybe never would.

Yet, if God had led her to him, didn't that mean there was still hope? Was it possible that Sky might yet come to love her?

But it didn't seem right to think such selfish thoughts now. It didn't matter if he ever loved her. She loved him and would always give everything she had to Sky. She mustn't expect any of her devotion to be returned.

The minister spoke as if he were reading Rose's thoughts. "We don't have an easy task ahead of us, do we? Healing his body, I think, will be the easy part. How will we ever heal his heart?"

"Why, Reverend Yates, don't you know the answer to that? Only God can do it."

Billy grinned. "I think you and I are going to get along wonderfully, Rose. I'm so glad you came."

"So am I, Reverend."

Together they continued the battle for Sky's life. Rose was

amazed at the minister's tireless commitment to Sky, and she was no less amazed when she heard the story from Billy of his relationship to Sky. If it was incredible that a stranger cared so for Sky, it was more amazing that his onetime adversary did so. And hearing these things also helped Rose understand much about Sky that she had only guessed at. She saw the roots of his bitterness, which had always seemed to go so much deeper than what simple bigotry could account for. She saw why he was afraid to love a woman . . . perhaps anyone.

Her heart ached when Billy said, "He was such a decent, fine person. I ruined that forever. No matter what happens, even if he comes to God again, I will have robbed him of his purity, that innocence he used to have."

"We all lose that eventually, Billy."

"Yes, to some extent. But it was ripped too violently from Sky."

"Perhaps it will one day give Sky a greater capacity to love others."

"That's my prayer."

She and Billy prayed often together and had many long talks as they sat by Sky's bedside. Once Billy commented on Rose's profound faithfulness.

"You are an example to other women, Rose," he said.

"I don't wish to be an example to anyone."

"But other women who have had similar difficulties with their husbands as you have had with Sky could be inspired by how you have never given up on him."

Rose thought about the time since Sky had left the camp. She knew she didn't deserve praise from anyone. There were times when she had wondered if she shouldn't just accept Sky's hasty divorce and move on with her life. She was young and still had a chance at a happy life. But always she remembered her conversation with her father before she and Sky had married, when Little Left Hand had asked her how long she would wait for Sky. The same answer continued to apply. As long as the love was alive in her heart she would wait. Being faithful to Sky was no great accomplishment as long as she loved him. But what if her love should finally grow cold? She was almost afraid to answer that question.

"I have felt in my heart I shouldn't give up," she said to Billy after some thought. "But that is me, Billy. Other women must follow their own hearts. And I can't say if I will always feel this way. What will I do if Sky recovers but turns away from me again and goes back to his whiskey? I can't say. I can only do what I must do now. I'm learning to let the future take care of itself. Who knows what tomorrow will bring?"

"I suppose that is the wise thing to do," Billy answered. "One step at a time; one crisis at a time."

"It's all anyone can do."

After three more days of constant vigil, a change finally came over their patient. Rose had been asleep in the chair and Billy had come in with a tray of tea. She woke slowly and languidly. It had been dark when she fell asleep, and now morning light spilled through the bedroom window. She felt quite rested, but said nothing for a moment, content in watching Billy set the tray on the table next to the bed. Her eyes wandered to Sky, and she sighed, wondering how much longer. Rose was about to say good morning to Billy when Sky moved and then his eyes opened. His eyes had been open before, of course, but he had been little aware of his surroundings. This time, before Rose could assess Sky's level of consciousness, Billy moved in front of her.

# 59

# BROKEN WINGS AND BROKEN MEN

It was Billy he saw first. "Bad penny . . ." Sky whispered.

"Sky?" Billy peered closely at his patient.

"Still here," said Sky.

"We both are."

"Yeah." Sky closed his eyes again. The light was so bright it hurt. But aside from that, he didn't feel as rotten as the last time he remembered. He recalled sitting in an alley, freezing and coughing and having a terrible time breathing, but content because he had a bottle of whiskey. Content, that is, until he had finished the liquor. Then he had felt really miserable. But he had no idea how he came to be back in Billy's bed nor how long he had been there.

"There's someone else here, too, Sky," Billy said.

Probably some do-gooder from Billy's church. Sky was about to say he wasn't up to visitors when Billy stood aside. He heard movement but stubbornly kept his eyes shut.

"Sky . . ."

It was a familiar voice . . . but it couldn't be. He must be dreaming, or maybe he was dead at last. Maybe all the angels sounded like that dear voice. Then an ironic practicality occurred to him. It was unlikely, if he were dead, that he'd be hearing *angels*.

He opened his eyes.

"Rose." A quick smile bent his lips before he could guard against it. "Where'd you come from?"

"Home."

"How——?" He stopped himself. "It doesn't matter. I wish you hadn't."

"Hush, Sky." She took his hand, and the warmth of her touch made Sky feel safe.

"I never knew such a stubborn girl. . . ." He closed his eyes again. "I think I'm going to sleep."

---

For the next couple of days Sky slept a lot. But when he woke, he was lucid. He felt strange having both Rose and Billy nursing him, yet he was too weak to argue. Deep down, he enjoyed being taken care of, enjoyed the human touch. It had been a long time since he had let anyone care about him at all.

He couldn't let himself get used to it, but for now, anyway, he was in no shape to insist on independence. He was so weak he could hardly sit up in bed without several hands to help and several pillows to keep him in place. He knew without even trying that his legs were too weak to stand, much less walk.

I'll accept their help while I have to, he told himself, but it's better for everyone if as soon as I'm able, I set out on my own. He refused to feel indebtedness toward them. Billy owed him because Sky had saved Billy's life. As for Rose—well, the best way he could repay her was to take his leave as soon as possible.

These thoughts lingered in his mind, but he didn't feel them as passionately as he knew he should. It was hard to get upset over anything when he felt so good—weak, yes, but good. He could breathe easily, and the coughing was far less debilitating. More than that, he wasn't shaking and his guts didn't ache as they so often did when he went without a drink. It was an odd sensation, but he didn't even crave a drink. He could hardly remember the last time he had felt that way.

*Since Wounded Knee.*

Sky pushed the unpleasant memory from his mind. He'd have to reckon with the past soon enough. He knew it wouldn't last, but for now, he just wanted to bask in the present.

---

Rose carried in a tray of food. She set it down and helped Sky sit up in bed. That was getting easier, at least. But Sky could hardly take it when Rose began feeding him the broth and gruel. When he came out of his coma, he had been too weak to grasp or lift a spoon. At first he resigned himself to his fate, but it was becoming

337

harder to do. He hoped that meant he was getting better.

As she brought the spoon to his lips he raised his own hand and laid it on hers. "Let me do it," he said.

Patiently she placed the spoon in his hand and helped him wrap his fingers around the handle. He slowly raised it, but his hand started shaking and the spoon fell, spilling broth on his nightshirt.

"Doggonit," he said.

"Don't worry, Sky. Your strength will come back."

"Not soon enough, I'm afraid."

"What do you mean?"

"Nothing. I'm just bored." He couldn't admit that he was anxious to leave. He believed it would be better for her if he left, but he knew it would hurt her.

"Sky, can you wait a minute for your dinner?"

Sky looked at the tray of bland, unappetizing food and nodded. Rose jumped up and left the room. In a moment she returned carrying a familiar large black case.

"My old guitar?" There was no approval in his tone.

Grinning, she nodded. He frowned at her.

"It was bad enough that you bought it once," he said. "Did you have to buy it again?"

"We argued once over this guitar," she countered. "Do we have to argue again?"

Before he could stop himself, he chuckled.

She smiled, obviously pleased by his rare mirth. "Take it, Sky, if for no other reason than to keep you occupied."

"I can't even hold a spoon. How am I supposed to play a guitar?"

"I'll set it here by your bed. When your strength returns, you will have it."

Rose continued to feed Sky his meal. When she wasn't looking, he watched her. And he decided that she had changed. She still looked the same, but somehow she seemed to be in sharper focus, as if he had always looked at her through cloudy lenses. Now the image was real, clear . . . and disturbing. It made him yearn for things that were simply too far out of reach for him, things that would only cause more pain if he tried to grasp them.

"Why are you doing this?" Sky asked suddenly.

"You mean the guitar?"

"No . . . everything. Why did you come? Why are you staying? Why, Rose? You know I don't want you here."

338

"Don't you, Sky?"

"I don't want to hurt you anymore."

"I will take complete responsibility if I'm hurt." She pushed a spoonful of gruel into his mouth so he couldn't reply immediately.

But he wasn't going to be silenced so easily. "You don't have to, Rose. I gave you your freedom."

"That's how you see it. But it's not so in God's eyes, nor in my own eyes."

"Do you think our Indian marriage ceremony counted to God?"

"The educated men at the agency debate this question all the time. Even they can't agree on an answer. I only know I married you in my heart, Sky. And my heart is still married to you."

"After all I did? How could you?"

"That is the nature of love, I suppose."

"I wouldn't know," he said, trying to sound cynical.

She gave him a quick smile. "I've forgotten what a hardened man you've become."

Sky said nothing in reply, but he thought, *I have to be hard to survive. If I opened myself up again, if I tried to love again and believe in something again and it failed me, I would die.*

Maybe that's what made him so uncomfortable over the next several days. He felt his emotional walls begin to weaken, especially around Rose. Feelings of tenderness would catch him off guard, and longing too—for what they could have together, if only he'd let it happen.

He knew he couldn't last long in the face of her unwavering love. Thus he threw what strength he had into getting well. He had to escape this place before he was caught in its insidious web of love and kindness. He asked Billy to help him exercise his arms and legs while he lay in bed. Billy also fashioned for him two tightly rolled dish towels which he could grip in his hands, even when he was alone, making and releasing a tight fist. Sky worked his hands every waking moment until after three days his hands were strong enough to feed himself without trouble . . . and play his guitar.

Sky played out of sheer boredom. At first his attempts were tentative. He played sad, quiet songs that suited his mood—"Red River Valley," "Lorena," "My Old Kentucky Home." Once when he was idly strumming the strings, not paying attention to what he was doing, he began playing the old tune he'd made up.

*"My warrior's song borne on the wind . . ."*

When he became aware of the words silently forming in his

339

mind, he shook his head but didn't cut them off. He let them flow through his fingers and mind like a balm—whether healing or not, he couldn't tell. Odd, how the song, made up while he was still young and relatively naive, so chronicled his present path. The dream of glory his father had instilled in Sky's heart was truly shattered. He was no longer a warrior. At twenty-five, he was a broken man, not even able to shed tears of hopelessness.

Still, he didn't change the last line as he used to do when he was drunk.

*"And hopes to sing his song at dawn . . ."*

Did he really think there was still a chance to repair all the damage that had been done? Sam would say, "Where there's life there's hope." But Sky wasn't sure if he *was* still alive. Sometimes he felt like a tomb filled with dead bones. And yet if he closed his eyes and let his mind go, he could see that white eagle in his song soaring with a broken wing. Sky had once seen that very thing in reality—not a white eagle, but a big brown one. Sky had been impressed at how it flew in spite of its injury. That's probably why the image had found its way into his song. Sometimes seemingly impossible things can happen. Sometimes even broken people can keep going—no, not just *keep going*, but actually *soar*.

He supposed it was up to him. But it was a big risk. Too big. And not only was he afraid of hurting himself, but he might hurt others also.

Bitterness and hopelessness were safe, if nothing else.

# 60

# THE SERMON

Sky clung to Billy's neck, hating the man's patience, resenting his strength. He took his first steps like a wobbly fawn or a feeble old man.

"You're doing great, Sky," encouraged Billy.

Rose was standing by the chair smiling.

"Only a couple of steps to the chair," Billy said.

"Forget the chair," said Sky. "I want to walk around the room."

"You don't want to overdo it."

"Around the room," Sky insisted.

He saw Billy and Rose exchange looks. Rose nodded slightly.

With Billy's help Sky hobbled to the other side of the room. He was panting and sweating by the time he dropped back into bed. An hour later when he was alone, Sky slipped out of bed and attempted once again to circumvent his room. He was exhausted after going halfway and leaned against the footboard of the bed to rest. Just then, Billy came in with lunch.

"You are a determined man, aren't you?"

"I'm sick of being a burden on everyone."

"You're no burden."

"I should think you'd be glad to see me get strong and out of your hair."

"I'm willing to leave it in God's hands."

"Well, I'm not."

"You've made that clear. But do you really have a choice? It looks to me like God has gone to a lot of trouble to keep you here."

Sky shrugged and continued on his journey until he reached the side of the bed. He scooted onto the edge and swung his legs back under the covers.

"If that's true," Sky continued when he was settled, "and I'm not saying it is. But if it were, then it seems to me you are wasting a prime opportunity."

"What do you mean?"

"You know, for preaching."

"Do you want me to preach to you, Sky?"

"No!" Sky answered quickly. "But I am kind of curious why you don't."

"What could I say to you that you don't already know?"

"If I know so much, why is my life in such a shambles?" Sky's words came out defensively, as if he were in an argument with Billy.

"I could tell you the answer if you really want to know."

Sky glared at Billy. He had been baiting him, and he was mad because Billy wasn't taking the bait.

"No, I don't want to know," Sky finally replied sulkily. He turned on his side with his back toward Billy.

Billy said, "I've got your lunch here."

"I'm not hungry."

"If you don't eat, you're never going to get strong enough so you can leave here."

Sky remained silent for a minute, then turned and sat up in bed. Billy set the tray in front of Sky and Sky ate as if every bite were a challenge.

"You're pretty smug, Billy," Sky said.

"I am?"

"You're flaunting your religion in my face just like you used to flaunt your bigotry."

"If I've offended you, Sky, please forgive me—"

"Stop it!"

"What do you want me to do?"

"Just get out of here."

Billy left without another word. Sky simmered and stewed the rest of the day. There was nothing more aggravating than to be denied a target for his ire. For days he had been waiting for Billy to start preaching at him; he had a great store of arguments to level at any theological tirade Billy might confront him with. But he couldn't argue with forgiveness.

He gave this a lot of thought and finally discovered a reason for Billy's reticence. He was ready for Billy when he came to take away the tray; but Rose came instead. Sky didn't see Billy until the next morning, but he picked up the thread of the previous conversation as if it were a dangerous rattler that needed to be killed.

"I've finally figured you out, Billy." Sky said with challenge.

"Have you?" Billy was helping Sky get out of bed for his morning exercise.

"You don't think I'm worth wasting your time on, do you? Why bother preaching at a mere Indian, eh?"

Billy maneuvered Sky so he was sitting on the edge of the bed, then he sat down next to Sky and faced him.

"Is that what you really think, Sky? Or are you saying it because you have no other way to explain it? Because if that's what you think, you are more deluded than I thought. Maybe I have been wasting my time—not because you are an Indian, but because you're a doggone fool!" Billy jumped up with his rising agitation. "I don't care if you ever thank me for what I've done for you, spending every minute I have nursing you and praying for you. I don't want your thanks; that's not why I'm doing this. But for you to accuse me of bigotry, well, that takes the cake! Even now, I'd still lay my life down for you, Sky, but that wouldn't be enough. Nothing I do will ever be enough, will it? That's fine, too, I'm not looking for absolution. But the least you could do is give me a little credit."

"Why should I?"

Billy ignored Sky's accusing tone. "Now that I think of it, I've got it all wrong, and so do you," he said. "This isn't about me at all. It's about God. You're just using me to shield yourself from Him. You want me to preach at you, Sky?" Billy's color rose with his voice. "Fine! Here's what I'd say: You can only push me so far, and I think I'm just about there, at the end of my patience. But you'll never be able to push God too far. You can't push Him, and you can't hide from Him. And once you leave here you're not going to have me to provide cover. Maybe you'll start drinking again—that's no doubt an effective shield, too. But sooner or later you're going to have to face God alone, without whiskey, without me, without even your bitterness to protect you. You're going to have to face God and answer for yourself. He's not going to want to hear your whining that people treated you bad because you are an Indian. He was treated bad, too—and he *forgave* those who mistreated him—"

Suddenly Billy stopped. "Doggone it! You made me preach, and I swore I wouldn't do it. Thanks, Sky," he added angrily, "I hope you're happy."

Billy turned and strode toward the door. "I'll send Reverend Harris in to help you exercise."

"Where's Rose?"

"She took a walk."

Sky said no more. He would have refused Reverend Harris's help, but he wanted more than ever to get strong. As much as he wanted to believe the worst about Billy, he couldn't shake his own sense of guilt over what he had said. In the month he had been under Billy's roof—sleeping in his bed, for heaven's sake!—Billy had never done anything to make Sky think he hadn't truly changed. Billy had not slipped once into the bigoted and mean character of the past. Sky could accuse Billy of anything and everything, but the truth was, Billy *was* a changed person. Really changed; completely changed; even miraculously changed.

Even that irked Sky. After all Billy had done, his life had turned out well. It didn't seem fair.

Maybe Billy was right. Sky was just using Billy as a convenient and safe target. It was a lot easier to hate Billy than it was to hate God. If he really admitted that it was God he hated for the mess his life had become—

Well, he didn't want to think about what would happen then. The image of the loving, forgiving God was too deeply ingrained in Sky for him to ignore it forever. If he came to terms with the real roots of his bitterness, he'd have to come to terms with God—the God of his mother, of Sam, of others whom he'd met and respected. He'd have to face the fact that God was pure love and forgiveness, that *He* hadn't brought evil upon Sky. The choice had been Sky's—it had always been his.

"I need a drink," Sky said aloud, licking his lips as if they were parched.

Was it true, then, what Billy had said? Was whiskey just another shield against facing the truth?

But Sky wasn't ready to answer these questions. He wasn't ready to let go of his bitterness.

When Billy came in later that day, Sky had gathered his protective barrier back around him. He had stuffed his confusion and questions back into a far corner of his heart.

"I'm sorry for getting angry at you earlier," Billy said.

"That's okay." Sky felt a twinge of guilt. He knew he had deserved Billy's outburst, yet he couldn't admit it.

"Reverend Harris said you were much stronger."

"Yeah, I'm getting there."

"The weather's cleared up quite a bit since you've come. The snow is almost all melted, and the farmers are predicting an early spring."

"Good."

"Rose said she found some wildflowers."

"What're you getting at, Billy?"

"Well, the doctor said if the good weather holds, you could walk outside a bit to get some fresh air."

"Now, that I'd like!" Sky said enthusiastically.

"I thought you might be getting a bit stir crazy."

"I'm not used to being sick and cooped up."

"We'll pray for the weather to hold up."

There was a moment of silence as Sky debated within himself. Something had been troubling him, and the mention of Rose brought it back to mind. He hesitated in mentioning it for fear of stirring up uncomfortable issues, but on the other hand he felt too strongly about it to simply let it go.

"Billy, how is Rose doing? You said she had been out walking; was it because things are starting to get to her?"

"I haven't had that impression," said Billy. "I think her faith keeps her strong."

"You would," Sky said with some disdain. Then he added, "Maybe you're right. How long is she planning on staying?"

"That's never really come up. Why don't you ask her?"

"Now that I'm better," Sky said, ignoring Billy's question, "I think you ought to encourage her to go home."

"Do you think she'll leave without you?"

"She has to, Billy. Even you must see that I'm no good for her. She thinks we're still married, but I divorced her, gave her her freedom. Anyway, it never was a Christian ceremony."

"I'm in no position to tell her what to do, Sky. Anyway, would she listen to me if I did?"

"It's useless for her to stick around. As soon as I'm well, I'm taking off on my own again. It's best . . . you know, for her."

"You'll have to tell her that yourself."

"I can't, Billy," said Sky miserably.

"There's still time," Billy replied with sympathy. "Let's wait and see what happens. Maybe she'll decide on her own."

# 61

# THE DRINK

In three more days, Sky was back on his feet. He wouldn't admit it, but he still tired easily, and he needed to put on twenty-five pounds to be back to his normal weight and rid of that skeletal appearance. He would have been quite pleased with his progress except that he could no longer put off a confrontation with Rose.

He thought it might go better if they were outside, so after lunch one day he asked her to go for a walk.

The sun was out and the sky was blue, but a chilly wind persisted. Sky had a new coat to wear, as well as new Levi's and a flannel shirt, sturdy boots and wool socks, and a wide-brimmed farmer's hat. His own clothes had simply been too worn out to salvage, but Billy's clothes were far too big for Sky, and Reverend Harris's were too short. Sky swore he'd pay Billy back for the clothes, although he didn't know how or when.

Everything Sky wore was new except the beaded collar Stands-in-the-River had given him. He didn't know why he kept it. Maybe he liked the peculiar mix, the way the combination of white and Indian ways mirrored his mess of a life.

The snow was gone, and the air was clean-smelling with mingled scents of blossoming trees, grass, and dirt. Sky realized how long it had been since he had been able to appreciate such good sensations. Long before his illness, alcohol had numbed his emotions and dulled his other senses as well.

Even better than the fragrance of spring was the pleasant sensation of walking beside Rose. He didn't want to notice the tilt of her finely chiseled chin as she, too, took in their surroundings. He wanted to ignore the shimmer of her black hair, with its thick braid swaying against her back with her every step. And he definitely tried to avoid her sweet umber eyes that were alternately glowing with fire or sensitivity. But he couldn't help noticing—and appreciating—her.

Maybe walking out here in the sunshine with Rose had been a mistake.

He felt himself weakening, considering fatal thoughts. Perhaps they *could* have a life together. Maybe he didn't have to go it alone any longer. How he hated the prospect of being alone again!

Rose interrupted his reverie. "You're doing so well."

"Yeah, I guess so. I feel much better."

"Even the doctor says your recovery is a miracle."

"I can't figure out why I made it."

"You can't?" Her brow creased in that peculiar way of hers— part scolding, part playful. She was making it so hard.

"Do you think God spared me for some great purpose?" he asked, his tone laced with mockery.

"You may make light of it, Sky, but, yes I do. I don't know why you fight it so. You must know God only means good for you."

"I *don't* know that, Rose, not anymore. But you wouldn't understand. You weren't at Wounded Knee. Any grain of belief I might have had was crushed there."

"Do you blame God for Wounded Knee?"

"I don't know. The only thing I do know is that it hurts too much to believe in anything. It's better to be—nothing."

"But God—"

"God, God, God! I'm tired of hearing about God. If it's not from you it's from Billy—or worse yet, from Harris. Why can't you all just give it a rest? I've chosen my path—let me take it."

"If I knew that's what you truly wanted . . ."

She turned and gazed at him, her eyes searching him so incisively he was certain she must see the truth. Uncomfortable, he looked away. When he spoke again, his words were marked with determination.

"It's what I want." Was his tone convincing enough? "Will you let me go in peace?"

"I'll try not to hound you about God, but I'm not ready to let you go—"

He broke in sharply. "Rose, you're wasting your time, do you hear me? I'm a lost cause."

"I am a Cheyenne squaw, Sky. Lost causes don't scare me!" She gave him that smirk again.

"Rose, I have given you nothing but misery. Why must you keep coming back for more? You should be scared—you really should! Do you think I've quit drinking? That's the only reason why I've been working so hard to get back on my feet. All I can think of is getting a drink. I haven't changed, Rose. I'll never change. If you think love will make everything better, you're wrong."

"You haven't given it a chance."

"For heaven's sake, woman! Why can't I make you see!"

"Do you love me, Sky?"

Her tone was quiet and confident, and the question came so abruptly it threw him off guard. She had never asked him so directly before, and though he had told her in the beginning that he didn't love her, he had never since been confronted with that question. He had to be convincing now more than ever. He didn't know the answer to her question; he only knew that how he felt was not important. Sometimes love just couldn't conquer all.

"No, Rose, I don't." But he couldn't look at her as he told the lie.

She was quiet for a very long time. They had walked some distance from town. A bluejay winged overhead, carefree on that fine spring day. From somewhere the fragrance of apple blossoms drifted into Sky's senses. He wished it were still winter. Spring was a dangerous time; it made you think hope was possible, and it dulled the harsh memory of winter.

When he could stand the silence no longer, he stole a glance at Rose and saw she was weeping quietly. Was there no end to his capacity to hurt her? Couldn't she see now why it was best to make a clean break?

"I'm going," he said suddenly.

"Where?"

"It doesn't matter."

He wanted to run away from her right then, to get as far from her as possible. But in his condition, he could never outrun Rose. And he didn't think she'd just let him go.

"Let's go back to Billy's," he said. "I'm kind of hungry."

They walked back to the parsonage, mostly in silence. The moment Rose went into the kitchen, Sky took off again, leaving quietly by the front door. No one saw him leave. He went to the little barn by the house where Billy and Harris kept a couple of horses. Billy would never turn Sky in for horse stealing.

Sky quickly saddled the chestnut and let him outside. This was too easy. It was meant to be. As Billy or Rose would say, it was God's will. And why shouldn't it be? What he was doing was as much for the good of others as it was for him.

348

When he was fifty yards from the house, he mounted and rode off.

————

The next town was ten miles away, and it was nightfall by the time Sky reached it. He stopped at the first saloon he came to. But when he entered the place, he didn't really want a drink. He was thinking of Rose, but not of the good life she had to offer him. He thought only that he had to show her once and for all the kind of man he had become.

He lugged in the saddle from Billy's horse and hoisted it up on the counter.

"You give me a bottle of whiskey for this?" he asked the bartender.

"I can't sell firewater to no Injuns."

"I'm not an Injun, I'm Mexican."

The bartender gave Sky a closer appraisal. Whether he believed Sky or not was questionable, but he obviously liked the idea of such a lucrative trade.

"You want to trade this saddle for one bottle of whiskey?" the bartender asked.

"Yeah."

"Okay." The bartender lifted the saddle and stowed it under the counter. He then produced a bottle and a glass.

Sky took these and went to an empty table in the corner. The saloon was quiet, with only three or four other customers. Sky uncorked the bottle and filled the glass. But he just sat there staring at the glass.

He felt as if he was looking at his future.

And he didn't much like it.

But was it any better reflected from Rose's eyes? Could it be better? Everyone was telling him that the choice was his, but was it? He hadn't chosen to be ridiculed and demeaned because of his Indian blood. It wasn't his fault that Jenny had been killed. He hadn't planned, or wanted, to leave his home. Others had thrust these things upon him. All the Billys in the world had caused his demise. What choice did he have?

It was their fault. They never gave him a chance.

And what of his choice to turn his back on God? Perhaps he could have gone the other way. Like Rose, he could have chosen faith over bitterness and hatred. Like Gray Antelope, who had seen so much more violence and bigotry than he ever would. Were they deluded, or the most courageous people he knew?

What if he did decide to give God another chance? Could God guarantee that people would not make him feel worthless for who he was, for what he could do nothing about? People would always hate him for being an Indian. So what good did it do to believe anyway? God had never protected him from hatred before, even when Sky believed. God had not changed the attitudes of others.

There was absolutely nothing in Sky's past to convince him it would be any different in the future. He would always be a worthless half-breed. God couldn't change that.

Suddenly Sky remembered something Billy said.

*"You're going to have to face God and answer for yourself. He's not going to want to hear your whining that people treated you bad because you are an Indian. He was treated bad, too—and He forgave those who mistreated him—"*

Was he really whining? The idea repulsed him. Seeing himself as a whining half-breed was far worse than the image of a drunken Indian. All his life he had only wanted to be a man of honor, a man with a warrior's heart. But look at what he had become!

He thought of the rest of what Billy had to say. Christ had also been mistreated. Like Sky, Christ had suffered unjustly for things He could not help. But what had His response been?

Forgiveness.

*"Love your enemies, bless them that curse you, do good to them that hate you, and pray for them which despitefully use you and persecute you."*

Those hadn't been just words, either. Christ had lived them out on the cross. Even as He died an unjust death, He had forgiven his murderers.

Before Sky realized it, images from his past began tumbling into his mind—things he hadn't thought about for years. Scriptures he had memorized as a child. Bible stories read to him by his mother. Sermons he'd heard Sam preach. Years ago Sam had given Sky that Bible. Sky had never read a word of it, thinking he could escape from God by ignoring Him. But Sky could do nothing about all the teachings that were stored away in his brain.

*"Be not overcome of evil, but overcome evil with good."*

Sky remembered the family tradition on Easter Sunday. The whole ranch would gather at sunrise and Sky's mother would read the Easter story, starting at the Last Supper and ending at the Resurrection. Tears would always fill his mother's eyes as she read about Jesus forgiving His executioners. Deborah Killion had fought her own battles with forgiveness. She had been imprisoned unjustly. Her beloved husband, Sky's father, had been killed, and her peaceful life with the Cheyenne destroyed.

Sky wasn't the only person to suffer hardship. Maybe it took a special strength to forgive—a strength he didn't have. Or did he?

Was it too late? Had he gone too far? Could he turn back? Could he find some of his lost innocence, or at least his lost spirit?

*Did he want to?*

He gazed down at the glass of whiskey. His drunkenness hadn't been all bad. He hadn't felt pain then. The whiskey did shield him from hurt. God had never done that.

"Hello, señor."

Sky's head jerked up at the sound of the voice. It was a barmaid. He looked at her with both annoyance and relief.

"Mind some company?" she said.

Sky shrugged, and she sat in a chair adjacent to Sky's.

"You buy that whiskey just to look at it?" she asked.

"No."

"How's about sharing some?" She set another glass on the table.

Absently, Sky picked up the bottle and filled her glass. He was tired of thinking, tired of going around in emotional circles. He'd never had to think much when he was drinking. Whiskey demanded nothing of him . . . except his soul.

The woman lifted her glass. "Come on, fella, you look like you need some cheering up. What'll we drink to?"

Sky placed his hand around the small glass and ran his fingers up and down the smooth surface—lovingly, as if he were welcoming his only friend . . . or, was it a gesture of farewell?

He hadn't known pain when he was drunk, but a corpse couldn't feel pain. He had heard of fictional creatures called zombies—the living dead. That's what he was. And that's what he would be if he had this drink. The most pathetic of all beings—not worthy of true death, not worthy of real life.

Was this, then, what Broken Wing's fine heritage had come to—drowned in a glass of firewater because his son was too tired, or too weak, or simply too beaten to do any better?

"White eagle soars on broken wing . . ." Sky murmured out loud.

"What?" said the barmaid.

He glanced up; he had forgotten she was there.

"I don't have anything to drink to," he said.

351

"I'll think of something, then."

"To the future . . . in a bottle or on a broken wing," Sky said.

"That's the strangest toast I ever heard. But anything in a pinch." The woman lifted her glass to her lips and tossed back the drink. When she saw Sky's glass still on the table, she said, "Hey, what about you?"

Sky hesitated, desperately looking for a reason *not* to take the drink. Suddenly the saloon door opened and a cold breeze swept in, followed immediately by the burly figure of Billy Yates. His frame almost hid the more petite figure that came in after him.

Sky could not believe what he saw. In another minute, he would have had that whiskey—and perhaps been lost forever.

Rose hurried ahead of Billy and reached Sky first. He looked up at her, sudden tears clouding his eyes.

"Rose, help me," he said.

Rose slid to her knees before him and took his hands into hers. "I will!"

# 62

# BELOVED HALF-BREED

Dew was still heavy on the new green leaves and the tender blades of grass when Sky mounted Billy's chestnut and rode out of town. This time he wasn't running away.

He was seeking.

After Billy had paid for Sky's drink and retrieved his bartered saddle, Sky had gone back to the parsonage with Rose and Billy. They had talked until the early hours of the morning.

"I don't want to be angry," Sky told them. "I don't want to hate. It's killing me. But I don't think I have it in me to forgive those who have hurt me, those who have hurt my people. How can you do it, Rose? Your mother was killed at Washita. Your sisters were killed by the measles that our people never had before the white man came. How can you not hate?"

"You gave the answer already, Sky," she said. "I don't want to die inside. Sometimes forgiveness is a selfish thing, a means of survival."

"It's too easy on them to forgive them. I want to see them suffer as I've suffered."

Billy interrupted, "As one of *them*, Sky, I can say I have suffered. Perhaps not nearly enough, but God did take me through the fire. But it was nothing you could do, Sky. God had to make that happen."

" 'Vengeance is Mine, says the Lord . . .' " Sky intoned.

"Something like that."

"I don't know . . ."

"Maybe if you started small."

353

"What do you mean?"

Billy faced Sky and looked into Sky's eyes. "I've tried to make up for all I've done to you by my actions," he said. "But I have never faced you and asked you for forgiveness. I ask you now, Sky . . . forgive me—" Sudden tears filled Billy's eyes. "Forgive me for hurting you. Forgive my hate and the hate I leveled at your people." Tears streaming down his cheeks, Billy dropped to his knees. "Before God, Sky, I am so sorry!"

"You don't have to do this," said Sky.

"Yes, I do. My whole life, all the changes I've made, will mean nothing unless I can hear those words from you, Sky. As you have had nightmares about me, Sky, I have had them about you. I've been haunted by the fear that I would go to my death knowing that the man I have most wronged had been destroyed by my hate. And, though I now love you, Sky, and I love the Indian people, there will always be a part of me that will suffer for what I've done."

"And my forgiveness will stop that suffering?"

"It will help."

"And if I don't, you will continue to suffer?"

"I think so."

"There was a time when that would have given me great joy, Billy. If I ever prayed at all, it was for you to suffer. My dreams that weren't nightmares—the good dreams—were of you, as you are now, on your knees begging me for forgiveness. And I would spit in your face." Sky paused as he thought of those dreams. How good he had felt in them when Billy Yates crawled away a broken heap of a man. But the reality was different. Sky was the broken man who would crawl away if he rejected Billy's plea—doomed to die inside, consumed by his own hatred.

"I wouldn't blame you if you did," said Billy.

"No, I don't think you would. You would love me just like you kept doing while I was sick. You made it awfully hard for me to keep hating you."

"But you tried."

Sky smiled. "Well, you've finally worn me down."

"Good." Billy returned the smile, as genuine as any Sky could have desired from his old adversary.

Sky now leveled his gaze at Billy. "Billy, I forgive you." And the words were not nearly as hard to say as he had feared.

Sky had risen the next morning before everyone else. His next step had to be taken alone. It would be even harder than forgiving Billy.

He had to face God.

He rode down to the banks of the river from which the town of Riverbend had derived its name. It wasn't much of a river, but here in the prairie regions any ribbon of water could easily attain such a status. Spring runoff made the stream more effusive than usual, boiling over river rocks in a merry, carefree way. You could throw a rock across to its other bank quite easily, and in many places the bottom was visible. But it supported a thick stand of cottonwoods and willows, now verdant with new foliage.

Sky led his mount down the sloping bank and rode along the edge of the water for a short distance until he found a spot that suited him. There he dismounted and tied the horse to a tree branch where the animal could graze on the sweet grass. Sky took his guitar and walked until he found a good place to sit. Everything was wet at that hour of the morning, but he found a big rock right at the water's edge where he could perch comfortably and have a good view of both the water and the surrounding glade of trees.

He took his guitar from its case, slipped Rose's beautiful strap around his neck, and began fingering the strings absently. He didn't have in mind anything particular to play but simply made up a melody as he went. Playing made him feel more at ease and relaxed his mind. He had to admit he was a little afraid of what lay ahead.

All his life he had been taught of a loving, merciful God. Billy and Rose were the most recent reminders of that God, but Sky had never been without *some* reminder. Even Wovoka had spoken of a loving, caring God. And, in reality, Sky had never stopped believing in God. He had often twisted God into whatever shape suited him at any particular time, but mostly he had written off God as "the white man's God." That had nicely explained away his mother's and Sam's faith. Rose and Gray Antelope were another matter. Explaining their faith had required a little more creativity on his part. But by immersing himself into the Ghost Dance faith, he was able to incorporate their God into his beliefs and not have to deal with the reality of the true God. And even if for the Indian peoples, the Ghost Dance was part of their search for the Wise One Above, it failed to take into account the one crucial facet of Christianity.

Christ died for *all* men, not just the Native people. God's mercy

355

was intended to be poured out on *all* who believed in Him.

For the moment, however, Sky knew he couldn't evade his personal confrontation with God by getting distracted with larger issues. For now, it wasn't "all men" or even the Indian people that concerned God. No doubt God did deal with nations and groups; there were plenty of examples of that in the Bible. But right now, God wanted to deal only with *Sky*. And even if much of Sky's degeneration could be blamed on injustices done to his people, he still had to answer for his own response to those injustices.

Like Rose and Gray Antelope, Sky could have responded with love and forgiveness. Instead, he had given hate for hate and returned his own kind of reverse bigotry for the white man's bigotry. Instead of allowing God to be his sword and shield, he had used his own paltry and vindictive strength. Rather than taking shelter in the everlasting arms of Christ, he had tried to hide in a bottle of firewater.

The choices had always been there. He had chosen the path that had led to destruction. No one, not even Billy, had forced him on that path. He alone had made that fateful detour.

Now he had a chance to turn it all around.

He had made a good start in forgiving Billy. Rose had been right; already he felt some of his own pain mended in that simple act. And because of that, he was here now. He wanted to take the next step. Forgiving Billy had made it easier, as Billy said it might. Yet Sky also knew that if he gave his bitterness and hatred to God, if he forgave those who had mistreated him and his people, it would not stop others from continuing the hurt and prejudice. Acts of injustice would continue. Other Billys would come along. Sky would still be refused service, and he would have to watch his children ridiculed and denied their basic rights. The pain would not magically stop.

Sky thought back to the many church services he had attended. He recalled a song Sam almost always had his congregations sing. Many times Sky had accompanied the piano, if there was one, with his guitar. As if it had been yesterday, his fingers quickly sought out the chords. His soft tenor had become a bit more rugged and deeper with the passage of time—rather like buckskin which looks beautiful when it is new, but becomes softer and better with age and wear. The words flowed from his lips without a single lapse of memory.

*"What a friend we have in Jesus, all our sins and griefs to bear! What a privilege to carry everything to God in prayer! O what*

*peace we often forfeit, O what needless pain we bear, all because we do not carry everything to God in prayer!"*

Sky had asked Rose what good was God if he didn't stop the pain? There were no doubt many good reasons why God didn't take away pain, but regardless, God did not intend that pain be carried alone. He offered to carry that heavy burden himself.

*"Have we trials and temptations? Is there trouble anywhere? We should never be discouraged—take it to the Lord in prayer! Can we find a friend so faithful who will all our sorrows share? Jesus knows our every weakness; take it to the Lord in prayer!"*

Sky could not believe how dense and deluded he had allowed himself to be. He had listened to those words dozens of times with a closed, hard heart. When he had been young and yearning for a friend, he had rejected the one true friendship, the friend who accepted him, troubles and weaknesses and all.

*"Are we weak and heavy-laden, cumbered with a load of care? Precious Savior, still our refuge—take it to the Lord in prayer! Do thy friends despise, forsake thee? Take it to the Lord in prayer! In His arms He'll take and shield thee—thou wilt find a solace there."*

"O, God!" Sky said to himself, and to the God he knew was listening, "I can't do this alone. When I tried, the only refuge I found was a bottle of whiskey. But it never gave me solace; it never gave me peace. I thought I had found peace in the Ghost Dance, but it failed me when I really needed it. It didn't protect the lives of my friends; it didn't protect my heart.

"I'm turning to you now, God, because I have nowhere else to turn. I'm giving you all my hate, all my bitterness. If you can't bear it for me, then I am truly lost. My best hope then is death. But I know you can bear it. You've done it for others, I know you'll do it for me if only I let you.

"I may be a worthless half-breed to everyone else, but to you I am your son. You were sort of a half-breed, too, weren't you Jesus? A Jew, but also the Son of God. What inner battles and confusion *you* must have known! Help me live out your example. Help me to return good for evil, blessings for curses, prayer for persecution. And when I fail, Jesus—I can't imagine not failing a lot!—forgive me and give me the strength to start over."

Then came the truly hard part.

"Jesus, you were perfect. You had done *nothing* wrong, yet you forgave. I am the most imperfect of men, and the Indian people are hardly perfect, either. So how can I do less than you did?

"God, I forgive the whites who have hurt me; I forgive the soldiers who killed my father and my friends at Wounded Knee; I forgive those who will continue to lash out unfairly at me and the people I love."

Sky's fingers, still resting on the strings of his guitar, began to move again, as if an extension of his prayer. The tune he had made up years ago poured out. *"My warrior's song borne on the wind . . . White eagle soars on broken wing . . ."*

Only God could make a wounded eagle soar. Indeed, that the wing was *still* broken only proved beyond all doubt God's power and goodness. Sky would always be a half-blood and an Indian. He would always carry with him the temptation to return to alcohol—these things God would not change. Yet Sky *would* take flight, broken wing and all, with a song of praise on his lips.

# 63

# WARRIOR'S SONG

With his guitar case in hand, Sky found Rose in the kitchen helping Reverend Harris prepare breakfast.

"Do you mind if I take Rose away for a few minutes?" Sky asked.

Harris eyed Sky, and a smile crept to his lips. Could he see the changes Sky felt inside? Were they actually visible? Had the peace in his heart smoothed out the taut angry lines around his mouth and eyes? Had God's refining fires turned the smoldering fire in his eyes to a loving glow?

"Go on," said Harris. "And take your time."

Rose dried her damp hands and followed Sky back outside. The sun had begun to warm up the morning. The glimmer of the dew had faded, only to reveal in more intensity the colors of springtime. Along the path, the lifting of the dew had allowed the vibrant orange heads of Indian paintbrush, the purple of bluebonnets, and the yellow of lupines to stand out in all their glory. Birds were fully awake now, fluttering from tree to tree, making carefree melody.

In silence they walked down to the river—not as far as Sky had gone on Billy's horse, but far enough to enjoy the similar sights. When they reached the river's edge, they found a dry, sunny patch of grass under the cottonwoods and sat there, still silent, as if basking in the delights of creation was as much as their fragile souls could take.

Finally Rose spoke. "I'm so happy for you, Sky!"

"About what?" He grinned.

"As if you could hide it!"

"I don't want to hide it. I wish I could gather every one of my people around me, like Wovoka did, and tell them all. But I'm no preacher. I'll leave that to the likes of Sam and Billy. I'll probably end up telling a lot of people, but just one at a time. And I'd like to start with you."

"Please do!"

"I've made my peace with the Wise One Above. I've fought my last battle, Rose. I'm ready to leave the rest of the battles to Him. I'm a different kind of warrior now—God's warrior! My weapons are love and forgiveness; my shield is faith in God—like it says in the Scriptures."

"I have never seen you walk straighter or with more pride."

"Do you remember the song I made up long ago?"

"Yes, the sad song. It made me want to cry. Have you changed it?"

"No. I don't think God wants me to forget my pain. It made me turn to Him, so it wasn't all bad. But as with everything Christ touches, it can finally end on a note of joy." Sky swung his guitar into position and set his fingers on the strings. "Listen . . .

> My warrior's song borne on the wind,
> Blows from the empty pale blue skies;
> Its chanting moan that has no end
> Sweeps teardrops from my heaven turned eyes:
> White eagle soars on broken wing
> For peace and glory long since gone;
> He leaves a lonely shattered dream,
> And hopes to sing his song at dawn.
>
> I sing of hands like silky pearls
> Touching my rough and darkened skin;
> Of sunlight catching light brown curls,
> Eyes that see my thoughts within:
> O prairie winds make our hearts blend
> And smother all our doubt and fear;
> If you should go my lovely friend,
> I'd lose the world that I hold dear.
>
> I sing of winding haunted trails
> Where snow-capped mountains touch the stars
> Through days of fasting, nights of prayer
> To lift my spirit, fill my heart;
> Come, Father, heal my broken song
> Wrapped in your arms where I belong;
> Dance in my soul to sweet release,
> Your arrows point the way, the way to peace.

O God, you shared my guilt and pain,
Caught in two worlds that tore my soul;
You taught my heart to love again
And then forgiveness made me whole:
Show me the pathway through the sky
With healing wind beneath my wings,
You heard this wounded eagle's cry
And gave the song my spirit sings.

"I can't be ashamed of who I am," Sky said, "whether Indian or half-breed. That would be the greatest injustice of all, because it would be against God himself and His will." Sky took Rose's hands in his and appraised her with eyes that he hoped mirrored what was in his heart. "Do you know what that means, Rose?"

She shook her head, but with a smile encouraged him to continue.

"I'm finally free. I can take the risks I was so afraid of before. Rose, at last I can love you as you should be loved. The words are no longer bound up in my self-hate."

"Yes. . . ?"

"I love you, Rose!"

"I knew you did."

"You knew all along?"

"There were times when I doubted. But you were not so hardened that you didn't let a few glimpses slip through every now and then."

"Is that why you didn't give up on me? Why you followed me here?"

"I did that because *I* love you. I could not do anything else."

Sky laid aside his guitar and opened his arms. Rose melted into them as if it was the most natural thing in the world to do, as if the things that had separated them in the past had never existed.

"Your father named you well," Sky said. "You were the bright, beautiful rose in the winter of my life. I'll always think of you with your pretty, red petals pushing relentlessly through snow and ice."

·  "You know what I like best about that?" Rose smiled. "The *always* part."

"And that's what I want for us—always to be together. That's why I now want to ask you to marry me."

"We are married, Sky."

"You were married, Rose. I'm afraid I never was. Would you marry me again?"

"And again, and again!"

"I'd like to have a Christian ceremony this time. Not because I think the Cheyenne ceremony wasn't valid, but because I think Sam and Billy would feel more comfortable with it."

"You want Billy to marry us?"

"Do you think he will consent?"

"I doubt you'd be able to stop him."

"There's one other thing," Sky said. "That is the matter of names."

"Another change, Sky?"

"The *last* change—if you are agreeable, and if Sam won't mind."

"What is it?"

"I feel strongly that my father's name should live on—and through his name, I want to always stay close to our Indian roots. I would like to be called *Sky Broken Wing*, and I would like any children we have to carry that name on. You know in our culture a name is supposed to show something about the person who bears it, or something about his experiences. My father first took that name because of the inner conflicts he had between two races he loved. I've never told you the story of the eagle with the broken wing. My father dreamed of finding a white eagle with an injured wing.

"My father said to the bird, 'You are hurt.'

"When the bird replied and said, 'I am,' my father in his dream knew he had found a medicine bird.

" 'Can I help you?' my father asked.

" 'That is why I have come, for only you have the medicine that can heal my wound.'

" 'What medicine is that?'

" 'It is the medicine of love in your heart.'

"In his dream, my father gladly helped the bird and somehow healed his wing, though he wasn't quite sure how he had done it. Then the eagle flew away. My father realized that the eagle stood for the white man, and that somehow he was destined to be used in bringing peace between the whites and the Indians. He took the name Broken Wing so he would always remember the hope the white eagle had given him. Later the eagle returned to my father in a vision, and the bird was not so kind or friendly. But my father kept the name. And I have only just come to see the greater significance of the name. Sometimes eagles *can* fly with an injured wing. My father continued to love the white man even though they had lied to him and cheated him. And that's the hope you and I can give—to our own children, if to no one else, that we must continue to hope and love no matter how much life may try to break us. And even if we are completely broken as I was, there is still hope."

"I will gladly take the name Rose Broken Wing. It sounds very right on my tongue."

"Now, I think we ought to go talk to Billy."

# 64

# HOME AGAIN

The three rode through Danville on their way to the Wind Rider Ranch. To strangers, they were a peculiar sight; to those who had known Sky and Billy, they were a shocking apparition.

The tall, husky Billy, with his blond hair, pale blue eyes, ruddy complexion, was dressed in cowboy boots and hat, corduroy trousers, and a denim shirt with a leather vest. He looked much the same as when he had ridden away seven years ago—outwardly, at least. His companions, the tall gaunt Indian man and the pretty Indian woman seemed a stark contrast. But all three had a glow in their eyes, an easy confidence of their bearing.

It was late afternoon and the Danville streets were quiet. They didn't plan on stopping. If they kept up a good pace, they could reach the Wind Rider Ranch by nightfall. There was no reason to stop, anyway. Sky had few, if any, friends here, and no business at all. Billy, too, had never been a person to gather lasting friendships; nearly all his so-called friends he had acquired through bullying. He had left fairly soon after his salvation, so no one ever got a chance to witness the changes in his life.

Billy looked over at Sky. "Doesn't look any different."

"It looks smaller, more run-down," said Sky. "But I guess that could go for all of us."

"They say you can't go home again. Maybe we're fools for trying."

"You nervous, Billy?"

"Yeah. How about you?"

Sky nodded. "I feel as skittish as a new-broke colt. I feel like I'm tempting my new faith just a mite too much."

"Were there any *good* memories here?"

364

"My family," Sky replied without hesitation. "There were good times with them."

"At least you can say that."

They rode on in silence, nearing the middle of town. Sky glanced at Rose as if to gather back his flagging confidence from her. She smiled encouragingly. It was all he needed.

Then someone yelled Billy's name.

"That you, Billy Yates?"

They turned in their saddles to see the speaker standing on the board sidewalk in front of the general store. Sky recognized him as the foreman of the Flying Y outfit—the Yates ranch.

"You still hanging around this town, Riley?" Billy said in a friendly tone.

"Could do worse, I reckon."

"Yeah . . . I guess so."

"Your pa know you're here?"

Billy took off his hat and wiped the back of his hand across his sweaty brow. He hadn't expected to answer questions like that so soon.

"I just found out I was coming a few days ago," Billy said. "How . . . is my pa, Riley?"

"He's here in town, Billy. Down at the saloon—if you want to see him."

Billy glanced at Sky, who shrugged noncommittally.

"Thanks, Riley," said Billy.

"I'm heading there, if you want me to tell him you're here."

"Well . . . I guess we'll head down there shortly."

"See you later, then." Riley turned and strode toward the saloon.

"I can't ignore him," Billy said to Sky and Rose.

"That wouldn't do, I suppose," Sky agreed.

"I was hoping . . . I don't know what I was hoping. I guess it's just as well to get it over with sooner than later."

"Kind of like taking a knife out of a wound. Better fast than slow."

"This is more like putting a knife *into* a wound. I know this is a lot to ask, but would you come with me, Sky?"

"My presence could just make things worse. But we're both going to have to face your pa eventually. So let's get it over with." Sky turned to Rose. "Maybe it would be best if you waited here."

Sky and Billy rode toward the saloon where Riley had entered a few moments earlier. They had tied their horses at the hitching

365

post and climbed the steps up to the sidewalk, when the saloon doors burst open and Big Bill Yates appeared, practically crashing into Sky and Billy.

"So, it's true. It is you." There was no hint of welcome or affection in Bill Yates's tone.

"Hi, Pa," Billy said.

Sky wondered if Big Bill Yates had withered, or if he, Sky, had just grown. But somehow Yates didn't seem as big and ominous as he had always appeared before. He looked old and weathered. There was much more gray than blonde in his thinning hair, and the lines in his forehead and around his eyes were deep crevices, more dismaying than dangerous. Neither Sky nor Billy was armed, but Sky thought that Big Bill Yates would have no qualms about using the six-gun cinched around his wide girth.

Yates let his eyes rest only briefly on Billy, then shifted his attention quickly to Sky.

"You're back, too." Yates growled, making it clear Sky wasn't worth a civil tone.

"I'm not looking for trouble," said Sky.

"You *are* trouble; you don't have to look for it."

"Pa," Billy put in quickly, "I'm on my way out to the Wind Rider Ranch, but I'd like to see you again while I'm here."

"So, it's true, then. You've become an Injun lover."

"I reckon I love all men now, Pa."

"Well, I don't want nothing to do with an Injun lover, or anyone that consorts with that white squaw woman—" Yates glared at Sky, obviously baiting him.

Sky had been afraid of this very thing, afraid that old wounds had not yet healed enough to stand the salt of scorn from men like Bill Yates. But, oddly, the words didn't bother him much. Something he'd heard once, probably from Sam, popped into his mind: *"If God be for me then who can be against me?"* It was really true!

He smiled ever so slightly at Yates. "Mr. Yates, I know how you feel, and you're probably not interested in what I have to say. But I'm going to be getting married, and your son is going to perform the ceremony. It'll be his first as an ordained minister. Anyway, we'd sure like you to come."

"You gotta be kidding," Yates sneered.

"Pa, it would mean a lot to me if you were there," Billy said.

Yates jerked his head toward where Rose still sat on her horse near the general store. "Killion, you gonna marry that Injun slut there?"

366

Sky tensed, and old anger flared. No one was going to talk that way about Rose—no one! But the words came to him again: *"If God be for me then who can be against me?"*

"That isn't called for, Pa," Billy said. "We're trying to make amends. It wouldn't hurt for you to come at least halfway."

"Wouldn't it?"

"Well, I see," said Billy slowly, regretfully, "that we're not getting anywhere here. You know where I'll be if you change your mind." He looked at Sky. "Let's go."

The two started down the steps of the sidewalk, but at the bottom Billy turned one last time toward his father. "Pa, no matter what, I love you."

Then he and Sky mounted and, with Rose, rode away toward the Wind Rider Ranch.

———

The sun was slanting toward the earth as they crested the rise overlooking the ranch.

"You know," mused Billy, "I've never been to your ranch."

Sighing, Sky gazed down at the buildings. Most of them looked the same. They had passed a windmill on the way in, and down below he saw a new stable. He wondered what had happened to the old one. But as always a couple of horses pranced about the coral, and cowhands were moving around probably finishing up their chores before the supper bell sounded. Sky knew he could expect a better reception from his family than Billy had received from his father, but he was nervous just the same. He thought about that last meeting with his mother, and about all he had put his family through over the years. Would there be resentments and awkwardness? Of course they would be happy over the change in him, but it was still very new, and he might have to prove himself to them. He could understand that. He had traveled an awful long time in mire for it to be completely gone.

"I feel like I need a bath," he muttered to himself.

Rose reached over and took his hand. "You have never looked better!"

"The blood of the Lamb makes you clean, Sky," added Billy.

"Well, then," said Sky, "no sense lingering any longer."

They bounded down the hill each at a brisk trot.

Yolanda was about to ring the bell when she saw them. She dropped the iron bar and cried, "Deborah, come quickly! We have visitors!"

In what seemed only a moment, the three riders had dismounted in the yard and were suddenly surrounded by a dozen people, all laughing and impatiently waiting for a chance to hug the newcomers. Deborah didn't care about anything except the fact that her son was home. She threw her arms around Sky and held on for a very long time. Sam didn't seem to care about manly reserve; he hugged Sky, then Billy, and finally Rose, kissing her on the cheek as if he'd known her all his life.

One person in the group waited as patiently as she could before she elbowed through the well-wishers.

"Carolyn!" Sky cried. And they embraced and wept.

Then Griff took Sky's hand and started to shake it. "Aw, shucks!" he said, and threw his arms around Sky, too.

# 65

# CIRCLE OF LOVE

Three weeks later Sky awoke early in the morning. The light of dawn was only beginning to break through the horizon. Next to him, Billy was snoring peacefully and didn't stir as Sky slipped out of bed and dressed in his Levi's, shirt, and boots. He picked up his guitar before leaving the room.

Sky wondered if Rose had been able to sleep. At least Carolyn didn't snore! But more than Billy's snoring had kept Sky awake. Today was his wedding day. It might be his second wedding day, but this one meant so much more than the one nearly three years ago. Now he loved Rose in a way he never could have before, and he felt a much greater sense of responsibility toward her. He was concerned about whether he would be a good husband. He had been such a terrible one before. Had God changed him enough so he could do better this time?

Sam had told Sky only yesterday that no one—least of all Rose—expected him to be perfect. All he had to do was be committed to keep coming back to God when he made mistakes. Sky hoped and prayed that would be enough. He didn't want to hurt Rose again.

Sky quietly made his way to the kitchen. There was some coffee on the stove left over from last night. It looked strong, but Sky stoked up the fire in the stove to heat it up anyway. When it was steaming, he poured himself a cup, brought it to the table and sat down. He took a couple of swallows, then lifted his guitar to his lap and began chording a tune. He had been working on a special song for Rose for their wedding; he had all the words figured out and just needed some refinement of the melody.

He was so engrossed in his music he didn't hear the kitchen door quietly open.

"Morning, Sky." It was his mother.

"Morning, Ma. I didn't wake you, did I?"

"Oh no. I often get up at this hour."

"Guess I forgot." Sky laid aside his guitar.

"Don't stop on my account. At least play while I fix us some fresh coffee. I'd like to listen."

Sky played "What a Friend We Have in Jesus" and two or three other hymns as the fragrance of freshly brewed coffee filled the kitchen. He stopped when his mother set another cup of coffee before him and sat down opposite him.

Sky sipped the coffee. "Ah, that's better!"

"Nothing like fresh coffee." She sipped hers but couldn't take her eyes off Sky. Before she put her cup down, tears were filling her eyes. "Don't mind me!" she said with a chuckle. She swiped away the tears. "It's just so good to have you here. I worried so that it might never happen. . . ."

"I'm sorry I put you through that, Ma."

"Let's not say another word about it, okay? I just can't help if I get a bit overwhelmed by God's faithfulness."

"I know what you mean."

They were silent for a few minutes, enjoying their coffee and the early morning quiet.

"Are you ready for today?" she said at last.

"As ready as ever, I guess. Sam and Billy are going to have to do most of the work."

"Watching the two of them with their heads together planning the service, I would guess it wasn't work at all to them. They are having a ball."

"Did you ever think Billy Yates would be conducting my wedding?"

"Never, but only because I don't have as broad a vision as God."

"It's too bad Billy's father didn't come around. But maybe that would have been just too perfect."

"Who knows what God may do—if not today, then some other day."

Sky finished his coffee, got up, and refilled their cups. "It's sure been great to have Carolyn here."

"She's been coming up pretty often since . . . well, since you left. I think she felt I needed her support—and she was right."

"Too bad Matt couldn't be here. I wish I could have gone to their wedding."

"Well, it's spring roundup, the worst time to get away from a ranch."

Sky nodded his understanding. "I haven't had a chance to really talk to you about what Rose and I want to do. Do you think we're doing the right thing in going back to the reservation?"

"From what I saw of your allotments, it looked like good land. I can see why you want to make a go of it there."

"We don't want to see the land slip out of Cheyenne control. That could happen so easily if we don't work it and make it prosper. My knowledge of ranching will help, and hopefully I can pass on what I know to some of the others and they can succeed, too. But I have to face the fact that there are certain risks for me in returning. Many of my friends there use a lot of whiskey."

"You would never go back to drinking, would you, Sky?"

"I don't want to. But you know how the reservation is. It can be pretty discouraging and frustrating. It hasn't been so long, Ma, since I was drinking just to avoid all that. I don't want to be too cocky for my own good. But on the other hand, I can't avoid whiskey. It's everywhere I look."

"Keep your eyes on Jesus, Sky, and maybe you won't notice it so much."

"I'll keep that in mind. But it would sure be nice to stick around here." He shrugged. "Maybe that would be too easy."

"You never did take the easy way, son."

"I want so much to make it work this time—not so much ranching, but life, especially my life with Rose. Sometimes I feel so confident. Sometimes I can see only the mistakes I've made. I suppose that's good, huh? It'll keep me humble."

"I was never much good at answering life's questions," Deborah said. "But there is one thing I'd like to do, and I'm glad it worked out that we were up before everyone else. I'd like to pray with you. I know we'll all pray together later, but I think there is a reason why it's just you and me now."

"I'd like that." Sky took his mother's dainty, work-worn hands in his. There had always been a special connection between them—springing, no doubt, from the common bond they held in the spirit of the Cheyenne warrior, Broken Wing. He had always been an integral part of the circle of love that drew mother and son together.

Hands clasped together, Sky and Deborah bowed their heads, and Sky knew that somehow his father was there with them, as was his heavenly Father.

371

Sky was waiting as patiently as he could in Sam's study next to the sanctuary of the Danville church. Griff tried to distract Sky with ranch stories.

"Be glad you weren't here for that twister three years back, Sky," Griff said. "It lifted the barn up and set it down ten feet away. 'Course it was kindling after it hit the ground."

"That'll be the third barn we've had."

"We was just thankful it wasn't the house."

There was a lull in the conversation, and Sky paced around a bit. He glanced over at the foreman who was watching him with a grin.

"Ain't too late to back out, Sky."

"That's the last thing I want to do."

"Didn't think so." Griff paused. "Anyway, it'd be a shame to waste all these fancy duds."

Sky couldn't remember ever seeing Griff so duded up. In a tan broadcloth suit, silk vest, new boots and Stetson hat, he looked more like a riverboat gambler than best man in a wedding. But Sky appreciated the sacrifice his old friend was making every time he wormed his finger around inside his tight collar.

Sky, also, had never had finer clothes. When he and Rose and Billy had stopped at the reservation for a couple of days on their way to the Wind Rider Ranch, several of the women had insisted on making wedding garments for them. The three intervening weeks and some financial assistance from his mother had allowed them to create a wonderful finished product. Sky's buckskin breeches were so soft and fitted so perfectly, he hardly knew he had them on. His buckskin coat, with its deep fringe and beaded designs, was a work of art. He still wore his uncle's beaded collar, which Rose had recently repaired and spruced up after Sky's years of careless living. In his long, carefully braided and wrapped hair he wore the magpie feathers, with the addition of the broken eagle feather he had once found. He was still an Indian, still Cheyenne. For now he was neither ready nor willing to change that essential fact about him. The world must accept him or reject him on his own terms. It had never mattered to God.

A knock on the door reminded Sky it was almost time for his wedding to begin. But when Griff opened the door, it wasn't Billy with the go-ahead. It was Carolyn.

"I don't know," said Griff. "This room is for menfolk."

Carolyn shouldered her way in. "When did that ever matter to me, you old blowhard?"

"Hasn't that man of yours taught you any respect yet?"

"He knows not to tamper with perfection."

The three laughed. Sky never missed his sister more than now as he realized their reunion would be drawing to a close. She was returning to Stoner's Crossing tomorrow.

"You two look prettier than a picture," she said, partly in jest but partly with admiration.

"Be careful what you say, Lynnie," said Sky. "When was the last time you wore calico?"

Carolyn tugged at the full skirt of the blue calico. "I think the last time was my own wedding. Only it wasn't calico, it was white satin—oooh, how I suffered. That more than anything proved to Matt that I loved him."

"What we'll do for love, huh?" Sky smiled.

Suddenly Carolyn's demeanor softened and tears filled her eyes.

"Oh, Sky!" She threw her arms around her brother. "I'm so happy for you. You have got yourself such a fine bride."

"Better than I deserve."

"No. *Exactly* what you deserve! I'm no expert, but even I can see you two were made for each other. And I want to see a lot of both of you after the wedding. There are plenty of trains, and I've got money coming out my ears, so there's no excuse, you hear? And all the little cousins are going be best friends, too."

"Let's not push things."

Carolyn blushed. Sky didn't think he'd ever seen his sister blush before.

Griff, who was always faster on the draw, reacted first. "Why, Lynnie, are you trying to tell us. . . ? Well, I mean—" Even Griff couldn't broach the delicate subject.

"Yes, you dear lug, Matt and I have a loaf of bread in the oven."

Both men whooped and Sky lifted Carolyn off her feet in an exuberant embrace. Then he remembered her condition and set her gently on her feet.

"I'm sorry, Carolyn. You okay?"

"I won't break, Sky. *Please*, don't fret over me. This is your day, yours and Rose's, so don't give me another thought."

Billy poked his head into the study. "It's time," he said.

Carolyn hurried out to take her place as maid of honor. Griff followed Billy to the front of the church, and then Sky went out.

He had never before seen the church this packed. Everyone in the county must be here, and then some. He wondered how many were just curious. But he shook away any bitterness in that thought. He'd be curious, too, he supposed, if the minister's wayward Indian stepson was getting married. What kind of gal would have him? Was she an Indian, too? Would she wear white? A wedding gown or an Indian dress?

But not everyone in those pews were merely curious. T.R. Lowell was there with his family—three strapping boys and another on the way. T.R. grinned at Sky as if to encourage him that there wasn't anything in the world better than marriage. About a dozen cowhands from the Wind Rider outfit were there, many Sky had known for years. Slim and Longjim were grinning like proud uncles. And Stands-in-the-River was there, too, with Stone Teeth Woman. He was sitting shoulder-to-shoulder with the Texas Ranger, Bob Tebbel. They were an awesome-looking pair, and Sky almost thought one was keeping guard over the other. How vividly they represented the past.

About a dozen Cheyenne from the reservation were there, mostly women. But Rose was very special to them, and Deborah had been generous in seeing that anyone who wished could make the trip. Sitting in the honored seat of grandmother of the groom, next to Deborah, was Gray Antelope Woman. Sky was looking forward to returning to the reservation if for no other reason than to care for her and honor her.

The notes of the "Wedding March" quickly diverted Sky's attention from the guests. He turned toward the center aisle.

Rose entered the sanctuary on Little Left Hand's arm. Sky had never seen the dress the women had made her, but it made his own fine outfit seem plain. The soft doeskin was a creamy white. Colorful glass beads and elk teeth were sewn in intricate designs down the sleeves, across the bodice, and around the fringed hem. In her hand she carried a bouquet of bright wildflowers. She was wearing the same moccasins she had worn for their first wedding; they were practically brand new.

In some ways this was the same Rose; it was fitting that she wore the same shoes. Adversity had seasoned her, of course, but that irrepressible smile still filled her eyes.

As she reached the altar, Sky motioned to Griff, who was holding out his guitar. With shaking fingers and a tremulous voice, he sang the song he had written just for her. Its simple lyrics, about his Winter Rose and the love God demonstrated in giving her to him, brought tears to her eyes—and to his. When the song was over, Sky breathed a sigh of relief, set the instrument aside, and turned to claim his bride.

"Who gives this woman to this man?" Billy asked.

With a proud grin, Little Left Hand replied, "I do." He placed Rose's hand lovingly into Sky's.

"Thank you, Nehuo," Sky said.

"It is my pleasure," said the old Indian.

Little Left Hand stepped back, took his seat, and Sky and Rose, arm-in-arm, turned and faced Sam and Billy. Sky hated to admit it, but the feeling of having Rose so close made the rest of the service a blur. The final words, however, were clear and delightful.

"Ladies and gentlemen," said Sam, "I would like to be the first to introduce Mr. and Mrs. Sky Broken Wing!"

Sam's voice betrayed no hesitation in speaking the name. Sky realized, perhaps for the first time, that Broken Wing had been a hero to Sam, too, and to him it was a fine thing that the man should be memorialized in this way.

Then Billy said, "You may kiss the bride!"

Sky forgot all about names and history. He thought only of the wonderful woman he held in his arms. And inwardly he praised God for the new song she was inspiring in his heart.

# A Word From the Author

*Warrior's Song* is a story. It is not intended to offer solutions or to substitute as counseling for the very serious problem of teenage drug and alcohol abuse. The highest aspiration of this story is to bring the problem into the light and offer the hope of Christ. Yet, because of the very nature of this story, it may attract readers either with addictions, or readers who are close to someone with an addiction. For that reason, and because I know getting help is both the most important thing to do and the hardest, I would like to contribute what encouragement I can toward that end.

Drug and alcohol addiction among teens—and even more so, addiction among Native American youth—is a widespread problem in this country. Most communities offer some kind of help program. Alcoholics Anonymous and Narcotics Anonymous are not the only organizations available, but they are among the most effective. Addicts who are most faithful to their AA/NA meetings have the highest rate of recovery.

Many churches are now coming to recognize that drug abuse is a problem (and alcohol is very much a drug) from which Christians are not immune, and some churches sponsor AA/NA groups. Many families in the Church are being torn apart by drug abuse, especially among teens. Godly parents like Deborah and Sam Killion are facing these issues on a personal level. That reality is not a condemnation of their parenting but an indictment of a society which advocates escape rather than responsibility.

This is not a time for Christian families to hide behind false concepts about what Christians are supposed to be like. Nor is it the time for judgment by other Christians who haven't been touched by these issues. Rather, I would encourage church families to roll up their sleeves, pull together, and confront the problem in a practical way such as can be found in the AA/NA 12-step approach.

I believe the well-known and oft-repeated prayer of Alcoholics

Anonymous is applicable not only to addicts, but to parents, church workers, friends and relatives of addicts:

*"Lord, grant me the serenity to accept the things I cannot change, the courage to change the things I can, and the wisdom to know the difference."*